Mindscapes Unimagined

An Anthology of the Supernatural,
Science Fiction, and Horror creeping out
of the shadows of your imagination.

Edited by Karen T. Newman

https://LeftHandPublishers.com
Twitter.com/LeftHandPublish
Facebook.com/LeftHandPublishers
editor@LeftHandPublishers.com
Cover design by Paul K. Metheney

Acknowledgments

Special thanks go out to Karen T. Newman, and her company, Newmanuscripts.net, for her tireless efforts in editing, formatting, and compilation. Many kudos to Paul K. Metheney and his company, Metheney Consulting, for invaluable assistance with our cover design and marketing.

Recognition should also go out to our friends and families who tolerated our working hours during the creation of this publication. None of this could have been possible without the creative imaginations and perseverance of the wonderful writers who submitted works to this anthology.

To the readers who purchased this volume, thank you.

Left Hand Publishers Books

Beautiful Lies, Painful Truths Vol. I & II BUNDLED
LHP's Web Site - https://bit.ly/2NoDgGI

Beautiful Lies, Painful Truths Vol. I
Amazon - http://amzn.to/2reSyIe
YouTube - https://youtu.be/4m1BR6BIBTM
The Reviews on YouTube - https://youtu.be/tTtdf0LQC7Q
LHP's Web Site - http://bit.ly/2FHXzw9
The Reviews on LHP - http://bit.ly/2FHhMlN
Goodreads - http://bit.ly/2BobVCi

Beautiful Lies, Painful Truths Vol. II
Amazon - http://amzn.to/2ngBq0i
YouTube - https://youtu.be/i8dAMSAbkAM
LHP's Web Site - http://bit.ly/2Dxu9n8
Goodreads: http://bit.ly/2slkBpP

Realities Perceived
Amazon- http://amzn.to/2Dbe1ny
YouTube - https://youtu.be/3SLjzDd9o3Y
LHP's Web Site - http://bit.ly/2Do87SE
Goodreads - http://bit.ly/

The Demon's Angel by Maya Shah
Amazon - http://amzn.to/2EVjj7V
YouTube - https://youtu.be/FZuvbiGjMcU
Maya Shah's Web Site - http://mayashahbooks.com/
LHP's Web Site - http://bit.ly/2DuXieD
Goodreads - http://bit.ly/2son5E2

Drawing from the Well by Rachel A. Bollinger
LHP Web Site - https://bit.ly/2LqIzER
Amazon - https://amzn.to/2th8WGE
Goodreads - https://bit.ly/2M8h57h

A World Unimagined
YouTube - https://youtu.be/2IO3rl0N_q8
LHP Web Site - https://bit.ly/2IG7Dea
Amazon - https://amzn.to/2yvJ4vS
Goodreads - https://bit.ly/2K7b6zj

Terrors Unimagined
YouTube - https://youtu.be/ow4XfWt2q7w
LHP Web Site - https://bit.ly/2MSohot
Amazon - https://amzn.to/2OsldAT
Goodreads - https://bit.ly/2LkLO17

CONTENTS

Hodag

by Steve Rouse

United States

The Bear 'n Boar's reputation as the best tavern within all of the Khandaran Forest has never been challenged. It invites its patrons in to knock the dust off their day and join in camaraderie with neighbors and travelers alike. With sturdy ales, smooth wines and robust meals of succulent meats, potatoes, and soft warm breads, the Bear 'n Boar satisfies all who enter, sometimes in ways they never suspect.

Bahlis paused washing glasses and grinned, knowing Rikar's latest hunting story had ended from the raucous cheering and applause coming from the great hall. As he anticipated, the crowd soon emerged from the main room, some chuckling and others expressing either amazement or doubts in whispers laden with ale. Whether elf or dwarf, human or gnome, they dispersed to other tables or to the bar to refill their glasses and continue the night. After serving their needs, Bahlis stacked clean glasses as the renowned hunter, Rikar, limped toward the bar and sat at his favorite stool, waving an empty mug.

"Ah, Bahlis, my friend! Too, too sad that the great days of my hunts are but a memory."

Bahlis cocked an eye at the old man. "And it would seem you certainly have more memories than most."

"What?" Rikar feigned surprise, right hand over his heart. "Do I hear doubt? Does the owner of the fabled Bear 'n Boar fear that I might be, ahh, too exuberant in my retellings?" He broke into a cough-ridden chuckle. "In my younger days, dear friend, I experienced the hunt like no one else. And, if it seems that my recounting of those

1

exploits is perhaps enhanced, then so be it. My listeners would be unimpressed with mere details." He gestured about the room. "Did you not just see what joy I brought to these less fortunate? They have broadened their lives, enriched their experiences through my eyes and my story."

"You do certainly keep them entranced, sir." Bahlis set a full mug of ale in front of him. "You should write down the magic of your experiences to preserve your, ah, truth, as it were."

"Then, it would seem, I am as gifted in my telling as I am in the hunt." He fell silent and sipped his ale as the tavern slowly emptied, light from the twin moons streaming in whenever the door opened.

Bahlis smiled and leaned across the bar top saying, "What would you say to a hunt? A real hunt as thrilling as one of your tales?"

"Alas my friend, I am past my sixtieth year and it is my body, no longer my bravery, that now tells me what it's willing to endure." Rikar drained his mug and set it upside down on the counter.

"There are forces, good sir, that can be of service to you. Powers I can summon that will allow you to experience the grandest, and yet most dangerous hunt of a lifetime. Powers that can even set aside the cost of time and replenish an aging body with one full of youthful ambition, strength, and skill."

"You have piqued my interest, old friend. At what cost?"

"Oh, you have more than paid that already. Your storytelling here has become a legend of its own. Many customers tell me they have come just to hear you. They stay longer, drink and eat more just to be entertained by one of your renditions. I guarantee your satisfaction in this, should you live to tell the tale."

"Now I am intrigued. How could I refuse? I put so much of myself into each story, admittedly more than I did in the actual hunt. But I tire of living only memories. I would relish such a chance to truly live again! When could this be done?"

"No time like the present." Bahlis ushered the last pair of customers to the door citing the late hour and bid them a fond goodnight, locking it after them. He returned behind the bar and signalled Rikar to follow.

*

Rikar hesitated. He couldn't say exactly why, perhaps because Bahlis looked different, the skin of his face seemed ruddier, his hair fuller and lighter, almost glowing. Bahlis reached behind some bottles and a section of the wall swung out, revealing a dark hall that dropped below the floor. The bartender smiled back at him and clapped his hands. Several small sconces lit, illuminating a stairway. He ducked low and entered the passage. Rikar followed, his senses heightened, despite the ale.

Descending half a dozen steps, Rikar came into a large chamber, its walls laden with spears, javelins, swords, dirks, hatchets, axes, and bows and arrows of every description. Bahlis gazed at him and gestured around the room saying, "You are allowed to select any two."

Rikar wandered for a few moments, admiring the arsenal. "What am I hunting?" he asked.

Bahlis turned and knelt at the room's center. A silver ring, as large as a shield, lay embedded within the stone floor. He muttered and gestured across the disc. Rikar stared, enthralled at the sight. He'd never suspected Bahlis of using magic and, while he hadn't experienced it himself, he'd heard others' testimonies. His heart raced, unsure of what he'd stepped into.

A small swirl of glowing embers appeared and floated before the bar's owner. He stood and then clapped. They fell within the ring and burst into yellow flame, forming the shape of a creature. Bahlis stepped back, extending an arm that drew Rikar away from the figure as well. As he did, the flaming shape grew.

"To know the true size of the beast," he explained. The flame swelled until it was larger than even Bahlis. Rikar noted the odd fire gave no heat, nor any sound as it burned. It then dulled to a soft blue and grew no more. "Behold the hodag. This is your quarry, my friend. Look at it. Learn it. Know that it does not die easily. You are allowed only one question about it."

Rikar stepped up to the image. It stood on four legs, the front two long like a wolf's but far more massive, while the back two were shorter and muscular, with squat paws like a 'gator. Its head reached to Rikar's waist. Two eyes were set in front, slightly recessed above a short muzzle. Dozens of long, sharp teeth and two impressive fangs jutted from its wide mouth. Its most remarkable feature was the collection of horns. A massive horn thrust from each side of its head, curling upward and slightly forward, about twice that of a bull's. Six more horns followed a sloping spine, rising up from the vertebrae, sharp and dangerous. They ended in a cluster of bony spurs pointing in many directions at the clubbed end of a long, reptilian tail.

From the side, Rikar saw it had no neck, the head fit snug between the shoulders with small squirrel-like ears below the horns. From head to tail, the creature was twice his height. He silently guessed its weight the same as a bear. *And probably as quick, too.*

"What weapons do you choose?" Bahlis asked.

"That depends ... where is the heart?"

Bahlis gestured and twin spots within the creature shown yellow, one high between the rear legs and the other just behind the head but beneath the backbone.

"And where's its brain?" Rikar continued walking around it.

"No more questions. Select your weapons. Be quick!"

Rikar stopped and eyed his friend. "Why?"

The hodag's image flared out as a wind filled the chamber, quickly whipping and rattling the weapons on the walls. "Hurry, my friend, or you will be sent to face the hodag with none."

Rikar inhaled sharply and walked to the wall. He picked a bow and quiver of arrows, slinging both across his back. The wind increased, now roaring around the room, a vortex with the ring at its center. Fighting against the wind's force, Rikar crossed to the swords and manage to snatch a sabre before being blown toward the room's center.

His hair and beard whipping about, Bahlis shouted to be heard. "Stand here," pointing to the now glowing silver circle.

Rikar struggled against the gale, but finally placed his feet within the radiant ring. Silence surrounded him. No wind touched him. He saw the wind forcing the weapons to wobble and blow off the walls and his friend covering himself against its force. No sound came to him until a soft, disembodied whisper reached his ears. "The hodag or you, one must die. That is the price to be paid, or there will be no returning." A flash of light enveloped him.

*

A heavy fog hugged the ground, clinging to every trunk and branch, swirling gently with any wisp of breeze. Clusters of snow dotted the forest floor and the sounds of nearby rapids filled the cold air, their mists shimmering in the early morning light. Rikar frowned. *What is this place?* A single yellow sun topped the distant hills. *Its color and size were wrong. This is not my world!*

Despite its strangeness, his nose filled with the familiar smells of a forest.

4

He found himself somehow dressed for the weather. Late autumn, he reasoned, with snow, yet unfrozen ground and river. Leather gloves and a hooded coat he'd never seen before kept him warm. The bow and quiver hung off one shoulder, a water skin and satchel on his other. Inside it, he found bread, fruit, carrots, and a soft roasted meat. *Thank you, Bahlis. Always looking out for me, eh? All I'm missing is some ale.* He sipped from the skin, hopeful, but then sighed. *Perhaps, when I return.*

He stepped ahead and looked around, finding himself at the base of a rocky outcrop half again his height. An odd five-trunk birch tree grew from its base next to him, its leaves still a pale green. The rest of the trees were darker. None had leaves, except the oak which always refuse to drop their dry and dead clothing until spring.

His eyes and ears picked up details he'd long just assumed were still there. *Age is a cruel taskmaster, but not today.* Rikar marveled at the clarity of the sight of a distant yellow bird fluttering its wings from branch to branch, the only spot of colour so far. He filled his lungs with cool, fresh air and felt young and powerful. Tugging his long hair from under his hood, he grinned at its deep black, without the gray he'd grown accustomed to. He squatted and rose, eliciting yet another smile for the lack of pain in his knees and hip.

Satisfied, Rikar repositioned his weapons and set out to locate any signs of this hodag. *Whatever this thing is, it dies today!* In all of his decades as a hunter and woodsman, he'd never seen or heard of such a beast. Given the magic that obviously sent him here—*wherever here is*—it would be possible that it, too, had some connection to magic. If so, caution would be a valuable tactic. It had looked like a nasty beast, one whose disposition could also warrant extra diligence.

He walked to the rapids, impressed by its roar. A massive cascade of water churned before him. He could heave a stone across it, but the whitewater tumult stretched above him to the bedrock's crest and below him around a bend at least an arrow's flight away. He turned and trudged uphill, the river to his left, keeping wary of the nearby trees along the way for what they could be hiding.

He easily reached the hill's crest, elated at not being out of breath. A crow cawed ahead and to his right, his eyes narrowed. *Not from above, but from the ground.* A thin trail of smoke rose from a clearing nearby. He called out "Hello in the camp," to announce his presence. No response. So, he walked slowly toward the clearing, making noise and calling out again so as not to startle anyone. Except for the smoldering campfire, there was no sound or movement.

Coming into the small campsite alongside a tent, Rikar stopped. A crow lay dead next to the fire. On the other side of the fire, Rikar's eyes locked on a man's corpse, sprawled on his back and grossly bloated. Between the tent and the corpse, the ground showed some signs that it had been dragged from inside the tent, bedding and clothing strewn along the way.

Rikar had seen his share of corpses, some animal and some human. If left alone, any body would swell, bloat, and eventually burst after death. Rikar instinctively sniffed the air and started to cover his nose. But there was no stench, no scent of death. Looking over the whole camp, Rikar surmised the man had likely died in the tent and then had been dragged out by some predator.

But no, that couldn't be. The swollen body looked to be two weeks dead, yet the campfire burned. He came closer and stirred the embers. He could still identify ashes from tinder and some of the wood had not yet burned. *This fire is only an hour or so old! Someone else had to be here.* He walked around the camp, looking for footprints or tracks. The campsite was hard and dry and left no traces. Rikar widened his perimeter and found a trail of overturned leaves and twigs, made by something with a wide paw, according to the spacing of the claws' indentations in the softer dirt. He followed them, a clear path of an obviously larger animal, but it was moving slowly away from the camp. Even if his appearance scared it away, these tracks were not of a running animal. *Whatever it was, this thing wasn't in any hurry.* He scanned the area ahead, but saw nothing of a predator.

Rikar returned to the camp and knelt next to the corpse. It was bearded, but the swelling obliterated the facial features. One eye had leaked. It had been punctured. Tiny scratches were on the forehead above it. Rikar glanced through the fire's smoke at the dead crow. They were known to start feeding on soft tissue, like eyes and lips. The only other obvious markings he could see were a line of discolored puncture wounds ringed by mutilated flesh just above the ankle, each with a dried blood trail. Whatever had dragged the body had hold of this leg. He walked to the tent, kicking at the bedding along the way. Inside, he found nothing he could make use of except for a sheathed two-edged dirk, its blade slightly longer than his forearm. He tucked it under his belt.

Still squatting as he came to the tent flap, he caught a movement to his left and froze, and then slowly backed up. He pulled his sabre and waited, watching. With low, heavy breathing, a great silver-tipped bear lumbered into the camp, testing the air with a raised head. It grunted and pivoted, scanning the site. It made its way to the body, sniffing it and pawing at it. Rikar could see more drool than normal for the bruin. *It must be really hungry, already drooling that much. I must have scared it away when I found the camp. Now it's back to claim what it hauled from the tent.*

The bear grunted a few times, seeming to hesitate, but then clamped its jaws onto the corpse's head and pulled the body toward it. The beast instantly let go and jerked back, howling and flailing, rubbing its face against into the dirt. It backed again and reared, coughing up blood and clawing at its throat. Within seconds, the fierce growl became an obvious screech of pain, blood bubbling through its muzzle. The massive bear suddenly gagged and fell forward, red froth spewing through its mouth and nose.

Rikar waited. Minutes passed before he ventured out, as of yet unsure of what just happened. He studied the bear from a distance and caught a bitter, acidic stench. His eyes watered from it, so Rikar moved to the other side of the fire. He found himself next to the dead crow and noticed that it too was bloodied. The beak appeared deformed and its mouth was filled with dried blood. Rikar paused, his mind working feverishly. He looked back and forth between the man's body, the dead bear, and the crow, puzzling just how they were as he saw them. Another noise, a low rumbling from the trees, grabbed his attention.

Startled, Rikar spun toward the source and saw the hodag coming from the brush. It paused, eyeing him, and then entered the clearing and strode up to the bear. Its gleaming white fangs and horns were a stark contrast to the dark bulk of a hairless body, looking like an inky cloud of night behind them. Everything he'd seen in Bahlis's chamber stood before him, in the flesh and strikingly more terrifying. Rikar had stared down wolves and had killed a charging buffalo, but never before had he felt real fear in facing a wild animal.

It opened its glistening maw and roared, shaking off globs of saliva in the process. Where those globs hit—plants, the bear carcass, and the ground—Rikar watched small puffs of steam erupt and heard their sizzling hiss. *What is this thing?*

Rikar stepped back quickly, keeping the bear's carcass between them until he reached the tree line. The hodag nudged the bear carcass. Disinterested, it then moved off at a quicker pace toward the man's corpse. As it did, its skin changed from the dark shadow color to the dirt and grassy color of the clearing. Rikar squinted at it in disbelief. *I never knew anything could camouflage itself so quickly!*

After sniffing the corpse, it bit down on the head and left shoulder. In a sickening crunch of breaking bones, the creature cut through the swollen flesh and shook them from the rest of the body. It tossed the bloody mass up slightly and chomped again, swallowing. Rikar watched with mixed fascination and revulsion as the hodag devoured the remains of the corpse within minutes.

It wasn't until the hodag sat cleaning itself that Rikar came to his senses and remembered his hunt. He had weapons and was to kill it. *This is already fodder for the greatest tale I could tell.* Still kneeling among the trees, he unslung the bow and nocked an arrow. The hodag turned and moved toward the bear carcass, quartering away from Rikar.

Now that'll be a good shot. He drew back, aimed, pursed his lips and blew a light exhale as he loosed the arrow. From one hundred feet away, the razor-tipped arrow struck the hodag in its side, just behind the front leg. Rikar heard the thud of the arrow's strike and saw the hodag twitch. It yelped and twisted around, but was unable to reach the arrow hanging from its side, the tip only half embedded in the thick flesh. Rikar checked the bow. *Yes, it's a hunting bow… good quality yew wood, nice flexion. This should be strong enough.*

Now behind the bear, the hodag turned to face him. Rikar quickly fired once more, but missed low, embedding the arrow deep within the flesh of the bear. The beast roared again and charged. Rikar slung the bow across his back as he ran toward the river. His heart pounded in his chest. He heard only that and the impact of his feet to the ground as he ran. When he got to the river, he glanced back and saw the hodag approaching, but only at the pace of a brisk walk.

He forced himself to control his breathing. *Calm. Consider. Calculate. My three "Cs."* Panic would lead to disaster. He had to keep his wits. Rikar looked about for options, needing to consider what would be the best choice for his escape. He looked to the river, but the rapids were far too rocky and swift, a certain death. The hodag blocked his way upriver, Rikar wasn't certain just how swift his quarry could be. It seemed somewhat cumbersome, but he had yet to test the beast. Rikar opted to run right, away from the river. He hated running into an unknown area. It was far too easy to get lost. *I'll use the sound of the rapids as my compass.*

He ran. The land rose slightly ahead of him away from the river, but down to his right as it followed the river's dropping. As he went, he entered an older part of the forest with thicker and taller trees, massive gnarled oaks that reached out and intertwined with each other, creating a canopy. Rikar put his younger body to the test and, while the hodag pursued, it fell further and further back until he could no longer see it.

He stopped, panting, and rested with his hands on his knees. He stood in the silence of the ancient forest and strained his hearing. The roar of the river had diminished to mere background noise. Rikar resolved to go no further from it or risk getting lost. He drank from the water skin and, sighing, decided he needed to rest. He backtracked a bit, watchful, until he found a broad, climbable oak.

Rikar jumped to reach the lowest limb, swung up and scrambled onto it. He shimmied to the trunk and climbed until he was about twenty feet up, and wedged himself into place where three branches forked. The sun had burned off the morning's fog and was now nearing its zenith. He adjusted his hood and weapons, and closed his eyes.

*

He startled awake and squinted, face to face with a wild animal. Sitting across from him was a squirrel. He kicked at it. His sudden movement spooked it, causing it to jump to a near branch and chatter at him, angrily. He smiled. The tree lurched. Rikar braced himself and stared down at the base of the tree. Something moved. But, more importantly, the trunk of the oak tree was either steaming or smoking, something spewing from the bark all around the tree.

It stunk, too. Rikar's eyes stung, just like they had from that bear. The realization came quickly that the stuff coming out of the oak's trunk meant that the hodag had found him. Rikar scanned the area around the tree's base until he saw it, standing about ten feet from the trunk.

Rikar had a clear view. *If I can see it, so can my arrow.* He drew back and loosed an arrow. It streaked down through the branches and struck the hodag between its shoulders. The shaft flopped to one side, dangling, only having penetrated an inch or so. The hodag squealed

9

and screeched, rearing up and shaking itself violently. The arrow dropped out.

Angered more than hurt, the hodag charged the tree and butted it, driving one of its horns into the trunk. Rikar felt the impact's vibration. So did the squirrel, which then climbed up and across to another tree on an intersecting branch. *Great idea!* Rikar followed his furry guide. The tree shuddered again and sagged, dropping a few inches before leaning away from the adjoining oak. Rikar stretched and snagged the other tree's branch as his tree's trunk split, dropping a foot before falling to the forest floor.

The crash sent debris, birds, and squirrels scattering in every direction. The hodag followed Rikar to the next tree. It immediately propped itself up, front paws against the tree and bit into the trunk, splintering bark and wood. Rikar could see the slaver oozing from its mouth as it covered the wood. Steam rose instantly and Rikar clearly heard the sizzle and popping of the wood as the creature's saliva destroyed the fibers like an alchemist's acid.

No wonder... He considered all that he'd seen in the camp. The man's bloated body, the dead crow, and the death of the bear. As he made his way to yet another tree using the network of intertwining branches, Rikar reconstructed a probable chain of events. The camper had started his fire, and then was attacked by the hodag while in his tent. It then dragged him out and went off, waiting for him to die.

Once the hodag's saliva got in the man, he died quickly, his body bloating. The crow came, attracted by death, and pecked the man's eye, the poison killing the bird. *By all that is sacred! That poor man had been dead less than an hour when I got there, not a few weeks! The crow was likely the one I heard, dead in seconds just like the bear.*

Rikar continued moving from tree to tree. The sun lay low against the horizon when he ran out of trees. The river's rapids began just beyond his last tree, starting its steep and rocky decent. He'd come a full circle, as he could now see the top of the camper's tent where this encounter had begun.

The hodag, not showing any sense of urgency, had not yet topped a hillcrest about three trees back, maybe forty feet away. It had seemed slow and tired. Their "chase" was easily in its third hour. Rikar rubbed his tender hands, dropped to the lowest branch and swung to the ground. He squatted behind a fallen log that still rested against its stump, readied an arrow and positioned a brittle stick beneath his foot.

Wait. He watched as first its horns, and then its head crested the hill. *It will stop.*

His patience paid off. Once clear of the incline, the hodag paused, breathing heavily. He drew back on the bowstring and held. He then pressed against the stick with his foot, breaking it with a clear *snap.* The hodag's head jerked toward him as the arrow Rikar had loosed dug deep into its left eye socket. Rikar watched the spray of blood as the hodag screamed, bolting up and back, throwing its head from side to side. It bowed, muzzle flat to the ground and pawed at the arrow shaft protruding only inches out of the bloody eye socket.

The hodag stood, again shaking its head, screaming and howling enough to hurt Rikar's ears. It staggered and fell, but then regained its footing and faced Rikar. A lower, angrier growl erupted from deep in its throat. The creature charged, roaring with its mouth wide, bearing dozens of long, knife-sharp fangs. Rikar had nocked an arrow right after the first and now let it fly at the hodag, diving to his right toward the stump. A heartbeat later, the beast struck the fallen log, knocking it free of its stump. Both splintered, sending shards of wood into the air in every direction.

Rikar rolled passed the stump, as fragments of wood rained on him, throwing him off balance. He knelt and reached for his bow and looked up to find the hodag. Its tail whisked just inches over his head, one of its spurs catching Rikar's hood, dragging him to his left.

The hodag spun, slamming its tail into the dirt as it turned. Rikar glared at the creature, searching for the feathered tail vein from his second arrow. Not seeing anything, he fled back to the tree and climbed frantically as the tail shattered the branch he'd just been standing on. Once high enough, Rikar adjusted his clothing and suddenly realized, *no bow!* He frantically scanned the ground below and moaned when he spied its splintered remains amidst the wood, leaves, and dirt near the stump. He did manage a slight grin when he saw the bloody streak in the hodag's mouth where his second arrow had penetrated deep into its tongue.

It can be hurt! But I'm truly limited without the bow. This last encounter came too close. Rikar concentrated on how he could get close enough, fast enough to do some damage to this creature with a mere sabre. He scanned the forest floor, but found nothing of the hodag.

"Where did you go, beastie?" Rikar called out. Nothing. *Could it have gone? Did it need to heal?* Rikar considered coming down for only a second, when he recalled how its skin changed coloration so quickly in the camp. *No, beastie, you're out there, just waiting for me to make a mistake.* So he waited, mindful of every movement, any sound. He waited until the sun had run its course and now rested beyond the western hills.

In the gloom of twilight, Rikar heard the hodag moving, but the light wasn't enough to see where. Rikar ate from his sack and lessened his thirst before wedging himself tightly for a cold night's sleep. Rikar relieved himself. To his surprise, the hodag charged the area where his pee splattered on the forest floor. "Lying in wait, eh?" Rikar taunted. "Stick around 'til morning and I'll have something else for you to attack!" he shouted, laughing.

Rikar expected the hodag to ravage the tree as it had done earlier in the day. He felt nothing and figured the beast needed to rest. *Great! So, come sunup, I'll still be on the run and it will have time to heal. Time to get some rest. If I'm lucky, the thing may just die.* He settled in and, despite his aches, fell quickly asleep.

*

The sound of splintering wood woke Rikar with a start. A tree was falling, but he felt no movement. Bracing himself and shaking the sleep from him, Rikar watched the tree next to his fall, ripping some branches free from the oak he sat in. Dawn had barely arrived.

Damnation! You are a smart beastie. Rikar considered his quandary. There was now no way but down. He studied the fallen tree next to him, anticipating using it to gain access to the next tree, and hence to the safety beyond. After the debris and dust had settled, a puff of steam erupted in the leaves within the fallen tree. Rikar focused hard, trying to discern any movement. *That white blotch there ... might be its horn or tusk.* He reached behind him and withdrew an arrow from the quiver and, like a dart, threw it. True to its mark, the arrow penetrated the branches and pinged off the white blotch. It moved, ever so slightly.

Waiting for me, eh beastie? Without moving, Rikar eyed the ground. The hodag had finally made a mistake. Hiding within the fallen tree meant it had to climb through all that foliage, slowing it down. *If I went that way, it'll have me for sure. But, any other way and it has to come around all those branches.* Rikar realized his best chance was to drop to the ground on the far side of his tree, nearest the river. He was a little more than ten feet up and would be dropping onto softer ground. *Maybe there's a way across the river downstream. I have to try.* He clenched his arms in and stepped off the branch.

He hit the ground and rolled, as he'd hoped. Springing to his feet, he sprinted toward the river, hearing the hodag crashing through the fallen tree. It, too, gave up on stealth and roared as it pursued him. Rikar reached the trail next to the river and ran headlong down it, pushing against trees to keep his balance. He kept his attention ahead of him, praying he would be fast enough. After a sharp drop, Rikar paused, seeing no change in the river. *No chance there!* He veered left into the woods, remembering a large oak he'd passed yesterday coming up the pathway. He reached it and scurried into its branches.

He spun, looking, but saw nothing of the hodag. No movement on the ground. *No growling either, but the roar of the river would drown out any noise.* He surveyed his surroundings and saw that the tree he'd run to wasn't the best choice. It stood alone, so he had no escape route, save for the rock face next to it. He estimated the lip of the rock to be another twelve to fifteen feet above him. Opposite that, another sheer drop to more oak trees and one with lighter bark and pale green leaves. *A big birch tree, the same one I saw when I arrived.*

Ever watchful, Rikar rested a few minutes. He then dropped two arrows, testing, but nothing moved. Knowing what the hodag did to the other trees, Rikar knew he couldn't stay, but also couldn't chance climbing down without knowing its whereabouts. Rikar spanned the branch to the rock face, but when he tested it, the rock pulled loose wherever he put pressure. *Can't climb this. I'll need to go higher than the ledge and jump down to it.* That meant climbing into the thinner limbs further from the cliff and leaping an eight-foot gap to the ledge.

He worked his way into the upper branches, swaying freely as his weight shifted. *Maybe I can use the sway to get me closer when I push off and try to grab hold of that log up there.* He practiced, leaning back and forth with the swing of the tree.

A massive roar blasted him as the hodag charged to the edge of the cliff, just feet away. Rikar startled and lost his grip, dropping several feet until his foot wedged in a joint. A sharp pain shot up his leg. He knew the ankle was broken. The hodag spun and whipped its tail against the closer branches, snagging them and causing more sway.

Rikar clutched at the limb and then reached to withdraw his sabre to fend off the hodag's spurred tail.

Another strike. This time, Rikar swung his blade, but too many branches and twigs deflected it. With the third swipe, Rikar stabbed out, pricking the tail's end. The sabre's tip pulled loose, but the violent movement of the branch loosened his precarious grip on both the limb and his blade. As he swung back on the branch, the sabre's edge dug into another branch. He lost his grip and the sword rattled loose and fell to the ground.

Now without bow and sword, Rikar grew anxious, but kept focused. *Since it's up here, I can retrieve my sword and get out of here. But, by the gods, I have to figure a way to kill this thing! For now, though, maybe find a way across the river.* The hodag approached the ledge again, growling and snapping in full fury. Rikar heard its tail slam against the ground behind it. It lunged and jerked toward him, its front paws slipping on rock at the lip. This close, he noticed the bloody eye socket. *It has no depth perception now! I wonder if I can make it mad enough to get too close?*

Taunting it in the hopes of its falling, Rikar drew the dirk, waved it at the hodag and screamed, "C'mon, you toxic lump! Can't get me, eh? C'mon, jump!" He snapped off a dangling branch and waved it at the snarling beast.

The hodag went behind the log near the edge and lowered its head. The log suddenly lifted into the air, and sailed off the ledge toward him. It wasn't out far enough to hit Rikar, but it dropped into the tree, causing it to swing wildly and pull him toward the cliff.

Rikar clung desperately to the branch and was tossed forward, almost following the log to the cliff base. The tree sprung back, throwing all his weight up and away. Rikar lost his footing and slid up the branches. He looked up and saw the hodag leap toward him, paws forward, and muzzle gaping.

Rikar's momentum took him aside the flying hodag. He managed to point the dirk at the hodag when it slammed into him.

Rikar felt its front paw rake the side of his head, and then the vise-like clamping of its mouth on his shoulder, at least one tooth ripping deep into his flesh.

They fell, hurtling and spinning down through branches that bent and broke against his back and side. Twisting foliage scraped his face, arm, body, and legs. He heard only the snapping of the wood as they dropped, seeing sky, then ground, then trees and then sky again. Immense pain seared from his shoulder with each jolt from the fall, until they hit the ground. A blinding flash exploded behind his eyes with a breath-stealing thud.

His mind reeled. Such pain he'd never known. He screamed and rolled away, reaching for his shoulder and finding only a bloody stump.

His vision returned as he knelt. He saw the hodag lying, unmoving, twisted unnaturally. Blood flowing from its mouth and head. Wedged in its teeth lay a bleeding chunk of flesh and a glistening bone. Rikar also saw the glint of the steel blade protruding from its skull. *That dirk is probably still in my hand.* He winced and leaned on the birch tree's trunk to steady himself, his ankle blazing from pain. He forced his eyes to focus on his shoulder. He bled freely. But his breath caught when he noticed his skin frothing. The stark realization hit him. *Gods! Hodag saliva! I'm dead! Can't let it ... have to wash it off. Water! ... River!*

Rikar staggered, hopping as he rushed headlong toward the river, aware of nothing but the pain and fear, visualizing himself as a bloated corpse. He tripped over rocks and toppled in, immediately swept into the swift current. Cold rushing waters surrounded him, swirling across his open wound, diluting the hodag saliva. The river tumbled him in its rush down the rapids, spinning him into its vortex.

*

Bahlis stood, refilling a customer's ale, when a roar and a cascade of applause came from the great room. He smiled. A mass of people soon emerged. Some finished their drinks and deposited their empty mugs on the bar. Bahlis wished them a good night and then refilled drink orders from those wishing more. Their conversations were casual, the customers expressing both surprise and doubt at the storyteller's tale.

Eventually, a hobbling older man emerged, an empty sleeve tucked under his vest. A satisfied grin covered his face. Bahlis took his mug as the man pulled out a stool and sat heavily onto it. "Bahlis, my friend. How are things tonight?" he asked.

"As long as you keep telling your stories and bringing in the customers, Rikar, things are going well. How are you feeling? Your cough is better."

"It is. It is, thank you."

"And your arm?" Bahlis asked.

"Ha! Well-rotted by now, I imagine! But my shoulder has healed, as I showed them." He paused after taking a sip of his refilled mug.

"You know, my friend, it is very odd. I remember every detail of my hunts, but of late, I can't remember how I got there or how I get back. I must be getting old." Rikar shook his head and took another drink. He then put his mug down and scratched the shoulder of his missing arm. "But, I am thankful. I've hunted most every kind of animal. Many a man would be jealous of what I've achieved. But, with only one arm, those days are surely gone." He raised his glass and added, "Cheers, Bahlis ... to the hunt!"

Bahlis clinked a glass with him and gave him a long smirk.

"What?" Rikar asked.

"I think you might be premature about that, old friend." He paused, glanced side to side, and leaned in, lowering his voice. "What if I told you I know a way for you to yet enjoy the hunting you love so much? There are forces, good sir, that can be of service to you. I am so graced that I am allowed to summon powers ... powers that can set aside the cost of time and replenish an aging body with one full of youthful ambition, strength, and skill even to the extent of renewing your arm. You would experience the grandest, and yet the most dangerous hunt of your life."

Rikar smiled, nodding. "You've piqued my interest. At what cost?"

***

Djinn and Toxic

by Jonathan Shipley
United States

"What about John Travolta in the back bedroom?" Floyd asked, still visibly flustered after ten deep breaths. "Hold him? Book him? What?"

I was still taking deep breaths myself. I made inspecting the corpse in the apartment's living room into a fine-tooth operation because I wasn't sure what to do with the kid. But letting a potential person of interest walk away from the crime scene wasn't an option. "Hold him," I said finally ... assuming he was holdable. Maybe he wouldn't just vanish in a puff of smoke the way he'd appeared. "I'll get to him in a minute."

I finished viewing the mess in the living room. Headless body and lots of blood. This was someone with enemies, probably with threads leading back to the East European mafia. No sign of any sharp-edged item capable of slicing and dicing, but that was the job of forensics. My job was to put the puzzle pieces together as they became available. With a shake of the head, I went back to the mystery in the bedroom.

The *Saturday Night Live* wannabe was perched on the edge of the bed with a vacant stare on his face. College kid to judge by the age and the letterman's sweater. But the rest of the outfit was pure time warp—t-shirt with white polyester bellbottom slacks and honest-to-goodness platform shoes with stocky four-inch heels. Either he'd missed the memo that the costume party was cancelled, or someone had a major '70s fetish. His face matched the clothes with long, wavy brown hair parted in the middle and mutton-chop sideburns surrounding a pleasant enough face with hazel eyes. As I studied the face, he stopped staring at nothing and shifted his attention to me.

"So how bad is it?" he asked with a glance toward the door. "Out there, I mean. Did something happen?"

I nodded. "Mr. Brogachek has been murdered."

17

The kid perked up, which was an odd reaction, considering. "Really? He's dead? You're sure?"

"No doubt about it. He's very dead all over the living room. No love lost between the two of you, I take it."

"I'm glad he's dead, if that's what you mean. He's been holding me prisoner forever."

Since the 1970s if I believed the costume. I pulled out my iPad and pulled up a query screen. "Then you should be in the system as a missing person. So you have a name, kid?"

"Probably," he shrugged. "I have no idea what it is, but I probably have one."

I frowned. "So you're a kidnapping victim with amnesia? What about a school? From your sweater, I take it blue and yellow are the school colors."

"Probably," he repeated. "But I can't remember that either. Same for family and friends. It's all gone."

So a nameless disco king. The captain was going to love this. And right on to the elephant in the room. "A few minutes ago, when Detective Floyd and I were searching this room, you seemed to appear out of nowhere. Care to explain that?"

He looked around uneasily. "I'm not supposed to say anything about that, but now that the consequences are ... well, dead, I guess it doesn't make any difference." He paused. "Actually, it could make a huge difference in a positive way. I mean, I could have been stuck inside for who knows how long if you hadn't been here. Now there's a chance to get free and get a life again."

"Not a clue what you just said," I said when he finished babbling. "The way this works is I ask a question and you answer. So let me ask again: where did you appear from?"

This time Disco didn't hesitate, just pointed to a low-slung antique teapot on the dresser. "From in there."

I raised a skeptical eyebrow. "From a teapot?"

"I know, I know—it should be a lamp, but apparently old oil lamps are hard to find. So someone improvised with the teapot because it's about the same shape."

"Lamp as in Aladdin?" And I thought I was skeptical before.

"Yes, exactly. Rubbing the lamp—er, teapot—evokes me and here I am."

I crossed over to the dresser and to take a curious look under the lid. Maybe it was *I Dream of Jeannie* reruns, but I was halfway expecting miniature furniture inside. But nothing. Just silver outside, silver inside. I picked it up, shook it to be sure it was empty, then rubbed my palm along its side. "Like this, huh?"

"Unh—"

And suddenly I was alone in the room. For a moment, I just stood there unmoving. I knew it had to be a hoax. Secret panel, trap door ... something. But I hadn't seen a thing. It had been, literally, now you see him, now you don't. Finally, I dropped my gaze down to the teapot. Checking under the lid again, I found it was still empty to the eye ... but somehow heavier. I rubbed it again.

And there he was, standing right where he had been a moment before. He seemed to need a moment to orient himself. He blinked a few times, then looked over at me unhappily. "I'd be obliged if you gave me a second to brace myself next time. Getting dismissed always feels like being pulled through a keyhole. So please don't do that any more often than you have to, and with ample warning. I'd appreciate it."

I was still working through all this. "So you're a genie? Or is that djinn for males?"

"Don't know, I'm not any of those. And I *cannot* grant wishes! Please believe that."

"Sounds like that's an old argument."

"It's a new argument every time the teapot changes hands. I've had some masters who refused to believe me and kept jerking me in and out of the pot as incentive until I was royally sick. I'd prefer not to have a repeat of that."

My mind had fastened on one particular word. "Masters?" I prompted curiously.

"Whoever owns the teapot is my master. His whim is my command."

"And you hated Brogachek for being your master?"

"I hated all the cooking and cleaning. No one ever used me as a maid before." Then he looked at me with narrowed eyes. "You're sure it was murder?"

"Definitely murder."

"Well, it wasn't me. I couldn't have murdered him because I was in the teapot."

That was true, but he sounded overly desperate to convince me of that. "Any idea who else might want him dead?"

"Hey, I'm just the maid, and conveniently disposable at that. He didn't keep me around for his private conversations. But from the weird invoices I'd find around the apartment, I figured he was into something."

That was a given. We knew Brogachek was connected to drugs and human trafficking even before he turned up dead.

Floyd stuck his head into the bedroom, bullet head swiveling on a stocky neck to take in the situation. "Everything okay in here, Lieutenant? Forensics is asking for you ... unless you need more time in here *by yourself*, of course."

Right. I was spending a long time in a room that had already been gone over and sealed up. This interview wasn't over, not by a long shot, but it needed to be better organized. "Be right out," I told Floyd and shot the kid a signal. He nodded and struck a pose with clenched jaw and clenched fists. Then I rubbed and he was gone.

"I am *not* writing this up," Floyd muttered. "I'd have no idea how to say it without setting myself for a psych evaluation. You need to give that a thought yourself, Lieutenant."

I grunted acknowledgement and followed him out to the living room. The body was still where it had fallen, but forensics had found the head. I stepped over and traded some details with them, but my mind wasn't on the murder. I had to figure out what to do with Disco. He wasn't exactly a witness and wasn't exactly evidence, but he was neck-deep in the situation, which made him part of the case. The problem was how to include him without looking like a loon. Floyd was right. The paperwork couldn't mention anything about genies and lamps. Too much truth in this instance would be stupidity. In point of fact, this had already turned into two overlapping cases—a murder and a weird kidnapping/imprisonment. The smart thing would be to concentrate on the first and completely forget the second, but I knew that wasn't going to happen. The reason I did well in this career was because I could not let a mystery go unsolved.

I caught Floyd's eye across the room and signaled "bedroom," then "corridor." He knew me well enough to catch the shorthand and looked distinctly unhappy. But he stepped into the bedroom and when he shuffled out again, his overcoat had one bulging pocket. I wrapped up my discussion with forensics and joined him in the corridor outside. I gave the uniform on duty at the door a nod and continued on down the corridor and around the corner, Floyd muttering behind me all the way.

"You know this is dumb-ass stupid, Lieutenant," he said, shoving the teapot at me as soon as we were out of sight. "Evidence tampering at the very least."

"Got a better idea?" I asked pointedly. He shut up. I "evoked" the kid.

"Listen up," I said. "We need statements about Brogachek, the apartment, visitors, and anything else that's relevant. So you are now the pothead neighbor he hired to keep the place clean."

"Why pothead?" the kid asked.

"Because you're dressed funny and that's what people will think anyway. We're marching right back in there and doing this as an official interview. Got that?"

"Name," Floyd prompted.

"And you need a name," I continued. "Since you can't remember your real one, just make something up and stick by it."

That should have been easy, but when we were standing in the living room in earshot of everyone and I asked his name, he answered, "Winston Salem, sir."

Beside me, Floyd rolled his eyes.

Later, when he and I were alone in the car with the teapot in the trunk, I asked, "So what do you think?"

"Complete mess," he snorted with a shake of his head.

"About Disco's reactions," I redirected. I refused to call him Winston Salem.

"Yeah, that. Not much shock at the blood and gore. I get that the vic was keeping him prisoner, but still pretty cold."

I nodded agreement. "We need to know who and what we're dealing with. You take the school angle. We have a blue-and-yellow letter sweater with four sleeve stripes. That ought to mean a senior. So we should be hunting a senior who disappeared within the last few years from a college or university whose colors are blue and yellow."

"Last few years?" Floyd gave a snort. "So we're officially dumping the '70s angle?"

"As far as we know, that's just a costume," I shrugged. "On the other hand, if you should happen on a missing '70s college kid who fits the description ..."

"A missing person's case, location wide open, that's forty years cold and probably not databased anywhere. Don't ask much, do you?"

"If you want to switch, I'll be running down lamps and genies. I know how much you like interacting with the occult crowd."

He gave me a sour look. "And cold case it is. What are you going to do with the teapot?"

"I'll hang on to it. Maybe some occultist might recognize it tomorrow."

"Huh," he grunted. "So the alleged genie goes home with you tonight. Am I the only one who finds that scary?"

"Strange, I grant you, but that's how it is. Until we know what's what, we have to keep that teapot close."

"Keep your friends close and your teapots closer," he muttered.

*

I spent half the evening fidgeting, unable to concentrate on the report forensics had posted online. Finally I gave in and rubbed the teapot. Out he came.

"Cool, new digs," Disco said, looking around. "I was pretty tired of cleaning those same three rooms year after year."

"How many years exactly?" I asked, keeping my tone casual. Sometimes the best way to collect data was to chum around.

"Five, ten—I lose track of time." He kept looking around. "You know, I could put a shine on this place that would do you proud."

"You said you hated cleaning."

"I did, but that was the master-slave thing. It's different when I'm offering on my own." He gave a shrug. "And I'm pretty good at it— practice makes perfect and all that. I would offer to whip up something to eat, too, but I haven't checked the fridge. Yours truly might be able to appear out of thin air, but I sure can't make dinner that way."

It was like he was moving in with me. "Don't get too comfortable, kid. As soon as things get sorted out, you're going back."

"To where? Brogachek's empty apartment?" he cut in. "Stuck on a shelf forever because there's no one around to rub the damn teapot? Come on, man, you can't do that to me. It's like solitary confinement for life. If you can't break the spell, at least you can be my new master."

Whoa! Suddenly the choice was breaking a spell or adopting him? How had we gotten here? "Breaking spells is not in my job description," I told him.

22

"Then new master it is," Disco continued with puppy dog eagerness. "So, dinner?"

"If you can find the makings of a dinner, feel free. I'll see if I can find you a change of clothes so you're not such a time warp."

Disco's smile faded. "Doesn't work that way. I am what I am, as in frozen exactly as captured. You want a maid, you're stuck with the look."

Who said I wanted a maid?

*

Next morning I woke up, let Disco out to make breakfast, and went back to the bedroom to finish getting ready for the day. There was something very wrong with that sequence of actions, I realized as I was brushing my teeth. Way too domestic. It was as if I was suddenly on track to wake up every morning and let out the genie like letting out the dog. Then the glorious aroma of an eggs-and-blueberries concoction wafted in from the kitchen, and I decided I could put up with a few days of domesticity ... for the sake of the case.

When I was ready for the world, I headed for the kitchen and found hot buttered toast and a blueberry omelette waiting for me. Disco was already in the living room, starting on the clutter. I gobbled the breakfast, fleetingly considered asking for seconds, then sensibly headed for the door. "You okay on your own for a few hours?" I asked, then quickly added, "Your omelette was delicious."

He grinned. "Omelettes are my specialty. And yeah, I have plenty to do for a couple hours. I'll stay inside and won't embarrass you— promise. But the omelette was about the last of the food. Any chance the neighborhood grocery store would deliver so we can have dinner tonight?"

Not much chance of a neighborhood grocery store, period, I thought. "The SuperEats on Houston Avenue will deliver if you pay them in blood."

Disco's eyes went huge. "You're kidding."

"Just a figure of speech," I said quickly. "I'll leave the number and some cash by the phone."

"A real phone, I hope. I never did get the hang of those little toys Brogachek used."

"It's an old landline," I assured him. "Is there any problem if I take the teapot with me? I'm doing research."

"It'll feel weird—like I should be somewhere else." But then he nodded. "Yeah, as long as I know what's happening, I'll be okay. Just don't leave town or anything. Too much distance will pop me back inside like a rubber band. And then your place won't get cleaned."

He finished on a light note, but I caught that separation from the teapot worried him a little. Interesting. "What about if I leave the teapot here and just snap some pix of it instead?" I suggested.

A certain tension cleared instantly from Disco's face. "Yeah, much better. Thanks."

Very interesting, I thought as I snapped a dozen shots with my "toy" phone and headed on out.

*

Contrary to Floyd's worst expectations, the local occult community was very civilized. For research like this, my go-to person was an academician at the local junior college. They called her an anthropologist specializing in religious artifacts, but it was a thin fiction.

"Lieutenant, come in," Professor Doherty greeted me when I reached her office. She was very professorial with graying hair and thin reading glasses that she never took off because she was always reading. "You said the category this time was antique lamps with special properties?"

I closed the door. "Genies, actually, but I didn't want to say that over the phone. Genies and whoever else might live in a teapot."

"Djinni, actually," she corrected automatically. "The more correct plural of genie is djinni." Then she gave me a sharp look. "Why did you say 'whoever else'? What have you gotten into, Lieutenant?"

"A silver teapot and someone who claims to be the occupant turned up at a murder scene. No idea if one is connected to the other, but now I have a homicide and a mystery on my hands."

"A teapot," she repeated. "That's not the traditional lamp myth, but it follows the same logic of an interior space for holding and a spout for coming and going. That's representational more than physical, you understand, shape implying function. What does the occupant look like?"

"Like a '70s college student, disco with a letter sweater. He says he's frozen that way because that was how he was captured. Does that make any sense?"

She had to mull that over a moment. "According to lore, a genie can take the form of an innocent-looking child or a sultry harem girl,

24

i.e. disguises that invite a person to let down their guard. Frankly, a disco teenager seems to be mixing in an entirely different universe. He really used the word 'captured'?"

I thought back to be sure. "He did."

"That's interesting because all the myths about djinni commonly known in our culture center on calling them up to gain wishes. To access lore on their capture, you'd have to abandon the English sources, go back to Arabic and Persian sources that talk about sorcerers a thousand years ago cleaning the wild deserts of djinni and devils and ifrits by entrapping them in little silver vessels."

"Where they were bound to their master's will, right?"

"Whoever possessed the lamp could evoke and dismiss, that's consistent in all texts. That in itself might have been enough to induce a genie to follow orders, i.e. grant wishes. When locked in a tiny cage, you would jump at any chance of freedom, even if only temporary."

"So," and this was back to the homicide, "there is no way for a genie, or genie-like being, to kill his master."

"Ah, but there are also cautionary tales about always keeping the lamp in hand when the genie is out because that is the only true protection. It's the vessel that has the power, not the master."

So if Disco was a genie, I'd done that part completely wrong. But that was a huge "if."

"And, theoretically speaking, is this the vessel of a real genie or just a college student?" I handed over my phone with the teapot pictures.

She clicked through them, then produced a magnifying glass from her desk drawer and reached for a reference book from the shelf behind her. She looked and referenced a moment. "According to the hallmarks," she said, panning the glass, "this appears to be French, post-Revolution. The Minerva's head indicates First Standard with a silver content 95 percent pure, which is finer than British or American sterling. That makes sense for an entrapment vessel, but this is a nineteenth-century piece, which is a thousand years after the genie-capturing era. So, theoretically speaking," she said slowly, "you're looking at a different animal completely."

"And what animal is that?"

"A lampslave, i.e. a human trapped in a lamp. For someone to pose as a genie is odd but explainable in terms of cultural knowledge. But to pose as a lampslave implies access to a whole different knowledgebase, such as an old Arabian grimoire."

I nodded, still sorting this out. "Help me out here. I get that you would never want to free a genie, but isn't a lampslave just the opposite? If you ran into one of those, wouldn't you try to free him ... theoretically speaking?"

Professor Doherty sat silently for a moment. "That might depend on why he was imprisoned. That could be a sticky decision ... theoretically speaking."

That thought followed me as I made my way from campus to the precinct. What I valued most about Professor Doherty was that she never pushed. She explained, advised, and warned without demanding any explanation back from me, not that I had any sane explanation in this case. "Theoretically speaking" got to be a thin fiction, but it was better than hitting the impossible head-on.

Floyd flagged me down the moment I stepped inside the precinct. "Lots to talk about, Lieutenant," he said, then glanced around at the busy nest of cubicles. "Privately."

There are no private places in the precinct, so we ended up driving down Uttica Street so Floyd could talk. "The colors blue and yellow might be Yale, or University of Rochester, or any school in the University of California system, but my instincts are telling me Rochester."

"Your what?" I had to ask because Floyd had all the instincts of a tree stump. Strictly facts and procedure, that guy.

"My finely honed instincts," he repeated stubbornly, then quirked an eyebrow. "Of course, this old missing person photo I found online helped a little, too." He handed me a black-and-white printout of Disco dated 1973. It could have been taken an hour ago. "Yeah, amazing, huh? The info was just sitting there, ready to come to papa. Downright spooky, actually."

Spooky seemed to be the flavor of the day. "Darren Haliper, huh?" I read from the caption underneath. "And now we have a name. Any family still living?"

Floyd held up a finger to forestall the question. "I haven't got to the good stuff yet, Lieutenant. Darren Haliper went missing just when the police wanted to question him about the Alphabet Murders—still unsolved, incidentally. Supposedly Haliper dated all three girls who later turned up strangled. Police thought he might have noticed some connection between the three."

"Or maybe *was* the connection," I suggested. "Did the Rochester PD like him as a suspect, or just as a witness?"

"None of the evidence linked him as suspect, but there wasn't much hard evidence to start with. When he went missing, police expected him to turn up as a fourth victim. They thought someone wanted to shut him up."

I gave a snort. "Well, stuffing him in a teapot would do that all right. But why not just kill him like the others?"

Floyd shrugged. "The murderer was ramping down and didn't want more heat? Or his murder would point toward the killer in a way the others didn't."

"A campus connection maybe," I mulled. "Who did he associate with on a regular basis?"

"Well, he worked as a TA in the School of Languages."

That clicked. "Arabic?"

Floyd looked impressed. "Yeah. The professor he worked for was their Arabic specialist. How'd you know?"

"The spell that put him in the teapot would be either Arabic or Persian, according to my occult sources. So it's a good guess *who* imprisoned Disco. The question is still why. That professor is ..."

"Dead decades ago," Floyd supplied. "But might still be good for questioning ... depending on your occult sources."

I could just imagine Professor Doherty's reaction to non-theoretical necromancy. "Then I see this backstory two ways. One, Disco was a key witness in a murder case and his nefarious professor teapots him so he doesn't talk to the police. Two, Disco was erroneously thought to be the murderer by his do-gooder professor, who teapots him to stop the murders."

"And don't forget three, Lieutenant," Floyd interjected. "That's where Disco is the murderer, but it can't be proved, so he's teapotted as a life sentence for his crimes. I'm leaning toward that one, personally."

"You just hate platform shoes."

"That, too," he nodded.

"The problem for us," I continued, "is that one and two carry a moral obligation to break Disco out of his trap, but three says leave him as is. And it's not like we can go to the DA with this one. We'd get about as far as 'man in a teapot.'"

"So how do we play this?"

"We get Disco to tell us. Not directly, but perps always give themselves away. He's either going to be pleased or scared that we've uncovered his true identity. I'll just let him react."

"And this is one-on-one in your apartment? Not liking that, Lieutenant."

"Has to be that way because you'll be handling Part B of the plan ... which starts now."

I parked the car and led the way into my apartment. Disco looked up from the floor where he was shifting piles of papers in an attempt to find enough carpet to vacuum. "Oh, company," he said with a grimace. "How optimistic of you to think I'd have the place the ready so soon."

"No, not company, just working the case," I assured him. "Your teapot has to go downtown for an evidence check before we try anything with it."

Disco perked up warily. "To free me, you mean?"

"Yeah, that direction. Detective Floyd here has uncovered enough of your past to give you an identity, and that's just the tip of the iceberg." I handed him the missing person's printout. "Welcome back, Darren Haliper."

"Darren Haliper?" He stared at the picture intently. "That was fast. Probably the miracle of the Unterweb or something, right?"

"Or something," I shrugged. "Let me get the teapot and we'll get out of your hair."

"And such a lot of hair to get out of," Floyd muttered in an undertone.

A moment later, we were heading out the door. "Special dinner tonight," Disco called just before I pulled the door shut. "Steak and mushrooms. We'll celebrate my having a name again."

"Hmm," Floyd murmured as we headed down to the parking lot.

"Is that a vote for one, two, or three?" I asked.

"Not so sure. He's real domestic, isn't he?"

My very word for him. "I'd almost consider keeping him around for his cooking, but that's a big almost."

"And you don't think it's weird that the first person puttering around the apartment since Cindy is ... him?"

My stomach knotted at the familiar name. "For the record, I think it's very weird. Probably it's not politically correct, but because he lives in a teapot, I don't consider him a real person ... not entirely." I shook my head. "But we've got work to do before my special dinner tonight."

*

When I walked into my apartment, I was assaulted by sounds and smells. I followed the smell to the kitchen where a pan of barbequed steak strips sizzled on the stovetop. I followed the sound to the back bedroom where I had hidden Cindy's spinet piano under a layer of blankets. No one had played it since she died.

But now Disco was attacking the keys with a vengeance to produce one of those big piano sonatas that my wife also loved. I set the pain of the past on hold to concentrate on the necessities of the present. "Not bad," I called over the wave of arpeggios.

Disco nearly jumped off the bench. "Didn't hear you come in," he gasped with a weak smile. "Guess I was really into the Beethoven."

"Pretty impressive for someone with functional amnesia," I grinned back. "But I have more news about your past."

"Save it for dinner," he said, scurrying past me. "There's nothing like steak to go with good news."

No response to my amnesia remark, I noted as I followed him out. Or maybe he forgot.

"We're in the dining room," he called from ahead. "I got the table cleared off and it's actually usable now."

Another first since Cindy's death. Again, I shelved the comparison of past and present, of the last time eating in the dining room and this time. Everything was cleared and cleaned and elegantly laid out, I had to admit. The candlesticks were a bit much, but I didn't say anything.

My phone rang. "Deadman's switch is set and moving," Floyd said at the other end. "And forensics came up with a zinger on the Brogachek murder. The head severed with a fourteenth-century sword. Yeah, you heard me right. Brings a certain name to mind, eh?"

One of the East European bosses collected antique swords. That case was turning out to be a pretty direct from Point A to Point B. But the Disco case was more than compensating in general murkiness.

"More news about me?" Disco asked, appearing in the doorway.

"No, about Brogachek. We're closing in on the murder weapon."

His face twisted in discontent. "I didn't really hate him, you know. Sure, he was abusive with the master-slave thing and kind of violent at times, but it was a pretty stable setup. But I'm not surprised one of the other *mafioti* killed him."

Which I hadn't said. Someone knew more about the East Europeans than they'd let on. But how could you live with a mobster and not know? Even in a teapot.

I seated myself and Disco brought out the steak strips smothered in mushrooms. Suddenly he paused. "I thought you were bringing the teapot back with you."

"Yes, I did. It's still out in the car. I'll get it later."

Disco relaxed and finished serving the steak. "Dig in. Be right back." He returned the serving pan to the kitchen and returned with a plate of strips and mushrooms for himself. "How is it?" he prompted. "Please tell me it's great."

"It's wonderful," I said between mouthfuls. "But I've never tasted mushrooms like these. They have a tartness, almost a bitterness that's like Asian sweet and sour."

He took that strange comment as a compliment as we continued eating in silence for a moment. "So what's new with Darren Haliper?" he asked. "You said you had more information."

"Yes, he was a senior at the University of Rochester. And a TA to a professor specializing in pre-Islamic Arabic. We think that's the genie connection. The professor must be the one who spelled you into the teapot." I kept talking and watching closely for reactions. So far I was only getting wide-eyed interest. "The question is why would he do that?"

"Hmm?" Disco nodded noncommittally, his mouth full of food.

I kept pushing, making sure one hand was free and close to the holster under my jacket. "It's almost a temptation to connect the teapot with the Alphabet Murders somehow."

He stopped cold. "It's a lie. That's what Professor Warren thought—that I killed all those girls—but I didn't. You can be emotionally distant without being a murderer. But he thought I should be locked up ... and that's what he did."

So the amnesia was a scam, and definitely not scenario one where the innocent student is potted by his evil professor. So either two or three—mistakenly thought to be the murderer or actually was the killer. But definitely a mental case. Should have picked up on that earlier. Long-term abusive relationship with a known *mafioti*, then moving in and getting all domestic right after the brutal end of Brogachek, not even blinking an eye at all the blood. The signs were all there for some sort of sociopathic co-dependency. So maybe two wasn't so different from three ultimately.

Suddenly the fork slid from my fingers. My whole hand trembled. "Something's wrong with the mushrooms."

"Oh, that's not the mushrooms," Disco smiled from across the table. "That's the Valium."

"Valium?" I choked out. My throat was closing up like a major allergy attack.

"Yup, that's me, child of the '70s. I may not understand your computers or be any good with your tiny telephones, but I do know my pharmaceuticals. People these days seem to have forgotten all the effects you can produce mixing mushrooms with simple drugstore drugs. Tonight's mixture of Valium and mushrooms, for example, produces muscular paralysis. It doesn't last long ... but long enough."

I grabbed at the phone in my pocket, but it fell to the floor from fingers fast going numb. Disco just kept chewing as I slumped forward helplessly. "I tried, you know, I really did," he said. "I thought you were going to be a great master for me. But then you started digging, and I realized you weren't going to be good at all. Other masters were like that—nice at the beginning, but then they'd turn on me. But this time I'm wiser, and I owe that to Brogachek. You don't get slapped around for years without learning a few things. All it took in his case was a damning phone call to one of his Romanian compadres and strategically leaving the apartment door unlocked. But now I have you to deal with. And Floyd. But with the two of you gone, I can start all over again. Someone polishes a forgotten teapot and, bingo, new master. Yeah, I can play this game forever, and I do mean forever. That freedom thing was just a sympathy ploy. Who needs freedom when you can be eternally young and—"

He twitched suddenly. Then his whole body shuddered. "It's not in your car!" he cried. He rose, pulling from his polyester pocket a thin silken chord. "Tell me where my teapot is!"

I whispered something and he came around the table to put his head close to mine. "What was that?" At the same time, he slipped the assassin's chord around my neck. "You damn cops think you're so clever, but I'm the clever one here. Now where's my teapot?"

Again I whispered and this time he caught the words, "Speeding to a toxic landfill."

It took a second for it to sink in that his all-important vessel was about to be buried in refuse and would never again see the light of day.

His face distorted into a mask of rage as he pulled the chord taut around my neck and kept tightening.

Hang on, I told myself as my vision turned black around the edges. *Just a few seconds more.*

Abruptly, his whole body spasmed. "Nooo!" he wailed, clutching at the table's edge with trembling hands. "Don't do this. I'll be good! I'll be —"

And he was gone, pulled back into his distant teapot.

I lay collapsed across the table for a long time. When my fingers started jerking on their own, I took it as a good sign that my muscles were returning. When the knock came at the door, I was recovered enough to stumble across the room and fumbled around until I got it open.

Floyd stood on the threshold, shaking his head. "Take it your part didn't go exactly to plan, Lieutenant."

"Not exactly," I managed to gasp. But the deadman's switch had worked perfectly. Floyd had sent the teapot toward its toxic grave when he didn't receive a call from me. Then because it had been a hell of a strange day, I had to say it. "Disco's dead."

Floyd cracked a rare smile. "Next time, just hire a maid."

***

Leapfrog Lager and the Little People

by Robert Allen Lupton
United States

Last month we brewed the first production batch of our new triple-hopped lager, a pale English style beer we named Leapfrog Lager. The humor of calling a hoppy beer Leapfrog Lager was more than we could resist. My label had ten fat men in Victorian-style clothing playing leapfrog while holding beer steins and all ten men were caricatures of American presidents or British prime ministers.

My husband, Bran, and I didn't plan to open a brewery. We came to England as foreign exchange students. I studied to be an artist. I'm Bara, a real Indian princess from the Jemez Pueblo in New Mexico, elected at the Gathering of Nations when I was seventeen. I designed and made my traditional clothing. The beadwork and sewing took almost a year. Bran was a musician and a Viking warrior—well, he would be if Viking warriors were five feet tall and polydactyl, six fingers and a thumb on each hand. There are notes in an alto sax only he can find.

Like all artists and musicians, we tried not to starve while we waited to become famous. It's cheaper to brew your own beer than it is to buy it. My husband could brew a gallon for what a pint of Guinness costs at the local pub. To our surprise, Bran turned out to be an outstanding brewmeister and I was a marketing wizard. By our first New Year's Eve, we sold beer to the entire neighborhood.

The next spring, we produced and sold three hundred gallons of Fuzzy Bunny Easter Ale. "It makes you feel reborn." I based the label on an old photo of Betty Grable.

We used the profits from Fuzzy Bunny to buy our brewer's license and rent space upstairs over a greengrocer. We crowd-funded enough money to buy professional equipment. We sold out of Coyote Odin

Microbrew in four days. Viking Six-Finger Discount Lager and Kokopelli Mountain Stout wouldn't stay in stock. Bran produced a thousand gallons of Ragnar Raindance Double Bock for Christmas. On the label, Loki and Thor wore feathered war bonnets and danced with Valkyries. One Valkyrie wore a full Kachina costume and looked a lot like me.

Bran designed Leapfrog Lager before we bottled and distributed the double bock. Leapfrog contained a special mixture of all three types of hops: aroma, bitter, and mellow. There are hundreds of different hops, and Bran tried several before settling on Amarillo, Warrior, and Tomahawk hops. Leapfrog contained 24 percent alcohol, about four times the amount in a typical beer.

It took three trial brews to get it right. It tasted amazing, but three glasses caused a worse hangover than Daddy's Dreamcatcher, the maple syrup infused corn whisky my father made in New Mexico. Both will kick your butt.

We ordered the hops and Bran sanitized the equipment. He mixed and boiled the wort and he followed his notes to ensure the hops were in the same ratio he'd used during the final test run. We waited impatiently through the fermentation and conditioning stages. It was perfect, the beer tasted great, and we bottled it before Lent.

The evening before the first cases of Leapfrog Lager were scheduled for shipment, Bran and I drank a couple of bottles with dinner. I saw the little people before I finished my fish and chips.

I'd read about people seeing pink elephants and little green men. Back home in New Mexico, young people on peyote-fueled vision quests see talking animals and plants. My brother claimed he spent two days soaring with eagles. I always believed it was the reason he became a pilot. I'd never heard of anyone seeing little people.

There were four of them, three little men and one little woman. They were about two feet tall and dressed like a Maxfield Parrish illustration. They were busy searching our rooms and didn't speak, but went efficiently about their business.

I reached across the table and tapped Bran's arm. I pointed at the woman and whispered, "Do you see her? Can you see the men with her?"

Bran answered in a slurred voice. Drinking 24 percent beer will do that. "Oh hell, yes, cool. Are they trolls or elves?"

"I think they're gnomes."

They can't be gnomes, they don't have little red hats. Why are they searching our place?"

"I have no idea. Do you think they can see us?" I waved my arms at the little woman and shouted, "Hey, Thumbelina, I see you. Can you see me?"

The little people froze and one of the men said, "They're talking about us. They can see us. No one should be able to see us in this frequency."

"We can hear you, too, Munchkin man. Why the hell are you in our apartment going through our stuff?"

The little people didn't respond, but talked among themselves. One of the men spoke to the woman, "Maia, they really can hear and see us. We have to go, but we can't leave without the Resonance Horn. They're drunk, but they're too big to fight."

Maia, the female in charge, answered, "We can run or fight later. Let's talk first, perchance they can help us."

Bran laughed and spit a mouthful of beer across the room, "I don't hang around people who say 'perchance.'" What the hell are you? You don't have pixie haircuts."

"I'm Maia. My ugly friend is Flick. These two young ones are Quin and Drim. That's who we are. As for what we are, we damn sure aren't pixies. We don't have wings and we don't shed that sparkly pixie dust crap. We have many names. In Germany, we're kobolds; the English call us boggarts, hobgoblins, and elves. In Ireland, we are known as leprechauns. The Scots say we're brownies or boogies. I hate that. Would you like it if people called you a brownie or a booger? Disgusting, who wants to be called a booger?"

She pointed at Bran and rattled on, "The big man looks Norse. His people call us dwarves or trolls. The big lady is American, where the native people have many names for us, but the only one I remember is kokopelli.

"We are never Munchkins and I am never Thumbelina. If you see a pixie or fairy around anywhere, I'll kick his little flower-sniffing ass. Those little flying monsters are mean. There are many legends about us, but no one can see us unless we're trapped permanently in your world. We're the movement in the shadows, the flicker in the corner of your eye, and the hint of an image that isn't really there. Cameras don't see us. We can see ourselves in your mirrors, but you can't see our reflections. We're not here to harm anyone, we just like to visit your world. I like motorcycles and pizza, among other things. That pixie crap isn't important. We're in real trouble here. We need some help."

"You make it sound ominous. I never thought fairies were scary." I answered. "Cover your ears, Peter Pan, but I don't believe in fairies. Before we talk about help, why can we see you and what's this frequency crap about?"

Maia and her companions climbed onto the chairs around our table, and sat with their chins at tabletop height. Maia said, "We aren't fairies. If you must call us something, call us kobolds. I hope you won't be afraid of us when you sober up. We mean no harm."

She shifted in the kitchen chair and smirked, "Drunk on two beers, you guys are lightweights. Talking's hard work, how about you give us each a beer." She leaned forward and her nose and eyes were barely above the edge of the table. "And some pillows to sit on would be nice."

Bram brought six bottles of Leapfrog Lager while I fetched four cushions from the couch. Maia took a drink and nodded her approval. Quin and Drim filled and smoked clay pipes while they sipped their beers.

"We live in the same places you live, except we live at a different frequency than you. We vibrate at a different speed than you do and our worlds are slightly out of touch with each other. Normally, we can't see, touch, or hear anything in your world. Most of the people in our world and all the people in your world aren't even aware of the other world's existence. Think about a merry-go-round. Everyone riding on the merry-go-round can see each other perfectly. People not on the merry-go round see the riders as fast-moving blurs and vice versa. This works the same way, only it's much stronger.

"Once upon a time—" She laughed and clinked bottles with Flick. "I like to say once upon a time, so sue me. Anyway, once upon a time, a kobold musician made an instrument we call the Resonance Horn. He carved it from an elephant's tusk. The horn has twelve holes running from top to bottom on the upper side and two holes underneath. This musician, unlike most of us, could use his toes like fingers. You could say he had prehensile feet. He played the twelve holes on top with his eight fingers and four of his toes. He used his thumbs to play the two holes on the bottom.

"He discovered certain notes changed the vibration frequency of every kobold within hearing range. The music modified our frequency to be close enough to yours that we could see you, but you couldn't see us. Since we vibrate only slightly out of harmony with your world, we can affect things. We can move stuff around, eat your food, scare your farm animals, basically do whatever we want, like in that movie about the poltergeist. We aren't magic, we just walk over to something, pick it up, and carry it across the room. Since you can't see us, it looks like magic to you.

"A different series of notes returns us to our vibration frequency and our world. I used the words 'vibration' and 'frequency' because I don't know better words. The effect of the first notes, the notes that move us unseen into your world, is not permanent, it wears off. If it wears off before the second note series from the Resonance Horn returns us to our world, our resonance continues to degrade until it completely matches the resonance in this world. Once we become perfectly in tune with your world, we're trapped here.

"You have legends about people like us who had to stay in your world. Some chose to live as house elves, virtual slaves. Trolls don't hide under bridges because they like the neighborhood, but everybody has to be somewhere. I have a great uncle who spent thirty years pretending to be a stone gargoyle on some cathedral in Paris. He finally made it home, but he's completely deaf. All those damn bells. We don't have the skills to survive in your world for very long and I don't want to live as a midget circus clown. We want to go home.

"So how can you help us? Dumb dwarf here," she said pointing to Flick, "Dumb dwarf hid the horn in a case of Leapfrog Lager. We checked the cases at your brewery and the horn isn't there. You brought three cases home with you and we hope the horn is in one of those cases."

Bran looked confused. "There's a magic ivory horn inside a case of our beer?"

"Not exactly, it's not magic, but we think our Resonance Horn is inside a case of beer in your apartment. It's not ivory. We haven't used ivory for hundreds of years. It's never a good idea to piss off an elephant when you're only two feet tall. We carve the horns from wood these days."

Bran drained his beer and stood up. "Let's check the boxes. I put them in the pantry." Bran took the first partially empty case from the pantry and sat it on the tabletop. He lifted two unopened boxes and put them beside the open case on the table.

The horn wasn't in the partial case. I opened the cardboard top on the third box and said, "I'm confused, if your frequency thing has degraded so we can see you, aren't you already trapped?"

Maia stood on the table and tapped her foot impatiently while I opened the box. "I don't understand why you can see us," she said dismissively. "Our frequencies haven't degraded. You shouldn't be able to see us, maybe your vibrations have changed. Open the box, open the box."

I folded the cardboard edges back and found the horn in the box. It was eighteen inches long and carved from a highly polished wood, yew. The finger holes were aligned like a row of shirt buttons on top of the instrument. The mouthpiece was carved from a deer's antler.

Bran reached for the horn and I handed it to him. As he took it reverently, he shared, "My degree is in music and I took classes in primitive instruments. I saw drawings of horns like these called 'lituus.' They were used during medieval times. Bach reconstructed a lituus and wrote the only piece of surviving music that requires a lituus horn. It was said to have a haunting but piercing sound. It's almost impossible to play."

Bran continued. "The horn looks similar to the ones snake charmers use in India, but this one has too many finger holes. Most people can't play this."

Flick pushed his pillow to the floor, stood on his chair, and shouted, "I don't need a history lesson from a drunk Viking. Give me my horn. Give it to me."

He climbed on the table, stumbled, and scattered beer bottles across the kitchen floor. He overturned my untouched beer and flooded the tabletop. Flick slipped on the foam and slid toward Bran and the Resonance Horn. He picked up speed and reached upward to grab the horn, but Bran lifted it out of his reach. The kobold helplessly spun his arms for balance and slid off the table and fell onto the broken glass and beer-covered floor.

Maia and the other kobolds laughed as Flick staggered to his feet and fell again on the beer-slick floor. The laughing stopped when he stayed on the floor. He lifted his left hand and it dripped blood and beer.

He stared at his hand in horror. I picked him up and placed him on the counter next to the sink.

I grabbed a towel, put pressure on his cuts, and then rinsed his hand so I could see how badly he was hurt. His hand was cut in two places and it looked like there was tendon damage to his first and second fingers. The little finger was bent backwards."

"He needs stitches on two fingers. The little one is broken. He needs a doctor."

"Rumpelstiltskin's wrinkled rear, we need more than a doctor," screamed Maia. "Flick is the only one who can play the horn. We can't go home without him. Do something."

Bran got sick at the sight of blood and he wouldn't be any help. "I'm not a doctor or a nurse. I draw illustrations, but my mother was the midwife on our Pueblo back in New Mexico. I helped her deliver dozens of babies and I grew up with three brothers. I know some first aid. I can pull his little finger straight and splint it with chopsticks. I can't guess how many beads I've sewed onto costumes over the years. If he can hold still, I can stitch his fingers with dental floss. It won't be pretty, but it will stop the bleeding. I'm sorry, I don't have anything for pain except beer."

Maia begged me to try. Flick drank another bottle of our 24 percent alcohol beer, Leapfrog Lager. He weighed about sixty pounds and he'd put away two Frogs in less than an hour. I figured he'd pass out in a few more minutes, if he didn't die from alcohol poisoning. He mumbled incoherently about some girl named Freyja and keeled over.

Mom always said to do the easy stuff first, so I grabbed his little finger and jerked it back into position. I could feel it click when the bones lined up. The bones popped together and Bran gagged at the sound. He really wasn't going to be any help. Maia held two chopsticks against the little finger and I wrapped it with packing tape, since that's what I had. "Don't let him roll off the table," I said to Maia and moved into better light where I could see to thread the dental floss onto a needle. My beer was wearing off, but it still took me a couple of minutes to thread the floss.

The little people were gone when I turned to the counter. Bran and I were alone in the kitchen. I stood, needle in hand, and looked around the room. Bran pushed gently on my arm and said, "What's the matter, they're screaming at you? Don't just stand there. Stitch up his fingers."

"They're gone. Someone must have used another different horn to send them back. I hope his fingers will be all right."

"What are you talking about? Flick's passed out on the counter where you left him with his head in Maia's lap. The other two are sitting in their chairs. Maia is screaming for you to hurry."

I shouted at Bran. "There's no one here. They're gone."

Bran moved to the counter and held one hand on a foot above the countertop. "She's right here. I can see her. I can touch her, I have my hand on her shoulder."

I stepped closer and waved my hand through the empty space between Bran's fingers and the countertop. "See, nothing there."

"Wow, your hand goes right through her. Wait, she says maybe something's changed your ability to see them. If we can figure out what changed, maybe we can fix it." Bran opened another beer and leaned against the refrigerator. He threw the bottle cap toward the trash can, took a mouthful, and then spit the beer on the floor. Between chokes and coughs, he sputtered, "It's the beer. You quit drinking beer. We can see them because of the beer. Something about the way I made Leapfrog Lager makes us able to see them. Drink my beer. Try it."

I took the beer from Bran and chugged it. I followed four big gulps with a very unladylike burp. Everything in the kitchen stayed the same, broken glass and beer were on the floor, Bran held the horn, and me, I stood there in beer-soaked shoes and held a needle threaded with dental floss. I finished the bottle and shadows swirled and congealed on the countertop. I heard Maia crying. One of the kobolds sitting behind me said, "Why doesn't she help him? Lady, help him. Please."

Maia and Flick coalesced and became substantial. I took Maia's arm and it was as solid as my own. I held Flick's injured hand and turned it over so I could stitch his fingers. "Okay, let's do this while I can see you."

I drenched Flick's hand with rubbing alcohol and disinfected my hands and the needle. I sewed the big cut on his index finger first. It took nine stitches. Not my finest beadwork, but I was three beers into the evening. Back home, when I decorated a pair of moccasins with ornamental beads, I wasn't drunk or distracted by little crying gnome people. If I didn't like the way a design turned out, I ripped it out and started over, but that's not an option with someone's finger.

There were two small cuts on his second finger. I closed them both, taking sips of Leapfrog Lager between stitches, and cut adhesive bandages into small enough pieces to fit his little fingers.

Maia thanked me and said, "He's waking up. Flick gets terrible hangovers when he drinks too much, but he'd better get over this one pretty damn quick. Give him the horn and as soon as he can play, we'll go home. What was wrong before you stitched his fingers, you said we'd disappeared?"

I explained that after I threaded the needle, I couldn't see or hear them. "Bran said it was Leapfrog Lager. Something in the beer lets us see and hear you. It could be the high alcohol content."

"Not likely. If all it took to see us was a lot of booze, every drunk in the world would know about us. The boys and I spend enough time in your bars and pubs to know better. Drunks see some pretty weird stuff, but they can't see us."

She shook Flick, but didn't wake up. "It could be something in the beer besides the high alcohol content. Anything special in it?"

Bran loves it when people ask about his beers. "Of course, it's special. There are three different hops, from three different countries on three different continents: South America, North America, and Europe. The North American Tomahawk hops provide the bitterness and a slight citrus finish. The barley is a mixture from three countries: Ireland, Germany, and Chile. The Chilean barley is from the highest elevation barley farm in the world."

Maia finally shook Flick awake and said, "Could be a mixture of those things. One version of the American Rip Van Winkle legend said Rip was drunk when he disappeared from your world and lived with our kind for twenty years. There are stories from many countries about people who can see and talk to us. I don't really know, but if it's your beer, save some of it and you'll be able to see us if we ever come here again."

Quin and Drim dried the tabletop and balanced Flick on the edge. They took off his shoes. Bran handed Flick the Resonance Horn and Flick positioned it carefully, holding the lower end with his feet and placing his toes over the bottom four openings on the horn. He looked like a koala bear hugging a tree branch when he gripped the horn with his short fat arms and legs. He tried to maneuver his fingers into place, but couldn't force his injured fingers into the positions necessary to play the recall notes on the horn.

41

After a few moments, he gave up. "It's no use, my fingers won't fit over the holes. Lady, take off the bandages. They're in my way."

I removed the bandages and the makeshift splint. Flick's hand and fingers were black and swollen. His little finger was as plump as an overstuffed sausage. He tried to flex his fingers, but they wouldn't bend.

Flick stared at his swollen hand. He looked sadly at Maia and said, "I can't play the horn. My fingers won't work. I'm sorry."

Maia took the horn from Flick and turned to me, "I can't play a note and these two boys are tone deaf. Our resonances will degrade to match this world's frequency in the next few hours. By morning, we'll be trapped here forever. "

Bran took the horn, "Maybe I can play it. Flick can show me the finger positions and I can modulate the pitch through the mouthpiece until I hit the right notes. We won't lose anything by trying."

Flick sneered scornfully. "I don't think so. How well do your toes work? Can you use your toes to cover and uncover four of the holes while you play?"

Bran held out his hands and spread his twelve fingers and two thumbs for Flick to see. "I don't need my toes, I have magic fingers."

"Pixie poop, I know I've had too much to drink." Flick observed. "He's got too many fingers. How many fingers you got?"

"Twelve fingers and two thumbs. I can do this if you'll show me the notes."

We moved into the living room and sat on the threadbare carpet. Bran crossed his legs and balanced the Resonance Horn. He looked like a fakir charming a cobra on a dirty Bombay street corner. Flick used his good hand to guide Bran's fingers into position and said, "Hold your lips like you are trying to blow high C on a bugle. Do you understand?"

"You bet, I can play a bugle. Okay, here goes."

Bran played the first note, an eerie high-pitched whine that squealed like a motorcycle engine revving too fast. Maia and the little men held hands and snuggled close together. "Too high," said Flick motioning downward with his uninjured hand. "Take it about three notes down the scale."

Bran played again and it screeched like chalk on a blackboard. "Sharp, too sharp," exclaimed Flick. "Flatten it a little more and you'll have it."

Bran tried a third time and the notes sounded the same to me as before. Bran held the last note for a few seconds and the horn vanished from his hands. Bran looked up from his empty hands and pointed to where Flick and the others had been seated. It worked— they were gone.

"Nobody's going to believe this," Bran said.

"We aren't going to tell anyone and we're going to stop distribution of Leapfrog Lager in the morning. If we don't, half the pub crawlers in Chelsea will see leprechauns tomorrow night. We'll claim the batch was contaminated and had to be destroyed."

We hurried to the brewery and spent the rest of the night pouring case after case of Leapfrog Lager down the drain. I called our distributor when he opened and cancelled all deliveries. I contacted our retail outlets and told them that our new lager would not be available for a couple of months. Better safe than sorry. No one wants people to get sick on contaminated beer. It's bad for business.

Bran and I saved five cases, one hundred and twenty bottles. We hid it in our apartment. You never know. Maia might visit us again. It might be fun the next time.

Bran confirmed the recipe for the beer we destroyed matched the recipe he'd used for our third test run. The production run made us see the little people, but the test run hadn't. Bran brewed four more test batches. None of them caused any effects other than what a 24 percent alcohol beer would be expected to cause. He decided to make another production run. I changed the label slightly. I added four little people watching the men play leapfrog, and the slogan, "LOOK BEFORE YOU LEAP," to the label.

The new production runs tasted great, but they didn't work. We didn't see little people when we drank the new batches. Bran developed a theory which made sense to me. Pick one of the three hops, for example, Tomahawk hops. The batch of Tomahawk hops we used in the first production run was planted, grown, and harvested on a specific farm. The amount of rainfall, the number of sunny days, the daily temperatures, and the bees pollinating those specific hops created a unique combination we couldn't quantify or replicate. The batch of Tomahawk hops Bran used was special because of the specific conditions that existed while the hops were grown and harvested.

It might not be the hops. The different crops that made up the barley mixture Bran used to brew the original production batch of beer were grown under once-in-a-lifetime conditions. The combination of variables occurring while all the ingredients were grown and harvested are beyond measure. It could be minor variations in the brewing process combined with the other variables. It could be as simple as boiling the wort for thirty seconds longer before Bran added the hops or as complex as the acid content in Chilean rain causing more limestone to leach into the soil. Perhaps it was the diet of the bees who pollinated the hops. It could be one thing, or it could be a thousand things. We were never able to produce another batch that had the same powers as the first one. Business was good. People loved Leapfrog Lager and we sold every bottle we made.

*

I hung a silver bell in the kitchen. I didn't know if Maia could read our language, but I left a note, "Maia, ring the bell."

We kept a dozen bottles of the frequency-changing Leapfrog Lager batch in a small, locked refrigerator behind the trash can in our pantry. We didn't want anyone to drink one by mistake.

*

Years later when our daughter was seven years old, she shook me awake in the middle of the night. "Mama, the bell in the kitchen is ringing. It's keeping me awake."

I nudged Bran and woke him up. He looked at me through sleep-filled eyes and asked, 'What's wrong?"

I shushed him with my finger on his lips. "Nothing's wrong, but the bell's ringing. We need to drink a beer. We have company."

***

Menagerie

by Tom Scanlan
United States

Then the dreams start.

Dreams, the boxes that hold sensations and images that bleed into one another. They are vague impressions of emotions that wake you up ready to gouge your own eyes out with fear or with a minute or two of false, ignorant happiness. I remember waking once, alone in bed— this is when I still had the house—with the deadly serious belief that Olivia, twelve years old and very much alive in her bed, needed to be grounded for not turning in a fifth-grade homework assignment. I lay there chewing on what words to use, how to be a good parent, careful not to be too harsh because she was such a good girl but needing to correct the misstep.

The recent dreams aren't impressionistic at all. They're like lived experiences.

In them, Olivia is sixteen and attends a boarding school in New England. She wears a uniform and seems to be in good health. I watch her study in the library, wearing a cardigan with the school's logo, brunette hair fixed in a bun, tapping a pencil on her laptop as she thinks. She plays field hockey, scoring goals and high-fiving teammates that respect her. Then she goes to her dorm, eats food in the dining hall with friends, talks about her day. A day-in-the-life type dream.

Only my daughter's long-since dead.

I tried discounting the dreams as projection. Each night for a week, I became a silent observer in Olivia's life. My heart ached that it wasn't real, but my dream-mind rejoiced that Olivia was beautiful and thriving, studious, athletic, healthy. Each morning of those seven days, when I scraped away my sleepy fog, I dealt with the truth, cold and rational, that Olivia had instead suffered untold human cruelties before being discarded like so much road trash, and was now mind, soul, and

45

calcium skeleton, part of the New England soil.

Two weeks. The dreams continue for two weeks. You can't ignore a dream that recurs fourteen times. I probably sleep six hours a night, so that's eighty-four hours of my life spent in a world still inhabited by Olivia.

Keep in mind that weird as it sounds, I remember almost everything from these dreams. You know what that does to a man? I'm no nut-job. I won't tell you that I'm starting to lose grip on what's real and what isn't. I will, however, have you know that after fourteen days of walking the halls of your dead daughter's school, of watching her laugh in the dining hall as she eats supper with friends, of watching her get hit on by prep school boys wearing polos and braced smiles, before sleeping peacefully—meanwhile, I'm accruing memories, syncing to the real-world rhythm of Olivia's routine—devastates a parent who has lost a child.

Three weeks. By the twenty-first night, I spend the entire dream struggling against the subconscious goo that makes up dreams to reach out and grab a hold of Olivia, and to talk to her. If I'm going to be in her life like this, I should be able to spend quality time with her. It pains me to wonder whether she senses me and knows that I care. Is my dream-blurred presence, detached literally and figuratively, enough for her young heart?

*

It's been a month of this now, which is why I'm about to use the old snub-nose .38 my father willed me when he died in 2015. A family heirloom. The bullets resting in the chamber don't even look large enough to penetrate my skull. I pray I won't go braindead, that a second trigger pull won't be both necessary and impossible.

The level of detail is what made me start to go nuts. Like here, the dream-autumn has started turning into winter. Leaves and pine needles line the roads as Olivia walks around campus in a winter jacket. The naked trees beside the field hockey pitch ooze the scent of sap as Olivia and her teammates run around, steaming sweat. The attention to detail staggers me, as if an artist devoted to veritas realism controls the levels of color, the textures, the sounds, the smells, with some higher aim than tormenting me. Why trouble with beauty? Or perhaps, as I've thought since the time I made the connection between the snub-nose .38 stored in my trunk for the duration of my stay at the Millham Limits Motel and an ending to my painful existence, the beauty was exactly the point. My cruel tormentor detailed the dreamscapes with such painstaking detail for the very reason that my suffering depended on my full immersion. The more I believe I cohabit this false world with Olivia, the more miserable I become.

After a month of recurring, and, I suppose, developing dreams, I can't even pretend that it's a coincidence. I must attribute nightly visitations with Olivia to some higher power that, while not necessarily benevolent, commandeers my mind each night for thirty days straight to show me this. I know it must have meaning. I haven't believed in God since Olivia went missing, but perhaps, if he exists and is truly a God of infinite love and grace, he senses how close to death I am. If the veil gets any thinner than white-knuckled fingers around the butt of a revolver, barrel parting the hair at your temple, I can't imagine what it looks like. Maybe in the slightly alien way a being like God has when relating to humans, where like a much older, larger child in a daycare accidentally hurts their younger, smaller peer, he thinks he's bringing me peace before I kill myself. The fact that I'll go insane is collateral damage, since for one month at least I'll get to walk in step with Olivia. I can picture him nodding in understanding at my wanting to leave the world, his enormous cheeks ruddy with embarrassment at what this world he's created has become.

The trigger, I feel its slack digging into the pad of my index finger. I'm millimeters from—

There's a knock on my motel room door. I wait until another occurs before believing that it's unimagined. The timing seems too unreal, too convenient. The minute I decide that I'm not going to continue to live the dreams any longer, my own personal hell—*knock knock knock.*

"Open up. It's Antonio."

Sheriff Antonio Boyce.

I slide the snub-nose under a pillow, whispering a promise that it'll get its time to shine tonight if it shows a little patience. I open the door.

"How'd you find me, Antonio?"

"You mentioned a while back at the diner you were staying here. You haven't come in. So, I asked the owner for your room number and here I am, doing a well-being check."

He must be disgusted at the state of my room, but as a true professional who's seen drug dens and dead bodies in homes belonging to hoarders, he doesn't balk at my casefiles on Olivia's disappearance, the pizza boxes and Wendy's bags, the empty handles of liquor—alternating between tequila and whiskey—with their sticky necks. He kicks some refuse out of the way with a boot and steps into the room, slides a window open to let in some fresh, early winter air, and then gives me a hard look.

Once the various police departments and media involved moved on from Olivia, Sheriff Antonio Boyce made a point of staying in touch with me. He lost a sister to murder as a young man and claimed our situations shared the same sudden brutality. His Mexican-American family left San Antonio when he was young, but, as he put it, he brought some Tejano mysticism with him. I remember his promise to me and its explanation. He told me he would check in with me at least once a season. New England's four seasons could dig at people who suffered incredible loss. Winter made them feel that the world was a cold, dead place, he'd say; spring made them cognizant of having nothing or no one to bloom with; summer nights long with sun made them mighty lonesome; and fall made them feel like they were dying. If not for the promise of having him in my life, however briefly, I would've followed my wife's example and killed myself long ago.

He appears younger than his age, but looking at me with his thick, black eyebrows knit together seems wise beyond both of our years combined. I feel he could almost see the pistol beneath the pillow.

"My mother used to talk about Hammurabi's Code, like in the Bible. Eye for an eye makes the whole world blind. I know cops are supposed to tell you to have faith in the system. I can't help but think that hope is something folks only find in the movies, and, you know, they tell you that anger will rot a hole in your gut. Well, anger's something to hold onto. And the drinking will take care of that other hole anyway, if you don't put a bullet hole in your head first. No more holes."

My chest tightens, and I can't speak. Antonio has always been happy to deliver on his promise, small-talking with me once a season, usually over dinner at the Millham Diner, for years. We'd talk sports, weather, and I liked to ask about his kids even though it made him feel guilty. He doesn't speak deeply like this unless there's a point.

"They found a body?" I say.

He shudders, fingers a belt loop. If he didn't have things on his mind, he might encourage me to continue referring to her as Olivia, not *a body*. "Ralph Skinner got out on probation."

"You said he had nothing to do with Olivia's disappearance."

Antonio nods. He gestures for me to move some of the files on the bed so he can sit. "The indecent assault on a minor and possession of child pornography he served six years for did connect him to her. I don't think I need to remind you how ..."

When Ralph Skinner got arrested the summer following Olivia vanishing, they found child pornography on his computer's hard drive. There'd been pictures of Olivia. I didn't understand how this comprised news. "And?"

"I think he knew more than he let on about the whole operation. If we'd had the technology back then that we do now, I know in my gut we could've leveraged him against the sicko responsible for that website."

"Thanks for coming all the way out here to share your useless theory," I say. "Just what I needed right now, Antonio."

Antonio stands over me, and puts his hand on my heart, as if he's saluting the national anthem for me. "Are you still harboring that anger?"

My eyes flicker to the pillow, the metal I know is beneath. I want Antonio gone. I want a .38 slug in my brain. I want the dreams to stop. Anger is far from my mind. "Sure."

"I have cared about this case right alongside you, Gavin," Antonio says. "I've come to know you and to care about you, man to man. I want answers about Olivia."

The annoyance of Antonio preventing me from suicide dissipates. It's true. I have seen him, in deed not just word, never give up on Olivia. He followed the cold case over the years whenever he could. "You've always been there for me," I say, humiliated by the sudden urge to weep.

"I've been following Skinner," he says. He averts his eyes, and I can tell he's gauging my reaction. I'm far from offended. In fact, there's a stir within me, somewhere deep and long-dormant, that flickers. "He went right back to his parents' house in Millham and he still drives that red '90s Firebird with the snout-looking hood. I've been tailing him, and I already caught him messing around with a girl. That's the best he can do, offer to buy booze in return for—we trust each other, right?"

I nod. If the context were slightly different, I'd tell him that he was the only other living being I had a relationship with, let alone trust.

"We might get into some bad shit, you and I," he says. "Selfishly, I think part of the reason I try to help you as much as I can is that I feel guilty about being too young and useless to have prevented my sister from being murdered. I also hold onto my anger. And right now, all of it is trained on Ralph Skinner, the only connection, loose as it may be, to Olivia."

I stand, wide-eyed and thrilled at Antonio's humanity, brutal as it is, founded from a deep place of love. "Did he tell you anything?"

"When I showed him the footage of him with an underage girl, yeah, he talked. I also failed to report, so trust between you and me is more important than ever."

"You want trust, Antonio?" I point to the bed. "Let me tell you something. There's a gun beneath that pillow that was seconds from blowing my brains out when you showed up. I would follow you to Hell if it meant finding the truth about Olivia. If I have to go to prison to find her body I will. Understand?"

Antonio pats me on the shoulder. "Damien Ridge. He gave me the name Damien Ridge. He told me that this guy lived in Mendon in the boonies near 146, and that for ..." Antonio clears his throat. "Ridge has been at it since before the Internet. For premium subscribers of his, he kept a *spank box* in his basement where he allowed them to watch VHS tapes of the girls. Apparently for these freaks it's vintage to use VCRs. That's what Skinner called it: the *spank box*."

*

On the drive to Ridge's home in Mendon, twenty minutes from Millham, I think about this man and the dreams, possible connections between the two. Like the horrible visions of Olivia in a strange place with evil people enduring unspeakable acts, my visceral anger has died down. The almost erotic desire for someone to hold accountable, to torture, has dissipated. I once wanted to take garden shears to digits and members and limbs, wanted them alive so I could tease them with the release of death by bathtub drowning with fits and starts. That's all gone now. My anger has long since been turned against the world, or at least the humans who inhabit it, evil, flawed, ugly—we like to pretend that the balance of good and evil once seesawed in favor of the good guys, but if history is any indication, that's false. My rage is dull and calm, the hatred of indifference, hate by lack of participation.

I can't help but consider that Damien Ridge is a figure of such grave sin that perhaps he transcends human evil. How can a *man* annihilate innocence? Yes, you're right that far too many other men have committed these atrocities before, but it doesn't stop me from suspecting that this strain of humanity is borne of different loins than the rest of us, seeded by a truly wicked patriarch, the king of the indecent, the swallower of innocence, the progenitor of child pornographers like Damien Ridge. Hell, not dying from the guilt and shame of such actions must take almost supernatural fortitude, or at least more than any of us care to consider. Why then would it be so ridiculous for me to suspect that he sent me these dreams as a taunt? He senses me faltering, conjuring an escape from my pain, and decides to exacerbate it with a simulation of what Olivia and I may have had.

The afternoon sun looks weak over the six-bedroom Cape perched on fifty acres of even land, with a horse stable in the back. The lawn looks landscaped. A clean Mercedes pops and clinks in the driveway. We park at the mailbox and begin the ascent up the long concrete stairway that splits the front yard. I've always pictured my daughter's kidnapper and killer to have acted for reasons, however depraved, desperate and needful. The apparent luxury of the house flips my stomach and freezes my spine. When a young, attractive blonde answers the door and says with a Slavic accent she's an *"au pair,"* I bark like an angry dog and push past her into the house, filled with some vague working-class anger at the fact that au pair is just rich-speak for nanny. Over my shoulder, I hear the young woman tell Antonio, likely because of the authority of his uniform, that Damien is in the backyard engaged in equestrian practice with a daughter named Anna and a horse named Brutus.

I open the sliding glass door onto the back deck and then take the stairs down to the sprawling but well-maintained backyard. Even in the cooler end of autumn, the green of the grass and the colors of foliage look unnaturally vibrant. I stand still, watching Damien Ridge, stalwart for his fifties, as he walks alongside Brutus, an enormous thoroughbred, mounted by a daughter who dons full equestrian getup. She laughs and shrieks with pleasure in the afternoon sun as they trot around the fenced-in pen. I smell Brutus's animal stink. Each of the horses' whinnies and snorts, and words of encouragement between Ridge and daughter, bring back all the rage from the past with such force I lose equilibrium, and Antonio has to catch me by an arm to keep me upright.

"DAMIEN RIDGE." Ridge notices Antonio's raised voice, looks our way. He mutters something to the girl up in the saddle, gestures for her to mind the reins, and then jogs up to us with brazen confidence in his stride.

"A county sheriff," he says. "How quaint."

Ridge sticks his hand out, first to Antonio, then me. We both leave it hanging.

"Okay. What do you need, sir?"

"To have an uncomfortable conversation. Away from any daughters or pairs you may have."

"It's an *au pair*, a foreign exchange student nanny."

I can smell bad on him. During some of our talks, Antonio's told me about the auras and scents and feelings that evil men give off. He says his Mexican mother used to tell him stories about monsters that fed off certain sins as a way to keep him and his brothers and sisters in line. She told him that all the crimes created energy around a person with different colors and smells and emotions attached to it.

"Do you remember Olivia McCauley? Pretty little brunette girl. You might've met her in 2003?"

The lids of Ridge's eyes tremble, subtly but perceptibly. His soul is suddenly bared out before me to be sifted through like cosmic dead space. Even so brief, the look is explosive. He blinks. The eyes change, the sclera turning yellow. I can't help but gasp when, as if he's not human after all, the face he wears turns pale. Just beneath the surface, like subdermal tattoos swirling there, I see patterns and shapes that would make sense if I could read the ancient hieroglyphs. His ears get pointed.

It's as if, under duress, he's lost control of his human form.

He regains the Damien Ridge face in an instant. He looks at us, understanding what's transpired, and gives us the look of a sentient deer meeting a hunter. I look at Antonio, who has piss forming a rivulet down the creased front of his khaki pants. He glances at me, dark, brooding Mexican features jaundiced three shades lighter.

"*El Duende* ..." he says.

Ridge, by whatever means, drops the pretense of his human flesh and bolts past us up the stairs to the deck and into the house. I've never feared death less than this moment. I give chase, entering the house through the sliding glass door in perfect time with a female shriek and a rambling string of Slavic words, and follow the au pair's quaking finger to the basement door in the kitchen.

The door's been left open and the basement yawns foul, unperturbed air up from its dark depths. I can't help but gag, the smell of feral inhuman—but human enough to be recognized—liquids and decayed filth. I pull my shirt over my mouth and stomp down the stairs to find Ridge grunting and cursing in a phlegmy tongue. He's shrunken by at least a foot, though his physical stature is somehow more impressive, however less human. The loose clothing swims on him and reveals more flesh with ancient calligraphy and symbols throbbing beneath its pale surface. He fumbles with a key and padlock and gets it open before I can grab him.

The air is thick beneath my tee shirt. I drop it from my mouth, needing a clean breath regardless of the stink, and when the particles that disperse from this newly unlocked room hit me like a reverse-sneeze, I retch, bile splashing at my feet. Three times. I sway, a dizzy, easy target for the creature, but he's in the room saying something. I focus. He's turned on an overhead light in there. He's whining.

"My girls," he says. The voice carries the nasally grievances of a spoiled child. "Oh, my girls. I am going to miss my girls."

The space is five feet by eight feet. An old big-screen television, with the heavy backend, rests on a wooden stand. Shelves line the walls above the TV, containing sheathed and loose VHS tapes, toppling over one another in disarray. A La-Z-Boy in the center of the room, like much of the floor at first glance, is covered with fetid food and open snack bags and the insects that have conquered. The creature squats on his haunches in the corner and rummages through a purple storage tub, creating a cacophony of plastic smashing other plastic, and reading the names of girls off the labels to himself in low nostalgic tones.

With the realization that he doesn't even care about preserving his own life, I comprehend how truly inhuman this thing before me is. Instead, the jig up, he wants one last moment alone with his collection of girls, all of whom were ripped from loving parents like myself and sent along a path of misery and destruction. For what? So this creature could enjoy them like pets? *Abused and exploited pets!*

Antonio hadn't flinched when I took the snub-nose .38 out from under the pillow and tucked it into my waistband before we left the Millham Limits Motel.

"Oh, my girls. Oh, my girls."

I can't take another minute. I pull the trigger, and a round blows through the creature's back. The hole produces a black liquid. The inscriptions just beneath its pallid skin dance violently, and I get the impression that the ink from the strange tattoos is what bleeds from the wound. He slumps against the wall, then turns himself to face me, his chest rapid in its rises and falls. He speaks.

"The dreams. I must work to keep them from you. Until you die. You were so close."

"Why sixteen? Why not make it the age she was killed?"

"Killed? I parented these girls." The creature feels his breast where a more powerful gun might have created an exit wound, the writing there squirming beneath his hand. "I gave them money, love, and education."

"That isn't love," I say. I smack a row of tapes on a shelf. "This isn't love."

"From what I've seen from humans, it seemed like it."

The pistol has five rounds left. I hold it up to the creature's head. From the way he pants, it seems like the round must've hit whatever lung-type organ he has in his torso. His breath comes ragged, heavy, wet. The fear is gone from his yellow eyes. He never feared death, only not being allowed a final goodbye to his girls.

"Olivia isn't dead."

The word *isn't*—IS NOT—hits me in the solar plexus. My mind can't even compute its meaning when placed between the name of my daughter and the so-final adjective, dead. *Isn't*. Years of hope being butchered from my heart like slices of deli meats; the better part of two decades hating myself for letting Olivia befall such a fate, and growing to loathe the world where that fate was possible; the last part of my life, numb, and then the dreams and the—

The dreams. They must not be dreams at all, but some sort of soul travel. The tether between father and daughter, blood-spirit flowing through it, must've shown me Olivia—real, living, breathing Olivia. No wonder the attention to detail became so maddening, and no wonder I seemed to accrue knowledge, night by night and day by day, of what I was seeing when I saw Olivia. It was real. *Real*.

The creature has faded on me. The yellow in his eyes has ebbed, the pupils starting to roll back into the skull. His breaths are shallow and the script below his flesh is becoming bleached, less pronounced.

He's about to die.

"The school?" I say. "Tell me the name of the school."

His lips are dry, and he parts them once, twice, tongue stuck to the bottom of the toothy mouth. I fear that he won't be able to tell me, and there I'd be, stuck with the task of searching every boarding school in the northeast for a girl who wouldn't even know me as her father. My life at once has purpose and with it comes the terror of again losing that reason to live, leaving me clinging to the creature to tell me the name of the school like a drowning man holds a life preserver in a hurricane. The creature rasps several times, and then manages words.

"Phillips Exeter."

"Phillips Exeter Academy." Antonio's behind me. "New Hampshire."

*

On the way to New Hampshire, daylight waning over rush hour traffic on I-495, Antonio explains El Duende. He tells me that parents in Mexico, in Latin America, and in Spain, use the bogeyman-type legend to scare children into behaving. He also tells me his mother never joked about El Duende coming to get him or his siblings if they didn't clean their rooms or get up for school on time, because their Tejano home, in San Antonio, hours from the Mexican borderlands, knew the stories of the creature kidnapping children to be true. "I don't *really* remember," he says. "It's one of those childhood memories that feels like it could've come from a TV show or a dream you had once, an impression. My sister Carmen was not murdered.

"We shared bunk beds. I remember her brief scream before El Duende covered her mouth." Antonio pauses, angry spittle hissing between his teeth. "The eyes, those yellow eyes flashed up at me, and the tattoos under the skin glowed and moved in the moonlight. We never saw her again. We decided to consider her murdered by the time we moved to Worcester. It was easier. For the longest time, I'd convinced myself that I'd created the memory of El Duende taking Carmen because I didn't want to think that human evil could've come into our home and taken her."

I relate to how there's comfort in considering the missing dead, especially the ones we love. Otherwise, they become disembodied nightmares, tumbling through the worst scenarios our minds can fathom, unspeakable anguish and cruelty the solitary emotions they know. I wonder what Duendes, for there must be many of them, want with our children. Maybe the reasons behind what they do are as complicated and legion as the motivations behind what evil humans do. Perhaps monsters, too, are individuals, with rotten natures and sinister behaviors. The Duende who took my Olivia thought the girls he took would be better served with him as their parent. He collected them—how many?—and used them, and then—what?—boarded them at prep schools or sold them off once they got too old to parent? Was his frail aim to act human? Assuming our flesh and acting the part? Did he not realize that raising girls is not a hobby, and that we are happy to parent them until we ourselves die?

Antonio helps me into the school's administrative building. A combination of anger and sadness, mixed with exhaustion of my heart, overcome by the idea that somewhere within these brick facades and green sporting fields ripe with the thin burning scent of late autumn, Olivia thrums with life, makes my legs buckle. Selfishly, I feel like I need another decade alone with my thoughts before I can be mentally prepared to see the girl I've been dreaming about. Death is strange in that way, assumed death anyway. It shows us the finite borders of the world, boxes the dead in. For years, my mind eulogized Olivia as a beautiful, well-tempered infant, showed her pink bow-tied head swaying its first steps into toddlerhood, the moments when she lay on Daddy's chest on lazy Sundays and I swore she'd stay as young and innocent and love-starved as she was in those moments forever. I now realize that the solace I've taken from that eulogy box has been the cruelest lie my mind ever told me. The walls of its cube tarnished and smashed by depraved inhuman hands.

And now, as I walk into the place where I'll re-meet my daughter, not in death or in dreams, but in flesh, I must do what all fathers— real, human fathers—do. The I, the me I use to navigate the world, needs to disappear. I need to think only of Olivia. I need to live for Olivia.

***

Gehenna

by Andrew Punzo
United States

William Wyeth Blanquefort was lying naked on his cell floor. The paperback Bible he was using as a headrest was soaked through to Isaiah, and when he sat up, several pages unfolded in a wet clump.

"Apparently Furman versus Georgia don't mean shit! Apparently the *Constitution* don't mean shit!"

Candles was shuffling under the escort of two guards, his leg irons dragging on the tan tiles.

"All those letters I sent to the goddamn governor and he gives us this fine fuck-a-ree!"

Candles' wife thought the stick of dynamite in her birthday cake was a novelty gag, even when he ran outside after he lit it. They arrested him in front of Saint Mark's in Shreveport, drunk on a Sunday morning and singing that one John Lee Hooker song. He was something of a legend at Angola, and with his notoriety came a commodity more precious than first crack at shower times or skin magazines: information.

"Senate passed the law this morning and it says we all get a date with Gruesome Gertie!"

The tension in Tier G burst in a cacophony of expletives and inquisition. Gehenna, as its residents had christened it, was claimed to be the hottest cellblock on Angola's death row.

Candles looked over, self-congratulation smeared all over his wrinkled black face. William wondered if he understood that he would get no special favors with Gertie's two thousand volts.

"Hey Ladykiller! Be seein' you in Hell!" he said over the noise.

William glared at him as he sat on the edge of his thin, uneven mattress and tried to think over the sound of the Wildman's pounding fists on the adjacent wall. Headline criminals would go first. Then the

57

kid killers. Candles was with them because his wife was pregnant with someone else's child at the time, unbeknownst to him. After that it was open season, but he was not concerned. He would be across the border or dead before he ever saw Gertie.

William knelt to the floor and his vision fell upon a passage of the open Bible. It said something about the carcasses of men that defied the Lord and how they shall be an abhorrence unto all flesh.

He laid his head down and closed his eyes.

*

They entered the half basketball court. A scuffed ball lay near the hoop, and some exercise equipment was set off in one corner. The high, grated window was large enough for this concrete cube to be considered outside by the State. William walked the perimeter, enjoying what token freedom it offered.

"On all levels," the chaplain began, keeping pace with William, "I'm opposed to the law and what is going to happen to you. No man or government should take the life that the Lord gifts you with. But there is the past that we cannot change and our future that we go towards with the power to control. Surely you can appreciate that."

William, who had spent every day of the past decade being told when and where to eat, sleep, shower, shit, and stand, certainly could not.

"And part of controlling that future, your future, is looking to yourself. Finding it within yourself to forgive and offering that forgiveness to the Lord."

"I forgave myself a long time ago," William said.

The chaplain halted. He was used to being stonewalled.

"That is terrific, William! Forgiveness is a very powerful thing. It's the first step to eternal peace. Do you give your forgiveness to the Lord?"

He shrugged. "Sure."

"Well, it's more involved than that."

"How so?"

"Are you baptized?"

"I think so."

"By the holy sacrament of Penance you can achieve absolution for your sins."

"Do I need to be sorry?"

The chaplain looked at him as if he had just asked his odds of being ordained bishop of Baton Rouge. "Yes, William. Contrition is essential to the sacrament."

"Then why were you talking all about forgiveness?"

The chaplain looked even more flummoxed. "Well, erhem, you do know that remorse is a necessary prerequisite for forgiveness."

William stopped in front of the hoop and looked through the window. He could see the cloudless blue sky and an uneven brush of green from the tops of distant trees. A crow flew by.

*

"Didjya convert?" the Wildman asked.

"No."

"That's right! Ladykiller doesn't change for no one!"

"Don't call me that."

The Wildman blushed and looked down at his bruised hands while William's cuffs were removed. William stripped and sat on his mattress, massaging the bridge of his nose.

"Hey, Damien."

Silence from the other cell.

"Damien ... it's okay, I'm not mad."

"You sure?"

"Yes. You wanna talk?"

"Well ... what do you think is gonna happen to us when we die?"

William opened his mouth, but then shut it and thought about what he was going to say.

Damien Thierry stood six foot six, weighed two hundred and eighty pounds, and was the only felon in the state on death row for a crime that was not murder. He was simple-minded, but only as far as that he thought in straight lines; he was not as stupid as most people supposed. Nor was this giant gentle. The authorities had wrongly assumed both when arresting the exotic animal trafficker.

With smirks and sneers, they agreed that his golden retriever, Curly, would go to a good home; his one condition for coming out of his backwoods shack willingly. While they were cuffing Damien, an agent wrestled Curly to the ground and muzzled him even though the dog had not so much as barked.

By the end of the ensuing chaos that involved a spitting cobra, a silverback gorilla, and a Bengal tiger, all of the agents had fled or were incapacitated. The one that put the muzzle on Curly was still in a coma, although Damien swore to the judge that it was the gorilla who did it and that they had the wrong primate on the stand. His shoulder length blond hair defied prison regulations because everyone knew it reminded him of Curly.

"I'm not sure what will happen when we die," William said, not wanting to upset him, "but I know you'll see Curly again."

"You really think so?"

"Hey, all dogs go to Heaven."

"Yeah! I guess they do! Thanks Ladyk—I mean Billy. Now I ain't so scared."

"That's good, buddy."

From down the hall they heard Candles say, "The fuck you mean enjoy my last shower?"

*

The chaplain and the warden came to William's cell three days later, but only the warden spoke.

"Blanquefort. You decide on last rites?"

"Don't need them."

"Son, don't you know you're gonna die?"

"Aren't we all?"

"Some a lot sooner than others, wiseass. You'll be movin' to the holding cell tomorrow night."

The warden walked away while the chaplain made the sign of the cross and said a prayer.

"Did those do Candles any good?"

The chaplain sighed and turned to leave but was stopped by Damien who began inquiring about the theological posture on canines in the Kingdom of Heaven.

William thought about Candles, who never bothered to help himself, and Gutierrez, the drug dealer who he had paid to help him. Unless he had skipped town and left him to rot or fry.

He sighed and traced patterns through the glistening sweat on his chest and stomach. *I'll know soon enough*, he thought.

*

The next evening William removed a plastic bag filled with slick, yellow-tinted liquid from a slit in his mattress. At meals all of the inmates would blot their suspicious meats and oily greens with a napkin. But William kept his. Every night since he thought of his escape he would squeeze a few drops into the bag while lying in bed

60

and then eat the paper. He spread the oil over his naked body, using his fingers as a basting brush. An hour later they came for him.

"On your feet, Blanquefort."

William lay in silence.

"Don't pull this shit now. Your ticket's been punched. Get up."

William did not move.

"On your feet!"

"You're going to have to come in and get me."

"Fucking Christ ... face the wall, hands behind your back," the guard said as he unlocked the cell.

He allowed him to cuff his left wrist before he spun around, slipping out of the guard's grip.

"Sweaty sonofabitch ain't y—"

William punched him in the nose with the entire weight of his body, sending him reeling into the other guard. They both collapsed. He grabbed one of their batons, initially losing his grip as the second guard screamed for help while the first groaned, and brought it down on their heads until the cell was silent.

He grabbed two pairs of rubber dishwasher gloves from his mattress and put them on his hands and feet and took the keys from the guard's belt.

"What're you doing?!" Damien asked.

"Get the other keys and get everyone out!"

William moved to the next cell. The others were clamoring at their bars, cheering William on as he moved down the line. The first freed prisoners ran towards the exit to the main compound. Alarms wailed as the door was unlocked and the men burst into another cellblock. One began to free more inmates while the rest clashed with guards in riot gear.

William ran to the opposite end of Gehenna.

"Wait for me!" Damien said. He ran to catch up with William who was unlocking the door to the basketball court.

"You won't make it out this way! Go with them!"

His gloved feet slapped against the concrete as he sprinted to the hoop and climbed up the pole. Standing on the rim he was jumping distance from the window, but the gap gave him pause.

"Oh," said the Wildman. "Hold on tight!"

"What are y—" William was thrust forward as he rocked the pole with his mammoth frame. It began to bend as it swayed in a widening parabola that built upon its own inertia. William clung to the bucking backboard until it came to a grating stop against the wall.

Red-faced and huffing, Damien smiled up at him. "There ya go!"

William clambered onto the wide sill and clawed through the thin bug mesh.

Over time the rebar had rusted and several of the welds that bound the rods into a grid had come undone. Heavy gauge steel wire was looped at each broken juncture, leaving nestled bundles of gleaming metal against the speckled, umber-colored rust. William thought nothing of it until he saw the crow.

It was cautious at first, pecking at the mesh and framing a doorway over several days. Then it would poke no more than its head through the gap as if keen to the stench of entrapment and hopelessness from the human animals inside, shrewdly surveying not just the beguiling wire but the men who came and went.

William would lie on his back while working out and watch the crow. The portent of doom became the promise of freedom as it bent and broke off bits of wire in its beak. It would leave with the treasure and then return for more until all of it had been stripped.

The rebar flexed encouragingly as William pressed his weight into it.

"Thanks for this Damien, but you need to get out of here." He nodded towards the hallway. "Besides, some of these guards go to dog fights, and the warden used to run a pound."

Damien's eyes widened and his jaw fell as he became horrified. Then angry.

"CURLY!" He charged out of the room, hair flowing behind him like the golden pennant of a battle knight. He heard cheers from the prisoners as the Wildman entered the fray. He also heard thunder, and saw dark clouds suffocating the treetops.

He put his arms through the gap that was no larger than their meal trays, pushing and squirming as the rebar flexed and grated over his oiled skin, but like a newborn, he was delivered easily after his upper body cleared the space.

When he stood, the crow streaked by, inches from his face and cawing. He flinched and struck his head on the top of the sill, causing him to lose his balance and fall.

He came to lying on his back. A ringing noise filled his head and over it he wondered why he was wet. *The rain*, he thought, *I'm outside!*

He rolled over and ran like he just rode the Tilt-A-Whirl, gaining speed even as he stumbled in the direction of an unmanned guard tower near the fence.

He scaled the ladder and stepped onto the railing, picking his way over the razor wire carefully to keep his dangling nether regions clear of the steel teeth. Dropping to the ground he ripped off the gloves and threw up dirt and chunks of grass as he widened his ungainly stride.

As he crossed the trim landscape of Prison View Golf Course and entered the woods, thunder drowned out his whoops of joy. He raised two triumphant middle fingers in the direction of the death row compound where a dim orange glow was spreading.

Black leaves and mud pasted to his bare skin, only to be washed away by the anointing rain that consecrated his freedom. His elation was swept away momentarily by a flicker of light from deep in the woods, but when he dove behind a tree he saw nothing else. *Lightning*, he figured.

Moving due east, he came to the triple oak and squirreled around its base, finding nothing. He began to curse Gutierrez, there was no package. Now he would have to figure out how to get clothes, cash, a gun, and the telltale cuff off his wrist.

Lights flashed again, closer this time, and he saw a straight line interrupting the schizophrenic geometry of the woods.

As he looked to his left, his vision blurred in a lag that rushed to refocus. A large tree limb with raw, white splinters at its elbow had crushed a section of fencing. On the other side of it, a rolled-up plastic tarp lay in a clearing. He grinned and took back his promise to kill Gutierrez as he stumbled over the tree limb to the bundle.

He trapped the translucent plastic beneath his knees and shimmied along as he unrolled it. William saw the outline of something black and long near his hands. It looked like the stock and barrel of a rifle. *Sweet salvation*, he thought.

Each rotation peeled back a layer of obscurity. He paused. The long black object in his palms did not feel like a gun. It was pliable, mushy even, and seemed to bend in his hands. It felt warm.

He looked up the length of the tarp and screamed.

Candles stared at him through his cheap shroud. A fog of moisture on the interior dampened his features, but the shock of white hair above black skin—now a sallow, sloughing gray—was unmistakable. Bloated in the process of purification, his eyes bulged and his wizened tongue stuck out as if he were trying to re-wet it with the rain like an old sponge.

More lights flashed as William stumbled to his feet and ran, slipping on the tarp. From behind him he heard a crackle as he imagined Candles sitting up and shimmying his shoulders to loosen the plastic. The scent of decaying flesh slithered through the heavy downpour and wormed its way into his fear-addled brain. His mind was flying faster than his feet.

Why is he here holy shit holy shit he was right the Constitution don't mean shit holy shit I thought they buried the dead what's goin—

Everything stopped when he heard the crow's caw. His tinnitus mixed with a jingling clink. He shook the cuff on his wrist; its cadence matched the sound that he decided was not in his head.

The crow sounded again and he raised his eyes. His bones reduced to powder as he moaned and clutched his head. There was Gutierrez, suspended, swaying gently on chains. His long, black hair fell forward on his face and scraped the large tattoo of the three-headed dog on his chest.

"No ... please no ... please ..." William said as he gibbered soft nonsense between the words.

The crow pecked at Gutierrez's eye and dove at him.

William's hope of freedom was subsumed by the conviction that he had left one hell for another. As he ran he saw more flashes, bizarre phantasms that arced and danced between the trees and turned from white to shades of red and yellow. He reeled as they tried to cloud his vision. The slick slap of tree limbs and vegetation were the fellow damned reaching out to hold him down. The ringing noise was gone and his head was now filled with the scrunch of plastic, the metallic tingling of chains, and the mournful tone of the crow as his personal angels of death pursued him. The peals of thunder were the bellows of God condemning him in righteous judgment.

He came to the edge of the swamp, not even realizing it until he was knee deep in a tepid pool and sinking into the muck. Beneath the ripples of rain on the water he saw a gleam of chrome and a red taillight. A car.

The tire iron, he thought. *I can fight them!*

He dove into silent tranquility. The water cleared his mind, purging the demons as it enveloped him. He pulled his way along the body of the cream-colored Chevrolet Caprice and groped beneath the steering column for the trunk release. It popped with a *ka-chunk*. Using one hand to stay submerged, he righted himself on the rear bumper and opened the trunk.

She rose from it with mesmerizing steadiness, swaying as she unfurled like a serpent to its charmer's music. Her arms reached towards him, longing for an embrace after all these years. As naked as the day he had last seen her, her skin was now the consistency and color of over-boiled chicken. It was contrasted by the gossamer strands of shoulder-length black hair that still clung to her peeling scalp. Her dead eyes and gaping mouth were full of hunger and laughter.

William's shocked rapture broke as he gurgled bubbles and swirled in a panicked torrent as *she*—the one they had gotten him on, the only one they had gotten him on—caressed his arm. He was kicking towards the surface as hard as he could, it was just feet away, but he was not moving. Her grip locked on his wrist and she dragged him down, down into the trunk to lay with her forever in a hell of his own making.

*

"No ... no! I have no idea! I told you already that the damned warden is here!" he yelled into the radio over the whine of the cable winch and the suck and drag of muck.

"Yes! As soon as I know you will!" He clicked off the radio and threw it into a bush.

"You didn't have to yell."

"I know but I'm PO'd! You have no idea how close the university is to cutting our funding over this. They've been hounding me for answers all morning."

Annette put on her waders and checked the camera. They stood separate from the warden and officers.

"Not to mention all that data we lost! We'll be lucky if we see stable humidity at those pre-storm levels once in the next five years!"

"Oh c'mon, Rog, you don't know that. Besides, Gutierrez wasn't moved."

"Yes, but we won't make it past the first peer review when the other forensic examiners get wind of this. 'Cross-contamination!' they'll say. 'Integrity of the scientific process!'" he said making air quotes. "And don't get me started on Matches or whatever his name was, we've never been able to get a male that old under plastic! And do you think we're going to get new cadavers easily? Man alive! How willing do you think the State will be to donate even the unclaimed bodies of shot-up drug dealers after the press has their field day? I can see the headlines now: 'No Body Escapes the Body Farm,' 'Lifer Swaps the Chair for the Trunk,' 'Out of the Frying Pan and in—'"

"Roger! Enough! It was a freak accident, a one-in-a-million shot. Let's just be thankful it was a guy on death row and not some lost hiker. And that line about no more cadavers! There are plenty of folks like Lydia Mortensen over there," she nodded towards the car, "who are more than willing to leave their body to science. We don't need the State." She softened her tone and patted his back. "It will continue. We're going to keep our jobs and our funding. This is important research and everyone knows it. Let the naysayers have their fun. It'll be forgotten about within a week."

The winch shut off and the warden came over in his own pair of waders. His mustachioed face was haggard.

"Let's see which one of my boys this is. Only three got out last night."

They waded out to the car where brown water still poured from the interior and sloshed over the bumper. Two naked bodies, one white and one gray, were entangled in the bed, parts of them sticking out. Annette shivered. The rear of the Caprice looked like the distended mouth of some mire-monster that was swallowing the corpses whole.

She began to snap pictures while Roger took notes. After she had covered all angles, the two men grabbed the white corpse by the shoulders, disentangling him from Lydia.

"Yep, had a feelin' it was Blanque—"

William's body jerked and fell. Annette screeched and immediately looked embarrassed. A commotion arose amongst the officers on shore as several drew their revolvers.

"Stand down! Stand down!" the warden ordered as he brushed water droplets off his shirt and pointed to the trunk. "Well, that explains how he drowned."

His handcuffed left wrist was held fast to the bumper. The opened jaw of the other cuff had snagged itself in the metal loop of the trunk latch.

Annette took some close-ups and dictated to Roger. "Deep lacerations on the left wrist. Numerous veins appear to be severed as well as the radial artery. Blood loss a possible C.O.D. concurrent with drowning."

William was facedown in the water. She bent over his body for more photographs and stopped at the back of his head, putting the camera aside and running her gloved fingers through his hair.

"Rog, check this out. Severe bruising along the cranial posterior." She massaged it probingly. "We'd have to get an X-ray to know for sure, but it feels like there are skull fractures. This guy took a serious hit to the head." She looked at the warden who shrugged. "He would have been extremely disoriented from a concussion this severe and may have experienced hallucinations. I'm surprised he was able to make it this far from the prison. Add it as another possible C.O.D."

"What'd he do anyway?" Roger asked as he tried to squeeze the words onto the crowded cause of death line.

"Raped and murdered Ellie Ann Conway back in '64," the warden said. "There'd been a string of disappearances of women around then in Baton Rouge, but they only got him on her and he never copped to nothin' else. Few years ago some fella out in the supermax prison in Colorado confessed to the others, but that didn't stop him from bein' called the Ladykiller by the inmates."

Annette shivered again.

"Funny enough that two of my boys are on your grounds. If we're lucky, maybe Thierry and—"

"Let's turn him," Roger interrupted, seeing Annette's discomfort and wanting to expedite their task.

They rolled William over like a log in a flume. Annette raised the camera, not wanting to meet his lifeless stare directly, but she lowered it when the lens came to rest on his neck.

"Rog ..."

"I see. I'll be goddammed," he said in awe.

"What? What is it?" asked the warden.

A thick collar of contusion wrapped around the front and sides of William's neck, purple and black bruises melding in an anguished, hypnotic mosaic.

"I've never seen such *force*," Roger said. "It looks like his Adam's apple was crushed."

"So what are you saying?" asked the warden, looking between the dumbfounded pair.

Annette's doe-eyes were watered with fear. "He was strangled," she said.

With incredulous synchronicity they turned to look at the woman in the trunk. From high above them, somewhere in the mist, a crow cawed.

***

The Sodbuster and the Spider

by Adrian Ludens
United States

*"Long ago, a Lakota Sioux spiritual leader was on a high
mountain and he had a vision. In his vision, Iktomi - the great
trickster - appeared in the form of a spider. As Iktomi spoke, he
took the elder's willow hoop and began to spin a web." —Lakota
legend*

Wade Norman's father drowned on dry land. It happened in the
springtime. When Walter Norman did not appear for supper, Wade's
mother, Edith, sent the boy out to look for him. Wade found his
father lying on his back in the barn's hayloft, an empty rye bottle lying
beside him in the golden straw. The older man appeared to have
finished off the bottle and fallen asleep. He'd vomited, his body
rejecting the bitter liquid, but enough trickled down his trachea that he
suffocated and died. Sturgeon's doctor, Douglas Stuart, had coined the
phrase that clung like a burr to Wade's thoughts. "I'm sorry, my boy,
but your pa found a way to drown on dry land."

Five months had passed since that bleak day. Wade had hoeing
and planting to keep him busy the rest of the spring and plowing
followed in the fall. The livestock needed tending every morning and
evening. Wade worked from dawn to dusk if the weather was bad and
longer when the weather was good.

On the September day that he rode his pony to Sturgeon for
supplies, his mother lay abed inside their homestead cabin, coughing
her life away a few burgundy droplets at a time.

Wade's lank brown hair tumbled down his forehead just enough
to provide his squinting blue eyes a measure of shade from the fiery
orb soaring imperceptibly across the sky. He did not own a hat, but
wished he did.

His sunburned, windblown features would have looked
appropriate on a thirty-year-old man, but not on a twelve-year-old boy.
His chest was white as cow's milk, but his forearms had browned
beneath the sun. His face was too gaunt to be considered handsome.
Only his eyes retained any spark of the lingering innocence and
exuberance of youth.

Wade reached town intent on his task. He was supposed to obtain
medicine, something to help his mother rest, from Doc Stuart. His
mother had also given him a short list of items to obtain from the
grocer. Wade's pony plodded to a hitching post and the boy
dismounted and wrapped the reins around the horse-chewed wood.

Townsfolk strolled along the boardwalks. Two dogs fought over a
chicken carcass stripped of its meat. From unseen trees, cicadas sang
their shrill song.

Then something remarkable happened.

An imposing-looking man rode into view. He sat on his saddle,
Wade thought, like a king on his throne. He rode down the middle of
the dusty street with chin up and chest out. The stranger pulled the
reins and his stallion—the color of the ash and coals of a dead
campfire—pranced a moment and then stood still. The newcomer
scanned the assembling crowd. One hand stroked a trimmed mustache
and goatee, then dropped and settled on the butt of a pearl-handled
revolver holstered low on his thigh. A reverent hush fell upon the
group that had assembled like ants around a dropped dollop of
strawberry jam. Wade stood among them. The stranger lifted his hand
from the revolver and brushed travel dust from the silver-colored star
affixed to his duster's lapel. Everyone waited in silence until the
lawman spoke.

"I am Marshal Eugene Masters," he boomed, "and I come to your
town to serve as God's wrath."

Gasps erupted from several of those assembled. Even the town
sheriff, a squat fellow with a ruddy face named Holst, dropped his
mouth open in astonishment. A few of Sturgeon's more notorious
drunkards put away their flasks. Gummy Kate, a soiled dove, looked
abashed and drew her ratty shawl over her mostly exposed bosom.
Even the cicadas fell into respectful silence.

Marshal Masters favored the assembled throng with a tight-lipped
smile and continued. "God's law has been broken. Man's law has been

broken. About ten miles south of here, as the buzzard flies, a family of homesteaders has been brutally massacred."

Shocked murmurs rippled through the crowd. Someone said, "God have mercy on their souls."

The lawman straightened in his saddle and cocked his head, as if listening for instruction from the heavens. A sliding cloudbank hid the sun and darkened the street. Masters picked up the thread of his narrative and yanked it forward with the words, "All massacred, except for one."

Masters waited for the excited murmurs of the townsfolk to subside before resuming.

"One young girl, Alice Chambers by name, was spared by the grace of God. She hid while the outrageous acts of violence were carried out upon her kin. I will discover the culprits and bring them to swift justice. This, I solemnly vow."

The crowd, like a congregation of evangelicals, had started responding with increasing zeal each time the marshal paused.

"I will bring the cold-blooded, bloodthirsty cowards to justice!"

The murmurs became angry shouts of approval.

"I will not rest until the murderers are dead themselves!"

Marshal Masters paused and used a bandanna to wipe sweat from his brow as the crowd shouted and clamored.

"People of Sturgeon, when the time comes, will you be prepared?"

Shouts of assent came, but the marshal wasn't done. "When I come to you with information about the murderers, will you be ready to volunteer? Will you take up arms and dispense justice?"

His chest heaved amid the swelling roar of the crowd. Some scattered, perhaps returning to their homes intent on retrieving their guns. Others pushed closer to the Marshal, trying to touch him, to touch his horse, or get in a word.

Wade let the frenzied men and women jostle past him. He gazed up at the lawman with unabashed admiration.

He'd found a hero.

*

That night, after completing his chores and giving his mother a teaspoon of her medicine, Wade fell upon his straw-filled mattress and plummeted into an exhausted sleep.

Reverend Gentry stood before him, austere and rigid. Wade had spent many Sundays watching in terrified fascination as the scowling reverend read long passages from his battered Bible, rebuking his sweating congregation with Old Testament tales of God's wrath. Now, however, the little country church, lit by a single guttering candle, housed only two occupants.

Wade sat ramrod straight in the front pew. The reverend addressed him in a hectoring, feverish tone. "It comes like a silk doll on rickety corncobs. His face pales to reach the color gray–dust dancing with dead leaves. The void increases when you get excited."

The words made little sense to Wade. Aware at a subconscious level that he was dreaming, he relaxed and simply nodded whenever Gentry paused.

Reverend Gentry gestured for him to come forward and kneel at the communion rail. Wade obeyed. The man of scripture held out a morsel of sacramental bread and the boy opened his mouth to receive it. Gentry pressed it onto his tongue and Wade felt an immediate change. His tongue was melting. Not daring to spit out the Lord's flesh, Wade swallowed the sacrament—along with the dissolving remnants of his tongue.

He gazed up at Reverend Gentry with wide and pleading eyes. The old man leaned in close and spoke in the voice of Walter Norman.

"From father to son, keep your ears open. God has taken away your tongue. Serve him well with these gifts bestowed."

Wade looked around with a sense of shock; a cool stream and rocky shore had replaced the darkened church. Wade had a moment to register the russet, craggy expanse of canyon walls. Then a giddy feeling of vertigo threatened to overwhelm him as the ground flew away from his feet.

Wade knew what would happen next. The hallmark of all bad dreams was the rapid ascent, followed by the terrifying plunge into wakefulness.

Instead, he rose only a few feet and the motion stopped. Wade found himself standing and staring at the wrinkled face of a weeping elder from one of the area tribes, Cheyenne, perhaps, or Lakota.

Wade meant to make a polite inquiry on the subject but snapped his mouth shut, his teeth clacking together like a steel animal trap. No tongue meant no talking. As Wade looked on, the wizened face dissolved and reassembled. Eyes blinked and revealed caves. The old man's skin became russet canyon walls, down which twin waterfalls fell. Black hair erupted into a murder of crows flapping past Wade, their wings battering the air. One crow shot straight toward him, its beak sprung open as if to pluck out one of his eyes.

Wade woke and sat upright, gasping. His heart rattled his rib cage like a panicked prisoner until his eyes adjusted to the darkness of the cabin. In the next room, his mother snored. Crickets chirped. Above him, shining in the moonlight, hung a magnificent orb-shaped spider's web.

Before sleep reclaimed him, the boy bit down on his tongue to make sure it was still there.

*

Marshal Eugene Masters, though no longer in town, was still on the lips and in the minds of most of the townsfolk. Most of the men admired and wished to emulate him. Several of Sturgeon's fairer sex daydreamed about his piercing eyes, broad chest, and commanding yet soulful demeanor. Silent, secret fantasies abounded.

As for Wade's part, he longed for a chance to impress the marshal. Two mornings after his startling dream, a remarkable opportunity presented itself.

He'd ridden to town to seek Doc Stuart's advice regarding his mother. The man of medicine, to his credit, went straight to the truth. "She has consumption, Wade," he said. "The medicine I prescribed isn't going to cure anything. It will ease her suffering and help her rest, nothing more."

The enormity of the revelation left Wade with a painful lump in his throat. He vowed not to cry in the doctor's presence. He would ride all the way home and ensconce himself in the privacy of the root cellar before he let his tears fall.

Dr. Stuart gave Wade a reassuring pat on the back. "Chin up, my boy. At least you're old enough to make it on your own." His voice dropped to a murmur. "Not like that poor girl whose family got killed."

At this, Wade looked up, interested despite his sorrow. "Alice Chambers?"

"Yes, she's staying with my wife and me until we are able to determine her next of kin. Never says a word, not that I blame her. Sheriff Holst tried to question her about what happened that night. Marshal Masters has too. She won't talk. This is rather vexing, and not only from a health and well-being standpoint. What if something she saw or heard could help bring the killers to justice?" The older man

73

regarded Wade over the top of his wire-rimmed spectacles. He took a deep breath, held it as if considering something, and then let the air escape his lungs. "Wade, Alice is eight years old. I know you're twelve, and I know you've had to do a lot of growing up lately, but do you think you might be willing ..."

Stuart let the question hang in the air unfinished because Wade had already nodded in assent. Perhaps he wanted Wade to play games with the girl in an attempt to lift her spirits. Or perhaps he wanted him to counsel Alice, to help her cope with her situation. Wade yearned to meet her. He hoped to be the one to get her to open up, to reveal something of importance. He flushed at the thought of gaining an audience with Marshal Masters and presenting newfound evidence. He'd be a hero. Wade wondered how old one had to be before they could be deputized.

Doc Stuart drew him back to reality by rising. "You could follow me there now, if you're inclined. You could meet Alice."

Wade nodded and rose. Outside, he mounted his horse and followed Doc Stuart's carriage, feeling both excited and nervous to meet the orphaned girl.

*

When they arrived, Alice Chambers cowered in a corner of the Stuarts' sitting room. She was so petite she looked to Wade like a doll someone had discarded. He felt a twinge of momentary surprise at the girl's dark skin. His limited life experience had led him to assume she'd look like him.

"Alice, this is Wade Norman." Doc Stuart gestured toward him. The girl eyed him with obvious mistrust. Stuart's wife, a tree stump of a woman with kind-looking eyes, came in from the kitchen, wiping her hands on a dishtowel. Sturgeon's doctor knelt before the girl. "Wade's lost his daddy too. He ... he wanted to say hello and offer his condolences."

The girl's eyes moved from her temporary benefactor back to Wade. His cheeks flushed. Not knowing what else to do, he walked across the room and sat down on the floor beside the disconsolate girl.

"Deep down in my heart, it hurts all the time." Wade wasn't aware he meant to speak until the words had left his mouth. Stuart gave him a curious look and Wade's cheeks burned even more. Then he felt the girl slide her tiny hand into his. She squeezed. He squeezed back. In

74

that moment, Wade knew an unspoken bond had forged itself between them.

Doc Stuart stood and followed his wife from the room. Soon Wade smelled coffee brewing. He and Alice sat in companionable silence, drawing strength from each other. He glanced at her and saw the telltale glisten of tears on her cheeks. He knew if she looked at him, she would see the same. Eventually, their breathing fell into a synchronous rhythm.

Time passed. The sun's path altered the shadows in the room. Wade felt his legs grow numb from the floorboards but didn't move. He didn't want to leave Alice's side. Doc Stuart looked in on them from time to time, but for the most part let them have their privacy. Wade never let go of her hand.

Then, at the sound of chairs scraping the floor in the kitchen, Alice shocked Wade by turning and urgently whispering in his ear.

"When it happened, I think I fainted, because I don't remember anything. I woke up hearing *pik, pik, pik*. Like coal miners swinging pickaxes. And then the sounds just faded away."

She sank back into her previous position. Wade felt too stunned to move. He tried to formulate a response but the concept of words seemed to have fled his brain. Doc Stuart entered the room.

"I shouldn't have kept you so long, Wade. Your mother must be worried sick." He grimaced, perhaps at his choice of words. His eyes moved from one child to the other. "I think you'd best be heading home."

Wade mounted his horse and rode back through town in the direction of the homestead. Chores awaited him, not to mention tending to his mother. She would need a meal prepared, water heated for bathing, her medicine administered. Wade urged his horse into a gallop.

*

Two hours later, Wade sat beside his ailing mother. After explaining the reason for his late arrival, he had brushed his horse and bedded it down for the night, fed the livestock, and collected eggs from the chicken coop. After completing his duties outdoors, he returned to his mother's side, feeling conflicted about being away from home for so long.

Edith reached for his hand and he took it. Her fingers were cold and seemed to be all knuckles. "I'm glad you sat with that girl. My heart just breaks for her. You're a fine son, Wade." His mother's voice sounded weak. "And you'll grow into a good, kind man. A mother knows."

Wade didn't know how to respond so he gave her hand a gentle squeeze and remained at her side until she fell asleep. Then he rose and set about putting the cabin to rights for the night. At last exhaustion overtook him, and Wade extinguished the last candle, kicked off his boots and stretched out on his own bed. He lay with hands clasped behind his head. The spider's web above him came into focus. Wade contemplated its complex, yet comforting pattern until sleep claimed him.

*

Wade stood in the barnyard. The sinking red sun touched the horizon. Wind sent dust and sand hissing through the overgrown weeds. He craned his neck, took in the enormity of the barn. Time and inclement weather had colluded to beat the boards to a disconsolate gray. How had he allowed this to happen? Wade reached out and pulled the barn door open. Dank, stale air filled his lungs. The sound of beating wings fluttered from rafter to rafter.

In the deep darkness, something moved and Wade felt his chest constrict with fear. Dread saturated his thoughts, deadened his limbs. The shape, a black-on-black shadow in the far corner of the barn, drew closer. Wade became aware of an unsteady shuffling. It grew louder as the shape emerged from the darkness, approaching him.

The hairs on the back of his neck stood on end. Animal fear escaped his lips in an inarticulate moan. He tried to run, but couldn't. A horse loomed, lurching forward on stiff legs. Hollow sockets of darkness hung where its eyes should have been. The horse's hide clung to its ribs. Hipbones and spine protruded. Clumps of mane had fallen out. Flies shadowed the beast in a loose cloud.

Wade recognized the coal-and-ashes hide of the marshal's stallion. The creature came to a stop a mere two feet from him. Wade could have reached up to stroke the stallion's emaciated muzzle if he felt like it.

He didn't.

The horse lacked eyes, yet seemed to gaze at Wade just the same. The boy could only stare back in awe. This horse had every appearance of having been locked in the barn to starve. Based on the state of the barn, it had stood derelict for decades. How could the horse still be clinging to life? And for what purpose had it miraculously staved off death?

Before Wade could formulate an answer to these questions, the horse turned away from him, as if satisfied. As its flank came between him and the setting sun, the red light of the orb shone through the stallion's rib cage.

The animal, he now realized, was little more than a reanimated skeleton, with tattered remnants of hide clinging to its bones. An object fell from a rear hoof as the horse hobbled back into the barn, swallowed by darkness.

Wade stooped and reached out for the object that had tumbled into the dust. It was a rusted horseshoe. Before his trembling fingers made contact, the horseshoe vanished.

Wade woke up in his bed. The cold gray light of impending dawn seeped in through the window. Chores awaited him. Sighing, Wade kicked his blanket aside and reached for his boots.

*

After working outdoors all morning, Wade looked in on his mother. He found her sitting up in bed, claiming to feel better. Wade thought he noticed a bit of color in her cheeks and felt grateful for the improvement.

He busied himself with minor cleaning inside the cabin, talking with his mother as he worked. He tried to improve her mood by bringing up pleasant memories from his childhood. He swept and scrubbed the floors, shook out rugs, and gave Edith a spoonful of medicine when she started feeling unwell.

Later, as she dozed, Wade entered his own tiny room. Here he also cleaned, needing to keep busy. He searched the ceiling for the spider's web but found nothing. He craned his neck trying to catch the web in the light without success.

Frowning, he gave up, pulled on a wool coat and went outside to get a head start on the evening chores.

*

When Wade crawled into bed that night, the spider's web came into focus. He thought about getting up again to dispose of it but his limbs felt heavy from the day's labors and he decided to wait until morning. He closed his eyes for a time, and then reopened them.

77

A spider descended from the web, and loomed large as it neared his face. Wade wanted to roll out of the way but found he could not.

"You are wise," the spider said, "and yet still have much to learn."

The orb-shaped web had blurred as Wade focused on the spider itself. The brilliantly colored creature's abdomen shimmered with silver-white, green, and gold.

"I shall tell you three truths and one lie," the spider said. "But we should relocate first."

Wade blinked and then gasped. He now sat in the hayloft where his father had died. His legs dangled out over the edge of the open hatch. He began to scramble to safety when the voice came again.

"No need to move."

Wade froze. He wanted to talk, to ask questions, but no words would come. In front of his face, illuminated by the moonlight, the spider swayed on a translucent thread.

"Listen to my words. You already have knowledge within you that can help save lives," the spider said. "The marshal is a good man who will listen when you bring him your message. Your mother will make a full recovery. Alice Chambers will soon be reunited with family."

Wade felt distress mounting within him. Which statement was the lie? Would his mother die? Or perhaps the quantification of "one" was the lie, and everything the spider had said would prove to be untrue. His mind reeled at the possibilities.

"Do you know how to wake from a dream, lad?" the spider asked. Wade nodded.

"Well then, you had better do it quick." The shimmering silver, green, and gold creature ascended into the darkness. Wade heard something rustling in the hay behind him. Rats? Boards creaked. No. Not rats. Dread kept him frozen a few moments more. Then he twisted his head and saw a silhouetted figure shambling toward him. Please don't let that be my father ...

But it was.

Terrified, Wade pushed off with his hands and plunged through the open hatch. Instead of breaking his neck on a hay rack, he awoke in his bed gasping and drenched with sweat.

Of the spider's web he saw no sign.

*

Wade knew exactly what he intended to tell Marshal Masters, he just had to find him first. This thought chased him through his day, like the catchy refrain of a Stephen Foster song.

Edith had taken a turn for the worse, it seemed, and Wade doted on her. As evening approached, he rushed through his chores, prepared a meal his mother barely touched, and then saddled his pony and headed for town. The man in the moon smiled down on him, as if proudly urging him onward.

The search for Masters proved to be an easy one; the noisy saloon was the only building still lit when he arrived. Wade recognized the marshal's stallion tied to a hitching post.

He dismounted, wound his pony's reins to another post and climbed the two wooden steps to the saloon's batwing doors. The unmistakable booming voice of Marshal Masters sounded, not from the saloon's interior, but from somewhere above Wade.

The boy moved out from under the awning and looked up. A feeling of déjà vu swept over him and for a moment Wade felt as if he were gazing up at the weathered barn.

The marshal's voice came again, and peals of laughter followed. Masters was not in the saloon after all, it seemed. Wade checked the side of the building and found a set of wooden stairs leading up to the second level. He ascended the stairs, not daring to look down. Something about elevated heights—discovering his father dead in the hayloft played a part—frightened him. Wade had important information to pass along to the lawman, however, and would not allow himself to turn back.

Inside the room atop the saloon, the marshal sat with a tumbler in one hand and a lit cigar in the other. Several women dressed like dance hall girls lounged around him. An assortment of other hangers-on filled the cramped quarters. Among them, Wade noticed a few hard-eyed men who looked like gunslingers. Cobwebs hung from the rafters, tobacco smoke fogged the room.

"What the hell is that kid doing here?" someone asked.

"Getdafukoutt," a scantily clad dance hall girl with straw-colored hair slurred.

Wade felt his cheeks begin to burn. He shuffled his feet and would have fled back down the stairs had the marshal not set the tumbler aside and raised a hand for silence.

"Do you have a message for me, kid?" Masters asked.

A tremendous wave of relief swept over him, but Wade still took several seconds to find his voice. "Yes, sir, I do."

"Well, let's hear it." Masters motioned him forward, like a king beckoning a page.

"Sir, it's about the Chambers family." Wade's tongue felt thick in his dry mouth. "I have some information about the murderers."

"Already know all about it," the marshal announced. "It was Injuns."

An angry murmur rippled through the cramped room. Wade shook his head. "No, sir. Indians didn't kill that girl's family at all. The girl, Alice, heard the clicking of stones against horseshoes. 'Like coal miners swinging pickaxes,' that's what she told me. Indians don't shoe their horses. That means someone else—"

Masters grabbed Wade by his lapels and yanked him close. The marshal's face, both menacing and repulsive, filled Wade's field of vision.

"Let me remind you of something, little sodbuster. That girl is not like you and me. She don't talk much because she's feebleminded. Her whole family was, if you ask me."

A belch from the marshal filled the air around Wade's head with the pungent odor of sour mash whiskey. "I happen to know that most of the men who did what they did are long gone. Half of 'em was so drunk, they don't even remember what happened. But folks hereabouts are hot for blood. They ain't gonna rest until they get some vengeance. We're riding out to an Injun encampment at dawn."

"B-b-but ..." Wade felt dismayed to the point of dizziness.

"You feebleminded too, little sodbuster? There's no use arguing. Sometimes this is just how the world works." Masters shoved him away.

Stunned, Wade opened his mouth to speak, thought better of it and took a step back. Like a sleepwalker, he turned and walked stiffly toward the stairs. Laughter and jeers rained down upon his shoulders.

Wade escaped the claustrophobic confines of the upper room and stepped back out onto the stair landing. The night was silent, and still.

Then he understood. It was just another bad dream. Marshall Masters couldn't be that corrupt, that cruel. The world did not work this way. Wade rejected the notion.

Justice would be served. He had to speak to the marshal—the real marshal.

That meant waking. Recalling his previous dream, Wade decided how he'd make himself wake up.

He lifted one leg after the other over the landing's wooden guardrail. The boy teetered for a moment, steadying his resolve, then pushed off, and tumbled into darkness.

*

The jolt of pain that came as a splinter of wood speared his sliding backside proved he was already awake. Wade twisted his body in an attempt to catch hold of the platform but missed by several feet. His outstretched arms, however, were in perfect position to collide with the long support beams that crisscrossed the posts. The wood shredded the fabric of his sleeves, and bit into his flesh, but it arrested his descent.

The boy hung at the crux of the matter in both a literal and figurative sense, bleeding and disheartened. He clung to consciousness, driven by righteous anger and the hope of seeing his mother again. When at last he'd regained his wind, Wade grasped the timber supports and moved downward, handhold by tenuous handhold. More splinters nipped at his palms but compared to the pain of his injured upper arms, the splinters were mere inconveniences.

At last he reached safe jumping distance and let himself fall for a second time. He landed gracelessly in the dirt, hoisted himself up and hurried back to his horse.

He decided to ride straight to Dr. Stuart's and rouse the entire household. He'd ask the good doctor to dress his wounds and suggest he send his wife or perhaps little Alice to fetch Sheriff Holst. He'd explain the situation to the sheriff who, though he could be a bit thick, had never been accused of being corrupt. Sheriff Holst could deputize as many honest townsfolk as he felt necessary. Perhaps even dour old Reverend Gentry could be enlisted to the cause.

Then they'd ride out to the Indian encampment to warn them about Marshal Masters and his men. If they had to stand by their side and fight in the name of justice, Wade hoped they would. He pointed his horse in the direction of Doc Stuart's and urged it into a gallop.

The world was not a perfect place, nor was it always just, and the forces on the side of good did not always win. Wade reasoned, as the night wind ruffled his hair, that a young man had a right to dream.

***

81

Every Single Day

by Sophie Kearing
United States

Every single day, someone tries to break into my house.

I have no idea why. I own nothing of value except for my T.V. and watch, and I'll be keeping those down here with me until this mysterious prowler stops his visits. I can tell it's a man by the sounds he makes. This is a quiet neighborhood, and when I leave my basement window cracked, I can hear his little grunts and weird, nervous throat-clearing. These noises have become more unsettling to me than the fact that he's trying to get in here. There's something familiar about them ... Are they the subtle sounds of a man I once crossed? Are they reminders of how dark regret can be, how perilous success? I don't know. I can't put my finger on it.

Thank god I don't have to worry about the garage.. I've never been one to lock it, but I sold my car a few years back, so luckily, there's nothing in there for this freak to steal.

I've gone to the police more than once. But the aspiring intruder always knows exactly when not to come. Besides, his efforts never go beyond him circling my house, jiggling the door knobs, and pulling at the windows. This makes it all the more pathetic that I hide down here instead of confronting him.

To my defense, the grunting man isn't the only reason I sequester myself in my basement. I have something of the utmost importance that I'm trying to accomplish. And since I've been at it for twelve years, I'm on one hell of a deadline. Let me explain. My thirtieth birthday is November 18th of this year. I know it's unforgivably cliché, but I've always feared that I wouldn't live past twenty-nine. I just can't see myself with a wife, children, a "dad" SUV, and a paunch. And it's okay with me if I never feel the sweetness of a wife and children, if I never drive a vehicle whose interior is peppered with Goldfish crumbs,

83

if I never acquire the soft belly that comes with the joys of family life. But it's *not* okay with me if I don't reach my goal before I die. That's why I stay down here, amidst the whirring space heaters and soothing dimness, doing my meditation, yoga, and special hand movements. I won't allow myself to go upstairs for my one small meal a day until I've completely exhausted the laborious routine that will eventually lead to the achievement of my goal:

Hours of a little-known mantra until the vision in my mind's eye is sharp and specific.

The achingly nuanced articulation of my body from pose to pose.

A complicated series of hand movements.

I feel most centered down here, with the doors locked and the windows too small to admit a grown man. Besides, I can't allow myself to become consumed with what's happening outside. I need to gain access to the power that my superconsciousness has over time and space. And the focus necessary to attain such a thing comes only with preparatory stillness followed by disciplined movement. I'm sure that I haven't yet succeeded because of some lack of depth in my meditation, a discordant pitch in my mantra, or an angle in my positioning that's off by less than a degree. It all has to be absolutely perfect in order for this to work. Very few have ever done it.

I move through my opening yoga sequence and proceed to increasingly difficult poses. My body buzzes and my mind goes in and out of blankness. My triumphant Kala Bhairavasana, the pose I do before I culminate in a sequence of esoteric hand movements, is interrupted by the pattering of sneakers up my front stairs and over my porch. Fuck. He keeps getting here earlier and earlier. And with how well everything was going, today could've been the day. I ease my leg from its folded position and go to the window. It sounds like he's fiddling with the mail slot in my front door. I can tell he's trying to be quiet even as he anxiously clears his throat.

When I no longer hear him, I trudge upstairs and prepare the only meal I can eat that won't act as an anchor: an odd mixture of lentils, quinoa, basil, apple, cucumbers, and berries that I've grown to love. I usually sit at the table, but today I carry my spoon and bowl around, munching as I peer out the windows. The windswept backyard, with all of its orange and yellow leaves slumped against the west fence, is indeed devoid of intruders. Through my side windows I deduce that the gangways between my house and the neighbors' are clear as well.

When I get to the foyer, I see the strangest thing. A note scrawled very lightly on the back of a flyer. It reads: STOP WHAT YOU'RE DOING IN THE BASEMENT AND YOU'LL LIVE TO SEE 30. This handwriting ... My saliva runs cold. I rest my bowl on the radiator cover. But my shock and confusion gives way to anger with uncharacteristic rapidity. I yank open the front door and fly down the steps. The street is deserted. I return to the foyer, slam my door shut, twist my locks, and apply the chain.

Despite my accelerating vendetta with the intruder, I won't stop my daily work. It is, after all, the very purpose of my life. To let him be a distraction would be to let him win. The next day, I begin my mantra thirty minutes ahead of schedule. I visualize the place. I visualize the time. I fill in the details with painstaking clarity. And then I deepen my breathing. It becomes unbelievably slow, and it consumes me. I'm suspended in nothingness.

I am nothing.

This is where I harvest the power. Without opening my eyes, my body automatically transitions into yoga. Everything flows with absolute perfection—until the intruder arrives. I'm pulled from my exalted state; I'm disoriented, then irate. Determined to catch the bastard, I fly upstairs. The mail flap creaks open. I rush to the door, intending to confront the trespasser once and for all. But then I see that he's left another piece of correspondence: a folded page from a coloring book. I pick it up and find scrawls written in blue crayon. Even taking into account the unsettling choice of writing implement and paper, what bothers me most is how feathery the letters have been drafted, as if the crayon had barely touched the sheet. Most baffling of all is the message: THE CORRECT MANTRA IS OM BHRAAM BHREEM BHRAUM SAH RAHVL NAMAH.

"*What* the *fuck*?" I mutter, eyebrows pinched. "Now he's *encouraging* me?"

The page shakes in my hands. I want to crumble it—no, rip it to shreds and feed it to my fireplace. I want to have the authorities stake out my house until they can catch whoever's doing this. That would require me to visit the police station, though, because I don't do cell phones, landlines, e-mail, or anything like that. Those things only lead to a constant barrage of unimportant interactions. Ultimately, I decide against contacting the police. As they had in the past, they would provide nothing but a massive disruption. I don't want them around, infecting my space with their obscene, worldly energy. And I can't show them the notes, as interested as I'd be in what information fingerprints could yield. The first note would lead them to ask what exactly it is that I do in my basement. And it's none of anyone's goddamn business what I do in my basement.

The next morning, I take out my trash. My neighbor, a woman in her sixties, is out raking leaves.

"Oh, hello, Jackson," she calls.

"Hello, Mrs. Bedeman."

She walks over to the chain-link fence that divides our backyards. "Beautiful day, isn't it?"

"Yes. Beautiful."

"You've gotten so skinny, Jackson. *Too* skinny. Probably all the jogging."

"Jogging? I don't jog."

"Oh, pardon *me*." Her eyes twinkle in the autumn sun. "You're just naturally svelte." She winks at me.

"I mean, I do get a lot of exercise. But mostly indoors."

Mrs. Bedeman bites her lip. After a moment she asks, "Are you all right, dear? Are you coming down with something? I suppose it *is* cold season."

"I'm fine, Mrs. Bedeman. I promise."

We exchange complicated smiles, and the woman returns to her pile of faded leaves. Once inside, I go downstairs with the coloring sheet to memorize and practice the new mantra. When the time comes, I begin my extensive sequence. Loathe as I am to use the intruder's advice, I use this new mantra and sink into an all-encompassing meditation. I'm not sure exactly how much time passes, but I find myself unwilling to transition to my special yoga moves. My numb body remains planted in lotus position, the syllables of the mantra falling from my lips. Suddenly, I'm running, out in the harsh daylight. Frantic. Why am I so frantic? Then I flash back into the basement, again aware of the low ceiling and the space heaters' toasty emissions. But I know that I'm not all here. Part of me is still out there, running. The mere acknowledgement of this fact casts me right back into the me that's hightailing it through the park. Oh, Christ. So *this* is why Mrs. Bedeman thinks she's seen me jogging. Because she *has*. And all this time, I had no clue.

I'm split. This is *not* the way I wanted to teleport—in odd, confused fragments, the most powerful part of me still tending to my basement ritual. There's enough of me out there to comprise a physical body, which, in terms of metaphysics, is not as particle-dense as most people think it is. In fact, it's mostly just the space between particles. When I'm focused on this outdoor version of myself, I feel unsafe and ungrounded. Unhinged. Desperate for cohesion with my full mental facilities, I briefly inhabit my meditating body. But instead of comfort, what I feel is another extension of myself manifest in the place that I had always intended to teleport: the Tibetan side of the Himalayas, where the great yogis live in enlightened solitude. This is the site of my intense visualization all of these years. But I can barely feel the solidity of the gritty terrain beneath my feet or the chill in the air. Still, I give a dry cough and wrap my arms around myself. A flash and then I'm back in tune with the part of me that's seated in the basement. I reach for my glass and drink every drop of water therein. I clear my throat, and the sound is echoed outside. I cock my ear. There's a scuffling out on the porch. A scuffling created by *two* pairs of feet. And then, a thud. Emboldened by today's progress, I thunder upstairs and out my front door. Nothing could have prepared me for what I see. It's me. Choking another me. I stagger backward.

The homicidal Jackson glares up at me. "Stop what you're doing in the basement. There are too many of us. With each new one, we're diluted. We fade. It hurts." As if to demonstrate his fragility, his grip on the other me weakens.

The other me pulls on the slackened hands around his neck and rasps, "Don't stop our project. This is the first day you've become aware of what's happening, and things can only get better from here. One day, you'll stop fracturing and start teleporting in your totality. It's what you really want. Just keep using the mantra I gave you. No yoga, no hand movements—engaging your body is what's been rendering you ignorant of your travels."

The other Jackson tightens his fingers again. "Shut the fuck up. Just shut the fuck up and die."

"*Both* of you shut up!" I hiss.

I look around, and to my great horror, I lock eyes with Mrs. Bedeman. She's staring at me through her living room window.

I turn back to the mes on my porch and growl, "Get inside. *Now.*"

Both obey. Once in the house, my panic only increases. Mrs. Bedeman, a nosy old bat and a member of the neighborhood watch, will surely be calling the police. Quickly, I must wring the other mes for more information.

"So both of you've been trying to get in here this whole time?"

The murderous me scoffs. "There are many of us. But we're not firing on all cylinders. We thought that if only we could get in here and commune with you, we could become whole again."

"*I* didn't come here for that. It's too late for that," the other me says. "I came here to help. I'm aware of things that I can tell you aren't. Maybe I'm a fragment of your superconscious."

"*You're* not firing on all cylinders, either, are you?" the murderous me blurts in my direction. "You clear your throat and cough almost as much as we do. You just don't realize it. You've got pulmonary issues ... because of all this."

I think of Mrs. Bedeman's assumption that I had a cold. "My neighbor ... I need to make sure she doesn't call the police."

"If she hasn't already," the murderous me calls as I leave out the front door.

I ring my neighbor's doorbell. She pulls her curtain aside, revealing her trepidation.

"I just wanted to explain ..." I say loudly, smiling and giving a little wave.

She opens her door but leaves her chain lock on, eying me through a three-inch gap.

"I hope my brothers didn't scare you. We're triplets, you see, and we haven't visited in quite some time. Roughhousing is how we say hello."

The woman draws her cardigan across her middle in two overlapping layers.

"You weren't ... upset at us, were you?"

"You mean, did I call the police," she states, voice chilly. Before I can answer, she continues. "You'll be glad to know that I didn't. I'm on in the years, young man, and I don't want to take on a reputation as a crazy old woman. Let's both just stay out of each other's way." The door clicks shut and the deadbolt engages.

I descend her steps. There's a newspaper partially hidden in the grass. I pick it up with the intention of lobbing it onto Mrs. Bedeman's porch. I'm not sure if it's the act of a helpful neighbor or a passive aggressive foe. Just before I pitch it, the date jumps out at me. November 18th. Jesus Christ. I'm thirty.

I don't know how I feel about this. I walk through the gangway between my house and Mrs. Bedeman's seeking a few moments of peace in the backyard before returning to Tweedle Dee and Tweedle Dum. I sit in a patio chair and breathe in the autumnal bouquet of wood smoke and forty-five-degree crispness. Seconds later, I hear a single scrape across cement. It's coming from my garage. I haven't even been in there since I sold my car. I reach over the short chain-link fence and snatch up Mrs. Bedeman's rake. I might have to fend off raccoons, or worse—skunks. When I pull open the warped aluminum door, it's too dim to make anything out. It isn't until I step into the garage and flip on the lights that I'm able to see the carnage that's been hiding on my very own property. Dozens of mes are heaped into the space where I used to park my car. Some of them look like they're sleeping. Some of them have been pummeled into unrecognizable masses of purple and crimson. Some of them have their heads cocked at unnatural angles, their eyes bulging grotesquely from their skulls. Some of them have been stripped naked, wedges of flesh and sinew having been chiseled away with garden shears. Blood has spread across the cement floor in a brown, sticky pool, though it's not as much blood as I would have expected from this level of savagery.

"Don't worry." The cannibal me, who had been standing flush against the same wall as the door, steps into view. "They don't stink. They're not real enough to stink, I guess."

"THEY *ARE* REAL! THEY'RE HUMAN BEINGS!" I scream, but then I clamp my hand over my mouth. My vision goes liquid. I blink away the tears and notice that some of the bodies have slightly merged together. It appears that the longer they lay stacked, the more they sink into each other, perhaps due to a lack of molecular density.

I glare at the cannibal. My god, he's carrying more weight than I am. There's a youthful fullness to his face and a healthy shine in his hair. His eye whites are bright and clear, his shoulders wide, arms bulky. Even more disturbing than his glowing robustness are the details that reveal his madness: the dried blood under his fingernails, the faint scratches across his cheeks and forearms (no doubt the product of the weaker mes' self-defense), and his effortless breathing (a wellness he's no doubt derived through using the weaker mes for

89

energetic sustenance). Something tells me that this predator is the most real thing in this garage. My assessment is confirmed when he lunges at me, subdues me in a chokehold, and kicks the door shut.

As I struggle pathetically, my terror is muddled by confusion: How on earth could this figment of *me* have developed such bloodlust? His very existence is due to my desire to live a life of reclusive spirituality, and to transport myself there solely with the power of my mind. Many other questions flood my brain, but all of them go forever unanswered. The only comfort I can possibly derive in my final moments is that technically, I *did* live to see thirty.

***

Drop by Drop

by C. R. Downing

United States

Present Day

Roger Frederick stared at the complicated figures on disorganized sheets of paper littering the top of his desk. Somewhere beneath the papers was a laptop.

His time in school paralleled the development of computers. His parents appreciated technology. However, they were not about to let any machine do a task that could be done quickly and without the help of a silicon chip.

He practiced spelling words and multiplication tables in pencil on lined paper. His friends were surprised and impressed that his manual calculations were as accurate and usually as fast as they could do on their calculators. A bonus was Roger's hard copy. Locating errors was much easier for him than it was for his hardcopyless friends.

At the end of each day in the lab, he scanned his pages of calculations into a program that converted his pencil marks into machine language. Every morning a data entry clerk moved his work into the collaborative database.

He tore the top sheet off his current legal pad. He considered crumbling it into a ball. He considered folding it into a crude airplane. In the end, he folded the page in half and tossed it toward his trashcan. It unfolded and landed like a pup tent, blank side up. He gave his head a resigned shake.

The laboratory housing his desk was dark except for the isolated island of light that surrounded him. The tomb-still silence was broken only by two sounds. The first was the gentle hum produced by his fluorescent desk lamp. The other just entered Roger's awareness—and it was ruining his concentration.

Drip.

91

There was a leak somewhere in the myriad of flasks, tubes, and connectors that filled the laboratory.

Drip ... Drip.

Droplets of liquid were leaking from some faulty seal, plunging Kamikaze-like onto a countertop.

Drip ... Drip ... Drip.

The tempo of the falling drops was increasing.

With a sigh, Roger pushed his chair back and uncoiled his lanky frame. He sighed again as he flipped on the overhead lights in the laboratory. After a final sigh, he began his hunt for the leak.

*

Seventeen Years Earlier

"Roger, darling, make sure you dry your hands after you wash them," Lila Frederick called to her son. Roger was notorious for splashing water on his dirty hands. He sometimes rubbed them together before rinsing them. But he never did more than shake them two or three times before leaving the bathroom.

"Okay, Mom," he replied. He turned off the water, paused, then shook his hands a dozen times before waving them in the direction of the towel hanging beside the sink. When he arrived at the dinner table, he sat down and rubbed his hands up and down the front of his pant legs.

"What is it about you and wet hands?" his father asked as he walked behind Roger and sat down. "Do you like wet skin or just dislike towels?"

"I shouldn't have to dry my hands at all," Roger replied. "I don't know why my hands stay wet after I turn the water off."

"Sounds like a good research project for this year's science fair," his father said. "Until then, I expect your hands to be dry before you leave the bathroom. Is that clear?"

"Yes, sir."

*

Roger named his science project "Why are you wet after taking a shower?"

The eighth grader planned to measure the time it took for different liquids to evaporate in a series of experiments. There was little science behind the choice of liquids. Easy to obtain was his main selection criterion.

92

His first stop was the kitchen. Cooking oil, soy sauce, and vinegar were his spoils of that war. The medicine cabinet in his parents' bathroom yielded rubbing alcohol and fingernail polish remover. His last foray was the garage where he collected a sample of windshield washer fluid in a coffee mug.

His outline of the experiment was as complete as most of his classmates' outlines. He added his personal hypothesis—water would be the next to the slowest to evaporate—as an afterthought. The hypothesis was based solely on his own experience with water.

Certain that he'd met the requirements for entering the science fair, he submitted the outline to his science teacher. Ms. Johnson returned the paper with "See me" written on it in red ink. She refused to allow personal experience to be the sole supporting evidence for his hypothesis.

"You need a scientific explanation for your hypothesis. Use your physical science book and a high school chemistry book if you have to," she told him. "After you do your research, I want to see at least four liquids ranked from fastest to evaporate to slowest to evaporate in your hypothesis."

"If I do that much research, I won't need to do the experiment," he complained. "I'll already know what's going to happen."

"Good scientists almost always know what they *expect* to get as results from their experiments. If they don't get what they predict, that's when discoveries happen."

In spite of his disappointment, Roger nodded. The idea of making a discovery had not crossed his mind until Ms. Johnson mentioned it. He had a new goal.

Although unaware of it at the time, the feeling Roger got by single-handedly supporting a point scientifically would be the driving force for the rest of his life.

*

Seven Years Ago

"Mr. Frederick, the proposal for your thesis is one of the most tightly written this committee has ever received." The chair of Roger's Master of Science in Chemistry looked up from his copy of Roger's proposal. He cleared his throat and looked to his right. "There is some concern in the minds of two committee members."

Roger's eyebrows arched in surprise. His thesis proposal was thirty-seven pages long. He could not imagine what concern there might be.

"Those committee members expressed doubt on the value of this research."

Roger clenched his jaw. They better not decline this based on a minority opinion!

"In spite of that, your committee unanimously approves your proposal. We look forward to reading the results of your attempt to weaken the intra-molecular polar bonds of water molecules."

"Thank you, Dr. Lewis," Roger said after a deep breath. "I won't disappoint you."

"I'm certain of that," Lewis responded. "Get on with it!"

"Yes, ma'am," Roger said through a forced smile.

*

Thirty-six months after the approval of his thesis proposal, Roger faced the committee a second time.

"I despise the use of the term *prove* in the reporting of results of an experiment. But, this is one case that merits its use," one of the doubting committee members intoned. "It appears that you are unable to accept that the objective of your research is unattainable."

"I'm certain that if I—"

"Mr. Frederick, the committee is willing to accept this thesis paper as fulfilling the requirement for the Master of Science degree." Dr. Lewis did not apologize for interrupting Roger. As his faculty mentor, she knew her mentee. She was certain Roger was chasing a figment of his imagination.

"What do I do now?" Roger asked. He'd based his life plan on successfully closing the evaporation rate between water and acetone until both values were identical.

"That is not a decision for this committee," the chair replied.

"If I might offer a suggestion," a member of the committee said. The chair nodded.

"Mr. Frederick, I recommend that you look at this problem from the other direction."

"I don't understand," Roger admitted.

"What was your goal?"

"Increasing the rate of evaporation of water to match that of acetone."

"Which terms in that sentence have antonyms?" the committee member asked.

"Increasing and evaporation," he answered, biting off each word to emphasize his displeasure.

"Very good. What options are possible?"

Roger's arms folded. I can work on reducing the rate or—

"That's a brilliant idea!" Roger enthused. "I'm trying to alter the fundamental nature of an inorganic molecule. Instead of working on the rate of evaporation, if I concentrate on increasing the surface tension of water, that could change—"

"That's a proposal for another set of letters, Mr. Frederick. If presented effectively, I can't see why any Ph.D. committee worth its salt would not approve it."

"Thank you," Roger said. He looked at the doubting committee member and added, "Thank you all."

*

Two Years Ago

Roger presented his Ph.D. proposal. It was accepted not only for his dissertation but as a fully funded fellowship as well. Coverage of his expenses was guaranteed for two years.

He started by hiring two laboratory technicians and one postdoc who would be the second name on the paper he knew would put them all on the physical chemistry map.

Less than one semester into the research, the fellowship ground to a halt. The four scientists proposed fifteen hypotheses. It was clear to all that none would generate a valid experimental procedure. Roger called a team meeting.

"There isn't any way to make this more palatable, so I'm going to get straight to the point. This research is headed nowhere. One thing we proved—"

He cut himself off at the shocked expressions on his team's collective faces. He knew what shocked them. He'd used the term proved as an absolute. He remembered the end of the recruiting speech he'd used when hiring each of the scientists seated around the table.

He'd violated his own protocol.

"I know you're shocked," he said as he resumed his statement. "But, in this case, 'proved' is the reality. What I thought was possible cannot be accomplished."

"Are you terminating your fellowship?" a lab tech asked.

"I'm not sure. I want to hear your ideas for restructuring the research objective. I hope we come up with one that will allow us to keep the fellowship solvent for the remaining eighteen months."

After several seconds of silence, the first idea for restructuring was tossed into the mix. After forty-three minutes, the flow of ideas stopped. There were seven ideas for research to flesh out.

"I'll copy the ideas onto thumb drives. You can pick up your drive in your mailbox after you secure the lab" Roger said.

Three heads nodded agreement.

"I'll research the least favorite idea," he added. "And I've got one I didn't share."

He waved off protests. It was his customary response to what he considered an invasion of his privacy.

"I've got a number eight that's so far out there, I'm afraid it might reach exit velocity and head off into the void of deep space. Let me be the one that enters the black hole."

*

In less than a month, the team agreed on Roger's black hole eighth idea as their best chance. The request to modify the fellowship was granted. The team dubbed RI-8 for "Research Idea Number Eight" to fail, although "Ridiculous Idea Number Eight" was a common iteration of the title when Roger was not around. Nevertheless, in a déjà vu experience, Roger Norman Frederick was awarded his Ph.D. in physical chemistry.

The team submitted five proposals to foundations and private firms as they attempted to fund additional research attempts. One private firm offered to fund nine months. Extension of the funding depended on providing marketable research results.

*

Ten Hours Ago

"You'll recall that adding RI-8 to any body of water that's open to the atmosphere and therefore subject to evaporation will cut the evaporation rate by 37 percent," Roger said as he neared the end of his sales pitch. This was his last shot at one of the major players in worldwide water management.

The scientist's business sense was mediocre. In the positive column was the fact that he'd leased the lab for eighteen months with his money from the private firm. On the negative side were several items, most notably the fact that his funding would run out before his lease.

"Remind me how I get rid of your additive when we need to use the water," the Chief Acquisitions Officer of Amalgamated Hydration Systems directed.

It was clear that the man was avoiding making a decision. Roger's postdoc, Sharon, ran the demonstration earlier. The CAO started and stopped the electric current himself. This was not a good sign. The team had to solve the math issue or no one would fund further research.

"Running an electric current through your solution pulls the RI-8 out with it." He pointed to the demo apparatus assembled on the lab table next to the small conference table that they'd moved into the lab for this meeting. "Amperage of the current required varies depending on the concentration of RI-8 in your solution."

"Hmmm." The CAO frowned. "Much of our work is done where there is no electric grid."

"We will offer a generator that runs off batteries charged by solar panels," Sharon answered the non-question. "You can customize that system to suit your needs."

"I've got all I need," the potential client said. "I'll run this by our technical division, but I have to be honest. We're not going to commit to much in terms of dollar amounts until we've seen the product perform as you describe."

"That's understandable," Roger lied. *The data I presented is enough to convince any open-minded entrepreneur of the potential of the product.* "We'll keep refining our research while we wait for your decision."

When it was just Roger and Sharon in the lab, she said what they both knew to be true.

"The math is the issue."

"But not forever," Roger said. He stood. "Have the lab techs run another variation of the process. Make sure they double-check every number they generate before they record it."

She nodded.

"While they're doing the grunt work, you review the math we used for the production data. I'll review the math for the experimental results."

"Roger, Roger," she said.

*

Tonight, after his most recent failed sales presentation, Roger worked alone in his lab. He'd sent the others home. He was experiencing persistent fatigue from fighting a feeling of hopelessness. He ordered his team to take an extended weekend.

"Don't stop by to see if I'm here," he told them. "As soon as I resolve one issue, I'm heading to my uncle's cabin on Deep Lake. I'm not taking my cell phone. There's no reception up there anyway. I'm leaving my computer here, too."

"It's not like you'll miss that," one tech said.

Everyone but Roger smiled. He looked each team member in the eyes as he added, "I expect ... the same ... from you."

Sheepish nods indicated understanding and a reluctant willingness to obey the boss's edict. They were tired, too, but not hopeless. They sensed that they were close to a breakthrough. Sharon spoke for them all.

"This trial should work. I've searched and searched and searched again for why it isn't working. I'm fresh out of ideas."

A ripple of laughter greeted this statement. Over the team's time together, "searched and searched and searched again" had become their personal definition of research. Sharon closed the meeting.

"I hereby decree the beginning of ye olde six-day long weekend!"

"For luck," she added as she tapped a water-filled cooling jacket on her way out.

*

Now

It was odd, Roger thought, how loud the dripping sounded when he sat trying to resolve the problem with his formula. He could barely hear the noise as he searched between the towering glass and rubber structures of his team's experimental set-up.

After several minutes of fruitless searching, he literally stumbled on the leaky joint. He slipped in a wet spot on the floor and reached out his hand to balance himself on the work counter to his left. Instead of a slap against the slate countertop, his fingers splashed into a puddle of water on the slate-topped work surface.

An inspection of the apparatus on the table revealed the culprit. A loose clamp on a hose leading to the water-filled cooling jacket that Sharon tapped for luck allowed water in the jacket to leak out. Judging from the amount of moisture in the general area, the leak was worse than he expected.

Some luck. He leaned in to check all the seals on the cooling jacket. *At least none of the RI-8 leaked from the apparatus.*

Roger backtracked to his desk, rummaged through one of the drawers, and pulled out a flat blade screwdriver. He hurried back to the leaky fitting and tightened the clamp. The drops stopped falling.

He was careful to avoid puddles until he reached the closest paper towel dispenser.

"This. Is. Not. What. I. Need. Tonight." He growled one word per paper towel as he yanked them from their hiding place. "If I didn't know better, I'd think someone had it out for me!"

After two swipes with bunched up towels, he paused to watch the water spread throughout a lone paper towel lying flat at the edge of the puddle.

"Water is sticky, but not like honey. A positive part of one water molecule attracts the negative part of another water molecule and vice versa. So, water molecules stick together. A drop is formed when many molecules stick to one another," he muttered. It was part of a speech he'd given many times to public school groups touring his facility.

"Surface tension is how tightly molecules are held in place by that positive and negative attraction. Water has a high surface tension. That allows some insects to scurry along the surface of a pond while hunting for food. It also helps aircraft carriers float." He made the rippling motion with his left hand he always made while delivering that sentence.

"The purpose of my current research is to develop a non-toxic substance with greater surface tension than water—"

"Too bad about the toxicity issue," a voice from behind Roger said.

"What the—"

"Sorry, boss," one of the lab techs said. "I didn't mean to scare you."

"I, it's, um ... that's okay," Roger managed.

"Is that what you tell school groups that visit us?"

"Yeah. Why?"

"There aren't enough illustrations. Water striders and aircraft carriers are a good start, but you should tell them why you want more surface tension."

"You think so?" Roger asked. No one had ever critiqued his presentation before. He wasn't sure he liked it.

"No," the lab tech answered. Roger relaxed until the employee added, "I know so. I listen harder when someone uses illustrations while explaining something."

"What are you doing here?" Roger asked after deciding that he didn't like being critiqued.

"Forgot my Thermos," the lab tech answered as he hoisted a shiny metal container. "If I leave this here, it'll be an unwanted organic chemistry experiment by the time we get back. What are *you* doing here? You said we were all on forced vacation for five days."

"I didn't say forced," Roger groused. "I'm finishing up checking a sequence of equations that have me baffled."

"On your knees between lab benches? Are you finally seeking Divine guidance?"

"Funny. I just finished stopping a leak."

"Any damage?" the lab tech asked.

"Not that I can see."

"Boss, you know those equations you're working on?"

"What about them?"

"They'll still be here in five days."

"Yeah, I know. I'm out of here after one more pass."

"You need to get away," the lab tech said. He turned and started toward the exit.

"I won't be here after 9:00 p.m.," Roger promised.

"Too late for that," the tech called over his shoulder. "Go home, already."

Roger checked his wristwatch. It was almost 10:30 p.m. The fact that he'd passed his self-imposed deadline for leaving was a bigger shock to the scientist than the lab tech's visit. He headed back to his desk, his mind roiling all the way.

It was clear that he'd never change the physical attributes of water. RI-8 was the additive his team proposed developing to increase water's surface tension.

The additive was non-toxic and recyclable. Separating the additive from water was cheap and easy. Running an electric current through a solution was all it took. A current of the proper amperage carried his new substance out of the solution as it passed through it. The RI-8 collected was reusable and, as far as they could tell, would have a shelf life of a decade or more.

That had been the plan.

A squish-squish sound interrupted his thoughts. He stopped. The sound stopped. He took two steps. The sound returned and stopped a second time.

The sound was his rubber-soled shoes treading on a thin film of water.

"This feels like a conspiracy," he muttered as he slogged along. He knew that significant damage to both the equipment and the experiment was a certainty if any cooling jacket leaked for five days.

He made a mental note to call the janitorial service before he left.

Roger flipped off the light switch. Darkness once more enveloped the laboratory. He dropped into the memory-foam cushion on his desk chair. The fluorescent lamp's hum reminded him of his goal. Seconds later, his sole focus was the mathematical problem.

It's common when one takes a break from an unsolvable task after hours of hard work for the solution to come soon after returning to the task. Roger experienced that moment of serendipity. The source of his dilemma was one digit in a universal constant. It was wrong each time it appeared in his computations. He opened a file on his laptop and typed in a note describing his discovery.

It's ironic. The only water spot on this page makes it hard to read that digit. No wonder we've been spinning our wheels for months.

He smiled and began refiguring each step in his formulae. I can feel it! Whoever would have thought that zero-point-zero-two is what blocked our progress for months?

The physical chemist worked feverishly with his calculator. He chuckled triumphantly as each new value got him closer to confirming his hypothesis. *Take that Amalgamated Hydration Systems!* He punctuated his thought with a giant checkmark beside his latest revision. *You'll be begging me to sell RI-8 to you at twice the price I quoted today after you slept through our presentation.*

While Roger rejoiced, a rather different phenomenon took place in the laboratory. A sizeable pool of water moved across the floor increasing the depth of the film already present as it approached the seated scientist.

The film paused at the legs of Roger's chair. Various droplets and smaller puddles of water flowed over and merged with the main pool.

There was a period of agitation on the surface of the pool. A faint hint of sound like that of delegates voting on a proposal in a roll-call vote was audible for an instant.

The agitation ceased. Three droplets of water moved away from the main pool. The action mimicked delegates at an assembly protesting a decision by walking out.

Several oversized drops split away, too. They moved with purpose toward the tables loaded with Roger's elaborate chemical apparatus. Other drops merged with them until each had the surface area of a doormat.

Then, drop by drop, the main pool of water began an inexorable climb up the scientist's chair.

Soon a thin film of water covered the chair legs and moistened Roger's shoes to the laces.

He didn't notice. Equation after equation confirmed his hypothesis as applied the mathematical correction.

So close! So close! How could I have missed this all this time? His excitement overrode his sensory input. He remained oblivious to the encroaching liquid.

Water saturated the scientist's pant legs and climbed toward his shirt.

Progress was slow. The pace ensured that water molecules reached body temperature as they soaked through each piece of Roger's clothing. The spread of body temperature fluid further delayed Roger's awareness of the developing situation.

The film of water coated Roger's hair and was oozing along the frames of his eyeglasses when he completed his mathematical remediation. He brought his fist down with a resounding thump upon the desktop and uttered a victorious cry.

"Finally! I knew my substance was better than—"

A mouthful of water cut short his shout of triumph.

Gagging and choking, Roger gasped for air. More water was all that filled his mouth as billions of water molecules accelerated their spread.

Desperate for oxygen, he inhaled through his nose. The only air that reached his lungs was that which filled his respiratory passages. A film of water covered his nostrils sealing out the life-sustaining atmosphere.

Roger tried to stand. The combination of excess water weight and the surface tension between him and the film of moisture covering his chair was too much for his cramped and surprised muscles to overcome. He slumped back and stared, horrified at the water flowing down his arms.

His fingers acted as overflow channels for water. Soon, the papers containing his calculations were saturated. The ink and pencil marks on the paper ran together. Shapeless blue blobs and black splotches replaced advanced algebraic formulas.

Roger flicked his eyes in the direction of his laptop. A gurgle escaped his lips as he watched a film of H_2O enter the high-speed dataport. A flash of fire and a puff of smoke left no doubt of the elimination of the hard drive as a data recovery site.

He forced his head around in the direction of the sound of glassware crashing to the concrete floor. The attempt to locate the source of the sounds of destruction succeeded. His floundering spirit sank further into despair. The merciless molecules were systematically eradicating his laboratory work.

There would be no evidence left, either written, or electronic, or experimental to document his success. Even his cloud storage would be of little use. The automatic data backup would not occur at midnight as scheduled.

His head began to spin as the lack of oxygen took its toll.

It is a ... conspiracy!

The last sound Dr. Roger Frederick heard on this side of eternity reminded him of a mocking laugh.

It *could* have been an audio hallucination.

My research ... never had ... a chance.

It *could* have been the ringing of his ears as water filled his auditory canals.

I should ... have asked ... for help—

But, it *might* have been the satisfied laughter of a trillion-billion water molecules as they protected their position of prime importance in the world as we know it.

Whichever the case, as Roger Fredrick's body went limp at the instant of death, the water began to recede from his lifeless form ...

Drop ...

       by ...

             drop.

***

Cleopatra's Needle

by Tom Howard
United States

She ignored the New Cairo mayor sitting across from her until he spoke.

"We are honored by your presence so soon after your last visit to the Western Lands, Your Highness."

Cleopatra, the forty-seventh pharaoh of that name, turned her attention from the gray skyscrapers outside the limousine window. The Royal Scribe sat beside her, his tablet on his knee. Natura, her niece and the Royal Handmaid, appeared deep in thought, but Cleopatra knew she, like the others, listened for an explanation of the unexpected trip. The Guard Captain, Rekeen, did not look at her. Of all her confidants, only he knew her true purpose visiting these chilly lands.

Never at her best after a long flight in her airborne palace, she forced herself to smile. The others relaxed. The mayor, a handsome, pureblood Egyptian from the Four Families of the Upper Nile, released the death grip on his knees. Of course, he was Egyptian. No outlanders held positions of authority within Cleopatra's realm.

"I enjoy New Cairo in the spring," she lied. "It's so ... industrious." She hated the cold clamminess of the New World, still so called after centuries of colonization. Her people had moved Greeks and Roman slaves across the ocean to extract the New World's bountiful resources. The pale immigrants had been fertile. They spread across the continent like ants.

She tugged her jacket, itching from the fur collar. Who would want to live in this dreary climate? At least Natura's perky breasts were covered, one benefit of being in the cold.

Amonaton, her portly scribe, cleared his throat, a sign he wished to speak.

"Yes, Amon?" She fought an impulse to throw her entire council out of the vehicle and finish the mission on her own. A blackmailer had summoned her as if she were a servant, and these prattling sycophants were delaying his death and her return home.

Amon cleared this throat again. "Our spies found two branches of the Anhutsep cult here, Your Excellency. Will you attend their executions?"

"Which cult?"

"Anhutsep, the sky snake, supposedly Anubis's daughter. New World commoners consider her a symbol of change."

"Is she part of the Christo's cult?" Natura asked, always eager to show her understanding of current events.

"No, no," Amon said. "We've successfully stamped out those heretics. Soon we'll do the same with the cursed Hebrews."

The mayor said, "We only worship sanctioned gods, Your Majesty."

Cleopatra fingered the cartouche of Bast, protector of pharaohs, hanging around her neck. "No executions. I'll attend a few official functions the short time I'm here."

She'd considered having the Royal Scribe, as her head of assassins, deal with the blackmailer, but she'd have to kill him afterwards, and Amon would be hard to replace.

"Perhaps you'd enjoy some rest and refreshments when we reach the palace, Your Highness." Natura didn't miss an opportunity to imply the pharaoh looked tired.

Although Cleopatra had lived forty years, she looked much younger, thanks to the Royal Surgeon. Kohl permanently lined her eyes, a tattoo done when she'd had her scalp depilated. Cleopatra glowered at her niece, but the girl had sense enough not to look up.

Since Cleopatra was the mother of three sons and no daughters for them to marry, her niece Natura saw her role as Royal Handmaiden as a stepping-stone to becoming queen.

Cleopatra had a surprise for her. As the current pharaoh, she intended to sit on the throne for many more decades. Her son would choose someone young and firm, neither of which Natura would be by then.

She ignored the girl. "What of the gold from the Southern Lands? Has production improved?"

"We've squashed the small revolts," Amon said, "but the overseers say they cannot force more work from the natives, no matter how hard they discipline them. Perhaps we need slaves from the Eastern Lands. They are good workers."

"Estimate the cost of transporting them," she said. "Then I'll make my decision."

Turning her attention to the mayor, she set her real plan in motion. "I suppose one gathering in my honor would be bearable, Mayor." Afterwards, she and the captain would slip away and deal with the blackmailer.

"Yes, your majesty," the mayor said. "At your convenience."

"This evening. Nothing too ostentatious."

"Five hundred people?" he recommended, and she nodded. That should keep things going until early in the morning. She would contact the enemy, meet him, and kill him. She smiled.

*

The night wind had a bite to it, and Cleopatra appreciated the heavy cloak that hid her identity. She stood at the foot of a giant "Cleopatra's needle" in the large city park. She hated the name; it created the impression that Cleopatra, like some menial, sat in her parlor darning socks in the evenings. The obelisks were named for a Cleopatra far of the past. The captain of the guard stood nearby, tall and broad-shouldered. She would have preferred to come alone. She rested her hand on the blade in her waistband.

The party lasted longer than expected. She'd been tired after her long flight, and even more exhausted after half of New Cairo showed their respects. She ignored the warmed blankets in her bedchamber. She had a man to kill.

Days earlier, in Cairo, her director of espionage had delivered an urgent message. She quickly scanned his written report, nodding that she understood.

"No one else has seen this?" she asked.

"No, Your Highness. Such messages are brought directly to me." An old man, he'd been a loyal servant since her father's reign. He would be missed.

She nodded and excused him, signaling the ever-present Anon to kill him when he left. She'd need the name of the field agent, too. She read the message again.

Pharoah,

Three cats bar the way, but Bast reveals all.

New Cairo archeologists have discovered an ancient container with three cats on the cover and the above inscription. It contains a scroll. Please advise in person, the third of Osiris, three a.m. at Cleopatra's Needle in Central Park.

A man's voice from the darkness jarred her from her recollections. "Good morning, Your Highness. Please follow me." Without waiting, he strode off, and she hurried to keep up. She gave the captain a no-kill command. This man could be a simple underling. She needed to find and destroy the scroll.

After leaving the park, the stranger stopped at a warehouse door, allowing her and the captain to catch up. He was tall and pale and dressed in dark clothing.

She touched the handle of the sword, confident he would be no challenge.

"Do as I say," the outlander warned. His beard held streaks of gray. He smelled of soap. Cleopatra had heard foreign slaves bathed daily.

They entered a large room, shrouded in shadow and empty from the sounds of her sandals echoing on the concrete floor. Against the far wall, two chairs and a small table sat in a circle of light. The purple tablecloth holding two glasses and a wine decanter made her angry. Only the royal family were allowed purple fabric.

"Please have a seat." He waved her to a chair and ignored the captain.

Rekeen moved two paces behind her and stood at attention.

She remained standing. "Do you have my ... possession?"

"Yes," he said. "I'm Dr. Logan, an archeology professor at the New Cairo University."

She didn't care. "Give me the artifact."

He laughed, pouring himself a glass of red wine. "I understand your haste, Pharoah. But you are not the only one who understands the importance of the three Basts."

She turned to the guard. "Stand by the door."

The guard moved out of earshot.

She took the offered seat. The wall behind the table appeared polished like glass, but she couldn't see through it.

"The container with three Basts is a family heirloom," she said. "What do you want in exchange?" She must discover what the outlander knew before she killed him. If he'd read the scroll and told anyone ...

He poured her a glass of wine. "The original drafter must have made two copies, one for the pharaoh and one if something happened to the original."

"I don't care." She ignored the wine. "State your price." Something felt wrong. After decades of listening to people who wanted something from her, she understood their body language. The professor was lying. He glanced at the glass wall behind her and licked his lips.

"We know your secret," he said.

She kept her face expressionless. The man wanted her to reveal something. She was reaching for the knife in her belt when something behind the glass wall crashed to the ground. Someone on the other side of the wall screamed.

The professor jumped to his feet and pulled a pistol.

She stood slowly. "What's this all about?"

The captain of the guard stepped forward and pointed his sword at her. "Please sit down, Your Highness. Tell us what is on the scroll in the Bast box."

Cleopatra couldn't believe her ears. "Are you mad, Rekeen? You dare pull a weapon on the pharaoh of the known world? I'll have you thrown into a pit of hungry lions."

"Tell us the secret!" Rekeen shouted.

"You've done your job, Captain," the professor said. "I'll show her we're serious."

He shifted his pistol and shot Rekeen in the head.

There wasn't a second scroll! This was all a conspiracy to make a fool of her. "Who put you up to this?"

Before the professor could answer, he jerked and collapsed onto the floor beside Rekeen. Another man dressed in black stepped into the light. He knelt to examine the professor and the captain before wiping the knife he'd used on the bearded man's clothing.

"What is the meaning of this?" Cleopatra pulled her blade.

The stranger was an Egyptian, a young man with strong features. "You are a stupid cow."

"How dare you? What are you doing?"

"I am saving your life, Highness. Now, come with me."

"Who are you?"

Instead of replying, he lifted one of the chairs and swung it at the glass wall. The one-way mirror shattered, covering the floor with shards that glittered like black diamonds. In the brightly lit room behind the glass, dead bodies and broken cameras lay on the floor.

"Who are you?" she repeated.

"Perat, the protector of Bast's secret. Someone wanted you to reveal the secret publicly."

"You can't know," she said. "Only the pharaoh has that knowledge."

The man nodded. "And the secret's protector. Now come with me."

"I must contact my people," she said. "My guards."

"Stupid cow," he said again. He ran for the door. "Who do you think wanted your secret exposed and you humiliated before the entire world? They are your family's guards, not yours. This was all a trap— the note, the trip, this room. Now that they've failed to make a fool of you, their next move will be to kill you."

In the alley, she caught up with him. She was tired, but her mind was abuzz with the events of the night. "Who would benefit from my secret being made public? The knowledge would destroy our way of life. The slaves—"

"Shut up," the man ordered. "Stay in the shadows." They were on an empty street.

She was surprised the sun wasn't up. She felt as if she'd been awake for days. She took some consolation that her rude escort wouldn't live to see another sunset. He'd called her a bovine twice. She'd enjoy seeing him suffer.

"Damn." He grabbed her and shoved her into a doorway. He pressed up against her, forcing the air from her lungs and keeping her from slitting him open with her knife.

A vehicle bearing the city guard insignia stopped at the curb. She'd have them imprison this man and return her to the palace. Amon would uncover whoever was behind this stupid charade and kill them. Before she could call for help, her companion placed his hand over her mouth.

"What do we have here?" The guardsman left the car. He wore the dark green uniform of the New Cairo police. "A late-night party, citizen?"

Perat turned, his hand still on her mouth. "Sorry, officer. I didn't realize we were past curfew. I wanted my money's worth."

The officer shined a flashlight on Cleopatra, still in her cloak. "I hope you didn't pay much. Still, it is late, and I'm willing to share." He smiled and unfastened his belt buckle.

Cleopatra froze. Was the city guardsman going to defile her? He wasn't some outlander criminal, but a man of her own blood.

"I'm sorry, officer." Perat pulled out his wallet. "Perhaps an offering would make sure the incident is forgotten. Don't want the wife to find out."

The guard smiled. "I'll take that wallet, sir." He swung his baton, catching Perat in the stomach.

The guard grabbed Cleopatra. Before she could pull her knife, the guard slapped her across the face. She froze. No one had struck her in her entire life.

Perat rose to his feet and wrestled the baton away from her attacker.

She pulled her thin blade and thrust it into the guard's chest.

The man stopped, disbelief coloring his face. His face muscles slackened, and he slumped to the ground.

"Nice to see you're not completely worthless." Perat clutched his stomach.

She stared down at the dead body on the street. "Why did he attack me? Is he part of the conspiracy?"

"Your mayor's city guard may be in on it." He lifted the man's shoulders. "But this man was just operating as usual."

"He acted like a criminal himself!"

"Welcome to the real world, Your Highness. Now help me get his body into the car."

"What are you going to do?" She lifted her attacker's legs while Perat carried his shoulders.

"New Cairo is surrounded by water on three sides. Convenient for disposing of vehicles and bodies. Even if the authorities find him, they'll think him a victim of organized crime."

"Organized crime?" she asked. "New Cairo doesn't have crime, organized or otherwise."

Perat laughed. "New Cairo is the crime capitol of your kingdom, Cleopatra. Most of it controlled by the mayor. Now, get in the front seat."

"This is some kind of nightmare." She slid into the car. "We must reach the palace. I'm not safe here."

"You're not safe anywhere," Perat said. "Not until I talk with my people and smuggle you out of the country."

"Your people?" she asked. "Who are you?"

"I told you. I'm the secret's protector. There's one in each generation."

"That's impossible," she said. "You're a liar, a rude, arrogant liar."

"You're not supposed to know about me. I'm trained to defend the secret as valiantly as you."

She shook her head. "You're part of the conspiracy. You want me to tell you what the secret is."

"Have it your way, Your Highness." He stopped the patrol car at the wharf. "We're here."

She left the vehicle, wondering if she could escape from this madman. With no one to trust and nowhere to go, she waited as Perat pushed the patrol car into the river. Arrogant or not, he had saved her life. Perhaps several times.

He didn't wait for the vehicle to sink beneath the water before he joined her. "Can you walk in those sandals?"

"Of course."

An hour later, she sat on a stone bench in a dimly lit tunnel and rubbed her blistered feet.

"Here." Perat took a sip from a cup and passed her the hot, black liquid. "This will keep you awake long enough to find you a cot."

"What is it?" she asked, too tired to argue.

"Something wonderful from the Southern Lands. They roast the beans and grind them before cooking them in hot water."

She took a sip and grimaced. "If you're trying to poison me, get on with it."

Perat smiled. "It'll grow on you down here."

"Where are we? Who are all these people?" Groups huddled together wore blankets and hoods to keep warm or disguise their features.

"Rabbis, escaped slaves, orphan children, priests of Christos, followers of Anhutsep. Most of them you'd have ordered killed without a second thought."

She shook her head. The tunnels were crowded. Little fires burned in alcoves, and the smell of food cooking made her mouth water.

"There are so many. I had no idea. They told me the undesirables had been wiped out or rehabilitated."

"Your people want you to believe everything is clean and perfect, Your Highness, but they are lying to you. It's only a matter of time before the Zionists band together with other undesirables and rebel."

"My people?" she asked. "Aren't you my people?"

"Look around, Cleopatra. How can you not be ashamed of our treatment of non-Egyptians?"

A baby crying in the distance distracted her. "I hate the New World," she said.

Perat laughed. "This culling of undesirables is happening everywhere. Since I follow you to ensure you do not reveal the secret of Bast, I see many lands. The rebels are everywhere. The Southern Lands are ablaze right now. We'll probably not receive shipments of their lovely beans much longer."

She sipped the hot beverage, feeling its warmth spread through her. "The small rebellions were put down." Her voice sounded small, almost pleading.

Perat waved at their surroundings. "You see what they want you to see. Does this look like a small rebellion? Open your eyes."

Her cheeks flushed in anger, and she considered pulling her knife. "You're one of the rebels! I'll have you flayed in the public square."

He shook his head. "This is how you thank someone who saved your life and possibly your questionable virtue?"

She thought about it. "Flayed."

A little girl missing her right eye approached and stared at Cleopatra with her good eye. She chewed on a brown bar as she studied the two strangers.

"What does she want?" Cleopatra asked.

"They don't often see one of the aristocracy down here."

Cleopatra pulled her cloak closer. "Do they know who I am?"

"Not your name." Perat smiled at the little girl. "But they can tell you've never worked a day in your life. They're curious but will respect your privacy as long as you're with me and the guards are looking for you."

The little girl pulled out what she was sucking on and offered it to Cleopatra.

"What is it?" she asked Perat. She was hungry but not hungry enough to accept food from an undesirable. No telling what diseases she might catch.

"Cacao." He took the offering and broke it into two pieces before handing one back to the girl. She smiled and ran back to her family. He broke his piece into two and handed one to Cleopatra. "Another nice surprise from the Southern Lands. They mix it with sugar cane and goat's milk. Perhaps you should wait for your Royal Taste-tester to arrive with whoever is trying to kill you."

Cleopatra grimaced and took the strange food. Before she lost her nerve, she popped it into her mouth. Who was this annoying man to think she was afraid of anything?

Perat chuckled at her expression of surprise. "Like with the coffee, our cacao supply may be cut off soon."

She couldn't believe how wonderful the cacao tasted as it melted in her mouth. What other things were the slaves keeping from her?

She swallowed, enjoying the blissful aftertaste. "Who wants to kill me?"

"Everyone you've ever talked to, I imagine," Perat said. "But my money is on Mellon-Ra, your oldest son. He and your handmaiden have something going on. Looks as if they've decided not to wait for you to die of natural causes. Amon and Rekeen worked for him. They'd all have had fatal accidents in the next couple months if you hadn't decided to take matters into your own hands."

She took a sip of the coffee. The unfamiliar liquid made her feel more alert. "How do you know what goes on in the palace? How did you find this place?"

Perat sighed. "I'm a shadow, Your Highness. I've been following you for years without you knowing."

She didn't believe his wild claims of being her protector, but she was in his debt. He'd still pay for the bovine comment. "Okay, secret assassin, what do we do next?"

"I've sent word to my people. We must stay hidden until the mayor and your conspirators make the next move."

She nodded. "What happened to the little girl's eye? Scarred in a battle?"

"No. Probably disfigured by her parents to keep her out of your brothels. They start training them about her age."

Cleopatra couldn't believe her ears. "Brothels? But she's so young."

"Your countrymen think the slaves work better if they have access to copulation occasionally. Of course, they have to pay for it."

She felt sick to her stomach. "You're still lying. No parent would ever do that to their children."

"No parent should have to do that to protect their children," he said. "Perhaps your time here will open your eyes, Pharaoh. Your world is corrupt and rotten. If it doesn't change soon, you'll lose everything."

She sipped her cooling coffee and thought of ways to refute Perat's words. His assertions could explain why her trips were planned down to the last detail and why she only met beautiful people and powerful representatives. Were her armies "training exercises" really frantic attempts to put down uprisings around the planet?

Or, as some small voice in the back of her mind prodded, was all this a plot to make her reveal the terrible secret of Bast only she knew?

Screams and popping noises in the distance brought Perat to his feet. "Damn. I thought we'd have more time. I hope you've had enough rest, Your Highness."

"What is happening?"

People shouted and ran down the tunnels, leaving their blanket tents and fires unattended.

"The mayor suspects rebels have sanctuaries hidden in the old subway system. He's sending guards into the tunnels looking for you."

"Will they turn us in?" It's what she would have done in their place. By sacrificing her, they could save themselves.

Perat shook his head and pulled her to her feet. "No. That's not what undesirables do. Their loyalty and integrity to each other are what make them undesirable. That's a lesson you could learn."

She pulled away from him. Would these people really die for her, a perfect stranger? "What do we do now?"

"There are a million ways out of these tunnels. Most of your saviors will escape. Come on. We've got some climbing ahead of us."

*

Hours later, Cleopatra sat in a small side tunnel, lit from daylight high above. Although it appeared the grill to the tunnel was rusted shut, Perat had opened it soundlessly and sat on a ledge while they caught their breath.

"If you are doing all this to make me reveal the secret of Bast," she said, "it won't work." She'd lost her wig during their torturous climb up unending ladders and felt naked without it. "What were those explosions?"

"The conspirators are sealing the tunnels. If they find your body, they can say you were killed by undesirables."

"But what about the people down here? There are children!"

"They want our secret badly. To them, slaves are expendable. My people should be waiting for us near here."

"Our secret? You can't know Bast's mysteries."

He wrapped his long fingers around her sore hands. "Like a lot of things you've learned tonight, the tales you've been told are not always true. You and I were never supposed to meet, but this could be a turning point in our history, Your Highness. It's up to you."

She looked away but didn't remove her hands.

Perat continued. "When the wife of Ramses III gave birth to a son, the court physician sealed the birthing room and summoned the pharaoh. He grew insane with rage when he saw his son had been born deformed with an enlarged head and a clubfoot. Such a thing should be impossible."

"Since pharaohs marry their siblings," Cleopatra said, "we ensure there are no genetic defects introduced into the bloodline. If there are abnormalities, it was assumed the bloodline has been ... tainted from an outside source."

"Even though we know now other factors such as gamma rays or caffeine can also alter genetic material," Perat said. "The pharaoh's wife hadn't been unfaithful, but Ramses assumed the deformed child could not be his own. In his rage, he killed them both."

The story unfolded in her mind. She'd learned the tragic tale from a scroll locked in her personal vault when she became pharaoh. Perat could not know what Ramses had done that dark night. Or what had happened next.

Perat's words hit her like physical blows. "The royal physician ran to the slave pens and returned with a newborn infant. Ramses, mad with grief over what he had done, believed his wife had died in childbirth and accepted the baby as his own. The surgeon recorded the secret on two scrolls. One he had placed in the royal vault, sealed by the sign of Bast, to be read only by Ramses' royal successors. The other, the doctor passed down to his descendants and tasked with protecting the secret. I am one of those."

Cleopatra imagined blood on her hands, the blood Ramses had spilled in anger. She saw the little girl with the terrible scar. "Please, it's not my fault."

Perat stood. "Tell me where the surgeon obtained the child, your ancestor."

"Please." Tears dripped down her cheeks.

"Tell me!"

She sobbed. "The Hebrew slave pens."

"Perhaps you can blame this cruelty and corruption on three thousand years of pharaohs, but Bast has brought you here for a reason. Free the people, learn about their lives and their dreams. Climb down off your maggot-infested throne and do some good in the world before it's too late."

She was exhausted, shocked at being so unaware of the world around her, and angry at being responsible for the entire world. She wiped her tears. Perat was correct. Something had to be changed, beginning with the descendant of a Jewish slave.

"If I'm to do this, I'll need you to come out of the shadows and help me, secret assassin."

Perat smiled and helped her stand. "That's a good beginning, Queen Cleopatra, a very good beginning."

***

The Bells

by Robert James
United States

He sat listening to the wind grate against the windowpane. Dirt particles tattooed against the glass. The shaft of morning light falling into the house dried up, surged brightly, disappeared. *Clouds passing overhead*, he thought. It was a safe thought, distant, blessedly remote from where his mind wanted to go.

He sat on the edge of the tiny, flower-printed bed with his hands clasped between his knees, head bowed as if in prayer. Those hands were scrubbed pink, almost raw, and they rasped as he drew them apart and braced himself. His right hand grazed Alanna's small foot. Touching her brought the reality back. It roared to meet him like a semitrailer—its approach a heavy and relentless finality. His eyes rolled toward the foot; he could almost hear his tendons straining as his neck followed. Then he was looking at her.

His sister was a small shape beneath the sheet. Almost nothing. A delicate steeple over her face—her nose. How many times had he tapped it lovingly with his finger before planting a kiss just there? How many times had she giggled when he'd done that?

"Every time," he whispered, and was sorry he spoke at all, because he'd been talking all night, to no one. "I'm sorry, Lanna," he said, and gingerly drew the sheet over the exposed foot. The nails were painted a bright pink. The rustling of the fabric seemed very loud in the tiny room. "I hope you like that color. I didn't know which one to use."

He touched the covered foot, hating how stiff it felt, then drew his hands together again between his knees. "You died at 10:02 p.m. Mom and I were there. I hope you know that. I hope you know you weren't by yourself. After—Mom couldn't stay. She couldn't—take care of you anymore. I hope she's okay. She hasn't come out of the garage since. Don't blame her. Please. I think she's sick, too. I think—" He drew in

119

a watery breath, let it out. "It'll be okay." He smiled at his dead sister. "You're safe, now. Right? Anyway, I gave you a bath, washed your hair, put you in your favorite dress. You know the one, with the yellow flowers? And I put that little matching clip in your hair. I hope you see it. I hope you can."

He rose from the bed, stepped toward the window, twisted his fists into the curtains, and peered out. The wind was kicking dirt and leaves across the road. Trees bent their limbs playfully over the many houses that marched down Henry Street toward the town square. The square, Jake knew, would be empty now. It was always empty at this hour. At least since people started getting sick.

When had that been? he wondered. The incidents began, so far as he could recall, not long after he'd come home from the university for a much-needed fall break. His mind snapped back to that day with the speed of a stretched rubber band suddenly loosed.

Jake had blundered through the door of the home he'd grown up in, his arms overburdened with two laundry bags and books that he couldn't fit into his pack. Alanna had been waiting for him on the steps.

"Jake!" she cried and rushed to him, bulling through his burdens and burying her face against his chest. Had she gotten taller since he'd last seen her? He knew she had—hoped she hadn't.

"Jeez, Lanna," he laughed. "C'mon, you're gonna give me a hernia." He dumped his bags and books in the hallway and gave his sister a proper hug.

"I missed you, Jake," Alanna said simply, and smiled at him, producing a small dimple on the left side of her face. She was looking more like their mother every day. She even had her naturally wavy hair straightened and cinched in a ponytail, which was how their mother wore hers to work at the restaurant.

"Yeah, I missed you, too."

Alanna stood bouncing on the balls of her feet, and Jake couldn't help but marvel at her energy, which made him feel horribly old—an absurd feeling for an eighteen-year-old, but he felt it just the same. "How long are you home?" she asked.

"About six days."

Alanna pouted. "That's not very long."

Jake nudged her shoulder. "Then we better make the most of it. You wanna take the bikes up to Miller's Park?"

Alanna bunched her fists and leaped into the air. "Yeah! Let's go! Let's-go-let's-go-let's-*go*!"

"All right. Go change. I'll put the bikes in my truck."

She pounded dutifully upstairs and past their mother who offered only a weak protest. Jasmine Cedici started down the stairs again and met Jake's eyes. She wore a terry cloth robe over her work clothes and a tired smile. "How you doin', kiddo?" she said.

Jake accepted her open arms and hugged her. She smelled of lavender shampoo, bacon, and cigarettes. "I'm good, Mom." They parted, and she stood with her arms crossed.

"Well, you're looking good. A little too skinny."

Jake offered an overt eye roll in response. "Are all mothers expected to say that?"

She gestured with a corrective finger. "Just the ones who care, Jacob."

Jake sighed. "Well, I'm fine." He bent to his bags, intending to take them upstairs. "I'm taking Lanna for a bike ride up at Millers. You wanna come?"

His mother's sudden silence gave him pause, and when he looked up at her and saw the way she was gnawing her lower lip, a habit his sister had also picked up, he knew his joyful homecoming was about to take a very sour turn.

"What's wrong?"

She wouldn't meet his eyes when she said, "Your father sold your bike."

Jake got to his feet. *Why?* was the first thought that came to mind, but it died before it could fully register. Such questions had been conditioned out of him over the course of long, disappointing years. He knew why.

He shook his head and shrugged. "Fine," he said, and that was all. He started for the door.

"Jake." His mother reached for him, paused. "Jake, you haven't ridden that old thing in years."

It was a lie. But Jake didn't have to tell her that. She knew.

He opened his mouth to say something, certain it would be terrible, then saw the drawn, worried look in his mother's face. It was a face much like his sister's, and he realized if he were to look at the two of them together, it would be very much like looking at some sort of sad timeline, a "before" and "after."

This is what you look like before you marry an asshole, Jake thought. *And this is what you look like after. Any questions?*

"Where is he, anyway?" Jake said.

His mother's brow furrowed. "You know where he is, Jacob."

"And so do you. And maybe if you spent more time defending us instead of him, this family wouldn't be up to its neck in shit."

He'd said the terrible thing anyway, and left without slamming the door.

The guilt clung to his back almost instantly, and Jake would rather lug all of his bags plus a hundred more ten miles through Miller's Woods and back than to feel this corpulent regret settling so heavily on his shoulders. He sighed, flicked through his keys, then went to the garage.

The door rolled up in its tracks with a hollow, rusty protest. Jake stepped toward the back of the space where he knew Alanna's bike would be. It stood leaning against their father's old workbench. Powder blue, chipped, but still in fine working order. She'd been taking care of the chain and crank shaft and keeping the bike out of the rain, like Jake had taught her.

His eyes ran over his father's workbench. Christian Cedici had been a hobbyist carpenter before Alanna was born, dreaming to one day open his own business and spend the rest of his life working with his hands. That day never came.

The tools that were left were those not valuable enough to pawn: a crusty hammer, dull hacksaw, and a chipped, rusty plane. The workbench itself was dust-coated, with a cubby door hanging open by one of its remaining weak hinges. Jake thought it too sappy to find a metaphor for his childhood in his father's neglected tools, but he found it anyway. He grabbed Alanna's bike and wheeled it out to his truck.

The truck—a beefy SUV, amply trunked—had taken him two years bagging groceries after school and three summers working at Saint Mary's Day Camp to afford—though it would've taken half that if Jake hadn't been forced into feeding his father's habits—and he cherished every moment he got to spend on the road, just him and his music, and he felt a very powerful urge to dump Alanna's bike, climb into his truck, and never come back. Then the sound of the front door opening and closing, and Alanna's soft-soled Keds on the steps, shattered the impulse. He lowered the backseats, hefted his sister's bike into the trunk, and shut the lid.

"All right, pipsqueak," he said as warmly as he could muster. "You ready?"

He looked at his sister. She stood unsmiling, gnawing on her lip. She wouldn't meet his eyes at first, and when she did, he saw something there that made his heart constrict: blame.

"What's the matter?" he said, taking a tentative step toward her.

Alanna shrugged. "Mom's crying," then, looking away, "again."

Jake sighed, glanced up at the westering light, and said, "C'mon. If we don't go, it'll be too dark to ride."

"Why'd you have to be mean?" Alanna demanded.

"I—I wasn't mean." Her candor always threw Jake off balance, made him into a liar, which he hated. "Look, let's get on the road and we can talk."

Alanna offered a curt nod and then climbed into the truck's passenger side. Jake, that guilt clutched to his back having grown in girth, looked toward the dirty bay windows of the house. His mother was peering out, one hand clutching the robe tight around her waist, the other covering her throat. He turned away, got into the truck, and pulled out onto the street.

It was a ten-minute drive up to Miller's Park—too much time to avoid the situation, not enough to talk it through in any meaningful way.

Alanna was watching him expectantly. "Well?" she prompted. "What did you do?"

Jake glanced at her, back at the road. She wasn't going to let it go. "Look, Mom and I had an argument. That's all."

"You two always argue."

"No, we don't." Another lie.

Alanna crossed her arms and glowered out the passenger window. They were passing through the town center where clusters of people scurried from one shop to the other. "I don't understand. If you're mad at Daddy, why do you have to be mean to Mom?"

Jake felt his hands bearing down on the wheel and forced them to relax, with effort. *Why does she have to be so damned perceptive?* he thought.

"It's complicated, Lanna," he said, and hated how lame that adult platitude sounded coming out of his mouth. "When I go away to school, I forget how angry I am at Dad. At what he does."

Alanna considered this answer. "I get mad, too," she said after a moment. "He makes Mom sad. A lot."

Jake nodded. "I don't know. I guess I just wish Mom would stand up to him once in a while."

"Dad sold your bike."

"Figured that out, huh?"

"Well, you only put my bike in the trunk, dummy."

"You're too smart for your own good."

Alanna ignored the compliment. "Why does Dad do it?"

Jake shrugged. "Who knows."

"Mom says it's an addiction."

Jake made a scoffing noise. "It's stupid is what it is."

"You know Mom tried to stop him from selling your bike, right?"

Jake flinched, or at least his heart did. "She did?"

"When he did sell it, she told him he couldn't come home until he got it back. That's why Daddy's not home."

"I—didn't know that. Mom didn't say—"

"Yeah, well, Mom can be weird."

Jake couldn't help but laugh a little at her assessment. "All right. When we get home, I'll make it up to her. I'll take us all out to dinner. How's that sound?"

"Oh! Oh!" Alanna was bouncing up and down in her seat. "Can we go to Puretta's? I want pizza!"

Jake said they could.

The rest of the ride was passed in idle conversation. Alanna told him all about her current science project and how the students had to make model simple machines—screws, wedges, levers, et cetera. She was making a scale model of a well with a drawing pail that could be raised and lowered with the help of a pulley. She also told him that Daisy Woods wasn't her best friend anymore. Now it was Andrea Patel. And did Jake know that Mom finally put in a wireless router that actually downloaded faster than a turtle?

Jake listened to all of it, responded appropriately, but his mind kept returning to his father. If his mother finally kicked the man out, where was he? Likely working off a hangover at Lenny's, the local sports bar, and sleeping nights at the shitty motel across the road.

Don't think about him, Jake thought. *Deal with it later.*

And he would have to, because, if this year turned out to be like last, Christian Cedici would have lost all of the family's available Thanksgiving funds on an idiot bet.

"Jake? *Jake?*"

Alanna pulled him out of his thoughts, and Jake was grateful. "What?"

"You missed the turn."

Jake looked in his rearview mirror where the southern entrance to Miller's Park was shrinking. "It's okay," he said. "I wanted to take you to the north end, anyway."

"Why?"

Jake thought for an appropriate excuse. "I want to see that new cell tower they put in."

Alanna blinked at him. "Oh. Why?"

Jake shrugged. "I just want to see it."

"Okay. There are some cool jumps up that way, anyway."

They pulled into a gravel lot that overlooked Buck Pond. A dirt trail wound its way down toward the pond then split north and west. Jake unloaded Alanna's bike, handed over her helmet, and then, when he was satisfied with the snugness of the helmet straps, they started along the trail.

Alanna did her best to ride slowly so Jake could jog alongside her, but he knew it would only be a matter of time before her feet and youth got away from her and she was riding full tilt down the next hill.

Should've changed into sneakers, Jake thought. His boots were starting to drag through the fine pebbles and thin dust that covered the hard-packed dirt path.

Alanna had pulled ahead where the path opened up a little and was riding in impatient circles. "You okay?" she called, and her cheeky smile made him feel older than he should.

"I'm fine," he huffed. "You don't have to wait for me. I'll meet you at the clearing past the picnic tables."

Alanna grinned and was speeding down the hill, her thin legs pumping with all the tireless energy of childhood that fades too soon, before her reply of "okay" could even register. Jake grinned, feeling an odd mixture of happiness and heartache. It was an adult feeling, and one he'd been forced to endure far more than he'd ever expected. Why did growing up have to suck so terrifically bad?

"Death and taxes," he announced obscurely, and then cut off the path, picking his way through the underbrush. The route was faster. He didn't want Alanna waiting alone for him longer than necessary.

Halfway along, the tree coverage broke, and he got his first glimpse of the aforementioned cell tower in the distance. It rose up through the distant trees like an alien monolith, aircraft warning lights blinking along its clean angles.

"That's a lot bigger than I thought," Jake said, and then remembered he was alone. He'd had no actual interest in seeing the tower, and his wonder of it was unexpected.

He navigated his way down the hill toward the clearing. He was nearing the bottom when his foot slipped on some loose soil. He came down the rest of the way on his back, cursing as he tried to regain his footing. He fetched up against a wayward picnic table, smacking his elbow against the bench. He lay there for a moment, rubbing the hurt out of his skin.

"Hey, you okay?" someone called over.

Jake got to his feet, brushed damp leaves from his pants, and looked for the source of the voice. A man, middle-aged with gray-feathered hair, stood nearby. A simple lunch was laid out on the picnic table where he was currently sitting. Next to the lunch was a pair of binoculars. Jake knew nothing about such devices, but they looked heavy and sleek and expensive.

"I'm all right," Jake said. "Just tripped."

The man nodded. "Well, I have an ice pack in my lunch bag, if you'd like."

Jake waved the kindness aside. "I'm okay. Thanks."

He started to go, already forgetting the man and looking to see his sister speeding around the lot up ahead.

"It's a lovely view, isn't it?"

Jake turned. "Huh?"

The man had resumed his seat at the picnic table, thoughtfully chewing a bite of his sandwich. He gestured at the skyline—hills bursting with autumn colors: red transitioning to orange and yellow and back again.

"I heard it was nice," the man continued, as if he and Jake were old friends instead of complete strangers. "But I didn't expect this. This town is so secluded. It's—refreshing."

"Yeah," Jake said, feeling suddenly wary and not knowing why. "I guess it's pretty nice."

The man swallowed the last bite of his sandwich, and set to packing up his bag with a sigh. "I wish I could stay longer." He shouldered the bag and pulled the binoculars over his head. Then he eyed Jake, his mouth drawn into a thin, disarming smile. "How long will you be staying?"

"Me? I—well, I live here."

"Oh? Is that so?" the man said, sounding doubtful. "You look old enough to be in college. So far as I know, Wind Creek Township has no local college."

"Well, I go upstate. But I'm home for the holiday."

"Ah," the man said, visibly brightening, and suddenly Jake wanted very much to get away. "So, you'll be here at least till Thursday?"

"Look, man, I don't know what you're getting at here, but—"

The man held up a steady, long-fingered hand. "I didn't mean to offend." He adjusted his bag and started away. "Enjoy your time."

Jake watched the man amble down the path toward the lot where Alanna was riding her bike back and forth across the gravel. Jake followed close. In the lot, the man climbed into an unassuming sedan and drove off. Jake watched him.

Alanna skidded to a halt at his side, but Jake hardly noticed her.

"The heck took you so long?" she demanded.

"Did you see that guy?" he asked.

"What guy?"

Jake looked at her, finally, saw the perplexed expression scrunching up her face, and realized he was... must be... had to be worrying about nothing.

"Forget it," he said. But he couldn't.

"Hey, you wanna watch me pop a wheelie?"

Jake nodded. "Sure. Show me."

They spent the next twenty minutes ambling around the gravel lot—well, Jake ambled and Alanna zipped—and all the while Jake's eyes kept returning to that monstrous cell tower, and his thoughts to the strange man with the binoculars. At one point Jake's cell phone rang, and, thinking it was his mother, he answered it without checking the caller ID. But there was only static and a faraway hum—no, not a hum, a chime, a kind of series of chimes. He pocketed the phone without thinking about it again.

When the light started to fade, Jake stood leaning against a safety rail that girded the embankment looking over the glen below. A man and woman stood nearby, watching the clouds skate across the evening. They were holding hands, and Jake felt lonelier than ever.

The man glanced over at Jake, saw him watching them, and

offered a friendly, if a little nervous, nod. Jake nodded back, then moved past them. He called out to his sister, and Alanna dutifully pedaled over to him.

"Time to go, pipsqueak. It's almost dinnertime."

"Oh, good," Alanna said. "I'm *starving*."

Jake, who hoped his sister never actually learned what it meant to be starving, nodded assent.

They walked up the path—Jake pushing the bike, now, and Alanna walking in her bubbly, almost-skipping way—and, as they were ascending, Jake heard a harsh, grating series of coughs come from behind them. He turned and saw the woman pounding her man on the back, a look of helpless horror on her face. Jake was about to drop Alanna's bike and hurry back when the man took a long, labored breath and gestured to the woman that he was all right, he was fine, just the wrong pipe.

So, Jake and his sister walked back to the truck. When they arrived home, Jake did as he had promised and took his mother and Alanna out to dinner at Puretta's. The restaurant was crowded. And not long into the meal it occurred to Jake that a pretty nasty cold must be going around. At least a dozen people were coughing or battling the sniffles.

*

The clamor of a bell broke Jake from the cage of his memory. He'd been gazing out the window for at least ten minutes, remembering. The bell, though, brought him back; it was a grim reminder of what had to come next.

It'd been three weeks since Thanksgiving. Few had celebrated it, Jake was sure. No one knew just when the quarantine had started. Some said it was right around the time that the cable and cell services went out. Whether that were true or not did not matter. The bell mattered. And everyone remembered when the bells started: Thanksgiving eve.

The personnel in charge of removing the deceased were not so callous as to call "bring out your dead" over a loudspeaker. The bell did the work.

Jake looked down from Alanna's bedroom window. The steady hum of a diesel engine droned beneath the intoning bell, creating its own kind of macabre music. And there, dressed in army green, was The Wagon. Folks called it The Wagon, but it was actually a heavy-wheeled dump truck run by four soldiers who wore respirators and sterile suits. The Wagon lumbered to a stop outside the Togtrens' house.

Benny and Jade Togtren were a middle-aged couple with three teenagers. Jake watched Benny Togtren greet two soldiers at the door. The man looked gray and sallow, and the finger with which he gestured the soldiers inside visibly trembled. Two soldiers entered. Then a third. Jake didn't realize he was holding his breath, and let it out in a sigh, or maybe a whimper, when the fourth soldier was promptly called in over the radio. A minute later, all four soldiers exited the Togtren home, bearing burdens wrapped delicately in white sheets.

"All of them," Jake murmured.

As the last soldier walked toward the back of the truck, the sheet shifted, disclosing a thin, pale hand. Benny Togtren watched from his doorway as the soldiers took away his family. Then the truck rumbled on, Benny Togtren closed his door, and Jake never saw the man again.

It took another ten minutes for the truck to reach Jake's house. He sat in an old desk chair with his raw hands clasped between his knees, his attention shifting from The Wagon's slow progress to the still form of Alanna on the bed. He had no intention of letting the soldiers in to take her. If his sister was going to be taken from the house where she'd grown up, he intended to be the one carrying her out.

The Wagon bell clanged. The soldiers had made it to his house. They'd collected ten additional bodies between the Togtrens' home and here. Jake went to the door, threw the various locks, opened it, and waved to the soldiers. They waited for him to signal how many, but Jake went back inside to collect his sister. The soldiers exchanged confused glances behind their respirators, then climbed down from The Wagon.

Jake paused in Alanna's bedroom, regarding her still form one last time. Then he gathered her gingerly in his arms and took her outside.

The soldiers waited at the door. One of them had drawn a semi-automatic rifle. Jake wasn't worried. He knew why the soldiers went around town armed, and it wasn't because of people like him. He stepped past them to the rear of the dump truck. The load was grisly. Limbs uncovered from the death shrouds were gnarled together. Jake hated the thought of his sister getting heaped in there with so many other dead.

"I'm sorry, sir," one of the soldiers called out from Jake's left. The respirator he wore gave his voice a tinny quality. "We have to move along."

"I just—" Jake began, but his voice failed him and tears ran down his cheeks.

"I'll take it," another soldier announced, and opened his arms.

Jake shook his head. It was only a matter of time, he knew, before the soldiers would be loading him up into The Wagon. He had made peace with that fate—or at least he thought he had—but that was not the place for his sister. Not for Alanna.

"I've changed my mind," Jake said. "I'll—I'll bury her myself."

He turned to leave, but one of the soldiers—the one brandishing his rifle—blocked his way. "We can't let you do that, sir. The protocol requires all corpses be collected *en masse*."

"And where will you take her?" Jake demanded, his voice rising. "To some mass grave? A stinking hole that's no better than a garbage dump?"

"Sir, I'm only going to ask you once more—"

"I'm not giving her to you!"

A bright light—blinding—exploded in his vision, and then darkness rushed in like an inky, midnight tide. Somewhere in all that darkness he heard a voice, a soldier's voice, *Sorry, kid, but they don't all die.*

When he woke, he was in his room. The window that looked out on Seeker Street was dark. A terrific ache pulsed at the back of his head and radiated down to his back. Looking around, he felt his stomach clench, and then he vomited. He hadn't eaten for some time, so he didn't make much of a mess.

Warm hands pressing him back down into the comfort of his mattress.

"Take it easy, Jacob," his mother said. "I don't know if you have a concussion or not, but you shouldn't be moving yet."

He grimaced against the throbbing in his brain and spine. "What happened?"

"You pissed off the soldiers," she said. "They were kind enough to carry you into the living room before climbing back into that godless wagon."

"You saw?"

She nodded, then paused, and when Jake looked at her he could see tears shining on her cheeks. "They took her."

Jake's fists clenched. "I'm sorry."

"What else could we have done?"

Jake didn't know if the question were rhetorical or if his mother genuinely wanted an answer. So, he didn't reply.

They sat in silence for a time. Then his mother called his name, softly. "Yeah?" he said.

"Just making sure you didn't fall asleep. They say if a concussion victim goes to sleep, they could fall into a coma."

"That doesn't sound so bad," Jake said, sounding tired, feeling helpless.

His mother gripped him by the arms, hauled him up, peered into his face. "No, Jacob. You're not lying down here. You're not getting stuck in this shitty town."

"Mom—" But what could he say? That everything was hopeless? That the government's quarantine was really just a death vigil? That, yes, all of them would die in this shitty town, and there was nothing to be done about it?

No, he couldn't say any of those things. Even in his grief, the thought of hurting his mother after she'd already lost Alanna was too much for his fractured conscience to bear.

He tried to meet her eyes, but she was looking out the window.

"They're waiting for all of us to die, you know."

"Yeah." Jake put his head in his hands, felt his eyes slipping closed, and pulled his head back up with effort. "I don't get why they don't just bomb the hell out of us and be done with it."

Now his mother did look at him, an expression of horror drawing her worried features tight over her skull. "What?"

"The longer they keep us in quarantine, the greater the risk that someone might break through the barricade. They can't have soldiers stationed in an unbroken radius around the town. Someone might slip through. And if they're infected—" Jake shrugged his shoulders. Somehow that gesture said more about his state of mind than anything he could have spoken.

"You think there's a way out?"

"What? No, that's not what I—maybe."

His mother's eyes were very bright in the dark and very wide. "Okay, then."

She rose from the edge of his bed and went to his desk. His book bag sat below it, still filled with books he hadn't touched since he had arrived. His mother dumped the books out, went to his dresser, and started shoving clothes inside.

"What are you doing?" Jake asked, getting unsteadily to his feet.

"We're leaving," she said without turning to look at him. "Here." She threw his bag at him. "Pack whatever you think we'll need. I'll do the same." She hurried to the door but was stopped short by a coughing fit. She collapsed in the doorframe, her face going bright red, the veins bulging in her neck.

Jake hurried to her, patted her back. "Mom? *Mom?* Come on. Breathe!"

She waved him off, finally gulping long gasps of air between coughs. "I—I'm—fuh-fine."

He waited for her breath to come back. And when it did and she looked at him, he hated the terrible vulnerability he saw there. His mother was afraid. Really afraid. It was a fear that paled in comparison to the long nights waiting for Jake's father to come home from a bender of drinking and gambling.

And as if the thought somehow summoned the man to his mother's mind, she said, "That lucky bastard finally got to cash in."

"What?"

She leaned heavily against the doorframe. "Your father. All his life he's been the unluckiest loser you can imagine. But now—now he's out there and we're in here, and I know it's because he went over to Raritan City to place a damn bet. Any other day he would've just gone to Lenny's." She shook her head. "Not this time. This time Christian Cedici won the fucking jackpot."

Jake didn't know what to say. He reached for her, but she shoved him back.

"You have to get out, Jake. The world doesn't know what's happened here. I'm sure of it. And you're not sick. You can get out, and disappear, and—do you hear that?"

Jake shook his head. "What?"

Jasmine stood listening, her head cocked. "Like—like bells—" Then her whole body seemed to clench. Her shoulders went rigid, tendons stood out in her neck, and her fists knotted so tight that Jake could see blood squirting between her fingers where the nails dug into the meat of her palms. She screamed, just once, and then pitched forward, collapsing in the hallway.

Jake stood motionless. He'd heard that the disease had affected people differently, that some succumbed in seconds while others took weeks. But to see it—

He went to his mother, called to her, but she remained still.

The tears would not come. Not now. He picked up his mother's stiff hand. She wanted him to get out. That was her last wish. And why not? He wasn't sick. Why should he wait here to die like all the rest?

"I'm sorry, Mom," he whispered. Then he bent to lift her, hoping to at least place her on the bed where she could repose with some dignity.

Her hand clenched down on his forearm—hard. Jake winced. She was looking at him. The muscles in his cheeks and jaw distended, preparing to loose a feral cry. But his mother shrieked instead, her other bloody hand hooked into a claw and swiped. Jake recoiled, barely, but her chipped nails gouged runny ribbons across his right cheek.

Jake strained backward, wanting to get out of that impossible grip, screaming something over and over, though he wouldn't realize until later what he'd been saying, *Stop, Mom! Stop! Stop, Mommy!*

He broke free and pin-wheeled to keep his balance. Jasmine Cedici was getting to her feet. Her contorted face dribbled an ugly, yellow fluid. And Jake remembered what the soldier had said, *They don't all die.*

She was blocking his way out. Standing hunched, his mother looked more like a predator than the woman who had made him chicken soup when he was home sick from school.

Jake set his jaw. "Move," he said.

Jasmine Cedici tilted her head; a thread of jaundiced spittle fell gleaming from her mouth. She took a step forward. Jake reacted. He grabbed the table lamp from his nightstand and bashed it against the side of her face. There was a meaty thud, the tinkle of glass, and then his mother crashed against the wall. Jake bolted.

He was downstairs within a second, then yanking on the front door. It wouldn't budge. He kicked it with a curse, pulled on the knob harder. He'd forgotten about the curfew—and the locks on the outside.

"No!" he shouted.

A guttural cry from the top of the stairs, and then the rapid and ungainly sound of his mother descending—*thud-thud-thudthudthudthud.*

Hitting the landing, she leaped at him. Jake tried to sidestep, but she caught him in the shoulder, dashing them both against the front door. The door rattled in its hinges but otherwise did not give.

Jake pulled his feet under him, fell, grabbed a curtain for balance, tore it from the rod.

Then his mother had him.

She wrenched his shoulder, flipping him onto his back. Jake cried out. Jasmine clutched his throat with one hand, bashed his face with the other. She hit him again, again—again. Jake didn't know how long it went on. Each hit drew a growing black corona around the world, and he knew he would lose consciousness soon, and then—well, he only had to look at the gibbering, horrid face of the woman who was his mother to know what happened then.

She released him. Jake felt his body wanting to go limp. His face was a sequence of swollen, wet heat. Jasmine, her mouth a toothy snarl, leaned over him, and then a peculiar pregnant bulge appeared in her neck. Her cheeks puffed and her lips clenched; she bowed and retched, retched again.

Fiery static in his arms and legs—Jake bucked beneath her just as the vomit came up, and rolled away from it. It was a gelatinous mass, viscid and somehow crawly, and it writhed across the floor where his mother had hawked it.

She shrieked at him, but now Jake was moving. He banked left into the kitchen, slamming his hip against the kitchen table, then he pulled open the garage door, went through, and slammed the door shut. There was no way to lock it from this side, so he hurried down the few steps, dashed to his father's workbench, and grabbed a hammer before ducking out of sight.

He was breathing very hard—hard enough for someone to easily hear—so he gripped the hammer, closed his eyes, and focused on the too-rapid thrum of his heart, demanding it to slow. And it almost worked.

Then the garage door banged open, and his mother's shadow—spindly and contorted—appeared on the wall. Jake's heart jackhammered. His breaths came in gasps that he tried to muffle with his hand.

She's going to kill me, he thought. *My mother's going to find me and kill me.*

The thuds of her shoes on the wooden steps were very loud, almost deafening to his ears. They seemed to vibrate some delicate equilibrium in the center of his head the way heavy thunder will vibrate a windowpane.

He sat squeezed behind the workbench. The space smelled dank and old and forgotten, and it occurred to Jake in this moment that this was how the whole town would smell in a year—maybe less.

A rattle of metal as his mother knocked into Alanna's bike, tipping it over. It fell into his view with a clatter. Then he could see his mother's shoes. She pivoted one way, the other, making a wet gurgling sound in her throat. He clutched his hand over his mouth harder, his eyes starting from their sockets.

The feet stopped, turned at weird angles. Then Jake's mother smelled the air—a distinct *sniff-sniff.*

"Jaaaaa-kuh," she wheezed. "Jaaa-*kuh!*"

He watched as hands lowered to the floor to join the feet. Then his mother's face appeared, tilted and twitching. Blood and yellow vomit streaked her lips and chin. She smiled.

"*Ja-kuh,*" she whispered. Then she scuttled after him on all fours, gibbering and snarling.

Jake shot left, but a hard hand grappled his ankle and squeezed. She was dragging herself out from beneath the workbench, reaching for him with the other hand.

Jake cried out once, then brought the hammer down on the back of his mother's skull.

His mother grunted, paused, then continued to pull herself toward him. He hit her again. Again. And once more. The final strike made a terrible sound that reminded him of crunching tree bark, and, horrified, he sent the hammer skittering across the cement floor, where it trailed a red, alien calligraphy behind it. His mother went limp.

Jake stood motionless, his bloody hand trembling. "Mom?" he croaked.

When she didn't move, he bent to her, touched the back of her head where the hair was matted against the dented bone. He barked a harsh cry, covered his mouth.

"What did I do?" he asked the empty cellar, his eyes seeking, needing to see a familiar face. He needed someone to tell him that he'd had no choice, that Jasmine Cedici died upstairs and this shell of her that he'd killed wasn't his mother.

No face appeared. No voice imparted these consoling words. So

Jake collapsed on his knees, pulled his mother's lifeless body into his lap, and wept. He wept for a long time.

*

The Wagon bell tolled on Henry Street like it did every morning, and the few people remaining—those who weren't killed off by the disease, which the government had lovingly named the Gene Detonation Protocol, or an infected individual—dutifully brought out their dead at the bell's sounding. In a week, the denizens of Wind Creek Township would all be wiped out, the army would collect what samples and information was left, and then the town—settled in 1835—would be razed to the ground. That was the plan.

When the four soldiers arrived at the Cedici home and sounded the bell, no one came to the door. A soldier named Higgins who rode on the back of the truck like a garbage collector, checked the tablet clipped to his belt.

He pressed the transmit button on his respirator. "Supposed to be two left," he called into his radio.

"All right," the driver called back. "Let's have a look, then."

Higgins and another soldier made their way up the porch steps while the other two rolled on to the next house. None of them enjoyed this particular tour of duty, and the sooner each morning ended, the sooner they could get along to forgetting about it.

Sergeant Higgins knocked loudly on the door. When there was no answer, he looked at the external lock. Staple hasps had been installed on all the homes at all the exits, each of which were secured every night with heavy padlocks after the mandatory curfew—the crew tasked with this tremendous undertaking were known informally as Keepers, and each night twenty of them went around town locking up the residents. Padlocks were removed promptly at five a.m.—only on the front doors—to allow the townspeople to get on with their dying in relative comfort. Sergeant Higgins didn't see the point of it. Leave the damned doors locked and bomb the hell out of the town—it would be much more humane. Jake would have agreed.

That thought reoccurred to him now when he saw that the padlock for the Cedici home was still in place.

Higgins grasped it in his hand, his thin lips drawn into a bow. "Who's the Keeper assigned to this sector?" he asked the other soldier whose name was Winston.

Private Winston flicked through his tablet. "Private O'Connell,"

136

he said.

Higgins didn't know why but the fine hairs on the back of his neck had started to stand on end.

"Do you want me to radio him?" Private Winston started to ask, but Higgins cut him off.

"No. Blow the lock."

"Sir?"

"For shit's sake!" Higgins shoved the private back, aimed his rifle at the lock, and with a burst of gunfire the door was loose.

The soldiers stepped inside. Over the radio the other two who had moved on in The Wagon were chattering, demanding an explanation for the shots fired. Higgins ignored them. He stepped into the gloom of the Cedici home. He recalled Patient Zero had not wanted Higgins and his men to carry out the girl yesterday, and for that Higgins had dealt him a swift crack to the skull.

Everything's fine, Higgins thought. *The kid's here. I scrambled his fuckin brains. He's probably lying upstairs in a coma.*

"Sir," Winston called. The static of chattering officers was audible through his face mask. Higgins had turned his radio volume down. He needed to be sharp. "What's got your ghost?"

"Just shut up and find the kid," Higgins said.

Stepping into the kitchen, Higgins felt the blood drain from his legs.

A man sat in the middle of the room, naked and lashed cruelly to a chair with various electronics wires. Duct tape had been strapped around his mouth so tight that his eyes had gone bloodshot. And those eyes were wide and staring and terrified.

Here's Private O'Connell, Higgins thought, and though his mind's voice seemed calm, Higgins knew the tone for what it really was. Acceptance.

He removed the tape with his knife, and Private O'Connell's words came in a gush.

"Knocked me out!" he shouted. "Patient Zero is loose! Do you hear me? Patient Zero is fucking *loose!*"

"How long ago?" Higgins asked, his tone still calm. He was, after all, still a soldier.

"Four hours," O'Connell said. "Son of a bitch ambushed me! Ambushed *me!* Jumped right off the goddamned roof!"

"Four hours," Higgins said, more to himself than anyone else.

"Hey? Hey!" O'Connell visibly vibrated in the chair. "Call it in! Do you know what'll happen if that kid gets into a town? A goddamned city! Hey! Are you listening to me?"

"Four hours," Higgins repeated. "And he took your uniform." He stood, rubbed a gloved hand over his mask. Then, Sergeant Julius Higgins removed his mask, which was just for show, anyway. When he removed the custom-fitted ear plugs, though, the soldiers erupted in panicked protests. "We're doomed," he said, and offered the men a smile. Then he shoved the barrel of the machine gun under the shelf of his chin and blew his hopes and dreams onto the ceiling of the Cedici home.

*

Jake figured the soldiers didn't think any resident would be stupid enough to jump from a second-story roof. Hence why they'd only bothered to board over the windows on the first floors of all the homes.

So when he'd crawled out onto the shingled roof of the garage from his bedroom window and pressed himself flat to the surface, he didn't expect the Keeper to notice. And he was right.

He spied the soldier approaching his house from the one next door and carefully crawled to the ledge on the opposite side. The rear locks were never unlocked, true, but the soldiers were still expected to check them. *Gluttons for protocol,* Jake thought.

He heard the soldier rounding the house—the respirator made that easy enough—and when he paused in front of the back door, Jake fell on top of him.

There was some scuffling and cursing, but Jake had made sure to land his feet on the soldier's head. Once he tore the respirator off and socked his forearm hard under the man's chin and squeezed, the soldier went still quickly.

Jake undressed the man, pulling the uniform and hazard suit over his own clothes. Next, he put on the respirator to hide his face. Surprisingly, the most difficult part of this entire endeavor was singling out the key to the padlock on the rear door of his house.

Once inside, Jake tied the man to one of the kitchen chairs with all the wires from behind the living room television. He paused for a moment, looking at the naked soldier. The steady rise and fall of the man's chest told Jake he was still alive, which was good—he didn't need another person's blood on his hands. But he needed to make sure the soldier couldn't call for help.

He went back into the garage. The respirator and helmet made his breath sound ragged, and for a moment he felt like some alien visitor. But when he saw his mother's body lying in the middle of the floor where he'd moved it, the reality of his situation, of his life, smacked him in the face like a sack full of quarters.

He went to his father's workbench, grabbed the old roll of duct tape, and then paused over his mother's body.

"I'm sorry, Mom," he murmured. "I wish I could've helped you, helped Alanna. But I'm going to keep my promise, okay? I'm going to get out."

He touched his mother's forehead, stroked his gloved fingers through the dirty hair, then, pressing the plastic of the mask against her cheek, he kissed her one last time.

Getting out of town was easier than he'd thought. He walked up Henry Street to Vintner Avenue, followed Vintner to Trask. Bright lights glowed near the entrance to the highway, and in all the quiet Jake could hear the periodic crackle of radios. But he wasn't heading that way.

The woods, he thought. *They can't cover all of that land.*

And then he was plunging through the eastern Miller's Woods, which would eventually lead to Highway 15. About ten miles through, the faintest trace of dawn started to bleed upward into the distant horizon. Jake paused—he'd jogged most of the way—and pulled off the hazard suit, respirator, and army fatigues. He glanced back, and, in the distance, he could just see the glowing frame of that new cell tower.

They shut our phones down, he thought. *Why's it still working?*

But the thought, he decided, was unimportant. He was almost free.

He came to the highway just before eight a.m., made it to a truck-stop diner before nine. At nine-thirty, and with a belly full of eggs and bacon, he ordered a taxi with the remainder of his emergency money.

At ten-thirty—just when Sergeant Higgins sat down in the Cedici kitchen with his gun—Jake was pulling into the parking lot of his father's favorite gambling house in Raritan City. After he thanked the driver—*you better get a icepack on that face*, the driver had said—and climbed out, he scanned the lot, and, sure enough, his father's car was parked directly adjacent to the front entrance, phony handicapped permit and all.

Jake made his way into the bar, which was always crowded on Sunday mornings for the games. As the cabbie pulled away, she leaned out of her open window and started hacking, hacking hard enough to have to come to a stop. Once she'd gotten herself under control, and, Lord, but her allergies were bad today, she peeled off, stopping at the next red light to pick up a random fare, who was going to the international airport.

Inside the bar, Jake found his father. The man looked up from his Bloody Mary, his hands visibly trembling.

"Jake?" Christian Cedici came forward. "Jake? What—how—" Christian grabbed his son's arms. "They wouldn't let me in. They wouldn't—wouldn't tell me what—"

Jake took a breath. "They're dead," he whispered. "Mom and Alanna."

Christian, his eyes watery, hugged his son.

"Oh, Jake—no, no, please—I'm sorry. Sorry I wasn't—" But words failed Christian Cedici. They flitted out of his mind like a field of butterflies suddenly disturbed. In their place, faintly, he thought he heard bells, a chorus of faraway bells ringing gently and discordantly between the darkness of his scattered thoughts.

Somewhere in the gloom of the bar, someone coughed. Then another.

***

Falling Like Rain

by Kat Pekin
Australia

I fly through the living room window feet first and land on Gran's rug. I'm still sweating. I can't catch my breath. Shit. Blaze has never gotten that close to killing me before. I'd managed to flood the ditch we were fighting in and he couldn't keep his flames burning.

"I'll find a way, Rainsong!" he'd screamed as I took off into the sky. "I'll find a way to hurt you!"

In Gran's apartment, I wait by the open window, listening to hear if Blaze followed me. All I hear is the bustling of late night in Brisbane city. Then I hear a tired, panting voice whisper in my mind.

Next time, Rainsong ...

I slam the window shut and yank the curtains closed. Blaze quiets in my mind. He must be as tired as I am, usually it takes way more concentration on my part to tune him out.

In the soft glow of my grandmother's apartment I check my outfit for damage. There's a tear in the arm of leather, plus I've lost the buckle off my belt, and then there's the shitload of scorching on my pants. My suit is supposed to be fire resistant.

It's usually a pretty cosy outfit. It's not a thin glossy spandex that coats my boobs like body paint. Mine is way more sensible. The navy fabric is almost like canvas, thick and rough. "Impossible to tear," as Gran used to say to my mother. I don't know who decided superwomen need cleavage to fight crime. My boobs, small as they may be, are covered and my look is completed with a leather jacket and blue scarf.

I check the time on the grandfather clock. It reads almost three. Gran has a habit of waiting up for me despite me telling her not to, so I'm not surprised when I walk into the kitchen and see her sitting at the table smoking her cigar and playing solitaire.

"You're late," Gran says as she slaps a card down. She's wearing her permanent expression of annoyance.

"Blaze," I tell her, hoping that's enough of an explanation. She knows my history with Blaze.

Gran stubs out her cigar. "Well, your dinner is cold."

"I'll reheat it."

Gran gives me a onceover glance. "Your suit's a mess, Anne."

She used to call me Annie. It still hurts that she can't find the heart to do it anymore. "I can fix it," I assure her.

Gran makes a chorus of grunting and groaning noises as she pulls herself up to her walker. "What time do you need my car?"

"I'll leave here at ten. My exam goes for three hours."

Gran sighs. "I'll go shopping this weekend, I suppose."

"I can go on the way home from uni," I offer, but she doesn't answer me.

"Did you change the lightbulbs in the study?" Gran asks.

Damn. Meant to do that this morning. "Not yet," I have to admit.

Gran sighs again and takes her time shuffling back towards her room. "Put your plate in the dishwasher when you're done."

After she's gone, I open all the windows to try and clear out the cigar stench. Why can't she just bake cookies like all the other grandmothers I hear about?

It seems that dinner was roast chicken; a plate of it is sitting on the countertop. After I stick it in the microwave, I levitate to get a bottle of whiskey from the top of the cupboards. I've got a nice selection of drink hidden up here. Since Gran's glued to her walker, it's not like she's climbing ladders anymore, so my little habit is easy for me to hide.

I don't bother with a glass; I just swig from the bottle and eat my dinner. I thought I had more whiskey left than what I do. I guess with the stress of my final uni year and Blaze burning havoc through the city, I've been drinking more than I should.

Drink up, little Annie.

Fucking Blaze. Feels like he's been able to do this forever, get inside my mind and mutter annoying bullshit. I take another drink.

Drink one, and then some more, Rainsong.

After a few more mouthfuls, his voice fades, so I replace my whiskey bottle on top of the shelves and put my plate in the dishwasher, then I head to my room to study. My environmental science books are stacked beside my bed. I can read as fast as I can fly, but that doesn't mean I absorb the info. Still, I can at least try.

The top book on the pile is my ecopedological principles textbook. I grab it and lie down on my bed to read. Tomorrow's exam is the big one, the 60 percenter that'll pass or fail me in this class. I failed the first assessment because I missed the deadline due to having broken both of my legs. A school bus had swerved off of a bridge and although I managed to stop it from smashing on the ground, I'd been crushed underneath it. I'd tried to plead my case to the student advisor, but she'd given me the whole "you know extensions need to be requested in writing at least a week before the due date, not the day after" spiel and I'd got a nice big "F" on my record.

At some point I must have fallen asleep because I wake up suddenly. My plan for a studying all-nighter was a complete fail. I'm still in my singed superhero get-up. I roll over in my bed and stretch out, surprised that I must have beaten my alarm. I check my phone.

It's 10:50.

I missed my alarm.

It's so cliché, sleeping through an alarm, that I almost laugh but I have no time. There's no way I can get to uni by car. I'll have to fly. I'm not supposed to fly unless it's for superhero business, but fuck it, I'll deal with whatever ramifications there are after my exam. I jump out of bed, whip off my costume, and dress in jeans and an old t-shirt.

"Did you set your alarm?" Gran asks me as I scoff down plain bread for breakfast.

"I slept through it," I pour myself a travel cup of coffee. "You could have woken me up."

"I'm not your mother," she snaps. "If you're grown up enough to save the city, you can get to class on time."

"I'll fly," I say as I secure the lid of my travel mug. "I'll still get there on time."

"Well," she buttons up her pale blue cardigan. "I guess this means I can at least go shopping."

A brief detour back to my room to grab my shoulder bag and then I'm out the window. Normally I enjoy every aspect of flying. The wind whipping past me, the dew that forms on my cheeks when I cut through clouds, the perfect view of the city. But today I have no time for anything. I tilt my head down and try to narrow my shoulders to gain speed. The blurs of a Brisbane city morning flash below me but I don't slow myself down until I see the familiar buildings of my campus at Brisbane City University.

I land on the roof of Building C and take the fire escape down until I can get inside. I make it to my exam room with a minute to spare and take a seat in the front row. The supervisor whispers to me to keep my travel mug on the floor, so I do, and then get out my pen, turn off my phone, and settle in.

After the preamble that comes with every exam— about academic integrity and turning off your phone, no open drink containers— I flip open my exam booklet, write Annie Raine on the cover along with my student number, and then I get started.

It doesn't take long for Blaze to come into my mind again. *Can you hear me, little Rainsong?*

I'm staring at a table asking me to classify soil minerals.

Soiling away, little Annie.

I can't remember what stems from the silicates. There are two main ones. Phyllosilicates and the other one ...

Silly soil, Annie.

Usually I'm good at muting out Blaze's inane ramblings, but he always seems to get into my head when I'm desperate to focus on something that isn't superhero related. Tectosilicates! I think that's the other one. Phyllosilicates and tectosilicates.

I feel my phone vibrate in my pocket. I'm in the front row in class, I can't chance stealing a look at who's texting me. The supervisors get really peeved when they see a phone. Rumour has it they chuck people out of exams if they're even caught with a phone. I resolve that it's probably an email alert and go back to my silicates table. Blaze is still blistering around my mind.

Silly, silly, silicone Annie.

I'm pretty sure I've got the six phyllosilicates down correctly.

Silly Annie. Silly Annie. Silly Annie.

I set my pen down and feign the need for some coffee from my travel mug. Really, I'm trying to put up a block on Blaze's commentary. I try to apply Gran's old advice.

"Think of water," she had told me. "Rushing, flooding water. Think only of water."

"I can't," used to be my reply.

"You have to or you'll end up like your mother," she said. "She'd still be here if she'd trusted her damn power and thought of earth. *Think of water.*"

So, sitting here in a room of my student peers, I think of water. Gran never talks about my mum unless it's to remind me what *not* to do in order to stay sane and alive. I wish she'd talk about her more. My memories of Mum feel translucent sometimes. There, but not there. I can see them, but I can see through them. I can't grasp them.

Silly Annie. There's no fool like the old one.

Water. I think of water. I think of that overwhelming rushing sound you hear when you're next to a waterfall, and the *whoosh* of waves hitting the shore. The insistent rhythm of a thunderstorm where all you hear is rain. The deafening silence when you submerge in a pool and you are within the water and it encompasses you.

My mind clears and I move onto the next question about soil profile analysis.

*

Three hours later, I'm done with my 60-percenter. But my plans for going home to sleep before heading out for tonight's shift as Rainsong are dashed when I check my messages and see one from Gran and one from my boss at EZ Electric.

"Can you come in just for the end of shift?" my boss asks when I call her back. "I'll pay you time and a half."

I'd rather go home and nap, but I need to pay for new tires for Gran's car. It's sort of unspoken between us that, since I use the car more than she does, I pay for the upkeep on it. So the extra money is annoyingly impossible to pass up. I tell my boss I'll be in as soon as I can. On my way I try to return Gran's message. Not surprising when I don't get an answer. I bought her a prepaid mobile phone from work but she refuses to learn how to use it. She still uses the house phone with the dodgy ringer she can hardly hear.

The ringers rang with a will.

Fucking Blaze. Water, water, water. Think water, Annie. Flooded rivers, constant rain.

Ten minutes later, I'm wearing one of the spare EZ Electric shirts and headed out onto the sales floor.

But soiling another, Annie, will never make oneself clean.

A young couple are scanning the big screen televisions, so I go over with my salesperson face on and start talking up the expensive

145

screen even though it's basically the same as the one five hundred dollars cheaper.

The blackest of lies.

I imagine Niagara Falls, tune out Blaze and continue selling. The couple leave with a hollow promise to think about it and return later. Next, I help a woman in a classic pantsuit who is browsing stereo systems. It's an easy sale. She just wants her stereo. Takes a nice mid-range one and heads off with a smile.

I fear you'll listen to tales, be jealous and hard and unkind.

Just after nine, my boss thanks me for coming in and lets me go. I catch a bus home to our apartment and take the lift to our level. I could levitate up, but I'm too tired. Blocking Blaze out drains my energy just as much as the everyday stresses of student life and selling electronics.

Our apartment is empty. "Gran?" I call out, but there's no reply.

I go to the fridge, but there's nothing exciting in there. I guess Gran didn't happen to go shopping yet. Maybe she's still out at the market. Maybe she's taking a bus home, she doesn't like to drive at night and has been known to leave her car locked in parking lots overnight.

All of an evening late ...

"Shut up," I mutter to myself. I stick the plug in the sink and run the water; that helps distract me. I click on the kettle, too. Maybe Blaze knew today was a stressful day and decided to really crap in my mind.

I go to dump my bag in my room and see my fixed superhero costume laid out on my bed. Gran's mended the scrapes, reinforced the fabric, and fixed those loose threads on my scarf. Guilt washes over me as it always does when Gran helps me out. Most of the time I think she just tolerates me because we're blood, but then she does something nice like fixing my outfit and I feel like shit for not doing what she asks. Like changing the light globes.

Gone for a minute.

Gran left the fresh light globes for me on the bookshelf in the living room. I ignore my tiredness and levitate to change out the globes in the ceiling chandelier.

Pattering over the boards, my Annie.

Globes changed, I make a cup of green tea, head for my room and flip open my laptop.

Patter she goes, my own little Annie, an Annie like you.

What is with him today? He rarely refers to me by anything other than Rainsong, and never so consistently throughout the day.

I'm not always certain if they be alive or dead.

My search engine homepage comes onto my screen. I click a tab to open my email.

Shadow and shine is life, little Annie, flower and thorn.

Shadow and shine? What is he on about? They almost sound like song lyrics. Curious, I click back to the search engine and type in what Blaze just mumbled to me.

The very first search result makes my spine run with ice.

On the screen I see the things Blaze has been assaulting my mind with all day. The lines, the references to Little Annie.

Why do you look at me, Annie? You think I am hard and cold ...

It's not a song. Blaze's ramblings are from a poem by Alfred Lord Tennyson.

The base little liar.

My heart stops. Our empty apartment. No food in the fridge. The missed call. The poem.

But the tongue is a fire as you know, my dear, the tongue is a fire.

A poem titled *The Grandmother*.

It hits me like a cannonball.

But stay with the old woman now: you cannot have long to stay ...

Blaze has Gran.

*

I undress and snatch my costume off the bed. The navy fabric instantly melds to my body and then I'm out the window soaring through Brisbane's night sky. I think of Gran, of water and Gran. Blaze's taunts have stopped. He must know that I finally figured it out.

I'm stupid. I'm so fucking stupid. I should have caught on to how he was teasing me. His taunts are normal to me now, but usually he's just nattering about whatever I'm doing at the time. I should have twigged when he started calling me Annie.

As I fly, I focus on Gran. My familial power bond alerts me to where she is. Her power has been fading with her age to the point where she doesn't bother wasting the energy to summon it, but I manage to hone in on a weak spark of her lightning. I see Blaze, too. His fire burns bright in my mind, but I follow Gran's lightning like a dimming beacon and it leads me to a warehouse in the middle of nowhere. Not a body of water in sight, nothing for me to draw from.

Blaze sure knows how to pick a location. Doesn't mean I can't use my powers, just means I don't have a river or lake or water tank to manipulate to my advantage.

I land quietly on the warehouse roof and scale my way down to climb through a broken window. I perch myself on the edge of a roof beam and scan the warehouse, and then I see her.

My grandmother is strapped to a pyre. Piles of wood are set around her like she's about to be burnt as a witch. She's still wearing her powder blue cardigan. Despite her dire situation, her annoyed glare is still plastered on her face. However, even from where I am I can see fear flickering in her tired eyes.

I hop off the roof beam and land on a metal catwalk that circles the top of the warehouse. I jump the railing and float myself down to the ground. "Blaze!" I scream when I reach the ground.

He appears from behind the pyre. "Took you long enough!"

"Let her go," I say.

He gives a lazy shake of his head. "Nope."

I clench my hands into fists and thrust them forward. Thick jets of water materialise and shoot directly at Blaze's body. He fires back at me with a flaming orb. I manage to deflect it and douse the flame with my jets, then he fires four shots in quick succession at my grandmother's feet. The pyre around her ignites.

"No!" I send a stream of water and extinguish the flames before they strengthen.

"Ignore him, Annie!" Gran yells at me.

For a moment, I falter and look over at my surly grandmother. She hasn't called me Annie since we buried my mother. I just figured it was her way of reverting our relationship back to a formal one since I killed her daughter.

"Say bye-bye to Grannie, little Annie," Blaze says. He extends his arms out to his sides and summons his flames. Fire licks around his body like hungry devil's tongues. The ground below him starts glowing shades of orange, and I see my grandmother start panting and sweating. Her head tilts sideways and her grumpy face is replaced by one of exhausted dehydration. She can't breathe. Her body can't take this. She'll be dead before she starts burning. She needs me. Now.

I try to focus myself.

All I can think to do is something I've never done before. My mother's power was earth; my father's power was air. Within me those powers turned to water, but maybe I can reach into those translucent memories of my family and find a way to tap into those powers.

I thrust my hands out at my sides and tilt back my head. My mother loved the earth. She loved gardening. She loved nature and trees and dirt and water. "Water and earth," she'd say to me when we planted roses. "We're stronger together."

I close my eyes, and I imagine water. But not water from above, water from below. I imagine the water heaving deep beneath my feet, underground below the rock of the earth. I feel the water surging and the familiar shiver over my skin. The ground beneath me starts to rumble.

I must look like a crazy witch summoning Lucifer, but all I think of is earth and water. I think of wind whipping around my ears so hard I feel like I might take off. I think of my father and how he used to spin me around and around so fast I couldn't hear. And how he'd laugh when I was younger and was able to levitate us just a little bit off the ground. I imagine myself fused to the earth beneath my feet. I imagine my face being blasted with air the way it is when I fly the skies as fast as I can.

Above me I sense the clouds darken the clear night sky and feel the tremble of thunder rolling in. A snap of lightning cracks over my head and the sky opens.

Beneath my feet the cement floor cracks and the raw earth breaths through. My heartbeat quickens with the sense of the rushing water churning up from beneath my feet. I inhale the air; I ground myself in the earth. I reach out for my mother and father.

In one loud burst, water erupts from the cracks in the ground and rockets into the sky. I keep control as best I can, contorting the water into thick ribbons that circle around me.

Blaze's fire is swelling, but my water is fiercer than flame. I clench my fists and contort the water into a roiling wave that swells and breaks over Blaze knocking him onto his back and into a gap splintered in the floor.

Blaze's flames fizzle away to nothing as my waves calm. I look and see Gran appearing brighter. Blaze is on his back gasping for air. I release my fist and the water around him begins to soak back into the ground. He props himself up onto his elbows, but he doesn't move to stand.

I'm panting. My heart feels ready to pop out of my chest.

I wade through my receding ankle-deep water towards Blaze.

"You ruin everything!" he splutters at me. "You took everything!"

"No, I didn't," I tell him. "I chose a different way. I chose to live with my grief, not be consumed by it.

"But we killed our parents!"

"It was an accident." It took me a long time to finally realise that, but I know it now. We were kids playing with burgeoning powers. We didn't know what we could do. I drowned our mother; Blaze fried our father. We thought they'd be fine.

Blaze lets out a languid laugh and lies back on the ground.

I shrug down at him. "What's your plan?"

"I'll kill her, then I'll kill you." Then he gives me a sad smile. "Then I'll kill myself. Then we'll all be done. Raines run dry."

I shake my head down at him. He knows he can't kill me. We're twins, our powers were created together and won't let one of us destroy the other. My brother knows this. He's grown more delusional than I realised. "It doesn't have to be this way," I tell him.

"With all I've done?" he scoffs. "This city hates me. Blaze bad, Rainsong good. It's a cliché good versus evil superhero standoff, and I can't win."

I reach my hand down to him to help him stand up. "We can change that."

"We can't." He looks to Gran and then back to me. "But maybe you can."

He clasps his hands together and ignites a furious flame that surrounds him.

Us Raines have our own personal kryptonite. We can destroy ourselves with the powers that make us superheroes. But it only works once our willpower is well and truly gone. And as I watch my brother burn within his own flames, I know his choice has been made. He lets out a scream of pain that has nothing to do with the fire. When we were kids he told me his flames tickled like feathers. My water won't extinguish him now. Siblings can't destroy each other, and we also can't save each other. Superpowers are for the greater good, and mine won't keep my brother from killing himself. Blaze's roar fades and the fireball that engulfed him extinguishes and the air takes the smoke away.

The ropes holding Gran come apart easy enough, and she even lets me help her walk down the ramp away from the pyre.

"I'll fly us home," I tell her.

"My car is still at the market," she says. "The shopping's still in it. He got me as I was about to drive home."

"I'll go back and get it after I drop you home."

Gran shakes her head. "I have food in the car. We'll go now."

I'm surprised she's so willing to let me fly her around, she usually complains it makes her nauseous and dizzy. I normally maintain that's because of her smoking but, after what just happened, I'm not going to start an argument with her.

I hold out my hand to her and, without flinching, she takes it. Her skin is surprisingly soft. I'm not sure when it last was that we held hands. We used to do it all the time, me on her one side and Blaze on her other. She was always the gruff, hardened woman I knew as Gran, but she used to have a softness in her when it came to me and my brother.

I thought it was long gone, but maybe it was just dormant. Hidden behind a thick veil of grief for my mother. Her daughter.

The storm is still circling and I try to keep Gran close as I fly us to the market. I don't want her to get a chill. When we arrive at the parking lot, Gran's station wagon is the only car left in the lot. I land us down right next to it. Even just from our little flight, she's looking a little pale.

Gran stops and finds her car keys in the pocket of her cardigan. "You drive."

I go to open the passenger's door for her, expecting her to bat my hands away, but for the first time in forever she's quiet and allows me to help her.

The engine takes a couple of tries but it turns over and I drive us out of the parking lot. My heart is hammering. My hands instinctively turn the wheel and shift the gearstick. My head hurts, and I can't stop clenching my teeth. My mind is racing, then I realise I'm searching. Searching for Blaze's voice. A voice I never thought I would miss.

"Are you hungry?" Gran asks me.

I turn right onto the street and try to push Blaze from my mind. It's strange, because I'm not pushing his voice out of my head like before. I'm pushing out memories of us as kids. Playing games with our powers, him making flames and me washing them out. Reading stories to each other. I don't want those memories, but he's solid where my parents are translucent, and I can't not see my brother in my mind. "I could eat," I manage to say to Gran.

"I bought a lasagne," she wipes a black ash smudge from her cheek. Or maybe it's a tear.

"I'll cook." Again, I wait for her to argue, to say she's more than capable of cooking a meal, but she doesn't. I thought Gran must be so familiar with grief that she had just gotten used to it, but I'm beginning to see losing Blaze hasn't only affected me.

"I'll make a salad," she says. Her voice is quiet.

"Sounds good," I check my rearview mirror and notice the shopping bags in the backseat. I can see a bottle sticking out of one bag. A whiskey bottle. My brand. So much for me thinking I was keeping my habit hidden.

"You couldn't have saved your brother, Annie," she says after a moment.

We drive the rest of the way in silence. At some point, I feel the almost forgotten warmth of Gran's hand clasping over mine.

***

Wide Open Spaces

by Joshua L. Shioshita
United States

It was brutally cold that December when I went home for Christmas break. There hadn't been a lot of snowfall that winter, but the inches that had accumulated refused to go away. The frigid cold froze what little had fallen into a permanent layer of sharp, biting, bitter white. When you walked across it, your feet made no indentation. It was that rigid. Here and there the limp, lifeless tops of prairie grass clumps pierced the permafrost layer like wispy strands of thinning hair, and the pitch-black skeletons of trees stood naked against the graying sky creating a dismally dead landscape.

I always forgot just how flat Bent Ford was, and how spread out everything could be in the great, open wideness of the world. It was funny. The rest of the nation seemed to have this concept of Colorado being nothing but towering peaks, snowy vistas, and nonstop skiing. They didn't realize that a large portion of the state was just as flat and nondescript as Kansas was always accused of being. It was actually kind of annoying, to be honest. The number one question I was asked by out-of-staters when they learned I was a native was, do you ski? As if that was the only pastime available to someone from the Centennial State. My answer was always the same. No.

It was a definite shock at first, coming back. Schooling in the big city of Auraria had desensitized me to the cramped, claustrophobic spaces and packed, city blocks of urban living I currently called home. I found the unflinching emptiness of my hometown overwhelming, overwhelming to the point of terrifying. It was like I was suddenly agoraphobic. The silence, the wide open spaces, they triggered spontaneous, intense, panic attacks that left me short of breath and light of head. It made no sense to my conscious brain but was

153

completely devastating to some more primal aspect of my id. That place made me feel adrift, adrift in a vacuum of bleak wilderness.

Even my house, or should I say my parents' house since I didn't live there anymore, even it felt strangely empty and depressing. I remembered it being so full of life and noise growing up, especially during the holidays, but now it just felt sad and vacant. The warm festive atmosphere must have been for show, for me growing up, and once I was gone the need for forced cheer dissipated. Now all that remained was a sort of reverse empty nest syndrome, and I didn't like how it made me feel, not in the slightest.

*

I was ruminating on this existential melancholy one inactive afternoon a few days before Christmas, absentmindedly staring out my bedroom window—or that is to say my old bedroom window—when I spied a small figure out near the tree line that bordered our property. It was a person, a small person, and that's about all I could make out. Whoever it was had layered up for the cold, and this layering obliterated any distinguishing features leaving only a strange, humanoid cocoon hovering along the perimeter of my family's home. This figure didn't move for as long as I watched them. They just stood there, a black shape against the white frozen ground, and as I stared, an unease began to develop in my chest until I couldn't take it anymore and had to turn away, my heart pounding. When I finally glanced back, the figure was gone, and the snowy landscape was unblemished once more.

Now by this time, I had been cooped up in the house for more than a few days and was getting a touch of the cabin fever. I had been planning on heading to town for a while, to see what was new, but had put it off for a number of reasons not worth mentioning. This strange incident at the window was the final push I needed to action. Rationally I knew there was nothing to be afraid of. I was taking some innocuous incident and blowing it completely out of proportion like I always did, and besides, this wasn't the big city. This was my hometown. Nothing bad happened in my hometown. This is where I grew up as a child. It was a place of innocence and simplicity ... which I repeated to myself like a mantra as I paced back and forth in an effort to convince myself of its legitimacy. It must have worked because the next thing I knew I was heading out the front door.

Outside, the cold made my forearm ache, and I itched absentmindedly at the rim of my cast in response. I waited in my car with the engine running for a little bit, waited until the air coming out the vents was a few degrees warmer than the ambient temperature in the vehicle. It wasn't much but it was something. It at least made me feel like I wouldn't freeze to death as I began driving.

As I passed through the front gate to pull onto the main road, I glanced at the spot where the figure had been standing earlier. It was empty. There wasn't even a footprint there to mark its presence, like it never existed, like it never happened. Unnerved, I turned the opposite way toward town, then immediately slammed on my brakes.

There, standing on the left side of the dirt road next to the barbwire fence was the figure I had spotted from my window. I laughed out loud in relief. What I had imagined to be some sort of terrifying entity was in reality just a boy of about eleven. He was wearing a large winter jacket with a bulbous fuzzy hood, puffy snow pants, clunky snow boots, and large mittens. I couldn't quite make out his face through the dense layers of winter wear, but I knew exactly who he was—Clint Knapp. His family lived up the road from mine, and more than likely he was walking home from town or something. Kids around here were very independent. I could see why his presence on my parents' property had unnerved me though. His winter wardrobe did make him look like a strange, inhuman, shapeless mass. It was off-putting. The only reason I was able to identify him as Clint was from the distinctive pattern on his coat, which was dark navy blue with three neon turquoise streaks running in diagonal lines down the back. The hood had the same markings on it, and there was a distinctive gold patch on the right shoulder in the shape of an upside-down triangle.

I rolled down the window and called out, "Do you need a ride?"

Clint just stared at me, at least I guessed he was staring at me. His face was hidden in shadow. He said nothing and didn't move. I gazed at the faceless hole between the fuzz and folds of his winter coat and waited for some kind of response. I received none.

"Okay," I said, rolled up my window, and continued down the snowy road toward town. I glanced in my rearview as I drove away and watched as his lumpy shape faded into the distance. What a strange kid.

*

My melancholy still hung about me thick as smoke as I meandered down Main Street. The depression I had felt upon arriving home seemed amplified here. I gazed at the modest buildings and quaint storefronts as they drifted past my car's view. They were as familiar to me as my own neighborhood back in Auraria, yet I couldn't shake the feeling that I was a stranger here, a visitor who had gotten lost and stumbled into some half-forgotten town in some half-forgotten land. It was a weird feeling, such familiarity mixed with such separateness.

When I spied the flat outline of Kelly's Supermarket on the corner of Maple and Main, sitting there where it always had been and probably always would be, my spirits lifted. I had so many fond memories of that old store, so many. I remembered how I would wait at the magazine rack near the checkout as my mother did her shopping. I would flip through fashion magazines, admiring how beautiful the women on the covers were and imagining how exotic the world outside my small town must be. Once or twice my mother actually bought me an issue. Those were magical moments, though for the life of me I could not remember what I did with the magazines when I returned home. Probably forgot about them. Who knows.

Kelly's was the only grocery store in Bent Ford. I always imagined it must have been named after some famous founding family who had built the business up from scratch when the town was newborn, but had no real proof to support such a claim and had never questioned it beyond this superficial whimsy. It seemed so big when I was growing up. I wondered how it would look now.

As I started to walk through the automatic door, the mechanism stuck for a moment and I almost crashed right into the glass. The thing seemed to judder hesitantly before continuing its slow angle inward, letting me pass. Kelly's was the only place in town with automatic doors like these, though it was obvious they hadn't been kept up in the time since I had been gone. When I was a kid I thought they were the coolest thing, like being in the future. Now they just seemed flimsy and antiquated. When I entered safely, I glanced to my left and smiled at the old, familiar bubble machine next to the exit. There were two machines actually. One sold a handful of stale Chiclets gum and the other some random, cheap plastic toy, temporary tattoo, or collection of stickers. It was constantly changing. When I was a kid the Chiclets cost a nickel and the toys a dime. Now the machines advertised it took the dime to get the gum and a full quarter to get the trinkets. My mother always thought they were a waste of money. I had to admit, I agreed with her now.

The first thing I really noticed upon entering was the smell. It was hard to describe but immediately recognizable, a sort of musty, greasy, dull odor. I knew that smell intimately, even more so than my brain recognized what I was seeing visually. Yet the odor wasn't so much triggering any specific memory in my head as it was triggering a strange sense of emotional vertigo in my chest. I took a deep breath in and let it wash over me. This was the smell of childhood.

Overall, the interior of the store didn't seem that much different from how I remembered it in my head, no big changes or renovations. That made me happy. I glanced down the few aisles there were looking for chips or some other, similarly junky food to get me through the next couple of cold days. The store was definitely not as big as I had thought. It was quite small actually, and it didn't take me long to find what I was looking for. Once my scavenge was complete, I headed to the front, my arms heavy with cans of pop and crinkly bags of salty goodness.

I was gazing at the magazine rack next to the checkout, a smile on my face, lost in memory, when someone called out my name.

"Holly? Holly, is that you?"

I stared at the pleasant face looking at me questioningly from the other side of the register, dumbstruck, my brain frantically trying to play catch up. I was caught off guard and had to stop myself from immediately going on the defensive. Then, like a lightbulb, it clicked.

"Maggie Blevins?" I said.

"Wow, yes, I can't believe it's you. You're in town? I wasn't sure it was you for a second but ... wow."

"Yeah, I'm here for the holidays," I replied.

"Really? Are you ..."

"How have you been?" I blurted out. I didn't mean to cut her off in that moment, but I got nervous. I went to school with Maggie. In fact, she had been one of my best friends growing up. She still had that bright red face and sunny blonde hair that I remembered as a kid. I wasn't expecting to run into her here. I thought she'd be miles away, living in some big city like New York or Los Angeles or something. That's all Maggie Blevins ever used to talk about when we were younger. I wondered what happened.

Maggie seemed to hesitate a moment, collecting her thoughts before replying. I hoped she didn't think I was being weird or anything. I wasn't trying to be. I was just in shock, that's all.

"I'm ... good. I just, it's surprising to see you. Um, are you okay? What happened to your arm?"

She pointed at the cast that covered my left forearm. I reflexively itched at it.

"Oh, this is nothing. I got into a little car accident a few weeks ago. Still healing up," I said.

There was a grumble behind me, and I glanced back to see an old man with a basket full of vegetables and fruit waiting impatiently for us to finish. Maggie saw it too and began ringing my items up, continuing to talk as she did so.

"It's so good to see you. I can't believe it. What are you ... are you doing anything tonight? We should get together and catch up."

"Yeah, that sounds great," I said, but didn't mean it.

Maggie quickly finished bagging my groceries, and I paid in cash. She slipped me a piece of paper with her cellphone number on it as she gave me my change.

"I get off work at seven. Give me a call then, and we'll make a plan."

"Sounds great," I replied and grabbed my plastic bags filled with junk food.

As I walked out the exit, I glanced back and saw Maggie running the grumpy old man's produce through the scanner. She looked my way as well. Our eyes locked. There was a strange expression on her face. I couldn't place it, but it seemed ominous. I hurried back to my car and drove home as fast and as carefully as I could with one arm.

*

My parents' house was always cold. I don't think they ever turned the heat on. Probably to save money. They did keep a fire stoked in the den, though, making it the warmest room in the entire house. This was where I found myself that evening, in the den, sitting in front of the crackling fire, munching on salty potato chips, and sipping on bubbly pop. As I gorged myself, I mulled over Maggie's invitation. Seeing her at the store had thrown me off kilter, mostly due to the look she had given me as I left, like something was wrong. Anticipatory dread had wormed its way into my breast and refused to leave. I hated it. I even entertained the idea of bailing on her, but I couldn't. This was why I was here, right? To catch up with old friends? To get back in touch with my roots? I was an adult, dammit, and so I gave her a call at 7:05 p.m., waiting long enough to not seem desperate but not so long as to seem uninterested.

Maggie wanted to meet up at a place called Scratch's Pub. I vaguely remembered where it was, or at least I thought I did. I knew where a bar was anyway. There were only two of them in Bent Ford, so I had a fifty-fifty chance it would be the right one. I really wasn't much of a drinker, so the idea of spending the evening in a smelly watering hole was not all that enticing to me, and it did nothing to alleviate my already buzzing nerves. It was a struggle not to conjure up some sort of flimsy, last-minute excuse to get out of the whole affair, and instead I found myself agreeing to meet her there at 8:30 p.m.

I spent the next hour in my room getting ready. I put on my cutest, warmest outfit. I didn't know why I cared so much about my appearance, but I did. It was like I was going out on a date, which was strange. I was just meeting up with an old friend. Why did I feel so awkward about it? Why did I feel like I was going to be judged?

As I ran a brush through my hair, I happened to glance out my old bedroom window again. It was dark now, but the moon was full and it gazed down upon the white, snowy landscape with its large, luminous face. It looked like a scene from a Christmas card. I started to smile, but my magical reverie was interrupted abruptly when I noticed the pitch-black, lumpy form of Clint Knapp standing motionless in the driveway. He was no longer hovering at the periphery but was now on the actual property, and he appeared to be staring directly at my window.

I felt a lump rise in my throat and a ghostly pressure push down upon my chest. Maybe it was because I knew who he was now and his presence was no longer unfamiliar to me, or maybe it was because I was just fed up with his creepy behavior. Either way I ran down the stairs in a flurry and flung open the front door ready to berate the boy with all manner of profanity I could muster.

When I stepped onto the porch, though, ready to unleash fury, I was shocked to find Clint had already run off. He must have known what was coming for him.

"What a creep," I said to the night sky and shut the door behind me as I retreated back into the safety of home to finish getting ready.

*

Scratch's Pub was exactly what I expected. The smell of cigarettes hung heavy in the air even though it had been ages since anyone was allowed to light up inside. The fumes must have permeated every fiber and grain of that cramped interior from back in the day when you could smoke wherever you pleased. It was accompanied by the slightly sweet and moldy scent of booze, which reminded me of my dad, not in a bad way, it just did. There was a country song playing quietly in the background from somewhere unseen, and a couple of older men hovering over a pitcher of beer in the far corner. Their eyes were glued to the TV hanging above the bar, and they paid me no mind as I entered.

Maggie was already there. She had changed as well. She was no longer in her frumpy clerk outfit. She was wearing a tight-fitting dress and had put her hair up in a messy bun. She stood up when she saw me and opened her arms to give me a big hug. I felt so awkward and was sure she was going to pick up on it.

"Holly, I still can't believe it's you," Maggie said as she embraced me. The smell of sharp perfume hung desperately about her in a smothering cloud.

"Um, yeah, it's good to see you too," I said. I felt the anxiety rising up in the back of my throat, but I swallowed it down and pushed through.

"Do you want something to drink?" Maggie offered as she gestured to a stool next to the one she was occupying. There was already a glass of dingy-looking white wine on a wet napkin in front of her.

"No, I'm okay. Thanks, though," I said as I sat down beside her.

Maggie gulped down the remaining wine in one fluid motion and asked the bartender for another. Then she turned to me, her eyes bright and excited.

"So how the hell have you been? What have you been up to? It's been forever."

"I've been good. Just school and work. You know, the normal stuff," I replied.

"School?" Maggie gave me a confused look, her face all scrunched up. It wasn't very attractive. "You mean like a teacher?"

"Maybe someday," I said. "How have you been? I thought you'd be out of here as soon as you graduated."

Me saying this seemed to sadden Maggie a shade, and I immediately felt a twinge of regret for blurting out such a thoughtless thing before thinking. I wasn't trying to insult her and hoped she didn't take it that way. I was just nervous. Hopefully she could sense that.

"Well, you know, I guess that's what we all thought back then, right? But life happened, kinda unexpectedly actually. For one thing I had a kid." Maggie smiled.

"Really?" I said in shock. I couldn't imagine Maggie Blevins a mother. "Recently?"

"Uh, no. Not exactly. Say, are you okay? You seem a little ... off," Maggie replied. She looked at me with a concerned expression on her face. It reminded me of my mother.

"Yeah, I'm fine. It's just been kinda weird since I got back into town. Things feel so different here now, and in such a short amount of time too."

"It just feels short, honey," Maggie replied.

"And that's not all. I had this weird thing happen. I mean ... do you remember Clint Knapp?" I asked. "He lives down the road from my house."

Maggie's brow furrowed in response.

"Of course I do," she said.

"Well, he's been loitering around my parents' property. It's starting to really creep me out. I don't know what his problem is or if he's just playing some sort of practical joke on me, but it's not cool."

"What ... what do you mean hanging around the property?"

"You know, he just shows up and kind of stands there all creepily. Doesn't say anything. I even asked him if he needed a ride today but ..."

"Wait a minute. Holly, where are you staying?" Maggie asked. That look of concern was back on her face, and that concerned me.

"I'm staying at my parents' house," I replied. "And Clint keeps showing up. Like I said, he just stands there and ..."

"No, no, no, no, no. Holly, honey, are you okay? None of what you're saying makes any sense."

"What do you mean, doesn't make any sense?" I asked. I was getting a little annoyed with Maggie's apparent confusion and was about to say just that when she abruptly took both of my hands into her own and stared me dead in the eyes.

"Your parents don't live there anymore, Holly," she said. "That old house has been abandoned for decades. You all moved away after the ... after the accident. Don't you remember?"

"What accident?" I said, a sudden sense of dread bubbling up from somewhere down deep within my soul.

Maggie squeezed my hands. She looked so sad in that moment, so sad it frightened me.

"The bus accident when we were in middle school. The one that killed ... Clint and everyone else in our grade."

"What?" I said. I could hear the words coming out of Maggie's mouth, but I couldn't understand what they meant. Was everyone in town trying to play a trick on me?

"Holly, you don't remember? When we were in sixth grade there was a field trip. It was winter, and the roads were icy. The bus rolled as it was crossing the Purgatoire River and everyone in our class was killed, everyone except you and me. I was home sick that day. You were ... you were on the bus, and when they pulled you out of the wreckage, you were in pretty bad shape but you, you recovered. At least that's what I heard. You were in a coma for a while, but then you came out of it. And when you did, your family just moved away. I haven't seen you since we were twelve years old. I can't believe I even recognized you."

"Why would you even say something like that to me?" I asked. The dread swelling up in my chest was growing. It felt like an actual physical force smashing my lungs against my heart. "I ... I was here. I graduated from here. I remember that."

"Do you?" Maggie replied. "Because no one in our class graduated. Not even me, at least not when I should have. They held me back since everyone else was ... gone. All that was left of our class was a sad, empty gap in the grades as our vacant spot moved up through the years with no living students to fill it. A constant reminder of the tragedy."

"But ... I saw Clint Knapp. He was wearing that stupid jacket he always wore when we were ... when we were kids." The dread was a crescendo, pressure seeping into my skull. My eyes felt heavy, like I could fall asleep and never wake up.

"Clint died in that bus accident," Maggie said. "He was your best friend. I can't even imagine what that was like. The two of you were inseparable. We all said you were going to get married, remember?"

"I don't remember," I mumbled, and that was the truth. I didn't remember. Any of it. All I did remember was a crash and then ... then I was here. This was my home. I was supposed to be here.

"How long ago was that?" I asked.

"That was thirty years ago," Maggie replied. She squeezed my hand again. "What happened to you? Can I call someone? Is there somebody who can come get you?"

My head felt like it was full of cotton. It began to ache, a sharp throbbing at the temple. There was a rush of heat, and my heartbeat echoed loudly from somewhere in the depths of my ear canals. I was swimming in a fog, thick as soup. Nothing felt real.

"No, I'm okay. I just need to—I just need to gather my thoughts," I replied.

"Can I drive you somewhere? Or you can come home with me, and we'll figure it out, whatever *it* is," Maggie said. She looked so concerned and so matronly. She probably made a great mother.

"I'm fine," I said, confused but adamant. "Sorry to bother you."

I rushed out of the bar and straight to my car.

*

I searched through every room of my childhood home, and every room was empty. A suitcase containing some crumpled clothes and various personal belongings sat open in the middle of my old bedroom. A few empty pop cans and some greasy chip wrappers lay scattered about the floor in the den. The embers of a recent fire sat smoldering in the fireplace, and that was it. There were no other signs of habitation. The house was derelict.

I took the suitcase down to the den and dumped the contents out upon the floor in front of the hearth. I sifted through the pile, not really knowing what it was I searched for. I didn't recognize any of the clothes or any of the belongings as being mine. It was like I was looking at a stranger's life in a stranger's house. It all felt wrong.

The headache that had started at the bar followed me home. It was now pounding mercilessly inside my skull. I wanted to find a sharp instrument so I could jab a hole into my temple thinking that would release the pressure and I would feel better. I even imagined the sound the built-up pressure would make as it rushed out of the hole. It would sound like a boiling tea kettle. That's the sound it would make.

I began to rub my temples over and over and over again. The tea kettle whistle was getting louder. As my fingers pushed against my scalp and prodded along the hairline, they encountered a scabby mass on the left side, right above my ear. There were a number of coarse, hair-like strands protruding out of this growth. It didn't hurt. In fact, it felt numb. The pain on the inside of my skull worsened, though, and I fell to the floor cradling my head in my hands.

*

I didn't know if I had fallen asleep or fallen unconscious. I didn't know how much time had passed or what day it even was. All I did know was that at some point the headache subsided, and I had dragged myself up the stairs and into my bedroom. I sat in front of the window and gazed out upon the cold, white expanse of my parents' property. I waited. Eventually I saw them. All of them, so I zipped my coat up and ran downstairs. I snuffed out the remaining embers in the fireplace and pushed the litter on the floor back against the far wall. I pulled on my big furry mittens and went to the front door. I waited.

Then the knock came, and I opened the door and stepped outside.

***

The God Portal

by William Ade
United States

Maggie had worked home hospice assignments before, but this new gig felt peculiar. She was to provide palliative care to a dying woman. The husband wanted her there for the duration, probably twenty-four hours, maybe longer. The odd part was that he had insisted on her, and was willing to pay triple rate to secure her services.

"He liked your résumé," the agency told her.

The taxi dropped her in front of a brownstone in Park Slope. The house had the look of one whose owner had long ago lost their wealth. After she rang the bell, the wooden front door opened with a protesting squeak from its hinges. The man welcoming her introduced himself as Dr. Bernard Price. He was short with a powerful-looking physique. She guessed he was in his sixties.

"Maggie Jefferson," she said, offering her hand.

Price stared at her with an intensity that she found disconcerting.

"Yes, yes," he finally said. "Please come in."

Maggie entered the hallway. Overhead a single lightbulb illuminated the vestibule. Other than a green umbrella stand in the corner, the room was empty, the floral-papered walls unadorned.

"Please join me," the man said, walking into a small room off the entrance.

Maggie followed and, as instructed by Price, sat in the one chair in the room. The only other furnishing was a video unit atop a cart. She wondered what those people spent their money on. It sure wasn't interior decorating.

"Miss Jefferson, let's begin," Price said. "I'm not sure how long my wife will be available."

Maggie frowned. In all her experience with families of dying people, she'd never heard anyone's death referred to as being *unavailable*.

"I do have a question before you start," she said.

The man's eyebrows arched in the middle of his forehead. Maggie suspected he wasn't used to being interrupted.

"Yes."

"Why did you insist on me?"

Price slowly smiled, revealing a crooked front tooth. "You were the perfect candidate. No one else had a nursing degree *and* a science background."

Maggie's mouth turned up at the corners. How ironic, she thought. Her adoptive mother, Momma Simone, had been unhappy when she enrolled in nursing school soon after earning her biology degree. They had argued bitterly, but Maggie did what she thought she had to do. The job market was terrible. Science teachers were unemployed. Nurses were in high demand.

"Your stubbornness is going to rise up and bite you someday," Momma Simone told her.

Papi, her adoptive father, enjoyed watching Maggie stand up to his wife. "A girl has to have some spunk," he'd say, "if she's going to survive this life."

God, she missed them both. Ten years since their passing.

Maggie heard Price take in a breath to restart his introduction.

"It's not clear to me," she said, unconcerned about again breaking into the doctor's prologue. "Why is that combination important?"

Price stared at her as if musing whether she'd work out at all. He dropped his head before sighing. "Let me give you some background and maybe you'll understand why I selected you."

He closed his eyes as he intertwined his fingers. Maggie imagined he'd given this lecture many times before.

"Until 1895, when you examined your hand, you saw the hint of veins underneath the skin. That year, the German physicist Röntgen worked with cathode-ray tubes, gas, and electric voltage to discover the X-ray. Then he built a device allowing people to see *beneath* their skin."

Maggie nodded, wondering how that bit of history was relevant.

"Until 1814, stars were merely twinkling lights. The glassmaker, von Fraunhofer, invented the spectroscope and discovered the secrets of refraction. Subsequent instruments gave astronomers ways of determining the characteristics of stars a million light-years away."

Wow, she thought, her instinct had been spot on. This *was* a weird assignment.

"Therefore," Price said, "our understanding of the physical world changed when an instrument was developed that measured things we never knew existed."

"Okay."

"That's what I do. I make machines that measure phenomena we can't see or feel."

Well, I'm feeling something, she thought, and it's not happy. Maybe it was best to drop her questioning and focus on the critical task at hand, addressing the needs of a dying woman.

"Perhaps I should meet your wife now."

The man grinned. "Of course, let me introduce my beloved. She has an important message for you."

Price pushed a button on the video unit, and the screen lit up. An emaciated woman appeared.

"Hello. I'm Rebecca Price." The woman's voice was raspy but firm. "Thank you for assisting me in my dying and after death."

Maggie held her breath. That was bizarre as hell, she thought. The woman was as strange as her husband. Thank God they found each other.

"Since I might be unable to communicate my wishes, I'm making this recording," Rebecca said. "My husband is embarking on unprecedented scientific inquiry. My strongest desire is to participate in his research. Please fulfill my final wishes by assisting him as he deems necessary. Thank you."

The video ended with a smiling Mrs. Price, her image frozen in zigzagging stripes. The doctor flipped off the unit and turned to Maggie. "As you can see, my wife was fully cognizant when she made that recording. I hope you'll grant her wish for a meaningful passage."

Maggie folded her arms across her chest. This gig was getting creepier every time Price opened his mouth. Her eyes shifted toward the doorway and back. It was best to know how many steps she'd need to get away if Dr. Strange made her feel too uncomfortable.

"I'll do everything to minimize your wife's suffering," Maggie said. "But I will not participate in an assisted suicide if that's what you have in mind."

Price looked horrified. "Oh no, I'd never allow something like that."

"Good. I'm glad we understand each other."

The doctor sniffed in affront, miffed at Maggie's implied characterization of his request. "Killing her would introduce an unknown variable which might ruin everything."

Maggie shuddered. That big paycheck she was getting for this job had better be worth all the bizarreness.

"Please come with me," Price said. "We must get started."

Maggie stood and followed him across the hall into a large, darkened room. A closed-up fireplace and three blacked-out casement windows suggested it might have been a living room at one time. A cut-glass chandelier hung between two supporting wood beams overhead, emitting a dusky light. The only sounds were the mesmerizing blips of a heart monitor and the swooshing of an oxygen generator. In the center of the room was a hospital bed. Maggie assumed the patient in it was Rebecca Price. Her anxiety climbed when she realized the patient was inside a body-length transparent plastic cocoon.

"I'm not familiar with that thing," she said. "What is it?"

"It's a linear electrodynamic trap," Price said.

Maggie shot him a look and stepped up to the bed, studying the woman enclosed in Price's so-called trap. She recognized Mrs. Price from the video, only now she was a shrunken shell of white flesh, her mouth agape. Maggie knew from experience that Rebecca was at the end stage of life.

"What does this device do?"

"It's a subsystem of what I call the God Portal."

Deep inside Maggie's brain, an alarm triggered. Something was very wrong here.

"I don't understand."

Price's face lit up. Maggie guessed another lecture was about to start.

"The human nervous system is a network of neurons transmitting information in the form of electrical signals. The brain alone has a hundred billion neurons, with a similar number in our nervous system tissues."

He paused and watched her, allowing her time to absorb his words. She had no patience for him mansplaining things, and she snapped, "I know that."

"Then you know those nerve impulses can be recorded."

Maggie stepped closer to the contraption, running her hand over the smooth plastic dome. "I'm guessing your instrument does that."

"Exactly," he shouted as if she were a dim student who surprisingly answered correctly. "The electrodynamic trap will gather the electrical discharges surrounding the biomass—in this case, my wife."

Maggie bit her lower lip. If there was a less sentimental man on the planet, she didn't want to meet him.

"Once the multiple receptors embedded in the trap collect the impulses, they're sent to the computing subsystem. That unit translates the electrical charges into usable data. Admittedly, it's not an elegant design," Price said with a sigh. "What's exceptional are the algorithms and programming code I created."

Maggie understood enough from the man's speech to guess what was happening. She was angry. "Don't tell me you're using your wife as a guinea pig in some experiment."

"Oh no, I'm not testing the concept on Rebecca. That would be unethical."

Price told her about the prototype testing on mice and rats. How he had progressed to the sickly cat he euthanized, as well as the two dogs, both animal shelter rejects.

"In every test, I recorded an electromagnetic event as the specimen expired and tracked the phenomena long after the animal body had stopped functioning."

Maggie shook her head. She knew enough biology and physics to push against his assumption. "Maybe what you observed was some desperate electrical arc, firing off as the nervous system died."

Price appeared irritated by her comment. "That's so obvious, why wouldn't I have tested for that possibility?"

His hostile impatience was unnerving Maggie. She had come today to nurse his dying wife, not engage in some scientific back-and-forth over something she knew nothing about.

"Maybe, Dr. Price, I'm not the right person to be here. We can call the agency and get someone different, probably within an hour."

Maggie's words stopped him cold. A look of apprehension blanketed his face. "I'm sorry," he said, mumbling like a repentant schoolboy. "I thought with your scientific training, you'd recognize the exciting opportunities of what Rebecca and I are doing."

"That looks like a bad assumption."

The doctor tossed his hands in the air and turned away from her. "Jefferson, you're impossible."

Then equally as sudden, he swung around to face her again. He sucked in a breath and smiled. "I'm sorry I called you by your last name. My beloved always told me I needed to be more patient with people. That not everyone could see or understand what I saw and understood."

Maggie resisted responding. This guy was a social car wreck, no doubt about it. Rebecca would have to groom him for a hundred years before he'd be fit for society. Best not engage him. She just wanted to get this over with and go home to a hot bath.

Unfortunately, Price was determined to draw her into his world.

"Let me expound upon the obvious, and I'm sure you'll want to stay," he said. "I believe our essence is part of some interconnected electromagnetic phenomenon that goes beyond our earthly existence. I intend to prove that concept by tracking the so-called soul from bodily expiry until and after entering what we call the afterlife."

"It sounds to me that you're messing with heaven and hell."

A smirk coiled around Price's face. "Heaven and hell are Judeo-Christian claptrap designed to frighten children and the feeble-minded into behaving."

"That so," Maggie said. Momma Simone sure felt different. She was a Bible-thumper of the first order, instilling in Maggie the fear of eternal damnation. It seemed to work; she had never been in trouble.

"Has anything like this been done before?" Maggie asked. "It all sounds crazy, if not immoral."

She wasn't surprised when Price's face colored and twisted with frustration. "Oh, that's insulting. My operating hypothesis is based on an exhaustive review of previous research."

Maggie shrugged, with more than a little attitude. "I wouldn't know. I'm just a nurse."

But she had to wonder. What kind of investigation was his theory actually based on, stuff done by former Nazi doctors living in Paraguay?

Price calmed himself and continued. "With my instrumentation, Rebecca will test my hypothesis by making visible what has always been hidden. History will be made with her passing."

Maggie parked her hands on her hips as she stared at the man. She wanted to slap that smugness off his face. "So why are you dragging me into this?"

Price shook his head and grinned. "I wanted a nurse here in case Rebecca needed medical intervention. And I needed someone with a scientific background who would bear witness to what I'm attempting to prove."

"I'm sorry, Dr. Price. I'll support your wife, but I'm not playing Igor to your Frankenstein." She wanted to leave. If only the money weren't so good. If only her car's transmission hadn't failed.

The man waved her off. "Don't be so quick. Let me show you how it works." He stepped to a computer console, swiveling a video display unit toward Maggie. "Once Rebecca's essence enters the electrodynamic trap, she should be able to fire off energy pulses that can be converted into letters. It's similar to how inkjet printers operate."

Maggie laughed. "So it's an electronic Ouija board."

Price's face darkened. "This is no parlor game. Rebecca will explore a realm of existence that up until now has been the domain of religion and myth. We will demonstrate the empirical existence of the afterlife."

"Why?" Maggie asked. "Why go there?"

Price refused to look at her, his fingers furiously tapping a keyboard. "To do what science always does. Free us from ignorance and superstition."

Maggie shook her head, now thoroughly revolted by the man. She'd ignore him and focus on comforting Rebecca as best as she could. When this was over, she swore to herself, she'd report this abomination to the authorities.

*

Maggie and Dr. Price shared few words over the next four hours. His attention was riveted on the instruments, while she monitored her patient's slow progression toward death. Sleepiness was beginning to overtake her. Her head was heavy and tipping into her chest when she was startled by Price suddenly appearing from behind.

"I thought you might be hungry," he said, offering up a paper plate dotted with dried fruit and crackers.

"Uh, that's okay," she said, her heart pounding in her chest from the fright. "I brought my own food."

Her refusal to dine with him failed to drive him back to his workstation.

"You know, my wife was the social person in our relationship. I always considered such exercise as bothersome."

"If you say so," Maggie muttered. He wasn't enlightening her with anything she hadn't already noticed.

Price placed the plate of food on a table next to the bed. He looked at his feet and then over at Rebecca before gazing at Maggie. She thought he wanted to say something but was uncertain how to engage in a conversation. She hoped he would give up and leave her alone.

Nope. She couldn't be so lucky.

"So I understand you're single and that your parents are deceased."

A wave of nausea rippled through Maggie's gut. How'd he know that? Who at the agency was sharing her personal information with him?

He added, "I'm guessing by what I read on your Facebook page, you don't have any siblings."

Damn her Facebook addiction.

"Yeah, but I have a serious boyfriend," she lied.

Price's eyebrows steepled in doubt. "You should update your relationship status, then." His gravelly chuckle suggested he knew she was being devious.

"Well, my neighbor Jeanne knows where I am," she said, with less of a snarl than she liked.

The doctor's face sagged. "I'm sorry, Miss Jefferson, I don't mean to alarm you."

Maggie nodded but didn't allow her muscles to relax. She was crippled by her own uncertainty. Obviously, the man didn't know how to interact with people. She could forgive that. Some folks aren't good with people. But maybe his social ineptness hid something more sinister. Her apparent unease did nothing to change the situation, however. Price stayed planted in front of her.

"I know what it's like to be alone," he said. "My beloved was the only woman who paid attention to me. I'm going to miss her terribly when she dies."

Although his words were wooden and unnatural, the tone of Price's voice seemed to be changing. To Maggie, he sounded less arrogant and more contrite. Was he sincerely opening up to her? Maybe she should show him some empathy. After all, his wife was dying. People often acted oddly in the presence of death.

"I know it must be hard," she said, "watching a loved one dying."

The man peered down at the floor. "Yes, it has been a most conflicting experience for me."

His oddly worded openness must be the best Price could do, she thought. Maybe she should build on it. As a hospice nurse, supporting the dying patient's family was part of her job.

"Your application for our services stated Rebecca was dying from advanced cervical cancer. Where was she being treated?"

Price's eyes jumped to Maggie and then to the woman lying in the enclosure. His lips squirmed, but he said nothing.

"She *was* under medical supervision, wasn't she?"

Price's eyes moistened. His right hand reached out and touched the plastic dome enclosing his wife. "Rebecca was ill for a long time before she told me. She never pursued treatment. Her death was a gift, she claimed, so I could test my God Portal on a willing and capable subject."

Maggie inflated her cheeks and slowly exhaled. Who were these people? Were they so devoid of normal human feelings that they could act this way without embarrassment? Why wasn't Price at least minimally outraged that his wife would give up her life for his pursuit of fame?

"I have to tell you, Dr. Price. You and your wife have one strange relationship."

Price didn't respond to Maggie's comment.

"Rebecca was an impatient woman." He sighed and slumped into the empty chair next to the bed. "She knew the cancer would eventually kill her, so she wanted to use it to our advantage. While she didn't mind receiving the Nobel Prize posthumously, she was damned if I was going to suffer that fate."

Maggie rubbed her hands over her eyes in a futile attempt to remove that man and his dying wife from her consciousness.

*

At about two in the morning, Rebecca Price's heart stopped and her brain function flat-lined.

"Dr. Price," Maggie called out. "Rebecca has passed."

The man jumped from his chair to the workstation and his fingers danced across the keyboard. At first, his expression was emotionless; his eyes locked on the monitor. Then he flushed, and tears snaked down his face. He kept whispering, "Oh, my beloved, my beloved."

Maggie was surprised by his tears, then repulsed. Those weren't signs of grief, driven by the loss of his wife. The man was smiling, his face radiating joy.

"Miss Jefferson," he called out. "Come see this."

Maggie closed her eyes and mumbled a profanity. That was it—she'd humor him and then she was gone. Her work was over. She'd alert the proper authorities, not trusting Price to handle the disposal of his wife's remains.

Her back ached, and her knee joints cracked as she walked across the room. Stepping up on the raised platform supporting Price's instrumentation, she peeked over his shoulder at the monitor.

"What the ..." she said in a barely audible whisper. There, on display in front of Price, letters were appearing on the screen, slowly assembling into words.

in light

"You see," Price gasped. "She's crossed over."

they here

Maggie mumbled, "Who are 'they'?"

"Who knows, maybe her deceased parents." Price's voice climbed an octave. "Hopefully she'll tell us."

A minute, then two, passed before a new word appeared.

afraid

Price groaned. "Damn, something is scaring her."

More minutes passed, and the display remained unchanged. Price stared slack-jawed at the screen, his fingers punching keys in a seemingly random manner.

"Come on, Rebecca, don't stop, please communicate with me."

Maggie stepped back. It looked to her that Dr. Price's experiment had fizzled. Whatever that was on the screen, whoever was sending those words was something she didn't care to know. You might mess with nature, she thought, but don't fool with God.

174

A rhythmic pinging sound slowly opened a beachhead in her consciousness.

"What's that?" she said. "My God, it's the heart monitor."

Maggie sprinted to the bed, unbuckling the plastic covering and pushing it aside. She was startled to see Rebecca's opened eyes, two blue crystals frantically searching for something.

"Dr. Price, Rebecca's alive."

Price thundered over to the bed. "Rebecca. Why did you come back?"

His wife's body shuddered, her anguished face rolling back and forth.

Price's voice grew loud and desperate. "What did you see? Tell me, tell me."

The woman gasped once for air before collapsing into lifelessness. Price grabbed at his wife's corpse, bellowing. "Rebecca, what happened?"

Maggie pulled the man away. "Dr. Price, stop. She's gone."

Price released his grip on the corpse and stepped back, his body going slack. Maggie scrutinized his face, wondering how he'd react, knowing that his ever faithful Rebecca was gone, never to assist him again in any form.

"I can't believe she gave up so quickly." Price sighed. "Why did you come back, Rebecca, why?"

Was that his eulogy? Maggie wondered. Was that all he had to say about his wife? What a disgusting man. She watched him wander in circles, mumbling. He was losing it, going bonkers. She looked around searching for her purse. It was time to go. There was nothing else to do here. She'd call a cab and, at this time of night, be home in less than an hour.

"I'm sorry for your loss, Dr. Price," she said. "If you need assistance arranging a funeral service, the agency can help you."

Price paused his pacing and stepped toward her, his fingers tapping his chin. "What do you think might have scared her enough to drive her back to this existence?"

Maggie huffed, her breath heavy with disgust. She didn't want to engage in another stupid speculative conversation with Price. But she couldn't resist offering an insight that popped into her mind. "Maybe she's wasn't the one terrified."

"What does that mean?" he asked.

She shrugged. "Explorers corrupt the beauty of any world they discover. Maybe those on the other side knew that. Perhaps *they* were the fearful ones."

Price's face twisted in anger. "Nonsense," he said. "We failed. I should've designed the portal to prevent her from returning."

Maggie couldn't take his behavior anymore. She spat out her last fearless words to Dr. Bernard Price. "You're crazy. I'm done here."

Before she could step away, Price reared, grasping her arm. "You can't leave. You have to help me build upon what we've learned."

"I don't think so." Maggie tried to pry the man's fingers from her arm. "Let go of me."

"No, Jefferson, we're doing historical, scientific work here, you can't walk away."

"You failed. You have to stop messing with the dead."

"No, no, no, surely you know science moves forward on failure as well as success."

"I swear, Price, I'll knock you on your ass if don't let go of my arm."

The man's eyelids fluttered in surprise, and he released his hold. Maggie dropped back a step, her eyes locked on Price's face. The bruises forming on her arm hurt, but she wouldn't rub the spot. Tears were trying to emerge from her eyes, but she refused to let them escape. That bastard wouldn't see any loss of control. Maggie Jefferson didn't bend to anyone.

The suddenness of Price's fist slamming into her face was Maggie Jefferson's last earthly fragment of awareness.

*

Bernard Price was exhausted. An hour earlier he'd knocked Maggie Jefferson out cold. After pulling Rebecca's corpse from the linear electrodynamic trap, he lifted in the unconscious nurse and strapped her to the mattress. He placed a vial of adenosine into a remotely operated IV and inserted the IV needle into the woman's vein. After securing the trap, he returned to the workstation. The doctor modified the code activating the receptor elements of the trap to ensure the flow was only one way.

No one was coming back to life this time.

The computer clock showed 3:24 in the morning. Price's lack of sleep was beginning to wear on him. The glow of the monitor was stressing his eyes and hunger was a distant ache in his gut. What to do with the women, one dead and the other about to join her never entered his thinking. He was utterly focused on the next stage of exploration.

With the touch of his finger on a key, the computer sent an electrical impulse to the IV device inside the linear electrodynamic trap. Multiple dosages of adenosine were released into Maggie Jefferson's blood system, producing serial heart blockages. She was dead thirty-eight seconds later.

*

How do you understand the unknown when it feels like nothingness? It's a dream of absolute clarity. Conversations are shared thoughts, void of accents or inflections, supplemented by a heightened feeling of anguish.

I sense you are Rebecca.

Yes.

Is this heaven or hell?

It's neither, Maggie.

Where are my parents?

They've been immersed into the One.

I don't understand.

You will, as your essence is absorbed into the universal.

Why are you still here?

To help you continue Bernard's mission.

He murdered me.

He gave you purpose, Maggie.

He sinned against me.

Sin is a corporal concept, it has no meaning here.

I can't accept that.

Focus your thoughts toward Bernard. You must share your sensations.

I don't want to be part of his perversion.

You must help him break the barrier between planes of existence.

I want justice, Rebecca.

Justice is meaningless. Please, Maggie, I'm being pulled apart.

*

The multicolored icon at the top right of the computer screen began spinning, signaling the transfer of electromagnetic charges from the body of Maggie Jefferson into the ether.

Bernard Price's exhaustion suddenly evaporated. "Excellent, she's off."

The first letter appeared on the screen, then the second, the third, and the first word became recognizable.

This ... hell

Where ... parents

Price gasped. Jefferson's transition into the afterlife had been almost instantaneous. Did time even exist there? Why would she think she was in hell? Was she communicating with other souls or were these her internal thoughts bouncing back to him?

"Be expansive, Jefferson," Price said. "Don't keep me wondering."

Additional letters, then words, formed.

understand

why ... you

murdered

Price stepped back from the monitor, unnerved. Jefferson seemed aware that he'd killed her. Had her unnatural demise altered her transition to the afterlife? Did people carry feelings of fear or anger with them after death? How much of the human memory was retained? Why would she even care?

"What's going on?" he mumbled to himself. "What does this mean?"

Price cursed the quality of the text responses. Jefferson's received words, he suspected, were scraps of longer text, like remnants of the Dead Sea Scrolls. Maybe the instrumentation wasn't sensitive enough to pick up the impulses she was emitting. But at least, Jefferson's words were arriving with higher frequency than Rebecca's had.

sinned

accept

"What does that mean?" Price asked. "She can't be *really* thinking about the concept of sin."

There had to be a logical explanation, he thought. The idea of a judgment day was ridiculous. Maybe one's religious orientation was reflected in the imagery of the deceased. Jefferson probably had a deep storage of Christian fantasies. But who or what was she communicating with?

i ... perversion

justice ... rebecca

"Rebecca," he shouted, "That's incredible."

Jefferson must be interacting with his wife. But why didn't Rebecca message him? What had happened? Oh yes, of course. She no longer could. Her second death was outside of the trap. But at least she was still there. Her essence, her understanding of what he wanted must be intact. What great luck! She could guide that obstinate woman to explore and report to him.

"Oh, my beloved," Price shouted, "We're going to do it."

*

I no longer sense Rebecca.
She has been immersed into the universe.
A warm tide is pulling on me, my disintegration beginning.
Revenge means nothing after death.
But my desire for it remains.
I don't care that the blessed and profane are the same particles.
I won't forgive.
Bernard Price.
Bernard Price.
This is your beloved.
Beware.

*

The more words that appeared on the screen, the greater Bernard Price's frustration grew. The textual bits were tantalizing clues open to any interpretation.

Longer ... rebecca

Immersed ... the

He should have anticipated that the thoughts of the dead might not transmit as efficiently as the vibration of the human vocal cords in an atmosphere. Not only would he have to fine-tune the sensitivity of his instruments, but he'd also have to coach the next traveler he sent in ways to communicate.

Pulling ... me ... disintegration

After ... death

What was Rebecca trying to tell him? Was that Jefferson who was disintegrating or her? What does "after death" mean? Was there something beyond death? Surely Rebecca could recall their many conversations about the nature of the afterlife. If she could send him a few words, she could confirm or refute any number of his arguments.

179

Had she lost her intellect? She had to be disciplined, focusing what she was experiencing through Jefferson.

desire

blessed ... profane

"That makes no sense," Price shouted. "Why would she be having such a conversation?"

The man punched the keyboard with no improvement in the quality of text he was receiving. The previous disjointed words remained quivering on the screen. What was Rebecca trying to tell him? So far she'd shown fear, curiosity, and some question about justice. Was she conversing with him, Jefferson, or something else?

Two new words appeared.

won't ... forgive

What does that mean? Who won't forgive? He wondered what absolution had to do with what Rebecca was experiencing. Was she being judged and if so, by what?

Price bent at his knees, his fatigue was now both emotional and physical. New words rapidly formed.

bernard

bernard price

"Oh my god," Price cried out, tears blinding his vision. Rebecca was directly speaking to him. She seemed to have a heightened single-mindedness. What did she want him to hear?

beloved

beware

Price's shoulders shook as an unexpected deluge of emotion overcame him. What did his beloved want him to be aware of? What had she learned about the world after death? Why was she warning him? Why was she afraid for him?

Three more words appeared on the screen.

*

The Crime Scene Investigator covered his nose and mouth with a handkerchief to block out the smell of decaying flesh, muffling his voice. "What do you make of it, Lenny?"

The detective he addressed dabbed his watering eyes with the sleeve of his jacket. "We got two deceased females, one who looks to be in her late sixties. She's over there on the floor, wrapped in a blanket. There's another female victim, early thirties, inside that damn cocoon thing. She must be the nurse the agency reported missing."

The detective pointed to the corpse hanging from a rope thrown up and over a ceiling beam. "The guy swinging by his neck is most likely Bernard Price."

"What you thinking, double murder and suicide?"

"I don't know. But that's a good guess."

"Hey, Lenny, look at this."

A street officer was standing in front of a collection of electronic equipment, waving the detective over.

"What you got?"

"Looks like a string of text messages."

The detective joined the officer. He pulled a pair of reading glasses from his vest pocket and placed them on the bridge of his nose. Bending at the waist, he read the words on the flickering screen.

bernard

bernard price

your beloved

beware

burning

for eternity

"What do you make of that?" the police officer asked.

The detective snorted. "Sounds like Bernie's beloved is burning in hell or something."

"That's some weird shit. Do you think it has anything to do with the dead women and all this computer stuff?"

Lenny looked around the room and shrugged. "Only God knows," he said, "and there's no way we're getting the Almighty to talk."

***

The Dionysos Health Spa

by Aaron J. French
United States

"Seems too New Age-y for me," Jane Russellfield said.

Shirley shook her head. "Hold on to it and maybe you'll change your mind. I'm telling you, girl, the place is magic."

Jane reread the front, then placed the pamphlet into her purse. She would take it so as not to hurt Shirley's feelings. Shirley had put on thirty pounds since her divorce, had sat at her desk gazing stupidly ahead each day, barely speaking to anyone except Jane. However, today she was wearing an expensive white dress and smiling ear to ear, all because of this *Dionysos Health Spa*.

"I'll think about it," Jane said, "but I won't promise."

"You'll go," Shirley said. "There's this fellow there, Thynantos, he's drop-dead gorgeous. He must be Greek—he's got the most beautiful eyes!"

Jane smiled politely. "I'm very happy for you, Shirley, but it doesn't sound like anything I'd be interested in. Honestly, what would I tell Max?"

She laughed. "Nothing, of course!"

"I wouldn't be comfortable with that."

She began turning her chair, but Shirley grabbed her arm. "You'll go. You won't be able to resist."

"I have work to do, Shirley," she said, shrugging free.

Shirley turned around, but as she did she muttered a determinative, "You'll go."

At five o'clock, Jane packed up her things. She saved her files, shut down the computer, and got up to leave, but Shirley intercepted her. "Promise you'll think about it?"

Jane sighed. "Shirley, you're just too much today. What's gotten

183

into you?"

She reached out and swatted Jane's purse. "You wouldn't believe me if I told you. Don't forget about the pamphlet."

"Goodbye, Shirley." She stepped around the woman and headed for the parking lot. Not twenty minutes later, she arrived at her home. Removing her coat, she placed it on a hook, then went into the kitchen for a drink of water.

Chelsea was at the table doing homework, a textbook in front of her, glass of juice by her arm. "Hi, Mom, how was work?"

"Don't ask." She got a mug out from the cupboard, filled it in the sink and drank it down. Beyond the window, backyard branches swayed in the breeze. Browns, golds, and reds. Autumn was here, and in no time Max's well-kept lawn would be littered with fallen leaves. Then the snow would come.

She turned to her daughter. "What about you, good day at school?"

"Sandy Penderson called Mrs. Finey a slut in front of the class and got sent to the office."

"Why'd she do that?"

"Because Mrs. Finey supposedly slept with, like, half the male faculty."

"Charming. Your father home yet?"

"In the study."

"Figures."

She gave Chelsea a pat on the shoulder and headed upstairs, slipping off her heels as she reached the landing. The study door was closed and a faint tapping came from inside. He always spent his afternoons writing. How anyone could work eight hours and then compose a novel was baffling. Only thing she felt like doing after work was eating dinner, drinking wine, and going to bed. But not Max. He still clutched his dream.

After this one he'll give up, she thought, entering the bedroom. *Three unpublished novels would discourage anyone, but somehow Max manages to bounce back. Not this time, though. I can tell he's putting everything into this one.*

She set her purse on the bed, grabbed a change of clothes, and went into the bathroom for a shower. When she came back out, the purse had tipped onto one side, spilling everything across the comforter.

Must've set it down too hard. As she began picking things up, her hand came across the pamphlet Shirley had given her. The picture on the front showed a mythical creature playing a set of pipes: half-man, half-goat, furry legs, two pointy horns. Below in bold black letters were the words *Dionysos Health Spa*.

"Ridiculous," she whispered. But she couldn't bring herself to throw it out. Instead she placed it on the dresser by her jewelry box and headed for the study.

After giving a knock, she opened the door. His back was to her. Books covered the walls and papers cluttered the floor, and before him on the desk sat his big black antique typewriter. She came behind him, placing her hands on his shoulders. He still smelled of the lumberyard.

"How's the writing?" she asked.

"Like you care."

"I care," she said, squeezing onto his lap. His face was stiff and blockish, eyes deep-set and brown, flecks of sawdust in his beard.

She brushed them away. "Can't you even wash the dead trees off yourself before coming in here? And when you gonna scrap this prehistoric clunker?"

He smiled and tilted away from her fingers. "I had a good idea and wanted to get it down before it escaped. And I'll join the damn technological revolution whenever I'm ready."

"You know that woman Shirley—the one I share my station with?"

"You've mentioned her. Went through a bad divorce?"

"Uh-huh. She was acting really strange. Smiling, chipper, her face made up, and she had this great dress on, too. Weird."

"It's obvious."

"What?"

"She's got a new man, probably got laid."

"I thought of that, but ... she just acted so different. Anyway, speaking of getting laid." She turned her body, straddling him best she could despite the arms of the chair, and brought his head down, hands in his hair, kisses to his mouth, trying to get her tongue in there. But when he didn't respond, she pulled away and noticed his fingers twitching nervously.

"Chelsea's downstairs," he said.

Her heart did that double-beat thing it did whenever she felt anger but suppressed it. Anger scared her because she didn't know where it came from, and she hated thinking about what might happen if she lost control.

She stood out of Max's lap. Planted both palms on his chest and shoved slightly, sending him back in his chair.

"I wasn't being serious, you ass," she said, heading out of the room.

"You'll never understand about my writing!" he called. "We have the rest of the night to be together. I only ask for a few hours."

"Fine, whatever."

"Don't you have dinner *to prepare?*" The end of his sentence rose toward a shout as she slammed the door.

She paused on the landing, hoping he'd pursue, hoping he'd take her and give her one of those apology kisses she loved so much, say he was sorry for spending so much time in that damn room without her.

But a moment later his typing recommenced. Each strike seemed to echo through the house like a blow to the head.

She went downstairs. Chelsea was gone. A letter stuck to the refrigerator informed her that her daughter was finished with her homework and had gone across the street to Margery's house.

"Great," she muttered, tossing the letter in the garbage. "You hear that?" she yelled, tilting her head toward the study. "Chelsea's not even home and you won't fuck me!"

Her cry went unanswered. The phone rang.

"Hello?"

"Jane? Shirley."

"Shirley? How'd you get my number?"

"Mr. Needleman gave it to me. I told him we were going to discuss the Reynolds account over dinner." She laughed.

"Shirley, that is unacceptable. I can't have you calling me at home. I'm hanging up now."

"Wait, I have something to tell you!"

"Better be good."

"I made you an appointment—all paid for and everything— tomorrow at noon."

She turned, faced the window, wrapping the phone cord around her wrist. "Appointment for what?"

"The Dionysos Health Spa. I got suspicious that maybe you wouldn't call yourself. So I decided to do it for you."

"That was inconsiderate, Shirley. And I won't be going to any health spa—no matter how much you pressure me. You might as well cancel."

A gruesome laugh. "Sorry, can't. Once an appointment is made, it must be kept. They'll send a car for you tomorrow at eleven. It might be a good idea to meet 'em outside or send your hubby out on some errand so he doesn't get suspicious."

"You gave them my address? How do you even know where I live?"

"Needleman again. But don't worry. You're gonna love it."

"No, Shirley, I don't—"

"Bye."

"Shirley!"

Click.

Rage welled in her throat, this time she could hardly contain it. She slammed the receiver into the cradle.

Who does this bitch think she is? Mr. Needleman and I are going to have a long *talk.*

She wrenched the refrigerator open, grabbed the bag of peppers, set them on the cutting board, fetched a knife, and started hacking. Sounds of metal against wood filled the room. She came close to nicking one of her fingers.

*

Saturday morning she awoke, rolled over, and tried to go back to sleep. But someone had opened the curtains, letting sunbeams into the room. The empty space in the bed beside her informed her that Max was already up. This set her mind in motion. It then became impossible to sleep. After a period of tossing and turning, she flung off the covers and went into the shower.

Max was probably in his study typing. Chelsea usually went to the mall with Margery on Saturday. That left her free to do whatever she wanted, maybe work in her garden for a while, or get a fresh start raking leaves—

The shower water seemed three times hotter as she remembered Shirley's phone call from yesterday. The bitch had made her a twelve o'clock appointment. What time was it?

She toweled off and went to check the clock. Just eleven, which meant she had an hour to figure out what to do. Should she ignore whoever came to pick her up? Or maybe ... fuck it, maybe she should just go.

That's stupid. Why should I do that?

Because it's paid for, came the answer. And then, a bit more sternly, *And because you have nothing left to lose.*

Frustrated, she marched down the hall to the study. If anyone could make her feel better, it was Max. She was a married woman. She didn't need health spa amenities. That was for desperate women. Like Shirley.

She tried the handle but to her surprise it didn't give; tried harder but still nothing. Inside the clattering typewriter ceased.

"What the hell?" she said, banging on the door.

Footsteps on the other side. It opened partly to reveal Max's bearded face. "Yes?"

"Since when do you lock the door?"

"Since you insulted me yesterday."

"I didn't ..." but she stopped herself. She didn't want to argue. She just wanted to spend some time with her husband.

She took a deep breath. "I'm sorry I got upset yesterday. It's just that I've been working so much and—"

"You think I haven't?"

"That's not what I mean, Max, dammit. I'm stressed out. I'm lonely."

He dropped his eyes and opened the door. "I'm sorry too. I know I get obsessive about my writing. It's just that I put so much time and effort into it—the last ten years of my life. I don't want it to be for nothing."

"I know, honey, I understand. I've put the last fifteen years of my life into this marriage, and I don't want *that* to be for nothing."

He smiled, nodding his head.

"Let's spend the whole day together," she said. "Like we used to."

His eyes dropped, his face slacked, he opened his mouth to speak but before he could she said, "I know. You have to work and this is the only time you've got. Max, I know. I know."

"I'm sorry. Just a few hours, then I'm all yours. I promise." He leaned forward to kiss her cheek, and she allowed it. Then he retreated into the study, and she turned and headed downstairs, and just as she'd suspected a note was waiting for her on the refrigerator and Chelsea was at the mall with her friends.

Good for you, honey, she thought, *go have a good time, I want you to.*

Max had brewed a fresh pot of coffee, and after pouring herself a cup, she went into the living room and stood before the window. "I'm so lonely," she whispered to the silent room. "I'm thirty-nine years old with a good job, a nice house, a daughter, and an attractive husband, but I feel totally alone."

She was about to go upstairs, lay flat on the bed and cry herself to sleep, when a sleek black limousine rolled up to the curb.

That's them.

Her blood ran cold. She glanced over her shoulder toward the landing. The study door was closed, clack-clack-clack from within.

The hell with it, she thought, setting her cup on the coffee table. *I'm not going to be afraid anymore. I can admit when I'm in serious trouble and need some help. I'm willing to try anything.*

Snagging her coat from the hook, she slipped on her sandals and quietly left through the front door. From the living room window she could be seen getting into the backseat of the limo, attended to by a man in a chauffeur's hat. A moment later, the long black car rolled away.

*

A moment later, another car came to a stop before the Russellfield house. This one not so black or so conspicuous. A pair of severe women dressed in strange clothes got out, approached the house, knocked on the door, and waited for an answer. When no one came, they knocked again. Finally, Max came plodding down the stairs, wondering where in the hell Jane had run off to.

*

Inside, the limo smelled like leather. The driver, who had introduced himself as Harold, sat up front, a short black man whose eyes occasionally found Jane's in the rearview.

"First time?" he said.

She nodded.

He chuckled. "Ain't that something. Always like seeing first-timers. I like to judge their condition going in, then see how it's changed when they come out."

She smiled, but had little to say.

"What's your name?"

"Jane. Jane Russellfield."

"And how'd you hear about us?"

"A friend."

Harold swung his head with a laugh. "Ain't friends great?"

Thinking of Shirley, Jane shrugged her shoulders. "If you say so."

The limo wound through the city streets, passing through the suburbs, then the downtown sector. Homes and buildings became increasingly less impressive.

When they entered the poorest part of town, Harold said, "Come down here much?"

She took her eyes from the window, from the miles of neglected slum rising like a tide of rubble, and shook her head.

"Can't say I blame you. Not when you got such a pretty house yourself."

His comment offended her. "May be pretty on the outside, but that doesn't mean it's pretty inside."

"No, I suppose it don't. And that's why you're sitting in this car, ain't it?"

"I don't *know* why I'm sitting in this car. I feel so lost."

Harold made a sound in his throat. "Don't you worry, pretty Miss Jane. The folks at the Dionysos Health Spa will fix you right up, guarantee it."

"It's Mrs."

"Excuse me?" He found her eyes in the mirror.

She thrust up her wedding ring and wiggled it. "*Mrs.* Jane Russellfield."

He grinned. "Sure."

They came to a long, black fence and pulled to a stop outside the gate. Harold pressed the security button, yielding a crackly voice from the speaker.

"Yes?"

"I'm arriving with your twelve o'clock," he said. Then, glancing back at her, winking, "A *Mrs.* Jane Russellfield."

"Thank you," said the intercom. "*Io Evoe.*"

"*Evoe,*" Harold replied. When the gates swung open, they drove through.

"What did that mean?" she asked as they pulled alongside a large gray building.

He glanced at her. "What's that? You mean the *Evoe*? Ain't nothing, sorta like a calling card."

He stepped from the car, came around, and opened the door, helping her out. She wished she had worn better shoes, instead of slippers.

Overcast here, with freezing winds. Everything was gray—the sky, the homes, the streets, even the trees. It was as if winter had come early.

A car door slammed and she turned to see the limo cruising away. *That's rude*, she thought. *Pleasure meeting you too, Harold.*

When she turned back, two women were coming toward her. Dressed in nurse uniforms, the kind from the fifties, starched with red edging, with those funny little hats.

They grabbed her by each arm, escorted her toward the entrance.

"What's this?" Jane demanded. "Why are you dressed like that? Is this a hospital or a health spa? I'm not sick."

"But you came to be healed," one of the nurses said.

What appeared as a crumbling wreck on the outside was a sparkling white haven within. Tile floors polished like mirrors. Walls and ceiling gleaming, stainless steel and glass panes rippling beneath halogen lights, a scent akin to strawberries and fresh yogurt.

The nurses left her, zipping away to either side and disappearing down the halls. She felt woozy and off-balance. Directly in front of her, a rounded desk jutted up from the floor, behind which sat three women.

"Yes?" one of them said. "You're the twelve o'clock, yes? Mrs.—um—" she rummaged through a stack of papers "—Jane Russellfield?"

"That's right."

"Says here Shirley Winkle drafted you." The women smiled at each other.

"What's so funny?"

"Oh, it's nothing," the middle woman said. "It's just that, well ... she can take a lot, that Miss Shirley."

The response made no sense. But before she was able to inquire, another pair of women emerged wearing plainclothes.

"*Io Evoe*," they said to the women behind the desk.

"*Evoe*," they responded.

Then the middle one, "Take Mrs. Russellfield to the prep station, please. Shirley Winkle has requested Brother Thynantos."

The plainclothes bowed their heads, then took up Jane's arms and escorted her down the hall.

"Not so rough," she complained.

The blonde on her left smirked. "I imagine you'll be singing a different tune shortly."

"What do you mean by that?"

But her question was met with silence. She was damn near dragged across the tile, doing her best to keep up, then literally thrown into a room. Once the door was shut, she felt a rush of anger and yelled, "Thanks a lot, bitches!"

She sat down on what could only be an examination table, glancing about for a magazine. But the room was mostly bare save for a purple countertop and a metal sink. After a moment a man entered wearing a white coat and a stethoscope.

"What is this place?" she asked him. "Why should I need to see a doctor for a health spa?"

He smiled. "Nothing to be alarmed about. Simple procedure is all."

"Well, you can forget about me removing my clothes."

He smiled again. "This is just to be sure you're physically and mentally able. Wouldn't want you keeling over from a heart attack."

She folded her arms. "I still don't understand what's happening."

"Don't worry. You will."

A nurse came through the door and helped the doctor perform a series of tests. He placed the stethoscope to her back and had her inhale, had her open her mouth and say *ahh.*

"Everything's fine," he said, dismissing the nurse. He then sat reverse in the chair, facing her, knees protruding. "Time for questions."

"Questions?"

"They'll go quick, I promise. Then you'll be on your way. First: How did you hear about us?"

"A friend from work named Shirley Winkle."

The ghost of a smile on his lips.

"You know her too?"

"I do. Examined her myself. She's a regular."

"Figures. Anyway, she was going on and on about this place. Saying how it had changed her life. Of course I didn't want to hear about it."

"Why not?"

She sighed, this was not a topic she wanted to explore. "No offense, but it sounded like a scam. Most of this New Age stuff sounds like malarkey to me."

"Don't you believe in magic?"

She laughed. "Of course not. Why, do you? Aren't you a doctor?"

Ignoring the question, he smiled and continued on. "So at first you didn't want to come?"

"Look," she said. "I know these places are popular with the yuppies. I'm a very grounded person. I have a job as an accountant, I don't drink or do drugs, I go to church, I'm married, and have a family—"

"And yet you're unhappy."

She stopped. Tried to think of a retort but came up dry.

The doctor smiled and rose to his feet. "I suppose that's enough," he said. "In my opinion you're more than ready to receive our services. I'm only sorry you've had to suffer for so long."

With that, he opened the door and let in the nurse on his way out. The woman pulled her off the table and led her into the hall. They walked for a while, for so long that Jane's legs were getting sore. Her mind seemed to go blank.

"How much more?"

"Not much," the woman replied.

Finally they came to a set of elevator doors. Jane glanced around but saw no one; the hall was deserted. The nurse pushed the call button, stepped back, waited. The doors parted with a *ding* and she said, "Please step in, Mrs. Russellfield."

Jane did. The nurse moved away as the doors closed behind her.

*

When they reopened, she was met with an impossibility. She stepped out, her hand pressed to her mouth, slippers squishing in moist dirt, and she thought *I must be dreaming* ...

A pinch to the forearm confirmed she was awake.

Amazing, she thought. *Absolutely amazing. I can't believe Shirley was right.*

Beyond the elevator doors spanned a magnificent forest. Maple, pine, oak, and spruce. Red and brown boughs full of leaves, thick knotty trunks, and a carpet of green grass. Blue and white birds flitting here and there. The distant drone of insects. A breeze, sweet and redolent, touching her face.

She wheeled in disbelief, but the stainless steel elevator doors were gone, replaced by red brick stonework rising high into the canopy, overgrown with fuzzy lichen.

Turning again, she padded to a nearby tree and pressed her hands to the trunk. *Real.* Not some illusion or gimmick. *Real.*

She slipped off her slippers and walked barefoot through the shady groves. Silken grass between her toes, soft earth beneath her heels. Lofty branches blocked out an unseen sun, yet the air was not cold. In fact she felt warm, and after a while she removed her sweater and hung it from a tree.

A sound came from behind her, from somewhere in the trees. A twig snapping. A rushing in the branches and leaves, a high-pitched twittering, flute-like.

She examined the forest hoping to find someone she could talk to who could confirm that this was indeed no dream. If this was a health spa, then there had to be other people around.

What she found was not another person, but a pair of eyes: yellow, slitted with red, glowing in the foliage.

She let out a gasp. Her heart palpitated. She tried to flee but her legs were unresponsive. She stood motionless as the creature uncoiled from the trees.

Not real; nothing like that could be real. It had to be a guy in a costume.

That's nothing, she told herself. *Asshole doctor sedated me. Am I asleep? I can't even tell. What's* wrong *with me?*

Tall, muscular, bearded, handsome. And naked—no, wearing pants. Were those pants?

Her eyes studied his lower half, and she giggled. Not pants, but wool, and feet like a goat. *Hooves.* She giggled again. It was the creature on the pamphlet Shirley gave her. The *satyr.*

"That's a nice trick," she said as the creature approached. He brought the pipes to his lips and played a melody—hopping suddenly, startling her, clacking his hooves together.

He began to dance.

Seems harmless, she thought. *So this must be what goes on here: men dressing up to show you a good time, like male strippers at a bachelorette party. Way to go, Shirley!*

Yet as the satyr danced closer, convincing herself of this grew to be a challenge, for the creature seemed almost *too* natural. The horns on his head too lifelike. And the coat of fur too shiny. And ... the massive phallus between his legs ... too sensual.

She wanted to be frightened. Wanted to scream and run back to the elevator. Back to her normal life. But she couldn't. So instead she laughed, swooned to the pipes, beckoned the creature to come closer.

He danced circles, skipping and twirling, lips laboring at his instrument. She could tell he liked her. And she liked him too. He was handsome in a primitive sort of way. His torso rippled with muscles; his biceps bulged.

When he had finished playing, he bowed and she applauded enthusiastically. His red eyes found hers, but she looked away. They were too intimidating, and they confirmed this was no man in a costume.

"That was wonderful," she said.

"Thank you, I wrote it for you." His voice was warm and it tickled the inside of her ears.

"Do you work here?"

He regarded her strangely. "I am Thynantos, a spirit of the forest. I've been waiting for you, Jane."

When he spoke her name, she wanted to leap into his arms. She was almost appalled for having this desire. "What are you?" she asked.

He reached out and caressed her cheek. Eyes closed, she heard him say, "I am everything you are missing in your life. I'm the before, the after, the beginning, and the end. I am the truth."

"And what is the truth?"

He brought up his other hand and cradled her face in his palms. His grip was strong, safe, enticing. Probing fingers entered her hair. She was lost to his touch, moving away from herself; the woman she thought she was was shrinking. In her place was a new woman, a woman without fear.

"The truth is that you are divine," he said. "You are the divine being, the essence of God, and yet you are ignorant. What have they done to you, my poor child? Who has made you suffer so?"

She kept her eyes closed, nudging against his hands. "They did it to me," she said, "all of them. They beat me over the head with their rules and laws, my whole life telling me what to do, how I ought to act. I don't know who I am anymore."

"Ah, but you do," the satyr replied. "I have already told you. But I will tell you again, for you are resistant. You are the divine being, the essence of the living God, the true source of the divine. Do not fight against it; let yourself go. Are you listening, my child?"

She sucked in a sob as tears filled her eyes. "It sounds so wonderful."

The satyr chuckled. "You already have it, and I will show you."

Hands groped her body, and she permitted them. Arms raised, her shirt was removed, and then her bottoms. Her bra unclipped, panties slid down her thighs, and she stood fully naked, the air tickling her flesh.

He pressed closer, his soft fine hair sending shockwaves through her body. She had never experienced anything so strange. It felt like she was being wrapped in an expensive rug.

His hard phallus dug into her stomach, and she could no longer contain herself. Her need was strong. Blind to the world, she cast her arms around his shoulders and pulled him down, guided him in. They made love in the grass with the other creatures of the forest dancing around them.

*

In a cold empty space she awoke, stretching her arms to investigate the grass beside her. The satyr was gone.

She lay naked staring up at the trees, gently stroking the hair between her legs. She could still feel his skin, his body, his touch.

This is how I always want to feel, she thought.

When she stood, she looked for her clothes, but they'd been taken. Good thing she didn't need them anymore, not in the forest with the animals and trees. Here nothing wore clothes.

She did wish Thynantos would come back. Why had he run off? Had she done something wrong?

She searched the maze of trunks calling his name, but he didn't come, and she worried he had abandoned her. Because she was different now—was born-again and renewed—she couldn't stand the thought of being alone. She wanted to share herself with everyone.

As night fell, she heard music in the distance, heard flutes and raised voices and boisterous laughter. She smelled roasting meat and glimpsed flickering torches.

Thinking Thynantos might be there, she followed the merry piping to a clearing where a large bonfire burned, from which smoke columns rose through the canopy. Stars twinkled above the branches; a bulbous moon peered down. Everywhere were bright torches stuck in the ground.

She found herself among a large group of people, embarrassed of

196

her nakedness until she realized everyone else was naked too.

Women danced around the bonfire, leaping, their breasts heaving in the torchlight. They carried strange pelts like deerskins, which they twirled as they moved. They wielded long wood staffs with white flowers sprouting from the tops.

A number of satyrs crouched in the background, beating drums, playing pipes. Hoping to find her lover, she made her way among them.

She didn't get far before a large woman with wild hair broke from the crowd and accosted her. Jane was frightened until she realized who she was.

"Shirley?" she said.

Her coworker nodded. "*Io Evoe*. I'm so glad you came, Jane. Isn't this wonderful? Did you meet Thynantos yet?"

Her heart fluttered at his name. "I did. In fact I'm looking for him now. Have you seen him?"

Shirley eyed her suspiciously. "I'll bet you are. Isn't he marvelous? I've had him more times than I can count."

"You—" she began, jealousy flooding her. Her cheeks turned red. She suddenly wanted to hit the plump woman in the face.

Shirley's expression changed. "Don't look at me like that. Everything is shared. That's how we keep ourselves separate from the outside world. Once we start acting like them, this place will be ruined."

Fuck you, you fat bitch, she wanted to say, but ventured, "Yes, you're right, I'm sorry. It's just that I miss him so much. Are you sure you don't know where to find him? I thought I saw a few satyrs over there."

"Oh, forget about them. There's plenty of time for that later. What you should do is focus on that angry feeling you're having instead of suppressing it."

"I thought you said—"

Shirley waved her hand. "I told you not to take it out on me, not to not have it. It's good to feel rage, anger, hatred; emotions are what set us apart from men. To be completely upset and immersed in anger—that's womanhood! Come on, I'll show you."

Shirley led her through the swarm of smeared naked bodies. They came to the satyrs and Jane searched for Thynantos but didn't find him. The goat-men crouched serenely in the shadows, watching the parade of female flesh, smoking elongated pipes.

They came to a shoddy wood crucifix poking out of the ground. Lashed to the beams was a naked man with a black cloth sack over his head. Sweat glistened on his body. A clump of leaves covered his genitals.

"Take it out on *him*," Shirley explained.

Jane looked the man up and down. There was something vaguely familiar about him. To Shirley, she said, "What am I supposed to do?"

The woman smiled and held up a large knife. She suddenly slapped Jane across the face, hard, splitting her lip. Spittle flew from her mouth.

Jane recoiled, her heartbeat double-fluttering. An army of anger marched along her veins. "You bitch!" she shrieked, preparing to strike the fat woman.

But Shirley thrust the knife into her hand. "On him! Use that fire within you and plunge it into his guts!"

Before she could stop herself, she turned to the man on the crucifix and stabbed him in the stomach. Buried the blade to the hilt. His skin tore away. Blood pumped down his legs, dousing the patch of leaves, as his body gave a quick jerk.

Then he began to scream.

Shirley was there to wrench the knife and open the wound deeper. She dug fingers inside the massive hole, causing his intestines to drop out.

"Oh my God!" Jane cried. "What have I done? I killed him! I—"

Shirley whirled and slapped her again, leaving a bloody handprint on her face. "Shut up, you bitch! You did what you were supposed to do. Feel the fire within, let go. Embrace the divine being. You are God and God kills his people without hesitation. Feed your soul, for it hungers!"

Shirley bent forward and bit the man's flesh; immediately he began to squirm, to scream.

"What are you doing?" Jane yelled.

Shirley glanced over her shoulder, jaw smeared with blood. "Feeding the divine being, you wench! Feeding Dionysos, ruler of all! *Io! Io! Evoe!*"

Jane fell to her knees as a group of crazed women answered Shirley's cry. A few came over, one of them looking down at Jane and asking, "Is this her?"

Shirley turned from her meal. "Yes, that's Jane. Told you I'd find someone."

"What's wrong with her?"

"Give her a break, it's her first time. Like I already told you, she'll make a fine addition."

This new woman leaned toward Jane and pulled her up by the hair.

"Let me go!" Jane cried.

"Show her," the woman said.

Shirley nodded, and with a whistle, summoned a satyr from over in the shadows. When he arrived, he boosted the fat woman up to reach the crucifix. She then removed the black sack from the man's head.

"Look," the woman said, yanking on Jane's hair. "Look what you've done to the one you love."

Even when she saw Max's face staring down at her, saw his mouth open, saw his severed tongue fall out, Jane could hardly register it. This was all happening to someone else, not to her, for she was asleep, dreaming; she had escaped to the farthest corners of her mind.

"He's dying, you killed him," the woman said.

Shirley laughed wickedly, climbed off the satyr, continuing to feed on Max's innards.

Jane was pulled closer, the grip on her hair tightening, her face brought before the ragged wound on Max's stomach. The woman said, "There is no going back from here. You know that, don't you? There's only forward. You might as well feed the divine being inside you: it hungers and it's suffered for so long. Feed it!"

Somewhere in the darkness of her mind, Jane somehow knew this was true. There was no going back, no hope of reclaiming her old life. And yet now that she had crossed the line, she was glad to be rid of her former, meaningless existence.

She bent forward, assisted by the clawlike hand gripping her hair, and for the first time—the first time in her shallow, petty, uneventful life—she fed the divine being within.

***

Two Months with the Lie-Smith

by Joachim Heijndermans
Netherlands

"How's the pasta?" Bal asked Aileen.

"It's great. What did you do with it? Is that basil?" she asked.

"Yeah, with only a spoonful of olive oil."

"This is amazing. You gotta show me how you did it."

"Really? You want me to teach you?" Bal asked, as he was all too familiar with Aileen's less-than-stellar cooking skills.

She hesitated. "Well, or maybe you can make it in front of my girlfriends. Cass and Barb won't believe it until they see it for themselves."

"It's nothing special," Bal said meekly. "Just tuna, pasta, sundried tomatoes, olive oil, basil, and a white wine sauce. Something I threw together on the fly."

"Mmm, simple, huh?" she said with a sly grin. "And where'd you get the pasta?"

"Made it this morning," he said, completely matter of fact about it. Sally, their Dachshund, sat up against his leg to beg for scraps. The little dog knew that Bal could never deny her.

Aileen smiled broadly. "You're adorable, you know that?"

Bal blushed. He did know that, in fact. He'd been told before by many, many men and women, and he loved to hear it nevertheless, he was still shy enough to feel self-conscious whenever Aileen complimented him. She made him feel young, which he really wasn't, despite his looks. She made him feel like the person he wished he could have been. Relaxed, loved, and the owner of a small apartment, a dog, and a fern in the corner, completely free from the judgmental eye of his father.

Suddenly, there were three knocks at the door. Sally ran to the door and began to jump, yip, and bark at their visitor.

"Are you expecting anyone?" Aileen asked.

"No," Bal said, as he stood up from his seat. "But I might know who it is."

"How do you know that?" she asked.

"The knock. I know that knock all too well."

Bal headed to the door. When he opened it, his suspicions were confirmed when he was greeted with the sight of his father's blood-brother in the hallway, soaked to the bone.

"Hello, kid. Can I come in?" asked Loki the Lie-Smith.

"How did you get here? And why are you wet?" Bal asked.

"Oh, it's a long story. Jory got into some trouble, and I got him out of it again. But your father isn't too happy with me right now. You know what he's like."

"Yeah, I do." No stranger to his father's infamous temper himself, he felt a twinge of pity for the man who clearly avoided the worst of it by the skin of his teeth. "C'mon in."

"Ah, bless you, kid. Really, I don't deserve this."

"No, you really don't," Bal sighed.

Loki stepped inside the apartment. Sally leaped up and pressed her tiny paws against the Lie-Smith's leg. "Who's this little fellow?" he said, endeared by the small dog, raising her up into the air. "Oh, I mean girl. Pardon. What's her name?"

"That's Sally. Try not to get her wet."

"Wouldn't dream of it, my boy."

"So what trouble did the snake get into this time? Did he bite off another hand?"

"The hand incident wasn't him. That was Fenny, my eldest. And no, it was all a huge misunderstanding."

"It usually is with you and your children."

"Hey, don't lump 'em all together," Loki grunted. "Sleipi is a good kid. Besides, your father seems very pleased with him."

"Her. Sleipnir is female," Bal corrected him.

"Really? Oh, who even keeps track anymore. It's great to see you, kid. The weather down here has done wonders for your complexion."

"Loki, I'm kind of in the middle of dinner, so—"

"Brilliant. I'm starving! Thanks."

"No, Lo—" Bal tried to stop him, but the Lie-Smith had already made his way to the dining area. He didn't even seem to take notice of

Aileen at first, only to finally spot her when he'd already stuffed two slices of Bal's garlic bread in his mouth.

"Ehm, hi?" Aileen said.

"Oh, hello. Baldr, you didn't tell me there were stragglers at the table. Can we perhaps get some privacy, blondie?"

"Wha—?" Aileen gasped.

"My boy, I'd prefer it if we could talk in private. Could we?"

"No, Loki, we cannot. Aileen was actually invited for dinner."

"You invite your servants for dinner?" he chuckled.

"Servant?" Aileen muttered.

"She's my girlfriend," Bal explained.

Loki paused, as a lump of bread still protruded from his mouth. He looked back and forth between Bal and Aileen with a dumbstruck expression. He then laughed. "Oh, oh my, how foolish of me. I must offer you my apologies, my dear. I am the son of the fire and the ice. Neither giant nor man, I am the great enigma of the Aesir. I, my dear child, am Loki."

"Hi," she said as she took his hand and shook it. "Nice to meet you. I'm Aileen. Are you a relative of Bal's?"

"Bal?" Loki chuckled. He repeated the name a few more times under his breath so to familiarize himself with its taste and tone, before patting Bal's shoulder with a heavy tap of his palm. "Ha, what a delightful little nickname, kid. Bal! Bal the Brave! Simply delightful."

Bal ignored the snipe aimed at him. He'd learned long ago that when dealing with Loki, it was best not to let him in the know when his actions or words bothered you in any way. He'd try to use it against you at some point, or worse, keep doing it until the last star vanished from the sky. Instead, he headed into the bathroom, as he knew exactly what Aileen would comment on and ask him to get in three, two, one—

"You're all wet. Bal, get him a—"

"Towel?" Bal finished, returning with three towels in hand. He threw one to Loki, while he placed the other two on a chair.

"Thanks," said the Lie-Smith, as he took his towel and wrapped it around his head like a pink fluffy turban. "You wouldn't believe what I've been through these last few weeks."

"Oh, you'd be surprised what I'll believe when it comes to you," sighed Bal.

"You got me there. I take it you're not interested in hearing how I ... got here?" he said with a pause, awkwardly skipping over the word *escaped.*

"How are you so wet?" Aileen asked. She rushed to the window and peeked outside. "Was it raining?"

"It's a long story, my dear girl. One with a killer whale pack and me forced to seduce the lead female for a month straight, swimming all around the arctic in the hunt for seals, avoiding oil tanker ships and Chinese hunters, before they finally passed by the shores and I could take my leave. Then I took a bus to Greenwich Village."

Bal pressed his face into his palms, groaning silently to himself, while Aileen looked at her boyfriend and his peculiar relative with confusion. The awkward silence was broken by the chime of the telephone. Bal picked it up without thinking twice, thus the greater his surprise when he heard a familiar deep voice, coarse and damaged by cold winds. "Hello there, lord of men," said the watchman of the rainbow bridge.

"Heimdall," Bal said, trying to sound surprised and be loud enough for Loki to hear, whose expression leaped from smug comfort to absolute terror in a nanosecond. "How are things back home? How's the bridge?" Bal asked, gesturing for Loki to calm down. The *I'll handle this* motion he'd gotten particularly good at over the years.

"Not well, lord of men. I must—"

"Listen, could you not call me *lord of men* all the time?" Bal sighed. "Bal is good enough."

"Oh, sorry. My apologies," mumbled Heimdall. "As I was saying, I must regretfully inform you that your father's blood-brother, Loki the Lie-Smith, has once again struck the Great One's ire. He is to be reported to our authority upon sight. Have you seen him in recent times?"

Bal looked at Loki, frightfully crouched behind his chair in some strange attempt to hide from the voice on the other end of the line. Loki's experiences with the guardian of the bridge had never been the most pleasant, as the all-seeing one always saw through every one of the Lie-Smith's half-truths. It was a good assumption on Heimdall's part that Loki would try and hide out with Bal, due to his reputation of never turning his back on anyone. It would've been so easy for Bal to just come clean and hand Loki over to the all-seeing one. Still, despite their troubled history, he couldn't throw the pitiful man who nearly crawled under the table to the wolves.

"Nope. Haven't seen him in years."

"Are you certain?" Heimdall asked.

"Absolutely," Bal lied again.

Silence. Bal knew the guardian stared that imposing silent stare of his that could break the truth from the tightest of lips, which was never as effective over the phone as it was in person, so Bal felt no urge to confess.

"Very well, lord of—Bal. If you should see him—"

"I'll call you right away. Promise."

"Fare thee well," Heimdall's voice boomed.

"See ya," Bal muttered. As he hung up, he and Loki exchanged looks and rolled their eyes at Heimdall's never faltering stoic state. To Bal's surprise, they even shared a laugh about it.

"Who was that?" Aileen asked.

"A friend of the family," Bal sighed.

"No friend of mine, that's for sure," Loki protested. "Thanks for covering for me."

Bal didn't reply. He sat down and sighed, forced to watch Loki continue to gorge himself with food. And as usual, like he adhered to some kind of demented schedule, the Lie-Smith only realized what he'd done after he emptied the last plate.

"Oh, I'm sorry," Loki muttered. "Did you want some?"

"Yes," Bal said. "But that's all right. You seemed hungry."

"I was. But I left none for you. How rude of me."

"Really, it's all right."

"Well, since we don't have enough for all of us, how about I cook up something?" Aileen suggested.

"Aileen, you don't have to—" Bal tried to argue.

"No buts. Put your butt back in your seat. I'm making us omelets," she said as she ran into the kitchen.

"Fierce little thing, isn't she?" Loki said, a toothpick clenched between his teeth. "I can see why you like her."

Bal recognized that look on the sky-walker's face. That hungry visage when something caught his fancy. A look that was the first sign of the oncoming storm, where all the good in Bal's life would be shred apart. But not this time. He grabbed Loki by his collar and pulled his face towards his own.

"Listen to me, trickster," Bal whispered. "You can stay here, but there will be conditions. Break any one of these, and you will regret it."

"What will you do?" scoffed the Lie-Smith. "Call your beloved daddy on me? Or better, beat me up and drag me back to the great hall yourself? I'd love to see that!"

"No. I will call up each and every man, woman, and other whom you have ever managed to piss off. We both know that is a very long list. And some of them will not abide by the laws of my father when it comes to delivering you unharmed. Heimdall is right there on top of that list, followed by some really pissed off trolls, giants, and that one guy in Copenhagen."

Loki's eye twitched, unaccustomed to Bal's harsh tone. "All right, all right," he relented. "What are your conditions?"

"One: no freeloading. You're getting a job. Doesn't matter what it is or how much it pays, you're getting one."

"What? Me, with a job? Kid, I—"

Bal continued. "Two: you do not touch or harm Aileen in any way. You will not lie with her. You will not steal from her. You'll do nothing that intentionally causes her any distress. Is that understood?"

Loki's face turned to an aghast expression. "I am shocked! Shocked that you'd think—" he began, but stopped when he noticed his words had no effect on Bal. "Oh, all right. I'll leave her alone."

"Swear it. Swear on your blood," Bal said through gritted teeth.

Loki sighed. "On the blood of my children and the blood of my own, I swear I will not touch Aileen, nor harm her, nor will I have my way with her pussy," he said.

"Crude, but all right. I believe you," Bal said. He leaned away from Loki's face and sat back in his chair.

Sally jumped up and down, begging for more food, which Loki was happy to provide in the form of strips of dried meat he revealed from inside his jacket. "Cute little thing," he said to Bal.

"My gift to Aileen for her birthday."

"And what a gift," Loki said, scratching Sally behind her ear. Aileen then ran in from the kitchen, coughing as she fled the smoke clouds.

"All right, so much for omelets," she said. "Pizza?"

"Pizza sounds lovely," Loki said with a wink and a grin.

*

"So, your uncle seems nice," Aileen said, as she prepared for bed.

"He's not my uncle. He's my dad's blood-brother. And he's not nice. He's just very good at making himself seem pleasant."

"Aren't you a bit hard on him?" Aileen asked as she crawled into bed next to a pouting Bal.

"Hard? I let him stay here. I fed him. I even lied to my father's soldier for him. He always does this. Gets into all kinds of trouble and then comes to beg at my door for me to bail him out."

"But the point is, despite everything, you let him into your home. Whatever he did, you still gave him a place to stay. He needed your help, and you gave it to him. That's what's important."

"I feel like I'm being suckered by him."

"I think you did the right thing," she said as she grazed her finger against his face. "You're cute when you pout, though."

"I'm not pouting," he argued.

"Yeah, you are," she said, as she grinned that self-assured grin that she always brandished whenever she knew she was right. Bal loved that grin. Normally his heart would be melt at the sight of it, but Loki's smug words still echoed in his mind, as did the memory of the way the Lie-Smith looked at Aileen. He needed to be vigilant around her at all times now, which would include locking their bedroom door every night, which he hated doing.

"Look, can we just talk about something other than Loki or my pout? Anything?" Aileen looked Bal in the eye and began to smile.

"What?" asked Bal.

Aileen then began to stroke his chest with her hand, while her fingertips tapped lightly against his bare skin.

"Maybe we could cuddle for a bit?" she asked. "See where it goes."

Bal smiled, but that smile quickly vanished when he remembered a vital part in dealing with their guest. "Actually, do you mind if we hold off on that for the time being?"

"Why?"

"It's Loki. You don't know what he's like. I'm not too comfortable making love while he sleeps just a few feet away."

"What, you've never done it with someone else in the next room?"

"That's not what I meant. I'm referring to Loki's reaction if he overheard us."

"Oh, come on!" Aileen exclaimed. "He can't be *that* prudish, can he?"

"Oh no, that's not what I'm worried about. I'm worried that he'll poke that nose of his into our business."

"Really? He seems so well-behaved."

Bal laughed a deep and hollow chuckle, trying his best to stay reserved and calm. "Well-behaved? He's anything but. Did I ever tell you what he pulled on my fourteenth birthday?"

"No. I thought you didn't celebrate your birthdays."

"Not anymore, I don't," Bal sighed. "My mother and father had thrown a large party together for me. They invited pretty much anyone who was someone from all the realms. As some sort of gift-slash-initiation ceremony, Loki tried to hook me up with this other young dark elf."

Aileen's eyebrow popped upward, as she wondered if Bal's story was going to go where she assumed it was. Bal continued.

"So anyway, the elf and I got along pretty well at the party. We chatted back and forth, he laughed at my jokes, he was cordial to my father. Then suddenly, he whispers in my ear about finding a private place where we can enjoy each other's company a bit more—"

"Weren't you fourteen?" Aileen asked.

"Different values and I was a horny teenager in the presence of the most beautiful man I'd seen in my life, so please don't judge."

"I'm not judging," she said, unconvincingly.

"So anyway," Bal continued. "He told me where to meet him after dinner, which, being the randy idiot I was, I did. There we were, inside the stables where all the steeds and other animals were kept when not being used. We went up this ladder where they stored hay and feed, a nice private spot out of sight from any prying eyes, which there are a lot of back home. We get comfortable and fool around for a bit when the elf pulls my pants down and begins to stroke me. I'm extremely nervous, frozen due to my own inexperience, so I don't know what to do or say."

"Aw, was he your first?" Aileen asked. She smiled while her hand grazed his cheek.

"No. And there's a reason for that. You see, as we're literally rolling around in the hay, I failed to notice something vital. But again, randy teenagers tend to overlook things."

"Like what?"

"Like the boards having their nails pried out, which created a makeshift trapdoor that I fell through, straight into a large pile of animal shit."

Aileen was stunned silent, not sure whether to laugh or show sympathy. She took the middle road by keeping her face as stoic as possible. "That must've sucked."

"That wasn't the worst of it. No, that came after I stumbled out of the stables, covered from head to toe in a mixture of horse, goat, boar, wolf, and cat shit. It turned out my elven companion waited for me just outside of the barn's entrance. He asked me why I'd suddenly vanished from the banquet and why I had shit on my face. That's when Loki, with a collection of nails between his teeth, leaped out of the barn and called for everyone to come. *"Come all, come all,"* he said. *"Come and see the son of Odin, fresh from his yearly bath in shit. Come see the smelly prince, Baldr the Brave!"* My father was furious, while my brothers laughed at me. It would be years before I would be comfortable opening up again to anyone like that again, during a time when Loki was trapped on a mountain somewhere. It was the most humiliating moment of my entire life. Around my birthday, my family still asks if I've taken my yearly bath yet."

"That must've been awful," Aileen said, still trying to hide her smirk, though she genuinely felt bad for him. "Why did he even pull a stunt like that?"

"Never ask yourself *why* he does what he does. He's Loki. We'd never understand the reasons behind his stunts if we lived until the end of time."

"But there has to be a reason why he would trick you like that. Did you do or say something to him?"

Bal shrugged. "I don't know what to tell you. Loki has just always had it out for me. If it's not pratfalls into dung, slathering me with honey to lure a bear, or murder attempts—"

"Wait, what?"

"—then it's some other stunt. And those usually irk my father, so he'll throw Loki back in some clammy cell, or worse. Eventually he forgives him, and the cycle begins all over again."

"What would your dad do if he found out you're hiding him here?"

"To us?" Bal said, trying to visualize his father's face before him. "He'd probably scream at us for a while and sic his birds on our living room couch. Then he'll buy us new cushions once he calms down and feels bad about his reaction. Loki, he'll probably punish with acid, again. My father is kind of set in his ways."

"You know, there are times I want to know more about your family. But every time you tell me a new tidbit, I want to know less."

"Believe me, I know the feeling," Bal sighed. "I'm sorry about all this, Aileen. I'm sorry that of all my relatives, he's the one you had to meet first."

"It's all right. Besides, he's only staying a week or two, right?"

"Of course," Bal said, as he desperately hoped the same. He then heard a light shuffle just outside their door.

"Is Sally in here?" he asked.

"Of course," said Aileen, pointing to the little Dachshund that laid comfortably at the foot of the bed. Bal sighed, sat up, walked to the door and swung it open to reveal a short little man crouched down before it.

"Go to sleep, Loki," he said.

"All right, all right. I'm going," Loki muttered, as he shuffled back to his makeshift bed on the living room couch.

*

The first two weeks of their guest's stay were mostly uneventful, apart from Loki leaving his undergarments on the bathroom floor and his daily raids of the fridge. But on the third week, Aileen's patience with their guest grew thin, culminating in the event that nearly broke her.

"What's the matter?" Bal asked when he came home from work to find Aileen angrily pacing. She pointed at the chair in the corner.

"Hi," said the naked young man handcuffed to the chair, shyly shrugging and embarrassed about his state of undress. Bal then noticed the pair of underpants that dangled from the ceiling fan.

"Who is this?" Bal asked.

"I'm Cole. And I swear, I had no idea Luke lied when he said this was his apartment. Should I explain again how—"

"Oh, I think Bal has a pretty good idea of what happened," Aileen said, shooting thunderbolts from her eyes.

"We should get him out of those," Bal sighed. "Where are the keys?

"Why don't we ask your uncle when he gets back from wherever the hell he is."

210

"Right, gotcha. Could we break the chair? Or get a locksmith?" Bal suggested.

"Oh no, we will not break a chair or pay someone to clean up Loki's mess," Aileen snapped. "This is on him, and he's gonna fix it."

"Again, I'd like to say how sorry and embarrassed I am about this," said Cole.

"No one's upset with *you*," Aileen grumbled, as she threw Bal another angry glance. "I can't believe he did this!"

"Really?" Bal asked.

"Actually, no, I can," she sighed. "But I'm pissed that he did!" She picked up Sally and cradled the dog in her arms, as she threw Bal another angry look. *Fix this!* her eyes said.

Bal sighed and walked to the naked young man, took hold of the handcuffs and whispered old words into it. Words that dated back to a time before the first of the Christian priests walked onto the beaches of the Northlands and credited Bal's deeds and adventures to their new human god from the south. Words that predated the mighty dwarven forges beneath the cold mountains. Words that could convince any lock to open and the strongest of spells to dissipate. And, knowing Loki, he would've needed to use them regardless whether or not they found the keys.

The handcuffs snapped open and fluttered gracefully to the ground. The young man seemed unfazed by this small miracle. No doubt Loki had practiced some of his lesser, albeit flashier, magicks to impress the locals. Bal also noticed how well-toned Cole was. Slim, tan, and no stranger to the gym; not really Loki's type at all. But that was no doubt all part of the scheme. The trickster knew exactly what Bal sought in a partner, any partner, and Cole was practically forged to fit his tastes. By all accounts, and under a less committed situation, he'd be absolutely perfect for the brave one.

Bal realized that Aileen saw his eyes wander. He knew that she didn't mind that Bal fancied both men and women. Hell, she'd been ogled by a few girls herself in the past and laughed about it. But she hated how everyone seemed to gravitate towards her boyfriend. Bal could feel Aileen's fury and fears, strong emotions he'd never felt from her until now. Those came hand in hand with the Lie-Smith, no matter how innocent his little tricks seemed. If he had to guess, it was all part of some greater scheme to drive her away. *Not this time,* he thought.

A heavy knock at the door. *Thank the world tree, a distraction*, Bal thought. He rushed over and swung it open, his eyes meeting a mountain of a chest. Bal instantly recognized it, even if the face of its owner was obscured by the door's awning. "Little brother!" roared the colossus, who needed to crouch down to enter their humble abode. "How've you been!"

"What are you doing here?" Bal gasped.

"Can't I visit the small lad I used to throw into the air for a good laugh?" the visitor boomed as he stroked his thick clubs of fingers through his red beard. "How are you?"

"I'm great. Fantastic. But seriously, what are you doing here?"

"Oh, just visiting. Having a look-see around. See if I come across anything peculiar," the giant said, winking his eye in the least subtle way possible.

"Who's this?" Aileen asked.

Bal turned and said, "Aileen, this is my half-brother, Thor."

"Oh, great. He's not—" *staying too* is what she wanted to say before Bal's widened eyes stopped her in time.

The mammoth of a man looked around, nearly scraping his head against the ceiling. One look at Aileen and the buck-naked Cole, who tried to cover himself with his hands, left him slapping his knee. "Same old Balley!" he roared. "Can't ever eat apples and pears one at a time. You randy little glutton, you!"

"Excuse me?" Aileen asked.

"I think he thinks your boyfriend wants to have a three-way—" Cole interjected.

"I do not want to have a three-way!" Bal snapped.

"I should hope not," Aileen grunted. "No offense," she grunted toward Cole.

"None taken."

"Is this a bad time?" Thor asked.

"Oh, an extraordinarily bad time," Bal groaned.

"I could come back later."

"No, please don't," Bal snapped, anxious to get rid of his half-brother. "I—uhm, I mean, maybe we can meet up elsewhere? For lunch?"

"Lunch?" Thor asked.

"It's like dinner, but in the afternoon," Bal explained.

"A third time in the day to dine? By the all-father and the many gray hairs of his beard! What will the little men think of next?"

"Little?" Cole asked.

"I think dinner would be better, brother," Bal said, as he'd hoped to move the conversation elsewhere. "How about dinner down the street. They have pizza there. You like pizza, right?"

"I don't know. Refresh my memory."

"Round flat bread and cheese baked together? Sometimes with meats on top?"

"Ah! Yes! Brilliant! Now if they could only make a decent ale!"

"Great, then we'll see you at the place down the street. Can't miss it. It has the red and white stripes plastered all over the décor. Meet you there after sundown, okay? Bye," Bal grunted, while Aileen and Cole watched the ridiculous display of Bal's attempt to move the man nearly twice his size.

"Wait, I still haven't fed and watered the boys!" Thor protested.

"Oh, you can bring them in here. We've got—" Aileen offered.

"Splendid!" Thor roared. He placed two fingers between his lips and blew. Bal had no time to protest, only able to utter the "N" part of "No", before two large goats ran up the stairs and stampeded into the apartment. Cole jumped up on the couch, while Aileen shrieked as the two animals began to feast on the fern.

"What the hell are these!" she roared out, taking off her shoe so to slap one of the animals against its head.

"My boys! The one on the left is Grinder. The right is Snarler. They're good lads!"

"They're goats! You could've mentioned—leggo of my shoe, Lamb Chop!—that you were going to unleash goats in my place!"

"Our place," Bal corrected her. The look she gave him afterward made him aware of the thin ice he treaded upon, and any further comment would indeed make it "her" place.

"You said they could come in," Thor mumbled dejected.

"And you never said they were goats!"

With a sigh, the thunder bringer took both of his steeds under his arms and headed out the door. "Will we still dine?"

"Yes! Yes, Thor. But please, get them out of here. We'll see you tonight, all right?"

"Shall I bring ales?" he asked.

"Bring a friggin' bar, but please, make haste before my girlfriend loses her cool."

"Ah, a child of the frost giants! Your tastes have changed, little brother of mine!"

Bal rolled his eyes. "Yes, now please go!"

"No farewell for the bo—" Thor began, but the door slammed in his face ended that sentence dead in its tracks.

Bal turned around, meeting the confused look of Cole and the furious sneer of Aileen. "So, uhm, that was my brother. He's a bit of a klutz, but he means well."

"Like your uncle?" Aileen snapped.

"Hey," Bal grunted. "I warned you that Loki would be a hassle."

"A hassle, yes. But you never prepared me for naked twinks—"

"Hey," Cole said, offended.

"—tied to my chair, or giant goats eating my plants. You never prepared me for that."

"Then what was I supposed to prepare you for? Him stealing from Nidhoggr, then stuffing mounds of treasure under our bed so an army of snakes would descend onto our apartment? Or having Ratatoskr sewn into our mattress? Because that's the thing with Loki; you can never prepare yourself for anything. Anything!" Bal snapped.

"Yeah, I wasn't prepared to get handcuffed to a chair," Cole said, meekly.

"Yeah, what was the point of that, eh? Feed you some eye candy?" Aileen grunted.

"What's that supposed to mean?" Bal asked.

"Oh, you know exactly what I mean," Aileen grunted. "He's obsessed with getting you into his bed."

"Eww," Cole grimaced. "That's your uncle, dude."

"He's not my uncle! And you stay quiet," Bal snapped. "Aileen, where are you getting this from?"

"From the texts he sent to you."

Bal paused. "Aileen, did you go through my phone?"

She gasped. "No, you asshole! They went to my phone because the dumbass doesn't know how to send a text. And fuck you for asking me that!"

"I should go," Cole muttered.

"Siddown!" both Bal and Aileen snapped in unison. Cole dropped down on the sofa as told, while Aileen turned around so to hide her face from her boyfriend. Bal began to calm down. He'd been down this road before, and like always, it was frustrating as all hell to deal with the fallout, aware that only way to dig them out of it was to remain calm.

He walked over to put his hands on her shoulders. "Aileen. Look at me. Loki is not lusting after me. He never has, and he never will. This is just his attempt to create a rift between us."

"Why? Does he hate me?"

"No, it's not personal. He just has it in his head that if you and I broke up because of his tricks, it would be hilarious. I don't know why. I just know it's not gonna work."

"Why not?"

"Because I love you too much," Bal said, which he realized was the most sincere thing he'd ever said to her. The room grew quiet, with all three of them frozen in place. A minute that seemed an eternity passed when the silence was broken when Aileen turned around and threw her arms around Bal's waist.

"I love you," she muttered into his chest. "I'm sorry I got angry."

"I'm sorry for my father's choice in a blood-brother. But I promise you, Loki will never come between us."

"Aw," Cole said.

Aileen laughed and wiped away a single tear. "Sorry I snapped at you, Cole."

"It's all right," said the young man. "I'd freak out if I found some naked stranger in my apartment. But could you maybe lend me some pants? The undies on the fan are the only thing Luke left behind."

"Sure," said Bal.

"Also, for the record, I wouldn't have necessarily said yes to the threesome idea, since I don't swing both ways, but you two are such a nice couple, I—"

"Kinda ruining the moment here, Cole," Aileen sighed.

"Oh, right. Sorry. I'm just saying—"

"We know what you were saying. And I think we're good on group sex for the moment."

Suddenly, the door flew open, and Loki the Lie-Smith waltzed inside. "Hey, everybody," he said, cheerfully. "Why all the long faces?"

Bal and Aileen shot their angriest looks at him, while Cole shyly waved. Sally scurried past them, her tail wagging as she ran toward Loki and begged to be picked up.

"I see you've met Cole. How've you been, my boy?"

"Can't complain," the naked man replied.

"Well, that's good. What's for dinner?" the Lie-Smith asked. He got his answer in the form of an empty pot, which once housed a nice fern, thrown by Aileen at his head.

*

It was the sixth week of Loki's stay. He'd laid low after the incident with Cole and the fern, and a mostly quiet status quo had returned. Bal and Aileen remained vigilant around Loki at all times. The added fact that they hadn't made love in all that time made their relationship feel new again. Even the slightest touch left them aching for each other. This came to a head that Friday night.

When he opened the door, Bal was greeted by the light of a hundred candles, placed all over the living room. Sally wobbled lazily past him, greeting him with a light yelp, before she walked off somewhere. Her weight had increased further since the arrival of the coconut trees, which she hid behind from time to time. Bal wondered how much their guest fed her on the side, and if Sally was the real culprit behind the constantly empty fridge.

"Aileen?" Bal called out as he walked into the apartment. "Are you home?"

"In here," her voice came from the kitchen.

"You're home early. Where's Loki?" he asked.

"He went out. Probably won't be home until tomorrow. So we've got the place to ourselves again."

"All right. Great," Bal said. He sat down on the couch carefully as not to singe his work clothes on any of the open flames.

"Hey there," said Aileen. She stood in the doorway, dressed only in her black lingerie and stockings. Bal felt his face warm up. He watched her dance around the sofa, grazing her fingers against the fabric. "Care for a drink?" she asked.

"I'd love one," Bal replied. Aileen took two wine glasses and poured a red merlot into them, handed Bal one as she took a sip from her own. Her lips caressed the edge of the glass, leaving an imprint on them. She placed her hands on Bal's lap and stroked them up and down his thighs. Her face grazed against his stomach, as she began to unbuckle his belt and unzip his pants. She unbuttoned his shirt and began to caress her hands over his chest.

"You're a wild one, tonight," Bal chuckled.

216

"Shouldn't I be?" Aileen asked as she let her tongue glide over his skin. "I want you. I've wanted you for weeks now."

"Yeah, I can see that," Bal gasped, as she pinched his erection through his pants. "I've wanted you."

"Yeah? How much?"

"You know how much," he laughed.

She stood up to sway her hips from side to side, grasping her breasts in her hands. "You like what you see?" she said in her huskiest voice.

"I do."

"What are you gonna do to me, baby? You gonna make me feel good? You gonna pleasure yourself as you watch me?"

Bal chuckled. "What would you like me to do to you?"

"Do whatever you like, baby. Pierce me with your mighty arrow," she whispered in his ear. "Take me however you want me. I'm yours."

"Are you quite done?" Bal asked in his strictest tone.

Aileen pouted. "What's the matter, baby? Not in the mood for some of this?" she said, her breasts cupped in her hands and squeezed together.

"I know it's you, so you can stop this charade," sighed Bal.

With a shrug of the shoulders and a swift pull at the scalp, Loki removed the long, blonde hair from his head, returning his face to its normal angular form. His feminine curves washed from him like snow in the warm rain. He still wore Aileen's lingerie, but with his thin, angular figure they caused him to appear as an aged *Rocky Horror Picture Show* fan in need of rehab.

"Where's Aileen?" Bal asked concernedly.

"She's fine. Overtime. She'll be home later," Loki sighed as he wiped the lipstick from his mouth. "Okay, I gotta know. How did you see through me? I've practiced my Aileen for nearly three weeks. I felt I'd gotten her down pretty well."

"Her voice and body language you mastered, I'll admit. But you giggle too much after every sentence. Also, that line about the arrow was a dead giveaway."

"I suppose you never told her about that," Loki surmised.

"Do you really think she would've let you stay at all if she knew that story?" Bal asked.

Loki shrugged. Downtrodden by his failed trick, he sat down and played with the straps of Aileen's bra, snapping against his bare skin. "Should I go and change?"

"Please do, before Aileen gets home," sighed Bal. "And destroy those garments. They smell of you now, and she'll pick up on that."

"Won't she notice that her stuff is gone?" Loki asked.

"Then you'll either conjure up some new things for her or buy them. You said you saved up some money."

Loki groaned. "But I worked so hard for that." Bal simply shot him a look that broke right through Loki's whines. "All right. I'll see what I can do." Loki sat up, undid the bra, when he suddenly chuckled warmly. "You know, you're taking this a whole lot better than most of the people back home would've. No axe to my head. No poison in my food. That's what I like about you, brave one. You don't judge."

"Oh, I judge all right. Just because I forgive does not mean I understand what goes on in that demented head of yours."

"You wound me so," Loki moaned. "And after I've been such a well-behaved guest."

"I wouldn't call eating the fridge empty the moment we leave for work being a good guest."

"Ah, but I did as promised. I did not touch Aileen in the slightest. Not a hair on her head."

It was then that Bal remembered a vital part he'd forgotten. When making pacts with the Lie-Smith, one would need to word it carefully, as Loki mastered bending the words to his own gains. Bal rushed over and swiped the blonde hair from Loki's hands to inspect it thoroughly.

Loki sighed and rolled his eyes. "Relax. I'd never pull the same stunt twice. That'd be dull. Besides, you're not as dense as half-brother Thor or as dim as that wife of his. You're too clever to fall for that old trick," Loki flattered. Despite this, Bal gave the collection of blonde strands a thorough inspection via a smell and testing its curl.

"It's human hair. Where did you get it?"

"I bought it," Loki smirked.

"You bought it?" Bal said, unconvinced.

"Okay, maybe not directly bought it. But I did pay the woman for it."

"What woman?"

"I dunno. Some woman. A blonde, obviously," Loki said, pointing at the clump of hair.

Bal sat down, sighed, and rubbed his fingers against his face. "Look, Loki. If you want to stay out of trouble or hidden from father's vengeful eyes—"

"Eye," Loki corrected him.

"Yes, eye, thank you. If you want to stay here without bringing his wrath down upon us both, you've got to make some changes. And that starts with no more raids of our fridge and maybe ..."

"Actually, I wanted to talk to you about that," Loki interrupted.

"Could you do that dressed in something else?"

"What? Does my body offend you?"

"No, but the image of Aileen's clothes with your head on top will wreak hell on my sex-drive. I want to be able to lie with her without your mug popping up in the recesses of my mind."

"Oh, sorry," Loki muttered. He rushed into the bathroom, only to reappear seconds later in a v-neck shirt and a pair of sweatpants, which Bal recognized as his. He didn't make a point of it, as it was a vast improvement over the Nordic drag version of *Chicago*. "I'll be moving out, actually," Loki said, continuing from where he left off. "I've gotten in contact with one of my kids. He's going to let me stay at his place and help me lay low for a while. I mean, hiding here was perfect, but we both know it's only a matter of time till someone from the family would come in search for me here again."

"Oh!" Bal replied, surprised by this sudden turn. "What kid? Nari? Fenris?"

"Billy. The one with the mustache. Runs a gas station in Missouri."

"Drawing a blank here."

"Hey, so was I when he called me up this morning," Loki said with a shrug. "So many kids these days. You really lose track after a while. Thank the world tree for their *book of faces*, right?"

"When will you head out?"

"Your mother's day. Sorry to jump it on you like this," he said, as he stroked his hands through his greasy hair.

Bal scoffed. "You try and seduce me in the form of my wife, and you apologize for finally leaving?"

Loki's reaction to that remark was an expression of genuine confusion. Bal lost count how many times he'd seen the Lie-Smith give him that look whenever he was confronted with the insanity of his schemes. There was something about Loki that no one from

Asgard, Jötunnheim, or Midgard could ever make sense of; his complete inability not to cock things up for the sake of a trick. As if he was compelled by some invisible force to make the lives of those around him miserable, with the small payoff of a cheap laugh and the hefty toll through the rage of Odin. Was the inevitable outcome of being chased by Thor or beaten by Heimdall or being tied to a rock even worth going through these madcap ideas? Bal doubted that Loki even knew anymore. It was just what he did, what he would always do, with only death to give him momentarily peace. His one great skill was to suck the joy from everyone around him, which included his own. It was his role in life, and he would play it regardless.

"I'll let Aileen know. At least let us make you a farewell dinner," Bal said.

"Will you be cooking?" Loki asked.

"Yes."

"Excellent."

"Loki, I think it goes without saying that I'd like it if you didn't tell Aileen of tonight."

"Of course not. I'm not an idiot. I swore I wouldn't hurt her. What kind of animal do you take me for?" he asked in a wounded tone.

"Then could you take the camera out from behind the flowers and give me the SD card inside?" Bal asked.

Loki rolled his eyes, stomped over to the flower vase in a huff, retrieved the small camera and tossed it gently to Bal.

*

"Well," Loki said, his duffel bag heaved over his shoulder. "I'm off."

"Did he have this many things when he first came here?" Aileen asked Bal.

"Don't worry," Bal assured her. "I checked."

"Ha, you two are quite the pair. I can see why she likes you, brave one," Loki said with a grin. "Still, you two have been such kind hosts to me. I didn't deserve such generosity."

"No, you really didn't," Bal sighed. He then leaned in and embraced his father's blood-brother. "You be safe out there, okay? Don't get into too much trouble."

"Do you need some money?" Aileen asked.

"No, he doesn't," Bal said sternly.

"He's right, I don't. But I really appreciate the offer and your hospitality. As a thank you, I've left a little gift for you."

"Really? That's so sweet," said Aileen. "Where is it?"

"Oh, you'll have to find it. But listen, I really must be off. Thank you again. Next time I drop by for a month or two, I'll call in ahead, okay?" Loki said, before he headed to the stairs. "Give my love to Sally."

Bal and Aileen waved the strange trickster off, as he hurried down the flight of stairs. Then suddenly, something about his guest's last words left a sensation of dread in Bal's gut. "Where is Sally anyway?" he asked.

"You know," Aileen said, suddenly realizing it herself. "I haven't seen her very much these last few weeks."

It was at that moment that Bal remembered the exact words of Loki's pledge. He swore he would not touch Aileen's pussy. Bal had totally overseen the alternate interpretation of that oath. "Oh shit!" he exclaimed, before he bolted back into the apartment.

"Bal? What's wrong?" Aileen asked.

Frantically, Bal searched throughout their apartment. He checked all the usual spots, until he found Sally in their bedroom closet.

"Oh no," he moaned, leaning against the frame of the closet door, the back of his head pressed against it. Aileen rushed beside him and gasped when she saw what whimpered at her feet.

"Oh my God! Puppies!" she squealed at the sight of her little Dachshund, who was preoccupied with cleaning her litter. "They're adorable. Oh, poor baby, I didn't know you were pregnant." It was then that the penny dropped. "How did she get pregnant? Did she get outside somehow?" She then gasped loudly. "We spayed her! Oh my God! I forgot we spayed her. Then how ... how did this even happen?"

Bal looked closer at one of the pups. Their eyes were barely open, but he could feel the fire that radiated from them. That same fire the burned within his father's horse Sleipnir; the snake, Jörmungandr; the wolf, Fenrir; the woman, Hel; and the many, many other children of the Lie-Smith. The family resemblance was, once again, uncanny.

"Loki," he muttered.

"What?" Aileen asked.

"Loki!" Baldr the brave roared. He lost his patience for the first time since Aileen could remember. With a righteous fury, Bal raced out of the apartment, bolted down the stairs, and leaped out onto the sidewalk. He frantically looked around, trying to spot the Lie-Smith in the crowds that walked up and down Eighth Street. He was gone, leaving them with a litter of dogs they couldn't afford, and they could never put up for adoption considering their parentage.

A woman bumped into his shoulder. Their collision caused her large black hat to blow off her head. Bal was quick to pick it up for her. "Sorry about that," she said shyly, as she took her hat and quickly covered up her baldness.

***

Courting Death

by Chris Dean
United States

It was a slow Saturday at the Tot Shop so Susan Patrick spent most of
the afternoon going over the ad copy for the following week. She
normally found poring over the advertisement proofs painstaking and
tedious. It was her least favorite part of managing the toy store. She
generally put it off until the last minute, usually scrambling late on
Sunday to finish. But the dreary weather kept the crowds away from
the mall that day. She was so bored that she'd pulled out the folder just
for something to do. Around four o'clock, she realized that she had
gone through the entire file and sat at her desk feeling smug.

She wanted to celebrate with a soda and decided to treat Mary
Ann to one too. Susan went up to front of the store. "What do you
want to drink?" she asked. "I'm buying."

Mary Ann looked up from the counter, "A Sprite, thanks."

The dark-haired girl was four years younger than Susan and still in
high school. Mary Ann always had a great attitude, but Susan could tell
the dull afternoon had worn her enthusiasm away. "You deserve it,"
Susan told her. "It's been a long day."

Mary Ann smiled. "I can't wait to get out of here today."

Susan agreed, "Me too. I'll be right back."

As Susan passed the mall entrances just outside the store, she
noticed a man sitting on one of the benches outside. It looked very
strange to see him sitting out there in the rain. Susan slowed down to a
stop and stared through the tinted glass. He was wearing a gray
hooded sweatshirt, sunglasses, and she could see that his clothes were
literally sopping with water. What was he doing out there like that?
Was he on drugs?

Suddenly she caught a sign of movement in the corner of her eye.
An older woman dashed across the wet sidewalk with her red coat

streaming behind her. As the woman passed the man on the bench, her coat brushed over him. The man didn't seem to notice.

Susan was about to turn away, when the woman faltered and stopped. She stumbled, sagging onto the bench next to the man. Her face looked very pale and Susan wondered what was wrong. A look of anguish covered the woman's face as she keeled sideways and slid down onto the sidewalk. Susan stared in shock.

Dashing back to the front of the toy store, Susan told Mary Ann, "Call nine-one-one! A woman just collapsed outside."

Without waiting for an answer, Susan ran through the mall back to the exit. Cold drizzle streamed down her face as she hurried to the woman's side. Kneeling, she tried to protect the prone body from the rain. The woman's face was deathly pale; Susan didn't think that she was breathing.

She wanted to do something, but Susan didn't know CPR. She was helpless. Leaning over the poor woman, Susan shielded her from the rain.

A man's voice came from behind her, "What's wrong with her?"

Susan looked up and saw a concerned face above her. She sobbed, "I don't know. I don't think she's breathing."

The man took off his raincoat and as he draped it over the poor woman lying on the sidewalk, Susan staggered to her feet. She shuffled backward as people began to gather.

There was a crowd forming. Someone was trying to feel the woman's wrist for a pulse, but they couldn't seem to find it. A tall woman wearing nothing at all but a short sleeve shirt and jeans was standing there getting drenched. Susan's clothes were soaking wet as she numbly moved back toward the mall entrance. A man was holding the door open and several people stood in the entryway. Susan pushed past them. The sound of a siren came in the distance.

That evening Susan saw on the news that the woman's name was Matilda Sinclair. She'd died of a heart attack. As she sat on the couch in her apartment staring at the TV, Susan felt like crying. The afghan did little to drive away the eerie chill that crept over her. She lay there hugging herself, trying hard not to think about that poor woman.

A month later Susan saw the man in the hooded sweatshirt again. The one that she'd seen sitting on the bench outside the mall the day Matilda Sinclair had died. Susan didn't recognize him at first, even though he was dressed the same and wearing sunglasses just like before. She was visiting her mother in the hospital and if the man hadn't spoken to her, she probably wouldn't have given him a second glance.

But as Susan passed by in the hall, the man cocked his head and said in a curious voice, "You can see me."

Susan stopped. There was something familiar about the man. "Are you talking to me?" she asked.

"How is it that you can see me?"

She was confused. "What do you mean?"

Wheels squeaked and Susan saw an orderly pushing a gurney past. She stepped back to clear the way. The bald man lying on the gurney was smiling and talking. The man with the sunglasses reached out a pale hand and brushed the man's arm as he went by. A moment later the man on the gurney ceased talking. He wheezed and gasped for air, his face turning an awful shade of gray. Alarmed, the orderly shouted something and moved quickly down the hall.

Suddenly Susan remembered the day outside the mall and she stared in horror at the man wearing the sunglasses. "What did you do to him?" she demanded. "And that woman at the mall?"

A smile appeared in the shadows under the hood. "That *was* you the other day. How on Earth can you see me?"

"What did you do?"

The man shrugged. "You know what I am or you wouldn't be asking that question. I am Death and I think you know that."

"That's impossible."

"No." A pale hand pulled the sunglasses down so a pair of dark eyes could peer over them. "You're impossible." The man moved past her and began walking away.

"Wait." Susan trailed after him. He didn't stop and when she followed him around a corner, he'd somehow disappeared. The corridor was empty and she checked the rooms nearby, but he was gone.

Susan made her way to the elevator in a daze. She convinced herself that the man with the sunglasses was a figment of her imagination. She'd been upset about her mother's operation for over a week and hadn't been sleeping well. Somehow the stress had caused her to have a hallucination. There was no other possible explanation.

The day before her mother was going to be released, Susan saw the man in the hooded sweatshirt again, outside the hospital. She was walking toward the front door when an ambulance came screeching to a halt. Two men dressed in white uniforms began wheeling their patient inside the building. The downcast looks on their faces told her that they'd arrived too late.

She stopped abruptly. Someone else was climbing out of the back of the ambulance. It was him! Wearing the same gray hooded sweatshirt and sunglasses. Dumbfounded, Susan followed him into the emergency room entrance.

The man went down the hall and entered a room on the left. Susan stopped at the door and saw a black woman covered in blood. Doctors and nurses surrounded her bed, working frantically to save her. The man with the sunglasses reached out a hand and suddenly the black woman's vital signs disappeared from the monitor above her bed. One of the doctors brought up defibrillator paddles as a nurse cried out, "Code blue!"

Susan stumbled back out into the hall. The man in the sweatshirt followed. He offered her a smile and asked, "Are you following me?"

They moved further down the hall. She asked, "Why are you doing this?"

"You're kidding, right?"

Susan implored, "They're innocent people."

The man moved faster. "You don't know how naive that sounds."

As they stopped at another room, Susan said, "You don't have to do this."

Inside the room, an old man was moaning softly. He wore a terrible mask of pain and anguish. A doctor was standing over him and a priest left the room as Susan and the man with the sunglasses entered. "Look at him!" the man with the sunglasses shouted. "He wants this. He *needs* this." He touched a spindly leg and the old man died.

Susan and the man went out into the hall again. Following him to the elevator, she asked, "But what about the people that don't want to die? The ones whose time isn't up yet?"

A frown appeared inside the shadow of the hood. "Do you think I get some perverse pleasure out of this? If I take someone it's because their time is up."

She didn't have an answer. The man behind the sunglasses was Death, but he was still a man. She struggled to comprehend.

"I'm glad I got a chance to talk to you," he said "I'd like to see you when I'm not working. But you shouldn't come with me. You'll see things you won't like."

Susan was touched. He was trying to protect her. She could tell that he was lonely and she said softly, "No. I'm coming with you."

As the elevator door opened, Death stared at her from behind the sunglasses for what seemed like a long time. He left the elevator and she followed.

In the next half hour, Death visited four other people in the hospital and each time, Susan felt herself grow more inured to the experience. She knew how terribly lonely the man behind the sunglasses must truly be and she didn't want to leave him alone.

Then, they got off the elevator on the fourth floor. The noise in front of them didn't register at first, but as they moved down the hall she asked, in a hushed whisper, "Where are we going?"

"I warned you."

She rushed in front of Death and told him, "No."

Death tried to sidestep her, but she swiftly backed up, blocking the door to the maternity ward. "No!"

Shaking his head slowly, Death reached a hand toward her.

The sound of the crying babies gave her courage and Susan said defiantly, "Go ahead!"

The hand dropped away. "You'd let me, wouldn't you?"

She nodded silently.

"Well, I won't," Death declared. "I like you. And you're the first person I've talked to in a thousand years. I can't hurt you."

"Then leave them alone."

"I thought you understood that I have a job to do."

"I can't understand *this*."

Death sighed audibly. He turned around and began walking back toward the elevators.

Was it some sort of trick? Susan followed him at a distance. When he got on the elevator she hurried behind him. He said, "You know, I'm really, really curious about you, Susan. Why can you, of all the people in the world, see me?"

He knew her name. Susan's heart skipped a beat and she felt a slick of sweat on her palms. "Maybe I'm here to help you stop," she said softly.

An abrupt laugh echoed inside the elevator. "A world without death. Think of what you're saying."

She didn't answer. Her eyes watched him step out into the hall on the sixth floor. Tiny hairs stood up on the back of her neck as she walked behind him.

Death stopped at room 614. He looked into the room and remarked casually, "She seems fine." His sunglasses glinted beneath the hood. "Maybe you should keep her company."

Her heart pounding, Susan moved past him into her mother's room. She sank into a chair as Death disappeared from the doorway.

A man came into the toy store a few days later. He had a young face and longish blond hair and Susan thought maybe he was looking for a job. She walked up to him and asked, "Can I help you."

"I wanted to apologize."

It was him! The sunglasses and sweatshirt were gone and he was wearing brown slacks and a dress shirt. He looked perfectly normal but she recognized his voice immediately. It was Death's voice. She couldn't speak. She could only gaze into the dark eyes and wonder at the humanity that she saw there. They weren't cruel at all. They were serious and sad and filled with expectation all at the same time.

"I wanted you to know," the young man said, "that I wouldn't have hurt her. Your mother. And I wanted to apologize for scaring you that way."

It was all so surrealistic. Here was Death. He'd transformed himself into a handsome young man with normal feelings and an apology on his lips. Susan's voice was soft. "I'm glad to hear that."

The man glanced around the store. "Can you get away? For lunch?"

Petra, one of the sales girls, was in the back room unpacking boxes. Susan *could* leave if she wanted to, but she hesitated. She usually ate with Petra every day and Susan had her plastic container sitting in the little fridge in her office. Her uncertainty had nothing to do with the chilled sticks of carrot and celery waiting to be eaten though. "I don't know," she said in a faltering voice. She was afraid of what the man was and what he did. But more than anything, Susan was afraid of the fact that she wanted to forget all about that and go with him.

"Please. I never get to talk to anyone." The man gave her a big smile. "Let's start this over. My name's Alexandre. Alex. I would very much appreciate your company for lunch, Susan Patrick. What do you say?"

"I can't be gone long." Susan glanced at door to the back room.

"We'll eat here in the mall. At that pizza restaurant around the corner. Do you like pizza?"

Susan began unbuttoning her work smock. "All right. But I can only leave for a half hour."

A short time later, they were sitting at one of those little tables in the food court with their slices of pizza and sodas and it was as though there was nothing strange at all about having lunch with Death. In fact, Susan found herself having a good time and she started to think that maybe she liked Alex. While sipping her soda, she studied his face. His pretty brown eyes.

Alex saw the look in her eyes and cocked his head. "Hmm?" he asked. "What are you thinking?"

"I—" Susan felt embarrassed. She said the first thing that popped into her mind." I was just wondering how you can be here. Aren't people dying?"

Alex gave her a conspiratorial look. "I can adjust time. It would be impossible to do my job otherwise."

"How long have you been ..."

"How does one become Death?" Alex laughed at her discomfort. "It wasn't by choice, I assure you. I was born in the early part of the twelfth century in Normandy. My family was poor and I was indentured to a potter and taken to live in a castle where Paris is today. It was there that I met my predecessor."

She nodded solemnly.

"It was a lot like this." Alex gestured between them. "I saw him by accident, and when I realized what he was doing, I tried to stop him. Lemieux was surprised that I could see him." Alex studied her face, then went on, "He was much older than I am now when he came to the conclusion that I was his replacement." Alex smiled. "I resisted at first. After all, who wants to become Death?"

"Why did he think you were his replacement?"

"Because I could see him. And I think he felt that it was the right time for him to be replaced. Although this job does allow one to resist the ravages of time, it doesn't make one immortal. I have aged several years since I started. I think Lemieux must have been Death for a very long time because his body was deteriorating."

"So you agreed to—"

"No," Alex corrected. "Though eventually I believed everything Lemieux told me, I wouldn't agree to take over the mantle of death. I just couldn't."

"What happened?"

"He gave me no choice. Lemieux urged me to accept the inevitability of the situation and then he simply touched his own chest and he died. I didn't accept what had happened at first. But then when I realized that nobody could see me and I saw the suffering—no one in the world was dying. I let it go on for almost a week and then I just ... I *had* to. I couldn't let people linger at death's door and suffer that way. Death is part of the natural order of things."

Susan's soda was empty. She took off the top and swirled the ice in the bottom around with her straw. "But why you?"

"I don't really know. Just a matter of chance, I suppose. A matter of timing. And since I could see Lemieux, he knew that it was fated to be." Alex stopped. "But this is different. I'm still young, this is something else entirely, you and I."

Susan looked down at the table." What do you think this is, Alex?"

He voice was soft, almost a whisper, "A different kind of fate altogether."

After lunch they took a walk outside. Susan told Alex about her two years in college and how she'd just up and decided to quit when the manager's job at the toy store became available. "I wasn't sure I wanted to be a teacher anymore and college seemed like such a chore after a while," she said. "I like working. I've been at the Tot Shop for five years and now I guess I'm stuck. I'll probably never go back to school."

"You like what you're doing. There's nothing wrong with that. College is for people who don't know what they want to do."

"Maybe you're right." Susan looked at her wristwatch. "I have to get back."

They started walking back. "I really enjoyed this," Alex said. "Can we do it again?"

She wasn't sure what to say. A part of her was completely convinced that she should thank Alex and wish him the best and never see him again. But when Susan looked at his face, into his soft brown eyes, there was no denying her attraction. After a moment, she heard herself say, "Yes."

Alex showed up at work again two days later. He was wearing an odd red shirt with three white pockets lining each side. Susan stared for a few moments. "Where did you get that?"

"You like it?"

"I'm not sure."

Alex shrugged. "It's the latest thing in Rome. Maybe I made a mistake." Then he laughed. "Well, at least you're the only one who can see how silly I look."

Susan looked at her watch. "You're too late for lunch. I get off in two hours."

"All right." Turning, Alex walked toward the mall, calling over his shoulder, "I'll see you in two hours then."

When Susan got off work, Alex was waiting outside the mall and this time he had a bouquet of carnations.

"Are those for me?" she asked shyly.

Presenting the flowers with a flourish, Alex answered, "Just to let you know how special you are."

She took the flowers. They smelled wonderful. "Then this is something special?"

"You're the first woman I've dated in a thousand years. I'd say that was special."

"Good." They began walking down the sidewalk. "I wouldn't want to get the wrong idea."

"Are you flirting with me?"

"Maybe."

Alex's hand slipped into hers and she gave it a squeeze. Suddenly Susan stopped and jerked away, her heart pounding with fear. "You touched me!"

"Don't worry," Alex soothed. "It doesn't work like that. I have to will it. I have to want to ... ah, you know."

She sighed with relief.

"I should have told you."

Suppressing a desire to punch him in his arm, she simply said, "Yes, you should have."

"I'm sorry."

Alex sounded so miserable, she gave him a little kiss on the cheek.

During the next week Susan and Alex saw each other every day. Most nights she'd cook them supper and then afterward they'd sit on the couch and snuggle close. Somewhere along the way, Susan realized that she was falling in love. Alex was warm and funny. When she was with him, she felt safe.

One night, Susan gave Alex a kiss on the neck and whispered, "I want you to spend the night."

He wrapped his arms around her, kissing her passionately. He gazed into her eyes. "You're sure?"

"Yes."

Over the next few weeks Susan and Alex spent all their free time together and he more or less moved into her apartment. They loved one another very deeply and Susan had never been so happy. Alex was the best thing that had ever happened to her. Everything was just perfect.

Then one evening Susan was reading the newspaper when she realized that something was wrong. She sat at the kitchen table for a minute, just staring at the wall. Taking a deep breath, she went into the living room to have a talk with Alex.

Alex was napping on the couch. She knelt down and gently shook his arm. "Alex."

Blinking his eyes open, he yawned and said, "Hi, honey." He pulled her up beside him. "I was *sleeping.*"

She teased back, "I know.*"*

He gave her a kiss.

She said, "I wanted to ask you something."

"What's wrong, honey?"

"Alex, have you been working?"

"Of course." He sat up and laughed. "I work all the time."

"It's just that in the paper it said that no one is dying."

"I told you." Alex was upset. "I can control time when I work. If I fall a little behind, I can always catch up, Susan."

"Yes, but—"

He took her hands in his. "I've gotten a little lazy." His lips brushed her cheek. "I guess I've had something else on my mind. Don't worry about it. I'll get caught up."

She let it drop. Snuggling into his arms, Susan sighed with contentment. It was natural to have to make some adjustments. Lately, she'd been a little distracted too.

But Alex never did go back to work. Susan saw it on the news and in the papers and everyone was talking about the *miracle*. All over the world, no one was dying. She knew that sooner or later the miracle would become a curse.

She found his work clothes on the floor behind the hamper one evening. Steeling her resolve, Susan went into the kitchen to talk to

Alex about the problem. She laid the sweatshirt and jeans on a chair and stood next to the table.

Alex was making popcorn in the microwave. Glancing over, he saw the look on her face and asked, "What's wrong, honey?"

"You lied to me, Alex."

"What do you mean?"

She pointed to his clothes. "You haven't been working all week."

Frowning, he turned back to the microwave. "I don't want to talk about it."

"Alex. You can't just stop."

"I just haven't felt like working lately."

She slumped onto a chair. "What's wrong?"

He leaned over the kitchen counter. His voice was a haunted sound. "I'm sorry."

"Just tell me what's wrong. People all over the world are suffering, waiting to die. You know that if you don't do your job, we'll have other problems. Famine, overpopulation. You know all this. What's wrong, honey?"

"I can't!" Alex wailed. "Don't you understand. I just can't do that anymore!" He sank onto the chair across from her and buried his head in his arms.

"Alex."

"I can't do it anymore." Alex lifted his head and she could see the tears on his cheeks. "I've tried and I can't."

Susan stood behind Alex. She draped her arms over his shoulders. "It's because of us, isn't it?"

"Yes," he croaked.

"But, Alex," she pleaded. "You can't just stop working. Too many people will suffer."

He gave her a haggard stare. "You don't know what it's like. I love you so much, Susan. I can't have these feelings and go out every day and ..."

Her arms trembled as she hugged him. "Alex, please. I love you too."

A hysterical laugh burst out of Alex. "I thought about giving you up. Did you know that?" He hugged her around the waist. "But I can't live without you, Susan. I love you! To hell with the rest of the world!"

Susan couldn't imagine being without Alex either. She thought about how impossible it would be to love someone as much as she loved him and wear the mantle of Death. To stop the beating of so many hearts when your heart was filled with bliss. It would be impossible. Susan knew what she had to do. This was her fault, and no matter the cost, she had to fix it.

Ignoring the fear that hammered inside her heart, Susan pulled Alex's hands onto her stomach, saying softly, "Take me."

Alex blinked in confusion. "What?"

She pressed his hands tighter onto her body. "You have to. It's the only way, darling. Take me!" Hot tears flooded over her cheeks.

"No!" Alex blanched. He pushed her away and got up from the table. "I won't do that!"

She took a step toward him. He had to do it or the world was doomed. Neither one of them had any choice. Her voice was a sad whisper, "You have to, Alex."

He covered his face with his hands and sobbed. Then Alex's fingers moved apart and between them, she saw the resolve inside his dark eyes.

Susan screamed, "No!"

The brown eyes dimmed and went blank. Alex slumped to the kitchen floor.

She dashed forward, throwing herself onto his body, sobbing desperately, "No, Alex, no!" Her fingers clawed at his back as she shook him. A river of tears flowed down her cheeks and she collapsed. A high lingering whisper fell from her lips like the tiny sound of a child, "Alex, don't go."

But he was gone.

Susan sat on the kitchen floor for hours. She wandered around the apartment in shock until the sun began to filter through the windows. Falling onto the couch, she sobbed and lamented, cursing the universe.

After a long while, she got up and stared at Alex's body lying on the kitchen floor. He had made this sacrifice for the world. He had sacrificed them both. She saw the sweatshirt still on the chair. She tugged it over her head. Spotting a pair of sunglasses on top of the refrigerator, she put them on and left the apartment.

***

The Mating Moon

by Chris Rodriguez
United States

Bucky couldn't will his eyes to look away. Ari Anansi was the most beautiful girl he had ever seen. She was huge. All bosom and bodacious booty. The moment Mrs. Craddock introduced the new girl to the class, his mouth dropped open in utter fascination. Spencer stabbed him in the back with a pencil. His mouth snapped shut, but his eyes were wide open taking in the wonder of her perfection.

"What a cow!" Spencer snorked. "Just what we need in this school, another mar on the landscape of Armpit High."

Bucky ran a tongue across his prominent front teeth, the ones that nailed his nickname in second grade. His mouth had gone dry, not unusual for him since it was difficult to close his lips without conscious effort.

"Ari is African American," Mrs. Craddock announced as if presenting a specimen for study.

Really? Bucky's pale blue eyes rolled in their sockets. Nobody in the room was blind. Ari's color was so dark and deep, it shone with the same inner light as the Apache Tear Bucky displayed in his rock collection. *Thanks for the label, Mrs. Craddock, you old bitch.* He shifted in his seat, embarrassed for the new girl.

Though totally entranced, Bucky held no hope this exotic creature would notice him. Not only was he, by far, the homeliest guy in the school, Ari never took her eyes off the floor. *It's okay. I like shy girls.* He felt he had a little advantage getting in a word or two before they walked away from him forever.

All eyes tracked Ari as she made her way down the narrow aisle of beat-up desks to choose a rickety seat in the back. *Crap! I won't be able to see her back there.* The other girls tittered as she walked by, no doubt feeling superior in their established place in the pecking order. In

235

Bucky's humble opinion, it was no contest. Ari's regal bearing, as she traversed the narrow aisles, proved she was easily a queen surrounded by a motley crew of throwbacks.

*

For the next few weeks, Bucky did all he could to get close to the girl of his dreams, to get her to notice him. A seat change in homeroom brought her nearer so he could watch her from the corner of his eye without anyone knowing. He stalked her in the hallways, hanging around her locker, following her to the lunch room where she ate quickly before disappearing into the girls' restroom where she didn't emerge again until the next bell rang. He had to meet her, talk to her, find out everything about this amazing female, this goddess from an unknown world.

Spencer followed Ari, too. He and his evil cronies tormented her, calling her names. They threw food at her in the lunch room. In the classroom, paper clips or spitballs tangled in her hair. The girls giggled, sneering at Ari, whispering, laughing. Bucky watched helplessly as Ari kept her eyes on the uncluttered desk, never responding to their unwanted attention.

A few weeks of this action and Bucky couldn't stand it anymore. He jumped up from his desk and threw his pencil at Spencer. It bounced off the bully's arm catching his immediate attention. The boy who had been his constant tormenter since kindergarten twisted in his seat to glare at Bucky. "What the fuck is wrong with you? You got a death wish or somethin'?"

Bucky went cold but stood his ground. He could feel his face burning, his teeth grinding behind his tight lips. "Leave her alone!" His knuckles cracked on the taut ridge of his balled-up fists. "Just leave her the fuck alone, can't you? She hasn't done nothing to you."

A slow smile spread across Spencer's face. It wasn't a friendly smile. "What's it to you, asshole?"

"I—I *love* her!" The words just spewed out as if someone had squeezed him too hard like a toothpaste tube. He was so angry, he didn't think, had no control over his mouth. All color drained from him. *What had he done? What in anyone's idea of hell had he done?*

Laughter filled the room. Students doubled over in pure glee. He dared to glance sideways at Ari, his gut tight with dread. Her glossy curls covered her face, but one eye stared directly at him. One gorgeous round obsidian eye.

236

She sees me! All the air escaped him like a deflated balloon. There was no anger, no shock, no embarrassment. Delirious hope filled his mind. At last, the love of his life knew he existed.

The raucous laughter in the room abruptly came to an end as Mrs. Craddock entered shutting the door with emphasis, her signal for the students to transition from childish pranks to serious treated-like-adult behaviors. Though not over by a long shot, Bucky had a reprieve. Time for him to further consider his next smooth move. *A lot better than this one, I hope.* Survival was key. He needed to make plans, both to win over Ari and the essential plan to avoid Spencer for the remainder of the semester.

The following Monday, Spencer was conspicuously absent. As far back as Bucky could remember, the only time Spencer missed school was when he broke his arm during a motocross race and it was only for one day. He wasn't the best student but was smart enough to keep his foothold in the hierarchy of the precarious social class of popular teendom, one in which the vacuum filled quickly. There were many willing to step in to take the lead. Rumor had it he had missed soccer practice Friday night. Spencer went out earlier with Marissa Beauregard, his steady—not his only—since seventh grade. Apparently, she didn't make it home either from their date conducted under the full moon.

Bucky listened to the students as they speculated. Maybe they stayed out all night and were afraid to go home? Maybe his truck broke down in the hills? Maybe they eloped? The girls voted for eloped, the romantic option. Bucky knew better. Spencer bragged openly in the locker room about why he kept Marissa in his string of fillies. There was just one thing she was better at than any other girl Spencer dated. That one thing was worth half a dozen of the others when he wanted to be serviced by the best.

Ari didn't seem interested in the banter. As usual, she sat calm and quiet, eyes on the whiteboard. Bucky's heart jumped, starting to race in his chest when she covertly glanced his way with a little smile. He no longer wondered what might have delayed Spencer. He no longer cared about what else was going on in the world around him. The room blacked out as his vision formed a funnel straight to the bright and dark face of his dreams. She held something out to him, low to the desks. In a trance, he took the paper from her long, slender fingers shoving it in his jeans pocket before anyone could see. It was as if the room froze in time making them the only two live beings in it, the rest a backdrop highlighting the moment their fate was sealed.

What absolute drivel! Bucky later reproached himself on being the lamest guy in school. He had to be marked for life as the biggest loser in history. In the privacy of his room at home, he couldn't help staring at the note, the map to his treasure. He ran his fingers over the paper, soaking in her essence. Finally, he opened it and read:

MEET ME BY THE CROOKED TREE IN THE PARK TONITE.

A full hour before the sun set, Bucky excused himself from the dinner table. He pedaled as fast as his skinny legs would go down the road. He wasn't going to take a chance on missing her. It seemed like he waited forever before he heard a soft movement behind him.

He turned to watch her float across the grass, bobbing like a helium balloon. Her graceful bulk swayed to the rhythm of the breeze playing through the treetops. She seemed a natural part of this place. She belonged here. In her habitat, she was confident, direct. Head held high, her shiny eyes burned through the blackness of the night. Bucky was enchanted by her proud demeanor.

They sat comfortably together on a large rock under the tree, Bucky content to be near this strange girl. He rubbed his shoulder against hers, the intimate contact sending sparks of pleasure through his affection-starved body. Once the overwhelming emotion subsided, he asked, "So where are you from? What brings you to Glendale? What do you like to do?"

Ari's laugh was a rustle of silk across his heart. "Slow down. We'll get to it." She reached across the narrow space between them and patted his arm. The touch burned through his skin like dry ice, creating an indelible tattoo on his memory.

For the rest of the evening they discussed her life in detail, her life only since Bucky's was pretty much dull and uninteresting. Plus, she didn't ask about him. A fact which never reached the protected part of his mind. The part cushioned by undying adoration.

Ari had moved around a lot. A new school in a new town each year of her life. "My parents are scientists, genetic engineers. They're self-employed. The work they do on projects and research takes us all over the world."

"Isn't all the moving hard on you?" Bucky asked with great concern. He leaned against her shoulder to show his solidarity.

"Not really. I'm used to it. I like to see new places, meet new people."

This statement struck Bucky as odd since she was about the shyest person he had ever known and she didn't seem to notice anyone around her, let alone meet them. *Maybe she has a secret life we don't know about.* It didn't matter to Bucky one way or the other.

When Ari said she had to go home to meet her curfew, Bucky followed her from a safe distance. He had to see where she lived.

The massive stone structure loomed over Bucky like a monolith of doom. He cringed against the threat it emitted by its very presence. Falmouth House was familiar to everyone in Glendale. It had been built by an eccentric in the 1800s as a wedding gift for his second bride. The first had died in childbirth before the couple reached the new frontier meant to be their home. The premature child was buried with her. Supposedly, the ghost of the first wife drove the second bride to hang herself from the top of the second-story stairs.

Why in the world would anyone want to live here? Except once a year when it was opened to the public for the annual "Haunted Halloween Tour," it had always stood empty. Her parents must be well off if they could afford to live in the biggest house in town. Bucky first felt a bit out of place, then puffed his chest out in pride. This princess in the haunted tower liked him.

*

The couple met in the park many more times during the spring, getting closer each time as shyness began to wear off.

"Did you hear about the other two girls in Mrs. Craddock's class?" Bucky threw his arm protectively around Ari's generous back. "I guess Kelly Ann was skinny-dipping with some boys up at the lake. It's not usually so warm this time of year. They found her clothes hanging on the bushes all covered in leaves and dusty spider webs." He shivered at the image. "They didn't find her body even though the lake was lowered. They dragged the bottom for days. How can someone just disappear like that?"

Ari nodded. "And Junior Garcia's sister disappearing from the public library where she had just been with her friends. Weird." Junior Garcia had filled in the open slot as head bully in less than two weeks after Spencer and his girlfriend disappeared. Ari and Bucky had both felt the sting of his scorpion tongue.

*

The whole situation was creepy. "The mayor has issued a curfew due to these disappearances," Bucky's dad announced at breakfast. "You *will* be home by dark from now on, young man." The curfew didn't help. There had yet to be a method invented to keep teenagers at home after dark. It was like trying to contain puppies in a cardboard box.

This was the strangest spring in Glendale's history. For Bucky, it all began when Ari came to town. It was strange a girl that beautiful, or any girl, could fall in love with him. For the rest, it was the mysterious disappearances of now four teens, all from Mrs. Craddock's class. Oddly enough, nobody missed those kids except their parents and the frustrated police department. The school was much quieter, nicer without them around. Still a dark undercurrent pervaded the students' daily life. It seemed to Bucky everyone's nerves were stretched tight as piano wire.

The week before summer vacation, the final spring full moon crept up on them. "I'm worried about it, Ari. I have to tell you, this business scares the mess out of me. Maybe we shouldn't be hanging in the park for now."

"It'll be okay," Ari rubbed his arm with her long fingers, the nails scratching lightly over his skin. Goosebumps of pleasure mixed in with the freckles. "We can meet at my house. Outside, I mean. My parents wouldn't like me being with a boy." She smiled slyly. "You know where I live."

Bucky gulped. *Busted!* He didn't deny it and was relieved she wasn't upset about his following her after their get-togethers. With all this disappearing business, he felt better about making sure she got home safely.

"Maybe we can get to know each other a little better," she added with a sultry smile. "Come on, it's totally private. Meet me tomorrow night by the big oak in our front yard."

Bucky squirmed with indecision. He wasn't in a hurry to become a crime statistic or to be anywhere near her creepy house. "I don't know. The full moon is tomorrow tonight. Are you sure you want to chance it? I would never forgive myself if anything happened to you."

"Yes, of course I'm sure. I wouldn't miss it for the world. My father calls this one The Mating Moon. He has a name for all of them. It'll be beautiful. Please say you'll come. I promise nothing bad will happen to me." She ran a fingernail from his knee to the middle of his thigh. "But, maybe something *good* will happen—to both of us, right?"

He nodded, his brain going all mushy at her touch. *What did she mean when she said that part about getting to know each other better and not missing The Mating Moon.* All kinds of images came to mind, most having to do with his overheated groin area. He squeezed her hand. "I'll be there. You know I'd do anything for you, don't you?"

Ari rewarded him with a dazzling smile as she leaned in and pressed her full, moist lips against his dry mouth. His semi-hard jumped in his shorts. *She* has *to mean we're having sex, right?* He hoped against hope.

Later, Bucky lay in his bed remembering Ari's touch. He involuntarily fondled other places on his body where he imagined her soft hands would visit soon. He fell asleep after tossing and turning for several hours trying to ignore the heat built up in his adolescent, hormonal body.

He walked across the patchy lawn of the Falmouth House excited about meeting Ari. The closer he got to the house, the more he wondered if this wasn't a big mistake. He glared at the crouching structure of the over-sized mansion. There was something wrong with a place like that. Ari appeared between him and the hideous building. Bucky rushed to put his arms around her, wrap her in a cocoon of safety, protect her from whatever threatened them in this place. His body froze in abject terror as the house, or whatever horrible creature it really was, moved. The edifice rose erect from its menacing crouch to become a towering behemoth like one of the Transformers in his little brother's DVD collection. Ivy covering the walls unwrapped and whipped around like tentacles on a jellyfish.

He held Ari tightly in his arms as the monstrous thing moved toward them grabbing at them with the sticky tendrils of ivy. Thorns on the vines impaled his tender skin and when he tried to rip himself from the grip, the live ropes wrapped more tightly around him. He was paralyzed with fear. Bucky felt himself being lifted from the ground, sure he would be swallowed by the monstrous house.

He looked down to see Ari on the ground. She laughed, pointing at Bucky writhing in the air and clapped her hands as if he had orchestrated this action for her entertainment.

Sweat rolled off Bucky as he sat straight up in bed, heart pounding in his ears. *Oh, crap! Did I scream?* He listened for his parents' footsteps in the hall and released a whoosh of pent-up air when all he heard was silence. He was too big to have bad dreams, but that house seriously creeped him out. How anyone could live there was beyond his understanding.

*

Bucky watched Ari glide over the dew-laced lawn toward the tree hiding him from view of the creepy stone fortress. *Damn thing looks like Dracula's castle.* His form melded perfectly with the shadow cast by the suspended moon, a super moon so large it backlit the entire house like a horror movie set. *Like I'm not nervous enough.*

He stepped from the shadows to greet her, pausing as she spread her arms. They opened wide to receive him. A niggling uncertainty froze his resolve to be brave, act like a man. Bucky regained his composure but was soon overcome with boyish lust. Drawn deep into the dark universe of her eyes, he didn't notice what she was doing as she walked. Ari was shedding her clothes along the way from the house to the tree. She was near naked. The small bulge in his jeans grew tight, uncomfortable. His overheated brain fizzled and fried, but he no longer had to think about what to do. His body took over.

The clothes he practically ripped off in his haste lay in a heap on the damp grass. He took a shaky step toward the magnetic pull, the promise of first-time sex. A warning siren from deep within distracted him. Although he longed to be held against her ample bosom, enfolded in the heavy drape of her arms, he hesitated. His warning radar switched on. *Are we safe? Why do I feel like something is wrong?* Was someone watching, hiding even deeper in the dark shadows? He glanced around, biting his lips.

Now Ari was closer, he could see her eyes, her lovely eyes. They looked ... hungry. Bucky's mouth went dry. *Why not?* He was hungry, too. Hungry to devour her, taste her flesh. He longed to become part of her, be inside her. His intuition could go to hell.

He stepped forward until Ari, with her arms stretched out, could touch him with the tips of her fingers. So close. *Wait! Something is wrong with this picture. What? What the hell is wrong with you? Isn't this what you want, you idiot?* Confusion swirled through his lust-fogged brain.

Bucky's brow furrowed. His head hurt with the effort to understand what he was seeing. Icy fingers ran down his spine as he watched alien appendages unfold down the sides of Ari's full-bodied torso, two on each side between her arms and hips. At first Bucky thought they were sticks she had attached. His mind snapped like a Black Cat firecracker when the sticks moved, waving freely, then formed the same horseshoe-shaped welcome as Ari's arms. The hair rose on the back of his neck. Before he could heed his instinct to back away from this bizarre display, she lurched forward, wrapping all eight ebony limbs around his thin body. He went rigid, eyes bulging from his head in disbelief.

Held hostage by the desperate need of his blood-engorged member and tightly secured limbs, Bucky closed his eyes and entered the deep heat of her body. After the past few months fantasizing twenty-four/seven of this moment, Bucky immediately lost control when the spasm beginning in his manhood sent shock waves to his befuddled brain. His body shook in Ari's clutch as if in grand mal seizure. An explosion in his groin sent a tidal wave of ecstasy to his head which bounced back as exquisite pain and also pleasure to the center of his universe. Heart pounding, chest heaving, he struggled to breathe, to make sense of the freakish events. Wasn't gonna happen. His eyelids fluttered open only to receive another assault on his sanity now hanging from a tenuous thread.

He looked into the eyes he loved so much, hoping she would see his suffering and release him. A high keening noise filled the air. *What the hell is that? What kind of animal makes that noise? Oh my god in heaven, it's me.*

Ari gripped him more tightly. Ice water ran through his bowels as two curved fangs unfolded from inside her cavernous mouth. Black, shiny fangs. Drops of liquid hung suspended at the needle-like tips. Ari, or whatever this unearthly creature was, bent her head to sink the sharp points into the soft tissue of his neck. His pulse pounded futilely against the pressure.

"Wait ... what? What are you?" he managed. He pushed against her bulk in an effort to free himself from further abuse. It was useless.

A pleasant flow of lava surged through his body like a fine opiate. His muscles soon refused to obey the adrenaline-fueled command to break free and run. He hung limp in her grip.

The deadly fangs retracted as Ari gently detached her body from his. Though he couldn't move a hand to cover himself, he felt the chill air on his naked, vulnerable body. His spent penis shriveled, sucked back into its turtleneck casing for protection. Some instincts never die.

"My parents created me," she whispered in his ear still pressed close to him. "They combined their essence with spider DNA. I am the beginning of a new world."

This isn't happening. It can't be real! His mind ordered his head to shake in denial. His head remained fixed in place. *What are you talking about?* His voice no longer worked.

Ari smoothed his hair, cooed in his ear. "All those others? The kids missing during the full moon cycles? They meant nothing to me. They were only food." Ari stroked him lovingly. "You, Bucky, you loved me, said you would do anything for me. Now you are my mate." She smiled in triumph. "Your body will feed our children. We will soon populate the world with our beautiful offspring."

Bucky rolled his eyes sideways tracking her movement as she stepped away. He stood on his own, frozen in place. His stomach regurgitated into his frozen throat as he watched her next inconceivable act. Two of her impossible appendages pulled some stringy substance from a hidden place behind her substantial backside. He felt the gentle impact on his skin as she threw it around him like a dozen lassos of sticky rope. She laid him gently on the ground, then moved to straddle his immobile head. Bile dribbled from the corner of his mouth still opened wide in terror. Bucky's eyes dilated as Ari, with great care, guided the eggs dropping like oysters down his open throat before sealing them inside with more cottony webbing.

There was no pain. Bucky was grateful to feel nothing, his mind at ease in the aftermath of panic. Forever immobilized, his silent silken scream was witnessed only by the fat orb of the pregnant moon. This nightmare was not going to end in his soft, cozy bed at home. Bucky briefly envied the victims who were merely food, as the spider thing picked up his stiff legs to drag him toward the dark, damp house of stone—her nest.

***

In the Dark, It Sleeps

by Bryan Best
United States

Charlie sat motionless in bed, paralyzed by terror. The black, eight-foot-long king cobra had wrapped itself around his body trapping his left arm against his side as Charlie tried to strangle the life out of the snake with his right hand. But he wasn't strong enough. His hand ached to the point of numbness as he realized their stalemate. The snake must have sensed his fatigue as it tightened its coils and opened its mouth, displaying its deadly fangs.

He panicked. With no visible lifesaving options left, Charlie screamed.

Something heavy thudded against the outside of his bedroom door followed by a muffled curse from a man's voice. To Charlie's amazement, the cobra ripped its head from its death grip, uncoiled itself, and dived from the bed to slither back into his dark closet as the bedroom door burst open.

*

"What in God's name is going on in here?" Reginald demanded.

Charlie sat straight up in bed as the overhead light came on. The fight with the snake couldn't have been real. Had he been dreaming? He shifted in bed feeling a saturated wetness on his waist and legs as if he'd showered in his pajamas. Realizing his bladder had released its contents sometime during his episode, he pushed the covers back and lowered his head in shame as he tried to stifle his sobs.

"I asked you what happened?" Charlie's stepfather repeated.

"Take it easy, Reg. He's had another one," Charlie's mother said as she sat down on the edge of his bed. "Tell us what happened, sweetheart."

"It ... tried ... to ... kill me," Charlie choked out between breaths. He stared past Reginald at the open closet door. "This giant cobra wrapped itself around me and was trying to bite me. There was nothing I could do, and I guess I just freaked out. When you all opened the door, it went into the closet."

"This closet?" Reginald turned on the closet light.

Charlie's dress shirts, T-shirts, and pants hung neatly on their hangers. Underneath the clothes, his shoes sat lined up in a row, and on the other side were boxes of action figures and other toys.

Reginald sighed and said, "I don't see any snakes in here, pal."

Charlie closed his eyes as he put his hands over his face and said, "I know it wasn't real but it felt real. I could feel the roughness of its scales and see the hate in its black eyes. I really feel like it wanted to kill me, Dad."

Reginald stepped over to Charlie and dropped to one knee in front of him.

"I'm sure it felt real, buddy. But we've been over this several times. These dreams—night terrors or whatever—are all just part of your imagination. And all week you've been coming home and telling us how your science teacher is covering herpetology right now, remember?"

Charlie nodded.

"Well, there you go."

"Honey, get out of bed and go rinse off in the shower while I change your sheets." His mother stood in his bedroom doorway holding a fresh pair of navy blue sheets and a clean pillowcase. "And I know we probably sound like a song on *repeat* to you, but the fact that your imagination can't hurt you will never change."

"I'm sorry I woke you and wet the bed."

"Don't worry about it, hon. We promised to help you with whatever you're going through the best we can, and you have no reason to be ashamed," his mother said as she felt his damp forehead, checking for a fever. "You have an appointment with Dr. Cromwell tomorrow after school and you can tell her all about your ... dream. And your dad and I will be there with you if you want us to be."

Charlie nodded and went to the bathroom and turned on the shower. He didn't have to look at his stepfather to know the man had rolled his eyes at the mention of the psychiatrist's name. As the warm water drenched his face and cascaded down his body, Charlie knew his parents were in his bedroom arguing over whether or not therapy was necessary.

His stepfather, ever the devout Methodist, swore that Charlie needed spiritual counseling, not mental medication from some recent college graduate who specialized in mindless blathering. Thinking of Dr. Cromwell made Charlie smile a silly grin. It wasn't a *let's just be friends* kind of grin, either. She was the hottest woman he had ever seen, way hotter than any of the girls in school. She meant well, too, and seemed like the only person who tried to understand his problem. His parents wanted to understand and help, but it felt mostly like the desire to help was for them and not his peace.

However, he understood that no parents liked being pulled from dreamland at three in the morning to the horror of their kid's screams, so he vowed to do everything he could not to disturb them for the rest of the night as he lathered the soap. He would be a teenager next year, and from the talk around school he'd heard teenagers were tough. But he didn't feel tough. Scared, but not tough. He felt on edge, like he'd done something he shouldn't have and was about to get caught.

Charlie couldn't help having a broad imagination. His parents would never understand that his imagination allowed him the freedom to move about in any form he wanted and to encounter things that couldn't be real in the *real* world. Then there was the endless harping about how they wanted him to grow up to be a responsible adult, unlike like his biological father. They wore on his nerves talking about their adult garbage. He would never tell his parents, but he wanted to be an artist just like his real dad. He thought of his Sketchpad as he dried off. Should he draw the snake that attacked him? But if Mom saw it, she'd have a fit and keep blaming the night terrors on his overactive imagination.

The thought of drawing comics for Marvel or DC made him smile at his reflection in the mirror. Yeah, if he spent the next few years refining his craft, he could draw for one of the major comic book companies when he grew up. His real father would be really proud of him then. After putting on fresh underwear and dropping his towel in the hamper, he went back to bed to lie on his clean sheets.

*

A young blonde receptionist led Charlie into Dr. Cromwell's office. He took his usual seat in a brown leather armchair. Unlike his stepfather, Charlie had nothing against Dr. Sydney Cromwell. How could anybody have anything against her? She kept her curly brown hair at shoulder length, wore business suits or skirts, and had the kind of nice large breasts every middle-school aged boy wanted to see without the confines of clothing.

"Good afternoon, Charlie," Dr. Cromwell said as she raised her head and made eye contact with him.

He watched her put her pen down as she leaned back in her dark leather chair and crossed her legs. She wore a red blouse with the top two buttons unbuttoned and he couldn't tell from where he sat, but he thought she had on a gray skirt. He hoped she would walk around the desk and sit in the other chair next to him as she usually did. And her lotion smelled like some kind of exotic flowers. Man, he loved that scent.

"Hi."

"How are you today? This session will be audio recorded unless at any time you wish for me to turn the recorder off. Do you understand that?"

"I'm fine. And yes, I understand about the recording." He thought it funny she said the same thing before every session.

"Would you like to tell me how your weekend went?"

Charlie sighed and said, "The weekend went fine, but I had another night terror last night. A bad one."

"Tell me about it." Dr. Cromwell propped her arm on the armrest and rested her chin on her knuckles.

Charlie told her everything about his episode except for the part about peeing on himself. A pretty woman didn't need to know about that, even if it was accidental.

"That sounds terrifying, Charlie. Have you always had a fear of snakes? Have you ever seen one in your backyard or while hiking?"

"No, we don't go hiking. I've never really had anything against them."

"Why do you think you had this awful night terror?"

"I don't know why I've had any of the problems I've been having. I wish I did because then maybe I could figure out a way to stop them." Charlie feared he sounded whiny. Not knowing the answer to something was a weakness which angered him. He felt color rising on his cheeks.

Dr. Cromwell scribbled notes as she asked Charlie how he dealt with his *problems*.

"Well, I've always loved to draw, so I've been trying to draw the things from my dreams and daydreams. Sometimes they're cool, but then sometimes they get a little scary. I get nervous because I don't know which of them will come or when."

"Do *they* ever come when your parents or other people are around."

Charlie shook his head.

"Do you feel comfortable describing *them* to me?"

"Well, I told you about the snake last night." He suddenly felt nervous. His hands needed something to do, so he began tapping them on his thighs one at a time. "Sometimes I see—I mean I think I see—things in my closet or any dark place around the house. And then if I concentrate, even a little bit, they seem to materialize right in front of me. I've heard something that sounds wet and slimy slithering inside the closet when the door was closed—that was the night I saw a black and brown speckled tentacle under the door—and then I woke up seeing a giant wolf with red eyes staring at me from the back of my closet. That one really scared me, but they always disappear when I turn the lights on."

Cromwell had made several notes while Charlie talked. "Do the things you imagine interact with you, if you allow the episode to go on long enough?"

Charlie shrugged. "Sometimes."

"What do they say to you?"

"They don't really *say* anything but it's more like they want me to do things."

"What things?"

"The bad ones try to get me to go into a closet, a corner, or some other dark place with them."

"Why?"

Sweat broke out on his temples and forehead. "I don't know. I've never obeyed them."

"How do you deal with these episodes when they occur?" Cromwell narrowed her eyes at Charlie. "Do you try to protect yourself?"

"Yeah, usually if I sketch whatever materializes in enough detail, it's like I've trapped it in the paper and I can then control it when I see it." Charlie sighed and shrugged. "I don't know if that makes any sense."

"Sure it does. Have your mother and stepfather become any more supportive of you drawing since these encounters began?"

"Kind of. I think they want me to get better but they get frustrated because they can't help me."

"That's very perceptive, Charlie. Do you understand the meaning of that word, perceptive?"

Charlie giggled. "Of course. I'm in sixth grade and have six classes a day including English where we have to work on vocabulary every week."

Cromwell smiled. "You're certainly a very bright, young man. I like that. Has anything or anyone upset you recently, or tried to get to you to go with them into a dark place that may have made you feel the need to create a parallel world in order to cope with some kind of event you don't want to remember?"

Charlie told her *no*. He gave a lengthy explanation of how his mother kept telling him his imagination couldn't hurt him and he needed to stay away from the sci-fi movies and scary video games.

"Your mother is right about your imagination, and she may be right about the amounts of stimuli you receive in a given day."

He watched her uncross her legs and then cross the one that had been on bottom over the former. He really wished she would come from behind the desk and sit next to him. The moment of silence lengthened, and he realized she had asked him a question.

"I'm sorry. What'd you say?"

"I asked if you have recently spent any time with your biological father," Cromwell repeated.

"Not since we went out to eat a few weeks ago."

The psychiatrist flipped back through her notes to read something. "You said your father took you out for pizza and gave you some money." Charlie nodded. "Do you remember discussing anything that might have upset you?"

"No. I mean, every now and then, he'll bring up him and Mom getting divorced and how he wished it hadn't happened, but then he turns around and says it was for the best. Whatever."

"It sounds like their divorce still bothers you. Do you think that's true?"

Charlie broke away from the psychiatrist's stare and immediately regretted it. It felt like he had just lost some kind of power struggle, and Dr. Cromwell knew that he knew. How could she thrill and intimidate him at the same time? He unconsciously shifted in his seat as he watched her draw a circle around something she had written and wondered what it was.

"It doesn't matter now. Nothing can be done about it."

"I see," Cromwell said, tapping her pen on the edge of her notebook. "Is there anything else you'd like to share with me about your *encounters* or your father before we bring your parents in?"

Charlie hesitated a moment, then nodded.

*

An awkward silence filled the car for most of the ride home. Charlie chose to ride with his mother to allow his stepfather time to calm down. His parents agreed, to an extent, with Cromwell that some of his episodes could stem from repressed anxiety over his biological parents' divorce and his mother's remarriage to Reginald. Even though that event occurred when Charlie was five. She explained Charlie had been at a very tender and crucial age when the divorce happened, and it angered him in such a way that his emotions had no other outlet than by being acted out through his imagination, and possibly, in his dreams.

Both these prognoses Charlie watched Reginald accept. It wasn't until his psychiatrist concluded her analysis with the suggestion of prescribing the anti-anxiety medicine Trailodine or some type of phenothia-something that his stepfather erupted from his chair shouting at the doctor with an index finger pointed in her face. Reginald swore by his life's blood he would never allow Charlie to take psychotropic drugs, and his counseling sessions with her were over. He finished his tirade by telling her that the only counseling Charlie needed was spiritual guidance from their pastor, and the drugs she prescribed were no less evil than cocaine or heroin the street dealers pushed.

Charlie had been so embarrassed his face turned red as he quietly stood from his chair and left the office.

"Why did Dad blow up at Dr. Cromwell like that?" He couldn't take the silence anymore. He could tell his mother had been just as embarrassed.

Jennifer sighed and said, "Reggie grew up here in the south and clings to the *old school* way of Nashvillian thinking. We're supposed to have faith and turn to God with our problems, but God also gave us science and individual brains to be able to use science to help

251

ourselves and others. Reg thinks when good things happen to us it's because God is pleased with us, and when bad things happen it's because God is mad at us or Satan's attacking us. And he couldn't be more wrong."

"I believe in God too, but he needs to be more pragmatic," Charlie said, looking out the window.

"How do you know that word?" Jennifer asked, laughing.

"From school, Mom."

"Well, you're right, he does, but it didn't help the matter any when Dr. Cromwell said that your night terrors could partly stem from a subconscious fear of Reggie's temper."

Charlie snapped his head toward his mother. They had all agreed a long time ago that he would address Reginald as *Dad,* since he truly was more of father to Charlie than his biological one had ever been. But his dad had no right to stop him from seeing Sydney Cromwell. The decision should be his.

"I'm going to send her a card apologizing for Reggie's behavior," his mother continued. "And I'll ask her if we can work something out where she can still see you without Reg knowing."

"Okay, good. But Mom, you've always told me my imagination could never hurt me, right?"

"That's correct," Jennifer said, putting on her left turn signal to turn into their subdivision.

"What if I'm special in a way where the things I imagine or the things I draw are not just pretend, but could really affect me or other people? What if that was possible?"

Jennifer slowed down and alternated between watching the road and looking at her son.

"I would say that Dr. Cromwell is right, you need to lay off the weird movies and video games. What would make you think something like that?"

"Nothing. Just wondering because I'm the only one who can see these things and it really does scare me, so I draw them and try to make storyboards out of them. In a way, it's like bending them to my will instead of them making me do what they want," Charlie replied with a shrug.

"Have you told Dr. Cromwell this?"

He nodded. "Yeah, I tried to feel her out to see how accepting she'd be, but she seems convinced my problem is yours and Dad's divorce, and horror movies."

"Well, is there anything about the divorce that still bothers you? We can talk about anything you want."

Charlie rolled his eyes. "No. Come on, Mom. All that was a long time ago. I just want to forget about it."

As they pulled into the garage, Jennifer looked at him and said, "Do me a favor and let's keep this little talk between us."

Charlie nodded.

*

Reginald brought home a feast from Kentucky Fried Chicken, and Charlie was thankful the dinner turned out to be much more pleasant than his visit to the doctor. His stepfather seemed his normal chipper self since arriving home. He was still pissed at his dad for embarrassing him in front Dr. Cromwell and hadn't said a word to Reggie since.

"Hey, pal," Reginald said, breaking Charlie from his thoughts. "I'm sorry if I upset you in Cromwell's office today. I kind of lost my cool, but none of that was directed at you. You understand that, right?"

"Yeah, I know. I knew you weren't mad at me, but I don't think you should've yelled at her like that," Charlie replied through a mouthful of mashed potatoes.

"Well, son, it's like this. She ran out of ideas on how to help you, which is why she fell back on her all-problem-solving drugs. We care about you too much to allow a doctor or anyone else to dump poison into your body. Then, to put the icing on the cake, she subtly suggested your night terrors are our fault for letting you watch movies and play video games.

"You know, I'd have a whole lot more respect for her if she just owned up and said she had no idea what was causing your problems."

Charlie looked at his mother who gave him a slight smile and nod, silently telling him to go along with Reginald's ideology. Reginald was a loan officer in a bank, what did he know about medicine?

"Well, I didn't want to take those pills anyway," Charlie said through a shrug. "I'll miss seeing Dr. Cromwell, though."

His parents laughed.

"Uh-oh, looks like our little boy has a crush on his former therapist. No wonder you liked going to her, you never heard a word

253

she said. You just liked to sit and look at her," Reginald chuckled, raising his bushy black eyebrows up and down several times. He cupped his hands in front of his chest and smiled at Charlie.

"Reggie! Stop it!" Jennifer blushed as she shook her head.

"What? The woman was busty. We can't blame him for noticing."

After supper, Charlie finished his homework and drew in his Sketchpad while he ate some chocolate ice cream. His parents were in the living room watching *Survivor,* leaving him alone in the kitchen. Movement from the corner of his eye made him stop drawing. He glanced to his left seeing the pantry door open and the light off.

Something moved!

It stayed in the shadows, just outside the reach of the ambient light from the kitchen. Charlie closed his eyes and ordered himself to stop looking into the dark pantry because there was nothing in there. He looked again and wished he hadn't. In the darkest corner, a pair of burgundy eyes stared back at him. They weren't glowing but were defined enough for him to see vertical irises.

No! This wasn't real. His imagination was on the run again.

Charlie turned a page in his Sketchpad and began drawing the pair of eyes staring at him from the pantry. He lost count how many times he looked back and forth from the pantry to the page, but in five minutes he'd drawn a perfect representation of the red eyeballs within an outline of the doorway. A sinister grin crested his lips. In another two minutes, he sketched the eyes again below the original drawing, but this time he drew them with large, closed lids.

He put down his pencil and turned to fully face the pantry before opening his eyes. There were only shadows. The red eyes were gone. He walked to the panty and turned on its interior light. The tiny room was empty save for the canned food, chips, and candy bars.

"Hey champ, you still hungry?" His mother asked from behind him. "It doesn't look like you touched your melting ice cream."

He had forgotten about the ice cream. But his fear was fading. He felt pretty confident about finding a way to control what he'd imagined, no matter how real it seemed to be.

"Sorry. I guess my eyes were bigger than my stomach."

"You feeling okay?"

"Yeah, just tired, I guess."

"Well, good, because it's time to get ready for bed," his mother said, pulling him into her side for a tight hug.

Charlie brushed his teeth and put a cup of water on his nightstand before crawling in bed. In spite of his protests, his parents put two nightlights in his room. He told them again that they treated him like he was in third grade instead of the sixth, but the lights stayed. Secretly, he was grateful.

His mother said she would leave their bedroom door open if he needed them. She tried talking Charlie into leaving his bedroom door open too, but he wouldn't have it. He declared he wasn't afraid. After his mother closed his bedroom door, he rolled onto his right side facing away from the closet. He refused to even look at it tonight and fell asleep before he finished praying.

At 2:48 a.m., he awoke with enormous pressure on his bladder. After flushing the toilet and wiping eye-snot from his eyes, he remembered he had to cross in front of the closet to get back in bed. Charlie stepped into his room and pushed the door closed behind him before taking three long strides and hopping into bed.

The closet door was open, just a crack. Hadn't it been closed when he went to bed? Yeah, his mother had closed it before leaving his room.

The closet light was off, making the cracked door look like a giant malevolent sideways grin hiding rows of sharp teeth. Charlie thought of pulling the covers over his head and going back to sleep, but the question of the open door bugged him. Wait, it was suction. He paid attention in science class. The suction from opening his bedroom door caused a change in the air pressure which pulled the closet door ajar. He giggled at what a dork he was for scaring himself.

As he pulled the covers to his chin, the closet door's hinges creaked as it opened a little wider. He stared at the ceiling determined not to turn his head toward the infinite blackness beckoning him from the partially opened door. He couldn't help it. He cut his eyes toward the closet and saw a shadowy figure within the darkness.

"What the hell is this?" Charlie whispered.

The silky shadow stepped out of the darkness into the dim light projected from the nightlights. Charlie stared dumbfounded at the familiar form standing just feet away from him in the threshold of the closet door. Dr. Sydney Cromwell stood half-naked wearing a dark-colored bra and thong panties with black thigh-high stockings. The flowery scent of her lotion permeated his nostrils, masking another odor. He thought he smelled the faintest hint of rot, like damp earth or dead fish.

He swallowed hard and thought, *This is so not happening.*

"It is happening, Charlie," the Cromwell-shadow said. "And whatever else you want too." Her hands caressed her stomach before gliding up her body and squeezing her breasts together. "You want to feel them, Charlie? Come here. I forgive you for banishing my friend from the pantry downstairs. Come into the closet with me and I'll let you feel and suck them."

Could she read his thoughts?

Charlie pushed the covers back and swung his legs out of bed. The bulge in his underwear made them feel too small as he took a step toward the closet but then stopped.

What would an attractive thirty-something-year-old woman be doing in his closet in the middle of the night? It didn't make any sense. He stepped back and reached under his pillow.

"Where are you going, Charlie? I said to come here," the Cromwell-shadow ordered as her hands unfastened the clasp of her bra.

"You're not real and I'm not afraid of you," Charlie stated as his whole body shuddered.

"I don't want you to be afraid. I want to show you how much pleasure we can give each other."

She pointed her index finger at him and curled it back toward her several times.

Charlie pulled his hand from under his pillow and lunged into the closet yelling a soldier's battle cry. Since his night terror with the cobra, he kept a four-inch dagger under his pillow which he thrust as hard as he could into the female figure.

His bedroom door opened and the overhead light clicked on. His mother stared at him in confusion as he stood with his arm in the closet.

"I heard the toilet flush and wanted to check on you. What's going on?"

He looked into the closet and saw that his blade had gone between two pairs of hanging pants and made a small hole in the sheetrock. There was no trace of his half-naked psychiatrist anywhere. He dropped the knife before his mother could see it, making sure it landed silently on top of a pair of shoes.

"Nothing, everything's fine. I must have been sleepwalking."

"You've never done that before." Jennifer walked in and put her hand to Charlie's forehead and slid it down his cheek. "You look like you're wide awake."

He shrugged. "I must have woken up when you came in, like the other night."

"Do you want me to make you some hot chocolate or anything?"

"No, I'm fine. I'll just go back to bed." Charlie faked a yawn as he crawled back under his covers. But he didn't sleep for the rest of the night.

*

Three nights passed without an episode, and Charlie had drawn in his Sketchpad every day. Then he dreamed of a huge man with a wolf's head chasing him through the woods. When the wolf-man caught him, he woke up screaming as his parents rushed in to find him standing in the closet doorway. He wondered, as he caught his breath, if his closet could be an entryway to some alternate world.

No, that was silly and childish. He had allowed his imagination control him again.

Tonight, an exasperated Reginald decided he would settle this problem once and for all. He would sleep in Charlie's room and Charlie would sleep with his mom to show him there were no bad things in his closet or anywhere else.

"Don't do this, Dad. Please."

"Son, I'm simply going to do what you do every night. I'll sleep with your bedroom door closed, but I will leave the closet door wide open. Tomorrow morning we'll get up and go to church and everything will be fine," Reginald said, pulling down the comforter of Charlie's bed.

"You don't understand. It's my imagination and I think my mind always wakes me up before anything bad happens. If you become part of it, I don't know if I can wake you up before something ... happens."

"That's ridiculous! You said you understood that your imagination can't hurt you or anyone else," his mother said, leaning against the doorway.

Charlie shook his head. "I can't tell you how I know this is a bad idea. I just know."

"Well, I can tell you it's a good idea because it'll help you in the long run. And in the morning your subconscious mind will understand the scary things you like to make up simply aren't real," Reginald said as he sat on Charlie's bed.

"Come on, buddy." His mother put an arm around his shoulders. "Tell your dad good night and let's get to our campout. We'll drink hot chocolate and watch TV until we fall asleep."

He and his mother slept in sleeping bags with the tent flaps open down in the living room. He drew in his Sketchpad more than he watched the movie. He drew his closet door from memory the best he could, but he added several chains crisscrossing in front of it before falling asleep to an old Adam Sandler comedy. He slipped into a deep sleep before the movie was over and dreamed he was watching his bedroom on the TV screen. His dream turned vivid, like the TV screen was a window into his upstairs room rather than a television.

Charlie watched a shadowy hand knock on the closet door while Reginald lay asleep in bed. Sensuous female laughter echoed through the room making his stepfather stir. Reginald sat up and rubbed his eyes. He glanced toward the closet and sat there staring at it for a long time, probably trying to decide if he was dreaming or not. The Sydney Cromwell silhouette darkened the closet door again. She still wore her thong panties and thigh-highs but this time she was topless. Charlie saw her voluptuous breasts and erect nipples quite clearly on his mind's eye TV screen, and he knew his stepfather could too.

"You're not Charlie, but you'll do. Come to me, Reggie," the Cromwell-being said, her voice barely above a whisper.

Reginald stood from the bed. Like Charlie, he only slept in his underwear and Charlie could see the idea of Sydney Cromwell naked excited his stepfather too.

"Well, it certainly doesn't feel like I'm dreaming, but I have to be." Reginald pinched his arm and let go. "What are you doing in my house?"

"Come in here and I'll show you what both you and Charlie have wanted to do to me ever since you first saw me." The Cromwell-thing held both her arms out to Reginald as if to embrace him.

Reginald hesitated before he said, "Oh what the hell? It's only a dream, right? You can't be unfaithful in a dream."

Reginald took off his underwear and strode into the closet. The door slammed shut of its own volition and Charlie couldn't be certain, but he thought he heard the sounds of growling, wet slithering, hissing, and screaming.

*

Charlie sat up in the tent and rubbed his eyes. He heard his mother leave the tent and then smelled the aroma of fresh coffee coming from the kitchen.

"It couldn't have been real. It couldn't have been," Charlie chanted over and over like a prayer.

He ran up the stairs and checked his parents' bedroom and bathroom for Reginald. Both were empty. He went to his bedroom and threw open the door. The bed was empty, there was no sign of his stepdad, and he found the closet door closed.

Charlie sat on the bed and let his Sketchpad fall open next to him. Flipping through the pages, he stared in fascinated horror at what he had drawn. There were pictures of wolf-men and other half-human beasts howling at the moon. He traced a finger over a drawing of some creature that was a combination of a squid, octopus, and Dr. Cromwell with its tentacles ending in snake heads. Next, a picture of Reginald— the likeness was striking—walking toward his closet with arms outstretched while several creatures waited in the background. Their eyes lusted with hunger. Feeling numb, he closed the Sketchpad.

Maybe now his father would be proud of him.

***

Pax

by Gustavo Bondoni
Argentina

Come to us. Stay with us. Feel the peace. You belong here.

Jack Hunt tuned the whining out as long as he could but, in the end, he had to concede defeat. He shut his notebook with an annoyed snap and looked up at his wife.

"All you ever do is play with that computer," she repeated. "You never have any time for me."

This was unfair on many counts. In the first place, he wasn't playing with the computer, he'd been trying to get some work done. He was the owner of a major oil company, with operations on every corner of the globe, and crisis in Asia didn't stop just because it was ten o'clock in Seattle. And besides, he spent every moment when he wasn't working on her. She had no cause to complain.

"I'm sorry, dear," he replied. "What would you like to do?"

Elena began to say something, but then stopped, frustrated. "I need to get out of this town. It's so provincial. Not one decent nightclub, no restaurants to speak of, and the opera house looks like something you might find in Bolivia. And it rains all the time!"

This, Jack reflected, was his own fault. He'd married the beautiful, blonde, Brazilian socialite essentially in order to annoy the political correctness fanatics in his peer group. She thought socialism was a disease, that wearing a size six meant that you were twenty pounds overweight, and that men had been put on Earth to buy beautiful girls pretty things. And he'd made the right choice. Not only had she completely baffled his American friends, he'd also known at a very early stage in their courtship that he could never love another woman the way he loved her.

261

Sadly, the only place in America where she felt comfortable was in Manhattan, and saw the rest of the country as a collection of uncouth nouveau riche being allowed to run the place from their gauche SUVs. And she was quite vocal about it.

"Where would you like to go?" he asked gently. He knew just the place. He had been holding it back as a surprise. It had been difficult to conceal, both because of the enormity of the undertaking and the fact that he'd very much wanted to tell her about it.

"Somewhere sunny. And with people you can actually talk to about important things." Things, he knew, like the ski season and Ascot.

"Would you like me to build you an island?" he asked.

This earned him a sharp look. Despite the fact that she played the empty-headed trophy role to the hilt, she was actually extremely intelligent—far smarter than he was. She was skeptical about the likelihood of such an offer being real, but also knew that such islands not only existed, they were well within Jack's means.

He smiled at her. "Ah, I see you like the idea. I'll build us an island, maybe near Borneo, so we can hop over to Australia if we need to see a big city. We'll spend the winter there. And we can invite all your friends over."

Her expression was still guarded. She wanted to believe him, but it seemed that it was just too massive for her to assimilate all at once. "When will we go?"

"Next week. I'll give you the instructions. Email your friends tonight."

She laughed, thinking he was teasing after all. "You're a beast, Jack. How could you build an island for me in a week? Don't be silly!"

He turned deadly serious. "If I tell you to email your friends, and that we'll be spending the winter on an island I had built for us, then you must believe me."

And now she was flustered. "But how can this be? How can we have an island waiting for us? How can it be built?"

Because, he didn't say, construction began the day I married you.

"Just make sure your bags are packed by Friday," was all he did say. "We'll all meet up in Bandar."

He smiled at her back as she moved off to prepare, having gotten much more than she expected.

*

We await you. We welcome you. Come.

The island was perfect. The contractors had delivered exactly what they said they would, and Elena was rapt.

"It's so beautiful," she said. "My cousin thinks it has to be the most spectacular place in the world. Even Joao is impressed, and you know that he's been all over the world driving those race cars."

Jack smiled. It was typical of her. She would always wait to hear what society had to say before emitting an opinion—letting the thoughts of others permeate her thinking, letting them color the way she felt about anything. Soon, anything that was said would belong to her, have been felt by her before any of the others. It wasn't something she'd do on purpose—she'd sincerely believe everything she remembered, even if everyone else remembered something different.

But soon, after everyone had weighed in, she would settle down and superimpose her own impressions on what others had built up inside her. She would see the beautiful, blue ocean, the lush, forested hills, the carefully sculpted bays, and come to realize with a sudden start that all of this had been built for her. That the entire island, this paradise on Earth that surrounded her and was approved of even by her jaded socialite friends, was a monument to the love that one man had for her. Jack knew her well enough to know that, when that moment came, her gratefulness would know no bounds, and the love he'd see in her eyes would move him to tears.

He also knew that it would come sooner rather than later. There was a certain peace on this island, something that allowed even the most hyperactive, stress-driven, and impatient men to feel at rest. Jack, among the worst of the stress cases, had felt it as soon as the contractor had anchored his boat between a large kelp forest and a slightly raised shoal and told him that here was the place where they would build his island.

Jack had agreed on the spot. There weren't many places on Earth where he could feel at peace. Its effect on less strained personalities should be magical.

After they settled in, Jack suggested they split up to explore the island. It was, he assured them, perfectly safe. All the fauna was interesting but harmless, every cliff face fell into deep but still water with access ramps back to the island, and the waves were controlled by an artificial reef built of large stone slabs.

Knowing what she wanted, he urged Elena to go off with some of her friends, watched her disappear into the carefully groomed jungle with Joao and his wife, and walked down the path that joined the Victorian-style manor house with the largest of the beaches.

The expanse of white sand fronted a large artificial bay on which the nearly perfectly crystalline water seemed as still as a mirror, courtesy of the artificial reef that controlled the fury of the ocean beyond. Only one channel, large enough and deep enough to accommodate a good-sized yacht, connected to the ocean through a series of buoy-marked convolutions.

Under the surface, he could clearly make out the kelp forest, which he'd ordered the contractor to retain, despite the man's original intention of creating a monumental rocky valley.

He sat on the beach, the beach he'd named Pax, and was immediately convinced that the feeling of well-being, the feeling of peace was coming out of that bay. There was nowhere else in the world where he felt the way he did here. It was all he could do to avoid walking into the water to be closer to the bliss of absolute tranquility.

He resisted that urge, but could never resist sitting there, a feeling of well-being washing continuously over him as if projected by a benevolent presence.

*

Sadness. Why did you go away? Come back to us.

Jack could do nothing but stare in disbelief and hold her as Elena cried into his shoulder, clutched at his arms and drove her nails into his back. Her grief was inexpressible; sobs racked her body. She'd known the man for years, they'd gone to kindergarten together, grown up together in Sao Paulo. He was like a brother to her, and now he was gone.

Joao and his pretty young wife lay on the white sand of Pax, immobile. They remained where they'd washed up the night before, where another Brazilian couple had discovered them half an hour before. Lying side by side, hands nearly touching, they looked like they'd decided to take a nap on the beach in full scuba gear.

Carlos, a doctor from Spain, who'd married yet another of Elena's countless school friends, was beginning his examination of the bodies. The first thing he did was attempt to find a pulse.

"They're dead, I tell you," Brigitte exclaimed. She'd been the one who first spotted the bodies, and her voice was raw from all the

264

shouting and crying she'd done that morning. "I can tell when someone's dead. Just look at them. They're dead. You can tell ..." Her voice faded into incoherence.

The doctor replied gently. "I'm sure you can. But you understand that I need to be absolutely certain before I begin any examination." He turned to Jack. "Who has jurisdiction over this island? Is there any police authority that needs to be informed, any paperwork that needs to be filled out?"

Jack shrugged. "I haven't got the faintest idea. I wasn't planning on having anyone die on me. As far as I know, this island is in international waters, under no jurisdiction."

The doctor stared at him, aghast. "So where are the deeds to the property? What happens if you get overrun by pirates?"

Another shrug. "I don't go anywhere without my security people," Jack replied, nodding towards the large yacht that had brought them in, anchored a few hundred yards beyond the reef. "It can be an imposition at times, but it also has its uses. When the island is unoccupied, I keep a small garrison on the premises."

The doctor nodded, accepting it as yet another lunacy of the ultra-rich—something that he'd been surrounded by since his marriage—and began his examination. He pushed things, peeled back nomex, and generally poked around before looking up once more. But this time, he looked out into the bay, as if studying the ocean floor and the kelp forest.

"What are you looking for?" Jack asked him. "Do you need our help?"

"I was just trying to see if there are any strange currents, anything that might have caused these two to drown. But all I see is a nice little bay which almost looks like a pool. Has anyone else gone swimming in this bay? Is it dangerous in any way that I might be missing?"

"They were the first to dive there, but it's not dangerous. The only movement of water is the tide."

"Then all I can conclude is that they must have been drugged or drunk."

"Why? What happened to them?"

The doctor tapped the tanks. "They ran out of air. And then they stayed down. And they died."

Elena, who'd calmed down somewhat, started crying again with renewed vigor. "But why wouldn't they come up?" she cried. "It isn't all that deep. And there were two of them! How could this have happened?" She covered her face, as if struck by a sudden thought. "What if they were murdered?"

The doctor looked at her gravely, but shook his head. "I don't think so. There was no sign of a struggle, no abrasions on the skin. Even the nomex is fine. And trust me, if you try to drown someone, they'll put up one hell of a struggle. There's no way they would have gone down without a fight—a fight that would have left marks, lots of marks."

"How can you be sure?"

"I get paid to know these things, but that's not all." He turned Joao's body over so that it faced the group. The dead man's face held an expression of absolute rapture, an obvious happiness that came through and sent a wave of peace over the gathered mourners.

"This doesn't look like the face of a man who suffered, does it?"

Heads shook. Even Elena, who'd calmed during her conversation with the doctor, nodded mutely, her sobbing forgotten. She dropped, cross-legged, to the sand, and, as Jack watched, the sadness, the desperation disappeared, to be replaced by a look of tranquility. The others soon succumbed to the feeling, sitting, each in his turn, on the beach.

Wave after wave of peace washed over them, calling them to join it. It was much like what Jack had always felt when sitting on this beach, but this time, it was tinged with a certain sadness, as if someone had lost something—something long wished for and finally achieved, but now gone once more.

*

Come to us. We move with the water. We feel the heart of the planet. But stay with us. Your visits are so brief.

In his more lucid moments, Jack wondered why none of their guests left the island after the tragedy. He knew it wasn't normal, knew that it wouldn't happen that way under normal circumstances. And yet he never truly worried about it.

The days passed in unnatural peace—enjoying the sunshine, frolicking under the forested canopies, making love on the shores of Pax, where the feeling was strongest. Every once in a while, one or two of them would go for a swim in the bay, and afterwards, the remaining friends would bury the drowned body without missing a beat. Nothing seemed to break them from their blissful stupor.

On the night of the storm, months after they first arrived, only Jack and Elena remained. Their hair was unkempt, and sunburns had given way to a beautiful bronze dolor that only retouched models in magazine ads normally managed to achieve. The tattered remains of swim trunks were all that was left of their once exclusive dress sense.

As the waves, higher than in any storm they'd yet encountered on this island, beat over the artificial reef and churned the waters of the bay, some breaking on the white sands of Pax itself, the whole feeling of the island changed completely. The sense of peace gradually ebbed as the waves grew, shifting to neutral wariness and, finally, to a sense of unease.

For the first time in months, Jack found himself able to think clearly, free of the sense that everything would be all right, that all he had to do was sit there by the beach and life would go on and on without problems. He suddenly realized that they'd been on this island for half a year. His board of directors must have been frantic. Hell, they might already have wrested control of some of the stock from his hands. He vaguely remembered answering frantic emails with inane pleasantries, and signing for supplies whenever the boat came in.

"Oh, my god!" Elena said. "They're all dead!" She seemed to have been freed from the feeling at the same time as he had. But her first concern had, understandably, been for her friends, her lifelong companions, now buried, one after another, in the small plot near the beach. She covered her face with her hands. "What happened to us?"

Jack didn't know. The only explanation he could think of was that the drinking water brought in by the supply boat was drugged, keeping them sedated like dangerous inmates in a psych ward. And yet, that explanation didn't feel right. It certainly wouldn't account for the deaths of everyone who ever swam in that bay. It wouldn't explain why everything had felt so peaceful, so right for all those months.

He also had no inkling as to why, all of a sudden, he felt sane again. More than sane—frightened beyond what he should. All he knew was, that as they moved towards the house to get out of the rain, the anxiety dwindled.

It was Elena who figured it out.

"The bay," she said. "There's something in the bay that makes us feel the way we do. The farther away we get from it, the weaker it is."

Jack nodded. "That would explain why we feel frightened now— the bay water is being rocked up good and hard. But the contractor did a pretty decent scan of those waters. There's nothing in that bay but the kelp forest."

It hit them both at once. The peace, the utter contentment they were experiencing was akin to what a big mass of seaweed might feel if placed in a bay of still water on which the life-giving sun shone all day long. Safe from the vagaries of currents and most storms. Of course, if those waters were churned up, they would be frightened, anxious.

"But how can it be?" Elena said, wonder and disbelief mixed in her words. "It's just underwater grass."

While Jack might not have agreed that the majestic leaves were underwater grass, he certainly admitted that it was an unlikely explanation for ... well, for anything, actually. But it was the only explanation they had.

Elena's expression, meanwhile, had turned from wondrous to angry. "And it's evil grass, it's been killing us off, one by one, and making the rest of us not care. The only reason we're still alive is because you wouldn't go into the water!"

Jack nodded dumbly. She was right.

"And what happens after the storm? Do we go back to how we were? Like cattle? No. We have to stop it. And if you won't do it, I will!"

"How do you propose to do that? If you swim into the bay, it will hold you in forever."

"No. It won't. We'll use a rope. You pull me up after ten minutes, even if I still have air for hours."

"I don't like it. I don't want to lose you."

"I know. But those things killed all my friends." Elena turned from him and began rummaging along the shelves, looking for a good sporting knife suitable for chopping down kelp.

*

We are still well. The violence is gone. Come back to us.

Jack pulled the rope hard. His sluggishness had meant that it took a little longer than usual for the alarm on his watch to get through to him. But even with the sensation of rightness threatening to lull him into inactivity, he managed to pull Elena back out in plenty of time. Nonetheless, he was still amazed by how quickly the peace had overcome him once they returned to the beach.

The first thing he noticed as Elena broke the surface was that she was struggling to get back into the bay. The expression on her face was indescribable, a mixture of rapt bliss and a mindless attempt to escape. As her feet slipped futilely on the sand against the pull of Jack's superior weight and greater strength, her hands reached out towards the bay. The knife she'd selected for the job, a vicious thing with a serrated edge, was nowhere to be seen; she must have dropped it in the bay.

Fighting against the encroaching listlessness, Jack took her into his arms and dragged her back to the house. The effect on this side of the island was much less pronounced, and Elena seemed to calm down, and recognize him.

"What happened?" he demanded, unable to believe how close he'd come to losing her.

"Oh, Jack, it was wonderful. Now I understand. Joao and the rest weren't murdered, nothing was done to them against their will! It was simply a question of not wanting to live if you can't feel the sensation of the kelp forest. It's like the peace we used to feel on the shore, but a million times more intense. It's ... it's just perfect."

He took her into his arms and whispered into her ear. "Don't worry. It's all right, it's all right. You're safe now. I'm here."

She pulled away, looked him in the eye. "I'm so sorry I was going to kill the forest. It doesn't mean any harm. It just wants to share what it feels with us. I got the feeling that it could sense my presence, know what I was feeling, and cure everything that was wrong with me. I've never felt anything like it." There was a sadness in her eyes that Jack couldn't quite explain but which made him suddenly afraid.

He went all out for her that afternoon. Margaritas on the beach—a different beach. A dinner that he cooked himself, taking advantage of the nearly untouched supplies and the unbelievable stock of well-aged red wine. He never let her out of his sight.

They made love that night like they'd never done before. A desperate, nearly violent coupling followed by another and another in which Jack let out all the pent-up fear of nearly losing her, and she, likewise, abandoned her sweet but tame bedroom personality. Hours later, satiated and spent, they'd fallen asleep.

Jack awoke alone.

He wasted no time with fear, didn't rush out to bring her back. He knew exactly where she was, knew that he could never bring her back.

So he took his time. He selected the meanest knife that Elena had left, and drew it across his forearm. He gasped as it drew a thin red line along his skin. Hopefully, the pain, especially when the saltwater got into it, would be enough to keep him sane. Only then did he shoulder the oxygen tanks, goggles, and weights. He would need lots of weights.

Then he walked down to the beach, and sat beside Elena's body. It seemed strange to him the way the high dawn tide always seemed to wash the bodies up onto the shore.

He had few illusions that he would be able to emerge from the bay—he wasn't even certain whether he wanted to survive—so he just sat beside Elena's still form one last time. His fingers traced the contours of her lifeless face, noticing how pleased she seemed to be. There had been no sadness for her at the end, no thoughts of the love she was leaving behind.

Despite the advancing sensation of tranquility, this thought galvanized him. Not only had the monstrous forest in the bay stolen his love, his one and only love, but it had taken him out of her mind. It had stolen him from her as surely as her from him. And that was simply unforgivable. He advanced to the edge of the bay, put his feet in the water, half expecting his resolve to disappear on contact—he now understood just how powerful this particular siren's call was.

But there was no sudden defeat of his senses. Even standing in the water he managed to glare defiantly at the vegetation clearly visible a few yards away, and a few feet below the surface. The peace wasn't enough to keep him from hating it, to defeat his resolve to do something about it.

Even when he sat, immersing more of his skin in the water, he could continue to concentrate on his hatred of the evil in the bay. Even as the peace crept over him, he could remember why he came.

As the knife slipped from his fingers, he knew there was something about the knife that was important, and something about the bay that was evil. He was satisfied with this knowledge: while he had it, he wasn't defeated.

Eventually, a voice—rough, commanding, obviously out of sync with the peaceful surroundings—broke through the fog.

"Jack! Oh, my God, it's Jack! Come over here, guys!"

And then a hubbub, a group of people, hands that helped him up, voices that asked difficult questions. Other voices that explained that they'd gotten worried when he failed to answer their emails. People exclaiming that he looked terrible, much too thin. People giving him water, which tasted surprisingly good. More questions.

Finally, strong arms helped him towards a waiting boat, and he felt the peace, the beautiful tranquility, ebbing. He knew there was something he had to tell the crew, a warning he should give them. And the time would come when he would. But for the moment, there was only one thing his addled mind was clear enough to explain.

He gripped the arm of the man nearest him, looked deep into his startled eyes and, painfully, began to speak. "I'm alive," he began, but broke down and coughed, and needed to be given water. "I'm only alive because I don't know how to swim," he said. Satisfied, he passed out.

***

David's Courage

by Gödel Fishbreath
United States

After my parents, my older brothers, my sister, and I were killed, we spoke, hugged, and went to the fur of our beloved Mother Goddess, whose name is Mercy.

As we went, we saw Her shape, a sky-sized wolf, so like us but with paws instead of hands and feet. She was bleeding power and presence as Her worshippers, Her people were being killed in genocidal numbers across the whole continent. The Deer Military had struck with uncanny accuracy, trashing our Wolf Military, leaving the civilians like ourselves to experience their unrelenting vengeance.

Being in Her fur is restful, healing, relaxing, but boring.

Twelve years later, still diminished, She spoke. "Justin? Cub? Would you like to live again?" Her voice came from in front of me, though I could not see Her.

I was surprised. It was common knowledge in Her fur that there weren't enough living wolves for more than a tiny few to reincarnate. I had no idea how I merited this if I did. Eyes bright, ears perked, and wagging my spiritual tail, I answered, "Yes, of course! What family do I get to be reborn in?" I would miss my own, clustered around me. Her voice had carried to them. They grinned and gestured silent best wishes.

"Not reborn—something new. Look at this."

She lead me through scenes. The outcome was that the wolves had a new acquisition: the deer's Two Souls spiritual technology, the ability to house two souls in one body. The spirits of wolves could now share deer bodies as compensation for the deer's wrongful and profane use of prophecy in targeting weapons. It would expand the number of Wolf Mother's and Her Husband's living worshippers.

The whole had centered around a high school age stag, David, and his love, who he lost to a merit-based population control lottery. In that incident, local military leaders, the Deer General and his defeated opponent and old friend, the Wolf Colonel, witnessed the Wolf Father appearing and prophesying that David would need to partner with a wolf spirit to give him the courage essential to face one of the important trials in his life.

"Me? Beloved Mother, please? I am just a cub."

Her smile was sweet as She licked my face. "Honey, I need a hero. I need you. Remember our motto, 'All wolves are heroes.'"

How could I refuse? Humble, I bowed my head, "Yes, Mother."

"David has motivation to accept you. We will see how that works." She looked at me again to fix my attention on Her. "Trust your Father. That prophecy is not just incentive. Don't dismiss it."

I hugged my family goodbye and went to spirit-follow David. In my joy and haste, I left many questions behind.

*

David's dead love chose to spirit-partner with her BFF. He mourned. But the prophecy kept him apprehensive, nagged him like an unscratchable itch.

A month later, between classes, he stepped off the concrete walkway onto grass and said yes to me. I was so happy! I slipped into his body, and the first thing I did was take a breath. It was so good I started crying in joy. I even wagged our tail. My tears found old grooves in his fur.

As I was merging into the body I felt "my" hand reaching up to touch my face. "Huh? What?" My mouth had moved of its own volition, and I realized that David had noticed me. My ears fell flat as my nervous demeanour returned. With panicked words, I began to ramble at top speed.

"Sorry about the tears. It was so good to breathe again that I could not help it. I have bad news. I don't know why They sent me. I think They should have sent my dad or maybe a soldier if they wanted to give you courage. I think I have less than most wolf cubs."

"Oh." David sighed heavily. "I guess we must trust your beloved Wolf Father."

"And the Mother more so. She picked me out. She woke me."

"Oh, okay. So, what were you like before you died?"

We talked so long David was late to class and got detention.

*

The Wolf Colonel and Deer General signed David up for the Hunter Junior Military training camp in response to the prophecy. They felt to do less would let the Wolf Father down.

A stag? To be sent in with the wolves? The hunters would either remember a prewar meal or view a member of the people who nearly eradicated their own.

*

In the months before the camp, I slowly got used to the odd both-sides-at-once vision, David's teen-stag body, and David as host. He would explain his high school lessons to me. Before this, I hadn't had the chance to learn to read. I learned other things, like the wonderful taste of grain and grass on his tongue. Then came summer.

*

At the high school military camp, the Deer General, with David and I, were behind the curtains to the right of the stage, awaiting our introduction to the camper-soldiers. It was evening, after the camp's supper. Some of the hunters, especially those in front on our side of the stage, were nudging each other while they sniffed and flehmened like they couldn't believe their noses.

The Wolf Colonel took the lectern in front of the Hunters Junior Army Camp's amphitheater. He explained the Two-Souls Tech—what it is, why it was wanted, and that the Wolf Divine Parents wanted it— and the result: a stag, David, would be in this camp, and he would host a wolf spirit.

He ended his speech with, "So welcome along with the cervine general, the wolf-cub spirit, Justin, and his host, David."

The general walked out; we followed. Since this was summer, David sported a set of half-grown dual-spike antlers, and the general, the start of a magnificent rack.

I saw a bunch of happy fanged wolf faces. David saw the ones who had to lick the drool off. He saw the ones who shut their eyes pain-tight and drooped their heads, not wanting to see a reminder of the deer's atrocity filled victory. Taking that walk was a gut check for him, one he later told me he previously thought himself braced for. He had wondered if I could have helped him as I was supposed to. But instead, he looked to the general and took courage. I don't know how the Wolf Father could say he wasn't brave. He managed to repress any

275

sign of his unease.

Some in the audience laughed nervously at this sight, and the colonel glared. We bowed, the colonel gestured for the hunters to rise. They did, bowed back, and sat down.

The general said, "Justin, please tell these troops how you died."

Shy in front of all, I studied David's feet instead. They could be clenched together to form a hoof. His were clad in rubber-soled shoes. I held my hands against the shallow of my back, like my older sister did at a poetry recital. My tail tucked, omega style.

From David's mouth came my higher-pitched cub voice. "I'm—"

Startled by my voice, the crowd laughed, cutting off my words; some laughed because of nerves, others, to mock, in spite of the officers present on stage. The colonel harrumphed and stared down the wolves. All changed their posture to show quiet submission. He nodded for me to continue. I found my own resolve and restarted. "Back when the deer were coming for our town, Daddy whispered in his stern alpha voice that we should be quiet and go to our hiding places. Mine was in the big basement trash can. Then Mommy and Daddy went outside. I heard much shooting, some short screams that sounded like them, and then quiet."

My voice shook as I held back my tears. "That's when they died."

An intense silence filled the auditorium, broken only by the occasional cough. All eyes were on me now, and shaking under their stares, I pressed forward.

"It wasn't quiet for very long because there was this big boom. It hurt my ears and stung my nose. The house fell down and crunched my hiding place so I couldn't move. Then there was another loud noise; everything started getting hot, and it hurt to breathe. I tried to be a quiet hero like Daddy asked, but it hurt too much. I don't think he had expected fire. We cubs were all screaming, but we could do nothing. My fur smelled burnt. It was too hot and painful around me. Then, the Mother was merciful and I died. I'm still six years old, just like I was on that day."

My eyes, the eyes of a stag, glistened.

All of the camp had heard their parents talk of seeing news of wolf civilians firebombed twelve years ago. If it had not been for the general accepting the colonel's surrender terms, it would have been the campers' fate too. They turned their ears down in sympathy.

"I felt I had failed my dad, and through him, the Wolf Father himself. I saw my family as we went to the Mother's fur. We hugged each other. Us cubs said sorry for screaming. Dad thanked us for trying and forgave us. I needed that."

"Justin, tell them how you feel," the general requested.

"I don't want anyone else to die that way."

"Tell them how you feel about David."

My voice might be a high-pitched cub's voice, but I was insistent. "I would not be here, I would not be breathing, if it were not for David. He accepted me. He needs to be brave, but ..." I whined, "I— I'm scared of fire, of the pain of being cooked alive, of guns, of spaces like the dark, closed one where I died. I'm just a cub. How can I give courage to David?"

The general said, "David, do you have anything to add to that??"

He looked up, using body language his audience would understand. He swept the crowd with a confident, forward-looking gaze, instead of his usual sideways prey-visioned one. His pose was self-assured: ears perked, pivoting, and alert, with his tail down, hiding the white alarm fur.

The camp soldiers were fascinated by the personality switch. This was the first time they had seen the Tech in action.

"I'm afraid of needing to have courage," David said. "The Wolf Father's prophecy scares me. And Justin, I'm not sure you can give what you haven't got."

David's body slumped, with ears drooping, as I took control. I whimpered, "I'm sorry."

His shoulders squared, and his tail wagged "all safe" in deer body language. His ears went high, eyes alert. "It's okay, little guy," David said.

*

The Wolf Colonel requested cabin mates for us. We gained a barracks full of comrades who sympathized. None of the ones who could not keep from drooling or who did not meet our eyes were included. Our fellow high school soldiers were then paired up in a buddy system. We were matched with a wolf, "Geo" Clawsharp.

As the other student soldiers left their seating, they speculated about the Tech. Many thought that bringing back and living with a favored friend or relative would be super. Others were skeptical about being "roomies" in one body. A few in our cabin asked us how it felt. We answered the best we could.

David found sleeping with so many hunters, even presumably nice ones, stressful. The body scents of the wolves, as well as the night noises as they tried to sleep, kept triggering his reflexive fears. He had to allow me to take over the body to get his rest. For me, being around my people was comforting.

In the morning, the campers reported that their dreams that night had been troubled by prospective spirits trying to sell them on giving another chance at life. Some had accepted one of their prospectives. Others prayed for a friend or relative they missed to be their partner.

Geo accepted a favorite uncle, Brett, a reserve officer who had died with his family.

After the campers chose, they needed time to adjust, to bond with their new buddy. So "Spirit" was the theme for the first week of the five-week Orient-elemental themed course. It was planned to help the campers learn more about themselves, how to communicate better, and how to deal with their new internal friend.

The focus of the course went beyond both the meditation and communications courses of the high school into sweat and smoke lodges, a junior level of psychology and self-help, and other techniques for self-exploration. The campers were urged to practice. The staff made available carefully supervised drug trips in safe, comfortable environments. Fasting and prayer were encouraged. This included offerings of the campers' own blood in the only prayers the hunter Gods took to be sincere.

David and I practised working as one. As fast as possible, we became good, trustworthy friends. We took to using "I" for ourselves, settling slowly but cheerfully into our partnership and body. I called myself DJ.

In the first week, my camp buddy, Geo-Brett, and I had long talks. GB chatted happily with me as Justin, but seldom as David. Even though David had only been a fawn at the war's end, for Brett and Geo, he represented the former enemy's people. Brett's kin weren't the only causalities; the carnage of the war had draped sorrow over Geo's family. But I helped all to reconcile.

Even before I had drawn breath again, I felt strongly that I did not want anyone to die as I had, and the next war should be prevented at a personal level. My example in forgiving the people who won the last war—and who killed me—helped plant the seeds for Geo and Brett to come to terms with their losses. This in turn nudged the cabin mates and, eventually, the whole camp towards accepting and acclimating to the postwar situation. At camp's end, I would feel that I had accomplished something grand. But that was to come.

*

In the first morning of the second week, our barracks mates grouped together and perused the "air" module training schedule. In the following days, the training would cover tree and mountain climbing, rappelling over cliffs, using zip and escape lines, and, finally, skydiving. Both GB and I saw it was going to be a challenging course for our strength and skill. Witnessing its magnitude, the crowd of junior warriors murmured their unease. As the instructors urged our teams forward, the scent of fear grew among us.

At every dangerous obstacle, I hid my nervousness by compulsively going through the safety checks with GB. Usually he and I would go first. David's and my anxiety showed, the body's tail was up and displaying white more often than not. The following hunters joked amongst themselves that they were chasing a deer. The joke removed some of the stress of fighting their instincts and allowed them to concentrate on their tasks, instead of their nerves.

Towards the end of the mountain course, the cabin sergeant was bawling out the laggards. To help my fellows, I went up to the sergeant and requested a halt to readjust my harness. It was a pardonable excuse given the camp's dedication to safety. The sergeant called "take five," and everyone got a breather. All relaxed and rested while checking their equipment, and they made it back from the mountaintop without mishap.

*

The next week spent learning and performing the "water" module activities was fun. Not so the following week: "earth/ground." Learning herb lore and geology was safe, but when we explored a local cave, I panicked. Enclosed spaces still scared me, so David retook sole control of his body and got through.

*

I was surprised by my reaction to the posting of the "fire" module's schedule. I thought I had worked through my death when we did "spirit" week. The remembered pain and smell ambushed me. I curled our body down into a squat, hugging myself.

I wasn't the only spirit who had died in a fire. Others were

279

reacting too. But I was the youngest.

Using the techniques we had gained in the "spirit" module, David and I explored my problem. He gave me what he could. We found that I needed further comforting and forgiveness from a hunter. After having gone through so much of the training together, Geo and Brett were our trusted friends.

David offered to intercede. I declined, wanting to talk hunter to hunter.

Still, approaching Geo was harder than I expected. Brett did not share my experience, having been machine gunned from the air. I was anxious.

Eventually GB noticed the pacing that was included in my bundle of nervous gestures and said, "Justin? Need something?"

He knew I was in control. David wouldn't have been so shaky.

I swallowed and nodded.

He sat up on the edge of his bed. "By the Healing of the Mother of Wolves, by Mercy Herself, come here."

I sat down next to him. GB licked my face as his mom would have and hugged me.

He must have gotten lost in his own past while we embraced. "I miss my own people. So many gone." He paused. "Why can you forgive?"

"Because Mercy would have done so, and Justice was happy enough with the deal He got. I've hugged my family after death. But the memory hurts, and I am afraid."

"Yes, it hurts. Cry it out with me."

And we did. We mourned in tears all the horrible deaths of our friends, our relatives, all our peoples all over the continent.

I was steadier afterwards. I had not known how much I needed release. And David helped me though the "fire" week, so we passed.

Camp ended, and all had a choice to make our bonds permanent. David and I, joyous, hopeful, and nervous, were joined for the life of his body in a group ceremony. It was much like what I have been told getting married is like. We lined up with music, and pomp, said a few important words that meant we agreed to be so joined for the lifespan of the body, and had a party. "We" formally became "I".

After the end, I did feel better prepared. But since I did not know what confrontation the Wolf Father would throw at me, I kept in shape.

*

A few years later, David met the beautiful doe, Elaine-Haseya Firehorn, at the gym. They found shared interests in action movies, books, athletics, and each other.

In a rare talk as separates, David reassured me that I was wanted in this relationship.

I had been using his eyes for long enough to appreciate Elaine's beauty and, on my own, her good heart. I fell in love with her as well as with her spirit partner, a shy coyote named Haseya.

David proceeded slower in his courtship this time. Haseya and I helped him win Elaine.

We all moved to the West Coast soon after our wedding. We are proud of the family our marriage created.

*

I still wanted to be prepared for my big trial. My friends, the Deer General and the Wolf Colonel, both exerted their influence to allow me to take every type of elite strength, skill, and courage training imaginable. These exceptionally varied courses were designed to be tough. I always had an extra reserve. When one of us was down, the other would take over and keep going, beyond what would be thought to be exhaustion limits.

I completed courses in firefighting and mountain rescue. I trained with the elite marine and army units and with the riot police. The paramedic and bomb-disposal courses were a change of pace: more nerves and smart action than stamina.

Along the way, I joined the Twentieth Wolf Regiment, the Rippers, who I continued to drill with, adding the first deer to their normally wolf-only group. They altered their insignia in celebration. It's now a fierce black wolf face in right profile, on top of a red right-facing deer silhouette.

I, Justin, needed some help getting through firefighter training, but I was growing, quickly catching up to David in knowledge, skill, and maturity. He continued my school remedial courses.

The training continued for almost six years. In some of the courses, just graduating was a high honor.

I was fearful and halfhearted about confronting what the Wolf Father had prophesied. I had been tested, but only on a mortal scale. Still, I rose to serve when asked. It was payback for the training as well as preparation for what the Father might send.

*

A wildfire raged across a local area, and firefighters of all types of peoples were called in. The response would be over mountains. Only the most fit would be considered. I answered the request. A short while later, a kitten went missing, and a storm was coming into the mountains where the youngster was last seen. I got called in and guided the child out. Flash flood, wind storm, lost—call after call, I was dependable and eventually promoted. My boast is I was directly responsible for saving over a thousand lives. Once in a while, I moved as though guided by intuition. Was it honed by my unusual pan-discipline training? Or a directing touch from the Mother of Wolves? Or maybe the Mother of Deer? I sometimes thought I had a hint of their scent with my spirit's nose, but was never certain.

*

I—well, really, David—had to stand against mating confrontations, a deer tradition. He found intimidation worked quite well. When he took off his shirt to reveal a peril-scarred body, tempered by a life of needing to be more than just strong, sometimes it was enough. But not always.

The interloper showed up equipped as military: lightweight armor with the Fifteenth Wolf Regiment insignia, and the steel knife horns of a soldier. And called out his challenge. "You! Smelly old stag! I have the spirit of a wolf and I have trained with their elites. I will take you down."

David threw back, "I was the first to partner with a wolf. I trained your trainers. I will not play fawn games with those who try to touch my wife. You challenge, you die. Still want to try?"

"You lie. You do not wear the knife horns of the soldier."

"I don't in civilian life. I have earned them, though. Talk to your trainers, fawn. Talk and live. Come back after, or find someone else. And do not attack those with only one wife. It dishonors your teachers."

One of the fawns handed out DJ's lightweight armor through the slightly open door. Elaine-Haseya tossed it to him. It showed the Twentieth's insignia.

David caught his armor. "The Fifteenths are the Firefangs. A good group. They know me. I'll report your death through them."

Though David was handling this on his own, I wanted in. I tapped his right arm with our left, a military signal, a request to change out.

The other stag's eyes went wide.

I stared him down and growled, "I have been alpha over alpha to many and taken them through danger and survived. My rank is specialist, doing what others do not dare. Can you say as much?"

The youngster backed down in the face of our combined threat, scared of our knowledge, my alpha status, and the family's support.

Neither of us thought that any of these were the confrontation prophesied.

*

Through my long and exciting life, as I gradually felt up to any demand, I kept looking for the Wolf Father's test. It would have to be awesome. I wondered if I would recognize it when it came.

As I finished defusing a bomb, the hidden charge below it went off. It was a new combination device designed to kill the responder. I—well, we—died abruptly. As two, we viewed with sorrow our shattered and scattered corpse.

David saw me for the first time then. We appeared as we each thought of ourselves, not our sixty or more actual years, but in robust middle age and clothed in identical uniforms. David sported an antler rack more splendid than he ever had in life. I displayed impressive muscles. Lost for the moment in our joy of seeing each other, we hugged and cavorted like long-strayed brothers; we licked each other's faces like fawn and cub greeting mom. Our elation was tempered by our body's death.

I asked David if he wanted to go to his beloved Deer Mother. He said he instead wanted to attend our transcendence party, then see my Father to track down the last riddle. I welcomed his answer. We have been buddies for so long.

*

Elaine-Haseya did not do the eulogy at our party. She broke down when asked. The service was crowded. All my crews, buddies, and command structures attended. Even some of those I had rescued showed up. My eldest son said that the whole family had kept awaiting and dreading this day. He also said I was a true hero, going beyond the call of duty all my life, the toughest and strongest. He had trouble completing his speech.

The sorrow of our beloved deer and coyote, of our family, cut our hearts. We wanted to comfort, to warm. But our flesh had been given to scavengers, our bones interred. There was no way of reaching our family; we on this side of death, and they on the other.

*

When we turned back to the riddle that had ruled our lives, we were puzzled and angry. As we were dead, the challenge must have happened, right? But when? It was supposed to be a matter of courage. Looking back on our life, at some time courage had become a habit. So when?

*

We presented ourselves to the Wolf God of Justice and Truth. We found ourselves in an area within a white cloud, facing a four-legged wolf three yards high at the shoulder. He smiled slightly. Then His smile spread to a grin. Naturally, we asked which of the many trials had been the prophesied test. He laughed and kept on laughing. Soon, He was rolling, tail and one forepaw slapping hard against the strangely solid deck. We felt hurt—was our life just one big joke?

The Wolf Father, after his bout of laughter was done, had no dignity—just a silly smile, as He looked at us from where He lay on His side. He said, "You never knew?"

His grin showed him still kidding. "All of them, sons, all of them."

We dared to frown at this answer. It felt incomplete, a joke, a cheat. We were about to call Him on it when the clouds swirled.

*

The Mother of Wolves slowly appeared as she trotted through the mist. She paused next to Her Husband, nuzzled His face, and shared His grin.

She turned to us as She sat Her back legs down and said, "There were two spirits united in a body and faced with a prophesied trial."

Our nods were coordinated; our actions have been synchronized for decades, and it showed. We knew this story and were set at ease.

"One based on the courage Justin would give to David. And they searched their entire life for the test." Her laugh bubbled up, interrupting. "They never found it."

We nodded again, staring at Her like children impatient for dessert.

"My husband loves that you *completely* missed it."

He gazed at us, chuckling. His tail thumped the cloud's floor once.

We exchanged a glance, both eager for an explanation and irritated at the delay.

"And so do I. But we got a hero and are pleased. You both have excelled, and if you missed something inconsequential, so be it." She kept smiling and started to leave.

"Wait! Wait!" We shouted together.

I asked, "Please tell us. What test? When?"

She turned back and sat down, still obviously happy. She moved Her paw left to right, and a glowing yellow-tinted light followed the slight motion, highlighting an incident in our memories for us. The color disappeared rapidly.

We stared at each other in wonder.

I said, "At the start? How? How could've we missed that?"

"We were looking," David said as he shook his head, "and it already had happened."

"You two didn't know Justin had any courage to give. He listened to his fears too much and to his self-image as a small, young, hurt cub. His courage was masked—as a kindness," the Mother said.

"But, wait! That's not sharing courage. I was not braver afterwards. He only took over the body and helped me through," David said.

"When you took over the body from Justin, because he feared fire or such, did you give him courage?" She asked.

"No, I got him out of a situation he couldn't handle."

"Then later, when he started to work with such predicaments, where did he get his ability to deal with them?"

David turned to me, his partner. "Do you remember?"

"Your example helped. The need to deal with the situation forced me to do so. And the slow familiarity with such both challenged me and made it feel more natural."

She asked, "Can it be said that David gave you courage, Justin?"

"A little near the start—the courage to trust, to go and confront on my own."

"Thank you. Good. Then I will say, likewise, Justin gave David courage, the courage to trust those who have traditionally preyed on his people. The prophecy was fulfilled."

She regarded David. "And, by the way? Justin gave you courage by forcing you to develop your own. And you never seemed to have noticed. Which was part of the joke too."

I answered, "We suspected a life of courage might itself count. But we never thought we'd already passed the test." I shook my head in wonder. "Such a simple thing it turned out to be: just taking the body when David was surrounded by predators at that first camp and letting our body get sleep. He did get used to them quickly."

I interrupted myself. "David? I know why I was selected as your partner."

David turned to me.

The Mother's eyes twinkled as She cocked Her head.

"Dad, or a soldier hero, would likely be condescending to a teen and hostile to what he saw as the enemy. Dad still regrets our family's death, even though all are in the Mother's fur, healed and comforted. As well, my attitude towards the war seems to have been an unlikely and unpopular one. The bond would not have been made permanent, and my impact on other's views would not have existed. Also, such a forceful personality would command so strongly that you would not have been given a chance."

Beaming with pride, Mother licked my face, then returned to the topic. "If it were not for sleeping that night, you would likely have refused or flunked the oncoming challenges. Your life would have been less, and, thus, civilization would have benefited less. You two started well. You have Our thanks for doing a good job and almost any comfort or reward you could ask for. We still keep for Ourselves the privilege of snookering you in your next life."

We planned to seek out Elaine-Haseya. She had said goodbye to her family and donated her cervine body to a wolf couple, so to follow David and me in her unbearable sorrow. The couple eased her through to transcendence and were honored and blessed by her gift.

While no one ever stops existing, all Mothers, all the various Mercys of the many peoples, discourage early returns. We would have offered blood prayers for Elaine-Haseya's reincarnation had we a body. She and her wolf helpers could be counted on to have offered all her blood and some of theirs in prayer.

We were anxious, our loves might not be permitted back. Would there be a baby for each of their souls? The deer are plentiful, but coyotes are not. And weren't the deer ruled by their own beloved Parents? Who could say if they would honor the Wolf Parents' requests?

I looked into my Mother's eyes and asked that Elaine-Haseya be allowed to live again. Mercy smiled as though She knew a secret joke. After She nodded, we watched as though on a split screen, a doe and a female coyote were born. Separately, they blinked into the light while drawing breath and then followed with feeble, wobbly fist pumps.

For all the rough play between us and Them, without the love of and for Mercy and Justice, the world would be horrible and bleak.

We chose to become two newborns, wolf and deer, similar to our sweethearts.

Mercy nuzzled us both before we left and said She and Her Husband would take note of our lives. We were at first happy, then dismayed. The saying "May you come to the attention of people in high places" was known to us. There are no higher. It had filled some with dread.

But we knew we were up to the challenge.

***

Toualetehydrophobia

by Kevin David Anderson
United States

I had no idea there were so many debilitating phobias. There are those that are terrified of right angles, Mexican food, the letter R, the metric system, and even a miserable few that fear Wednesdays, becoming incapacitated every hump-day. There is even a phobia of elastic. Can you imagine being afraid of your underwear?

Irrational fears are life-altering, and it broke my heart when we found out about my son's. We discovered his while at the mall. My son had to go to the bathroom, so we started our quest. Why department store bathrooms are located in the place farthest from where you start looking for them is a mystery for another time, but we found it. My five-year-old made a mad dash for the closest stall, and I knew by his pace that we'd just made it. I stepped over to the sink but before I turned the water on my son screamed.

I pushed on the stall door, but it was locked. "Jacob, you okay?"

"Daddy!" There was terror in his voice.

I kicked the door. It didn't budge. "What's wrong?"

"It's trying to eat me."

"What's trying to eat you?"

"The water. Daddy!"

Had to be a joke. Do five-year-olds make jokes like this? "Can you unlock the door?"

"I can't reach. It won't let me."

"What won't let you?"

"The water. Help!"

I put my shoulder into the door. It popped with a metallic ping, and water splashed the floor. My son, tears on both cheeks, stood to the side of the bowl, hands clasping the toilet paper dispenser. He waddled, pants around his ankles, into my arms. I held him close.

Water soaked through my shirt, transferring from his body to mine. At first, I'd thought he'd peed himself, but there was water all over the floor, the toilet, even the walls.

"Did you fall in?"

"No, Daddy, it grabbed me."

I pushed him from my embrace. "I don't understand. What grabbed you?"

He wiped his nose, getting the tears under control. "The water. It wanted to eat me."

I looked into the toilet. Other than it needing a good cleaning, nothing seemed out of sorts.

"Jacob, water doesn't eat people."

"I felt its teeth." He turned, pointing at his butt. "Right here."

I looked at his skin, blinking a few times, hoping I'd find nothing. But on his left cheek in a circular pattern, six-inch diameter, were tiny red marks. An image from an animated '80s film *When the Wind Blows* came to mind. A rat in a toilet feeding on feces attacked a character, and even though a cartoon, the image has haunted me.

Again I examined the bowl, this time for rodent hair and found nothing. By the time I looked back at my son, the marks were fading.

"Do you still have to go?"

He shook his head quickly, eyes wide.

Whatever had happened, I decided he'd been through enough. I wasn't going to let on that I knew he was lying.

"Sometimes after a man pees, he has to go again right away. Think that might happen?"

He nodded, so I carried him to the nearest urinal. He wasn't tall enough for the important part of his anatomy to reach so he stood on my feet. Unsure of how this new peeing arrangement was to work he pondered for a few beats before letting things flow.

It was about this time that my wife, Gayle poked her head in. "What's taking so long?"

"We're fine," I said over my shoulder. "Had a situation."

"Is it going to take long?"

"A minute. Why don't you head over to gift-wrapping and we'll meet you."

"Fine," she said, disdain in her voice. "Oh, and I ate your cookie."

"Goddammit. The only reason I come to this mall is to get a cookie."

"That's a penny for the swear jar, Dad."

"Okay. Take care of it later." I sighed. My marriage was shit. There are only two times in life a woman will eat a man's cookie without his permission: one, when they just start dating and she knows that he's more interested in getting into her cookies rather than eating one, and second, when the woman doesn't give a rat's ass about the consequences because the marriage has gone to complete and utter shit.

I cleaned Jacob up, no small chore thanks to the save-the-planet hand drying machines. If environmentalists spent less time saving us from ourselves and more time cleaning up after kids, we'd still have paper towels in public restrooms.

While Jacob picked out wrapping paper for our presents, Gayle asked me what had happened. I recapped it as best I could, even offered my rodent explanation. Hearing myself tell the story, I realized how strange it sounded, ridiculous, even surreal, but my wife didn't react as I'd expected. Normally she would have taken the opportunity to point out how inattentive I was as a father, or lambasted me for not watching the situation closer like any good parent.

But it didn't come. She just held a pensive look.

"What're you thinking?"

"Not sure. He really said that the water tried to eat him?"

I nodded. Without another word she turned away and joined Jacob.

It was a quiet ride home. We arranged the presents for friends and relatives under the tree, my wife heated up dinner, we played a board game, and that was it. We didn't talk about it for weeks. Not until we had too. It was a Wednesday when Gayle called me at my office. I work in internet security as a consultant and was in a meeting telling a medical company how they were hacked, and what I was going to do to ensure it wouldn't happen as easily next time—and rest assured, there's always a next time—when my assistant interrupted.

"It's your wife. Jacob's in the hospital."

I excused myself and picked up the line in the waiting area. "Gayle?"

"Where the fuck've you been?"

"In a meeting. What happened?"

"Jacob collapsed at school in horrible pain."

"Jesus."

291

"The ER doctor says his kidneys are backed up, and his colon is impacted."

"What? How?"

"David, he hasn't gone to the bathroom in almost three weeks. Not since that day at the mall."

"That's ridiculous. How is that—"

"David, just get down here." Gayle sobbed. "They're gonna put a catheter in him."

I left the office in a daze, and don't remember driving to the hospital. I sincerely hope I didn't hit anybody. The next thing I knew, I was at my boy's side as he howled in pain. Ever watch your child being fitted with a catheter? I don't recommend it. They flushed his kidneys and ran tests to check for long-term damage. Toxicity levels in his young body were alarmingly high, but hadn't become lethal.

"How could a child, a five-year-old, keep from going to the bathroom for weeks?" I said to the attending physician, Dr. Adams. But even as the words left my lips, I knew it was the wrong question. *How the hell could we, his parents, not know he wasn't going to the bathroom?*

I could tell by the doctor's hesitant response that he'd like to know that as well. Instead of asking the question, he said, "There's no physical reason why Jacob can't go to the bathroom. Everything's in working order. Any lingering discomfort he may experience will dissipate in a few days with the antibiotics I've prescribed. But there is nothing physically wrong with your son."

"Okay. So that leaves us where?"

"I can only conclude that your son's problem is physiological. I recommend he see a child psychologist."

"Jesus." I ran fingers through my hair.

Adams retrieved a card from a pocket. "Here's the number of a wonderful therapist. She's helped lots of children."

I didn't take the card. I didn't want to. I didn't want Jacob to need me to take the card. I wanted things back the way they were. I was in a loveless marriage, stuck in a lackluster job, but a proud parent of a great kid. And that was all I needed. I could live with that. But not this. "My son's not crazy."

"Nobody is saying that," Adams said. "But he needs help."

"We're his parents. We'll help him."

Adams closed his eyes for a few beats as if this wasn't the first conversation he'd had with a father in denial. He returned the card to his pocket. "We're admitting Jacob for overnight observations. Barring any unexpected test results, he can go home tomorrow."

An hour later Jacob was moved upstairs to a room, where exhaustion set in and he fell fast asleep. Gayle and I watched him for almost an hour without saying anything. We just sat and watched him breathe. After it seemed we were both convinced that he'd continue breathing even if we looked away, I finally spoke. "How did we miss this?"

"Miss what?" Gayle said.

"How did we miss that he wasn't going to the bathroom?"

"By we, you mean, *me*, right?"

"No, Gayle. I really want to know," I said trying not to sound accusatory. "Did he give you a reason why he wasn't using the bathroom?"

Gayle closed her eyes. "Said he was afraid."

"Of the bathroom?"

"The toilet water," Gayle said. "He thinks it wants to eat him."

"The water. Crap, this goes back to what happened at the damn mall."

"What happened that day, David?"

"I told you everything. Even my rodent theory."

"He wasn't bitten. I checked when we got home," Gayle said. "The marks you described were gone or were never there."

"He really said he feared the water? The water, Gail?"

Gayle nodded and then must have seen something on my face as the wheels in my head began to take me back. "This has nothing to do with that," she snapped.

"No, of course not," I said more to avoid a fight rather than stop my thought process. "I just think it's interesting, that he said water."

When we started dating—and I use the word dating loosely, as it was more a string of uninspired hook-ups—I learned about Gayle's gift. There was a group of us out one night, discussing useless talents. My roommate demonstrated his ability to turn his eyelids inside out without touching them; Gayle's sorority girlfriend could clip her toenails into a shot-glass, which she unfortunately demonstrated, and I did my impression of a tap-dancing mouse with the full musical score. But Gayle's talent was the topper of the evening. We sat mesmerized as she twirled her index finger over a glass of water. Without coming in physical contact with the glass or the liquid inside, the water move.

It spun, mimicking the motion of her finger, swirling around like in a toilet bowl. If she changed direction, the water too changed.

During our six-month relationship, before she got pregnant, I'd seen her do a few other things inadvertently. Once at the beach, I swear she took control of a wave that was about to hit her. At least a foot over her head, and only seconds from crashing into her, Gayle held up her hands defensively and the wave split down the middle dissipating to either side of her. Later a speeding car drove through a huge puddle sending a shower of dirty water our way. We both saw it coming, but I was the only one who got soaked. There are other examples, but what we realized was that this talent, or gift, call it what you will, was one she could only summon when slightly intoxicated. She had to be drinking in order for it to work, not stoned, we know because we tried them all. It had to be alcohol.

We were always inebriated when together, but when she got pregnant, she stopped drinking, and so did I. It's amazing how sobering a pregnancy test could be. It took some doing because as we were to find out, we were alcoholics, or at least heading down that road. Jacob changed our lives and we found sobriety. And with sobriety came a fresh look at one another, resulting in more than just the loss of her unique talent.

"I can't believe you're bringing that up," Gayle said. "It's been fucking years. How dare you."

"Goddammit, Gayle, I'm not accusing you. Shit, I just want to know why this happened."

"And I don't? I'm his mother."

"Why're you so fucking defensive?"

"I'm not—but everything is not my goddamn fault."

"I ..." I took a deep breath. "You're right. Let's just focus on Jacob. He needs us. Why don't you go home, get some rest. I'll stay with him tonight."

Gayle nodded. "Think they'll let you spend the night?"

"They'll have a hard time stopping me."

Gayle picked up her purse, kissed Jacob then moved over to me, hesitated, and gave me an obligatory hug. I squeezed her shoulders and wondered how long we could keep this up.

When the sounds of her footfall had faded down the hall, a groggy voice spoke from behind me.

"Hey, Daddy, I lost track ..."

I turned to find Jacob's eyes open. "Lost track?"

"I lost track, but I think you owe about ten dollars to the swear jar."

I laughed. "Probably right, son. Take care of it when we get home."

Jacob sat up. "Are you and Mommy gonna get a divide?'

"A what?"

"This girl in my class, her parents got a divide. Now she gets two birthdays and two Christmases."

His question was like a punch in the stomach. "You mean a divorce. And no, we're not getting one."

"But if you did, can I live with you?"

The weight of his words caused me to sit. I scooted closer to his bed. "Why wouldn't you want to live with Mommy?" I asked, not really sure if there was an answer I wanted to hear.

"Mommies should always come when you call," he said.

"What does that mean?"

His mouth opened to speak but paused, and I got the sense he was rethinking his answer. After a few beats, he said, "She doesn't know anything about *Star Wars* and thinks Pokémon is dumb."

"Well, now," I said. "I understand. These are pretty serious issues. Maybe we should talk about them at the next family meeting." I took a deep breath. "Right now I'd like to talk about why we're here, and not at home."

"It's because I hurt myself. I didn't go to the bathroom."

"That's right. Mommy told me that—"

"It's the water, Daddy. It wants to eat me," Jacob's voice rose, agitated.

"But, Jacob, you know that's—"

"I'm not going near that water, ever again."

Before I could respond there was a knock at the door. I turned as a nurse poked her head in. "Knock, knock," she said, stepping inside. "Dr. Adams recommended we try this."

"Is that a bedpan?" Outside of a movie I don't think I'd ever seen a real one.

She nodded. "It's kind of big, I know, but we don't have a children's ward at this hospital, so we don't really have his size." She looked over at Jacob. "Do you want to give it a try?"

Jacob looked at me for guidance.

"Give it a go."

Jacob sat on the thing in his bed. He seemed to like that there wasn't any water in it, and although he didn't go, it gave me an idea. I called Gayle and she said it was worth a try.

The next day upon arriving home we showed him what Gayle had bought. It was the largest toddler training toilet chair we could find. A kid's version of a bedpan that sits on the floor in the bathroom while a child learns to take care of their business. On the packaging, it said for use with ages six months to two years, and it was odd seeing my five-year-old on it, but no weirder than a six-year-old in diapers, or a ten-year-old breastfeeding—all things I've seen. Gayle had even found a Pokémon one.

"Check it out, buddy," I said. "You can take a crap right on Pikachu's face."

Jacob laughed. "Swear jar, Dad."

"All right, but you have to clean it. You're a big boy, and that means dumping out your business in the toilet. Your mom and I will help you the first few times, okay?"

Jacob nodded, less enthused. He looked over at the toilet as if it might grab him, then scooted the training chair as far away as possible.

And that was that. Over the next few days, Gail and I helped him with the dumping and cleaning and then he took over. We had our solution. It wasn't perfect, like a square band-aid on a round wound, but in my mind, it was over. A temporary fix, until he grew out of whatever the hell this was. But as I would soon learn, this wasn't the kind of thing you grow out of.

Less than a month had passed, and I had all but forgotten about Jacob's irrational behavior when Gayle met me at the front door one evening. In our five-year marriage not once had Gayle ever met me at the door. "Come with me to the backyard," she said.

"Hello to you too," I said.

I followed her around the side of the house. She pointed to a spot by the fence. I could see flies. Hundreds. "Something die back there?"

Gayle shook her head. I could see she'd been crying. As I moved past her, the smell hit me. I gagged once, twice, then used my tie to cover my nose. Plastic beach shovels were scattered around, covered in what looked like mud. But it wasn't mud. The stench of human waste overwhelmed me. I vomited, just missing my shoes.

296

I staggered back to Gayle, unable to deal with the realization that our son had been burying—or doing his five-year-old best—a month's worth of excrement.

"Back at the hospital, Dr. Adams gave me a child psychologist's number," Gayle said. "He gave it to me because you wouldn't take it."

"Make an appointment," I said.

"I already did. Tomorrow, ten a.m.," Gayle said, walking away.

I gagged. "Good call," and threw up again. This time my shoes weren't as lucky.

*

Jacob saw the psychologist, Karen Mathews, three times a week for almost a month. I liked her. A bit young but really knew her stuff. After one initial meeting with all of us, she met with Jacob alone. After about session nine or ten, she asked to meet with Gayle and me while Jacob sat in the waiting room. There was a receptionist out there so Jacob wouldn't be alone, but Jacob protested. There was a bathroom right next to the waiting area. When the toilet was flushed, the sound of the swirling water caused Jacob to tremble. He was now at the point where he couldn't even be within ten feet of a toilet.

Karen allowed Jacob to stay if he promised not to listen. He sat in the corner with headphones and played a game on my phone as we began.

"I think he's getting worse," I started. "We keep his potty in the garage now. Hell, he brushes his teeth in the kitchen."

"I know," Karen said. "And you're correct, his situation is becoming paramount."

Gail's eyes were wet and red. "What's wrong with him?"

"When we first met I mentioned a possible diagnosis, and one of the reasons I called you in here today is because I'd like to make it official. He is suffering from an acute case of Toualethydrophobia."

"Jesus," I said. "The fear of toilet water? How is that even a thing?"

Gayle began to sob silently.

"I don't wish to spend our time focusing on the phobia itself," Karen said. "What Jacob and I have been working on in our last few meetings is dealing with what triggered the phobia."

"The incident at the department store this past Christmas."

Karen shook her head. "It goes further back than that, and Jacob and I have been getting close, but every time we approach the event, he becomes blocked, very agitated, and shuts down."

"Is there a way to get over this block?"

"Yes, and that's the next thing I'd like to talk to you about. During our last few sessions, we've been working on EMDR therapy—Eye Movement Desensitization and Reprocessing. It's a technique which will allow Jacob to approach the event and reframe how he feels about it. I hope we can alter his fear and turn it into a source of strength. Today I'd like to push past his block, deal with the event of origin, and start the process."

I can't say I understood everything she said, but it all sounded positive. Any improvement in my son would be welcome. "Are you asking our permission to do this?"

She smiled. "I just wanted you to be aware of where we're at and what I'm hoping to accomplish today."

"Is it all right if we watch?" Gayle asked.

"Of course," Karen said. "Let's get started."

We sat in the corner of the room closest to the door while Karen prepared Jacob. There was a long serious of questions, asking Jacob about the colors and smells in the room. After fifteen minutes of this, Jacob leaned back and put his hands behind his head. He took long steady breaths. I hadn't seen him this relaxed in months. He smiled, even when the conversation turned to the trauma at the department store.

"And what did the water try to do?" Karen asked.

He responded casually. "Tried to eat me."

"But it didn't, did it?"

"Nope," Jacob said.

"Why is that?"

Because water doesn't eat people, I wanted to shout.

Jacob held up his hand as if he were thrusting a sword into the air. "Because I am strong. Way stronger than water."

"That's right, Jacob." Karen pulled something out of her pocket. I couldn't see what it was because of where I sat, but I could see that Jacob's eye's locked on it. I leaned to catch a glimpse. Karen held a small toy. Kid's call them fidget spinners. She used an index finger to give it a slight turn every few seconds, and with another finger, she started tapping on its center. So there was a turn, a tap, a turn, and a tap. It continued like this for several minutes. "Can you remember a time when you were going potty, but you didn't feel strong? A time before the water tried to eat you at the department store."

With his eyes locked on the toy, Jacob nodded.

"Can you tell me where that was?"

"At home."

"Are you alone?"

"No, Mommy's home. But she's sick. I keep calling but she won't come."

"Did you need her?"

"Yes. Mommy help me. I'm falling."

I looked over at Gayle. She was shaking. "What the fuck, Gayle?"

Without meeting my gaze, she got up and left. I followed, stopping only to shut the door to Karen's office. I grabbed Gayle by the wrist.

She whirled around. "It's not my fault."

"What is Jacob talking about?"

She covered her face with her hands. "Oh, god, oh, god, please don't let this be my fault." I guided her to a couch. The receptionist's eyes were on us, but I didn't care.

"What happened?"

Gayle wiped her nose. "It was over a year ago, almost two. We told Jacob he couldn't use the toddler practice seat anymore. He had to be a big boy and use the toilet without it. You remember?"

"Yes."

"Well, one time, when ... he ..."

"Gayle, what the fuck happened?"

"He fell in, lost his grip or something."

"Was he hurt?"

"No, but he was stuck. Couldn't lift himself out."

"Okay. So he called out and you came and got him."

"I heard him calling. Over and over. Mommy help," Gayle cried.

"You helped him, right?"

She looked at me clearly reliving the scene. Her lips tightened.

"Why didn't you help him?"

"Because I was drunk! I collapsed on the couch and just listened to him. I was sick of him. Sick of you."

"Jesus, how long was he in there?"

She put her hands over her face. "Three hours. When I finally got him out, I made him promise never to speak of what happened. Bury it. Just bury it."

"Shit, Gayle."

She dropped her hands and faced me, eyes angry. "You want to know why I was drinking?"

I stood up. "I don't give a fuck."

She grabbed my hand. "I unpacked your suitcase from your Boston trip. There was lipstick all over one of your shirt collars. Jesus, David, how cliché can you get?"

I leaned down, bringing my face close to hers. "You stupid bitch. Our client took us to a strip club. A stripper sat on me, kissed my neck, tried to sell me a lap dance. I left and took a cab back to the hotel."

"You didn't ..." She slid off the couch and fell to the ground. "I'm sorry, David."

I pulled my hand away. "Go home," I said, then walked back into Karen's office. I shut the door quickly. I didn't want Jacob to hear his mother cry.

"Calm down, Jacob," Karen said. She was on her knees in front of Jacob's chair.

Jacob kicked wildly with both feet. "I can't get out. I can't."

"That's not where you are right now. Tell me what colors are in my office."

"Mommy, where are you?!"

I walked over to Karen's side. She held a hand out indicating not to interfere.

"Jacob, I need you to listen to me." Karen put her hands on his shoulders.

"Mommy should come when I call."

A crash came from the waiting room. It sounded like furniture being flipped over. It was punctuated by a bloodcurdling scream. Gayle's screamed. I assumed Gayle was throwing a tantrum, but then there was another scream. Distinctly not Gayle's. The receptionist. I moved toward the office door and looked back at Jacob.

"Help me, Mommy!"

Gayle screamed again, and like an echo, so did the receptionist.

I hurried into the waiting room, and my left foot instantly slipped on the wet floor. I kept myself from falling by grabbing a coffee table that had been upended. I stepped on drenched magazines. The receptionist was on the floor, clothes and hair wet, one shoe gone. But Gayle was nowhere to be found.

"Where's my wife?"

The woman didn't say anything, just pointed toward the short hall heading to the bathroom. I jumped over the table and turned the corner just as Gayle screamed. I saw a pair of hands holding onto the doorframe inches from the ground. She pulled her head up into the hall and caught my gaze. "Help me, David!"

I dove, grabbed her hands and held tight. We were both pulled into the bathroom sliding on the wet floor. My head slammed into the sink and I lost my grip. I laid back and looked up in horror.

A funnel of water had encased my wife's legs. As it swirled around, sharp ripples gouged into her thighs. Blood streaked the water, winding around, red stripes on a candy cane. The funnel lifted her up and slammed her against the stall door. Gayle reached for me, eyes pleading. But all I did, all I could do, was watch as the funnel swallowed her hips, then her torso. The twisting water pulled her into the stall, and that's when I noticed where the tornado of liquid came from. The toilet.

The funnel began to sink into the bowl, getting smaller and smaller. The water made almost no sound, which seemed to amplify the snapping and crunching of Gayle's bones. As it pulled my wife in, she said the last thing she would ever say to me. "David, it hurts."

The lid came down with a slam. Water dripped down each side of the bowl, clean and clear. When I was finally able to take a breath, I felt something in my hand. I unclenched a fist and found Gayle's wedding ring resting in the center of my palm. It must have come off when I had a hold of her hands.

Dizzy from the blow to my head, I crawled over to the toilet, lifted the seat. The water was still, quiet. No sign of Gayle. No blood, hair, bone, nothing. Not even her scent. She was gone. I looked at the ring in my hand and tried to remember when we bought it. Where we bought it. Anything. I couldn't. I let it drop into the bowl. Watched it sink. Then flushed.

*

Jacob and I are Canadian now. It's not so bad. Bit cold. Nice health care. Made the sudden move up north when I began to realize the police were not on board with the "toilet ate my wife" story. I don't blame them. I did think that the receptionist's corroboration would help, and it did until parts of Gayle began showing up in different sewage treatment plants across the greater plains. To put it mildly, it horrified the public, and police were pressured to find a suspect. Since there was no one but me, up to the Great White North we went. Not a difficult job for an internet security expert. In fact, the only hard part was convincing Jacob when we changed his name to Luke that our new last name couldn't be Skywalker.

We've been up here a year and Jacob shows no signs of his toualetehydrophobia. Like my wife, it's gone. I've given it a fair amount of thought and I'm still not sure if Gayle's gift was the cause of Jacob's phobia. Did she manifest something that terrorized him? I don't know. But when it comes to Gayle's death, I had a theory, and it was comforting for a while. I liked to think her guilt over what she may have done to Jacob took physical form through her gift and sentenced herself to her own form of punishment. I used to believe in some way it was kind of redeeming. She wasn't a great mom, but at least she knew it and felt bad about it. Anyway, I don't think that anymore.

On Jacob's birthday, we went out for steaks. Like men. As we waited for the food to arrive, I thought I should check in with him about his mom. He hadn't talked about her, and honestly at the time with all the covert relocating, I was glad. I had my hands full. But we were settled now. It was time.

"Hey, Jacob."

"Luke."

"Right, Luke. Ever think about Mom?"

"No," he said, as he put a finger on the rim of his water glass.

"Well, do you miss her?"

"No." He started moving his finger in a slow circle over his glass.

"Okay. Why not?"

He looked at me, eyes narrow. "Mommies should come when you call."

A chill moved through me as I stared at his glass. The liquid was moving.

I opened my mouth to ask him a question, one I did not want to ask for fear he might answer. *Did you hurt your mom?* But in the end, I didn't need to. The answer was in his eyes, and in the liquid in the glass, now swirling like water in a toilet bowl.

***

The Whole World in Their Hands

by Clark Roberts
United States

We've all seen the beginning of the end—a giant fucking hand.

There are gods, and now we all wish there weren't.

The setting of the first *Taking* was not a coincidence. The fact it happened on the stage of the World Cup was without doubt deliberate. Here in the USA, the single most-watched event is the Super Bowl, but every four years the entire *world's* eyes turn to the World Cup. It was here that *they*—whoever *they* are—sent us a message. One second the German standout Klaus Albrecht was speeding on a breakaway. The next second he was gone, snatched out of our existence while the soccer ball rolled harmlessly off course. The Brazilian goalie didn't take one step towards corralling that ball. Like all of us, he was frozen with fear.

The message was heard loudly and clearly by humanity. *You are not safe. You never have been, and you will never again feel safe.*

A giant hand.

A giant hand of a god made Klaus Albrecht look the size of a toy figurine, and it stole not only his glory but also him from our existence. That giant hand might have stolen sanity from all of us.

There was no door opened, at least none discernible. On playback there was no shimmering of the air as science fiction and horror movies have led us to believe. The footage revealed no crack in the fabric of our reality, no peek into what is on the other side—except for the hands. Watching it in slow motion only revealed the hand literally transpired from nothing. First the fingertips and then the inner hinges of the knuckles, a palm with a lifeline not unlike our own.

Everyone was looking for answers, because it was almost unbelievable.

Except it wasn't, because then the second *Taking* was caught on video a week later. This one a grainy cellphone recording from an Indian family visiting the zoo. The father is seen holding his baby, extending his arms out to a wire fence while a black buck antelope approaches. The antelope puts his nose through the fence nuzzling at the baby's bare feet. The baby is overcome with giggles, and its legs pedal the air. The father erupts with laughter as he looks back at the mother. We hear the mother from behind the recording cast an admonishment in a language I do not know, but I know that tone. All fathers know that tone. *Be careful!* The father gives a look all fathers carry in their repertoire saying *come now, let us have our fun.* Then the hand appears, dwarfing the baby. A giant thumb and finger snap closed on the baby plucking it from the father. The antelope rears and kicks its forelegs before bolting. There is a moment where true terror registers on the baby's face before it is taken. The father is left holding air. The recording clatters to the cement pavement. Screaming ensues.

Next up was Inukjak. All of the lights of that small Inuit village in northern Quebec were put out in one single night. I looked it up on the Internet the next day. The population of that village was 656. All 656 of those people vanished without a trace in a modern day Roanoke mystery. Except it wasn't a mystery. We all knew what happened.

The *Taking* happened, and because there were no answers on the horizon, the world held a breath. The Pope attempted sage advice, "We must continue to live piously and wait."

It seems many people cannot simply just wait. People are frightened. In the past year the suicide rate has more than quadrupled. People want to meet the god they worship rather than the gods behind the fabric of our reality.

I used to believe that anyone who followed through on that act was a selfish coward.

Now I know otherwise.

*

On a blustery winter night half a year ago, I was surrounded by brightly colored owls—a wiry statue of an owl on the nightstand, owl figurines lining the shelf, even an owl clock with oversized and shifting eyes hooted out the hours above the head of my daughter's bed. Our Ellie loved her owls. My wife and Ellie were both on the floor as was customary for what had become their nightly ritual. They both held

306

playing cards fanned out before them. Between them the rest of the cards were spread out in a haphazard pile.

"Ellie," my wife said, "do you have a jack?"

"Go fish," Ellie said.

Darlene reached and pulled a card from the make-believe fish pond.

Ellie studied her cards with her features momentarily twisted in earnest. "Mommy, do you have a ace?"

"It's *an* ace," I said, stressing the *an*.

"Huh?"

"*An* ace," I repeated. "When the next word begins with a vowel you use *an* not *a*."

"Sorry, Daddy."

"Technically he's right," Darlene said, passing over a card to Ellie. "But for now just ignore Professor Dork."

Ellie giggled. Darlene glared questioningly at me. *What the hell are you talking about right now?*

I took the clue, turning my attention to the bedroom window where sleet was already beginning to patter against the glass. The winter storm that had been predicted was beginning to froth. A steady breeze had kicked up and could be heard whistling around the corners of the house. An oncoming northern winter storm after dusk can feel downright ominous at times, and my thoughts turned to the *Takings*.

Since the tragedy of Inukjak, there hadn't been any more incidents of entire settlements vanishing. Still, worldwide, the *Takings* had progressed to an average of one or two a day. Our town had been spared up to this point. The nearest incident I could recall was in a town over a two-hour drive away. A pediatrician had been snatched as he unlocked his practice.

A gust of wind blasted the bedroom window. The bedroom light flickered perilously.

After the light steadied, Ellie had her eyes shielded with her cards.

"Maybe you should round up some flashlights," Darlene said to me. She was staring up at the bedroom light as if it was a giant icicle threatening to break loose and deliver a death blow.

"Good idea," I said. "Right after we put Ellie down I'll do that."

The game of Go-Fish progressed, and, like 99 percent of the previous games, when it was finished, Ellie had piled up twice the amount of sets as Darlene.

In the past I'd expressed to Darlene it wasn't wise to let our little girl win every time. We didn't want to be responsible for developing a winning complex that would crush Ellie when life actually challenged her. Darlene's response of defense was a challenge to me to challenge Ellie.

Beat a four-year-old in a game of Go-Fish? No problem.

So I'd challenged Ellie.

I'd lost hands down.

Darlene and I had always thought of our child as special, but the crushing defeat Ellie dealt me in a simple kid's game made me ponder it differently. *How* special is she? When I mentioned it to Darlene as we brushed our teeth, Darlene had given me a look in the mirror. *So you finally see it.*

The discussion had continued when we went to bed. We even went so far as to discuss the exorbitant amount it would cost to send her to a school for gifted children. Darlene, always a believer in the supernatural, had tossed out the term clairvoyant.

With the current game wrapped up, Ellie tucked herself into bed. Darlene promised to come back for a last 'goodnight' when I finished a bedtime story.

I scanned Ellie's bookshelf, asking her, "Which one?"

"Little Red Riding Hood!"

"Again?"

"It's spooky. It feels like a spooky night."

I reluctantly pulled the Brothers Grimm edition and sat down to read.

"Watch this," Ellie said, taking the book from my hands.

She proceeded to read through the entire story without making an error. This was no child's picture book interpretation of the tale but the original and complete Brothers Grimm version. Certainly there are a couple pictures to help flesh out the plot, mostly crude sketchings which don't even thinly veil the wolf's predacious intent, but for the most part it is a true short story.

She closed the book letting it drop to the floor.

"Good Lord," I muttered, and dropped my jaw.

"Do you think I'm special, Daddy?"

"Under all of God's grace I think you're special."

"Daddy, if the power goes out in the night, can I come in and sleep with you and Mom?"

"You sure can, Elli-owl." I tussled her mop of blonde hair. I glanced at Darlene who was back and leaning against the doorframe.

"I'd really like that too," Darlene agreed.

When the *Takings* first began, Darlene and I had brought Ellie into our bedroom each night. We'd slept better knowing Ellie was by our side. It only lasted a week and ended on Ellie's terms. Despite my concern, and Darlene's almost imploring, Ellie had amazed us both when she returned to her bed without batting an eye.

I patted Ellie's head. "In fact, I'll go down and get that flashlight to put on your nightstand." I leaned down to kiss her cheek goodnight. She tilted her chin up, and I turned to receive her reciprocating kiss on my cheek. This time she reached higher, kissing my forehead. She let the kiss rest there for a second. Parental. Recalling that kiss makes me think of paintings of the Mother Mary holding her baby Jesus.

"That was different," I said, squinting my eyes.

"I love you, Daddy." Kids are strange, and I chalked it up to that. If only I'd known.

I joined Darlene in the doorway and reached for the light switch. The heaviest gust of wind yet assaulted the house. The light once again flickered of its own accord. Sleet pelted the window like handfuls of thrown stones.

The room fell decidedly black. Immediately my fingertips tingled. I've always dreaded the initial sensation of helplessness that washes over me when the power fails completely.

The blackout only lasted a couple seconds, just long enough to draw out a yelp from Darlene, before the house hummed back to life.

The hand, large enough to palm a small sedan, hovered above our daughter's bed.

Nothing can compare to the loss of your child. When parents stand over a child succumbing to cancer and state they'd gladly take their child's place, I can testify to the truth of their conviction.

I won't write down in detail what next happened. Certainly I could recall it in full detail as I've dreamed the sequence almost nightly. At other times, when Darlene forgets to take her pills, I've been wakened by her thrashing the bed sheets, and I know it's the nightmarish memory we share that also ruins her sleep.

But no, I won't put that down here.

I cannot do it.

I simply can't.

It's enough to just acknowledge that the *Taking* had finally occurred in our town.

*

Just nights after our daughter's *Taking* the town organized a vigil. The community turned out in droves to light candles and whisper prayers. Darlene and I were hugged by both friends and strangers.

The days turned into weeks, the weeks into months. We refused to have a legitimate memorial service. Instead we chose to play the part of Sisyphus, pushing our rock of grief through each day that was our hill. The memory of Ellie's *Taking* haunted our dreams. I would wake from these dreams and tumble back down that hill with a bottle of liquor in hand. Darlene would rise in the middle of the night and stand next to the window. Often she'd stay there just staring into the deep of space until the morning. I never found any answers at the bottom of those liquor bottles. The moon's phases never delivered any mercy to Darlene's soul.

*

Last night was different. Last night I had a different dream.

I was seated at the back of a school bus full of young children. Outside my seat's window the dark of night pressed as the bus barreled at warp speed down an empty but winding highway. Around each curve the bus careened onto two wheels threatening to roll. Inside the bus was a madhouse of wails and terrified screams. Children spilled into the aisle while others clung to their seats for dear life. The driver of the bus was undeterred by any of this madness and continued to straighten the curves, then flooring it on the short straightaways at breakneck speed to the next upcoming bend. Through my feet I could feel the frame of the entire bus rattling, breaking apart.

The little girl I shared the seat with was dead. Her head had banged against the window with such force the pane of glass had spiderwebbed. She flopped into my lap. Her head rolled. Her tongue stuck out. Her eyes lifelessly stared up at me. I decided I couldn't stand for any more of this.

The center aisle jerked to and fro like a rope bridge snapping in hurricane winds. Somehow I managed my way over and around the mass of entwined bodies being tossed about as I stumbled down the aisle to the front of the bus.

310

"Slow down!" I yelled.

The driver looked up at me blithely. His eyes were missing, replaced by only darkness as if they'd been cleaned out with a deep-digging scoop. He worked the shifter and somehow the bus found a higher gear. I actually felt the bus momentarily lift from the road. Behind me the children were screaming bloody murder. I glanced back. The emergency door had swung open creating a vacuum that sucked the children out in clusters. My daughter was one of the children; she was suspended in air like Supergirl. Trying to fight the forceful vacuum, she clutched to the top of a seat for all it was worth. The bus jolted as we hit a bump, and my daughter lost her grip. She was sucked out of the bus with hands and feet splayed before her.

"Better brace yourself," the driver intoned.

I turned my head in time to see the headlights bearing down on a massive tree before we smashed into it.

I was thrown forward and shattered through the bus's front window. I struck the ground with the force of a meteorite. Despite feeling the impact rattle through every bone in my body, I raised to my feet to discover I'd survived the crash unscathed in a way that is only possible in dreams. Behind me the wake of carnage from the wreck was nothing short of apocalyptic. The children had not survived. Their bodies and limbs were strewn over a burnt wasteland. I was surrounded by a blackened and worthless landscape. Smoke coiled from gigantic craters in the ground. To the west, far in the distance, I could see massive fires lighting the sky. To the east, not one, but three separate suns were rising. Their discs were unsettling against the horizon. They were too near the Earth, too large in the sky.

My mind tried to compute what had happened, tried to elucidate the why of it.

"Because why not? I guess some of us just don't give a fuck anymore."

I turned to the voice. The bus driver was slumped beneath a charred tree, his eyes closed as if he'd only been stirred from a nap. The tree was a nightmare unto itself. Despite having been burnt crisp, the ends of what few limbs remained blossomed before my very eyes, and the fruit of each blossom was a fungus-like disfigured effigy of my daughter. It was a heavy fruit. Hanging the branches low, the fruit-fungus stirred pendulously in the hot breath of the air.

I ran to the bus driver. I curled my fist into the man's coat, shook him violently, and drew his face near mine. I screamed, "Why did you do this? What was the point of all this?"

The driver's eyelids fluttered momentarily before popping open. Again, his eyes were only darkness from which ribbons of smoke escaped.

"You've got me all wrong, Daddy-o. But let me ask you something, you ever step on an anthill?"

"What does that matter?"

"It *won't* matter." He pointed my attention back east where now the three suns collided and absorbed into one gargantuan, blazing orb. It was so immense in the sky it couldn't be seen in its entirety. Though what could be seen, and felt, was mind numbing. Massive fiery whorls as flames consumed flames, infinite fusillades of explosions each more nuclear than the previous, heat, heat, heat. "That's your end game right there. So why not?"

I woke from this dream shaking. The house was silent. For a time, I stared up at the ceiling trying to regulate my breathing. My body trembled, and the sheet below me was sopped in cold sweat. The back of my throat was dry. Beside me, my wife's sleep continued in a steady cadence. I rose from the bed knowing if I closed my eyes I would only be haunted by horrific images of sprouting fungi that would grow into the face of my little girl.

I went downstairs and straight to the liquor cabinet. I poured a double shot of Scotch into a tumbler glass. With a trembling hand I drank it all in two swallows. I gave the liquor a chance to steady my nerves before I pulled back the kitchen window's curtain. Outside, all was still and quiet with the world. The moon hung in its appropriate place in the night sky. Our neighbors' houses were not the frames of smoking skeletons as I'd feared they'd become.

"Hello, Daddy."

The tumbler glass dropped from my hand and clattered into the sink. Turning, I saw the small figure in the next room. She was seated straight-backed as a book binding as my wife had taught her was proper at the dining table. I stepped around the kitchen island. With each heavy breath a step until I reached our dining area. My hand flailed, sweeping the wall behind me until it hit the light switch.

"I'm glad you and Mommy didn't throw my juice boxes out." She was dressed in the same purple owl pajamas she'd worn the night of

312

her *Taking*. In front of her was the juice box of which she'd spoken. With sheepish and innocent eyes, she leaned over sipping from the crinkled straw. "I found it in the fridge. I know you guys always told me to ask first, but I really wanted some juice. I hope you're not mad."

My legs had gone numb. My hands were once again trembling uncontrollably as a mixture of relief and shock burst through my systems. I gasped, "No way, Ellie-owl. I'm not mad at all."

"Daddy, why are you crying?"

I sobbed, "Because I've missed you!"

"I missed you too, but I'm not crying."

Next she giggled, and then in straight Ellie fashion, she put a hand over her mouth to conceal her smirk. This had always been her go-to move when she laughed at something she thought was funny but possibly inappropriate. This was truly my daughter, my Ellie. I didn't know why or how, but she had been delivered back into my life.

I rushed to her gathering her petite frame in my arms. I hugged her tightly to my chest and squeezed not only her but also the tears from my eyes. I rocked back and forth in an outpouring of emotion while she rested her head on the sweep of my shoulder. It reminded me of the first time we'd spent an entire evening at an amusement park. She'd tuckered out at the end and I'd had to carry her to the car.

"I'm sorry if my dream scared you," Ellie said.

"What do you mean by that?" I asked, truly perplexed.

"The dream I sent to you tonight." Beneath my palms I felt the small knobs of her spine straighten as she pulled back so as to assess my reaction. "I could feel you were scared."

I set her back onto the chair and brushed a fallen lock of blonde hair from her forehead. "We don't have to talk about my dream right now."

"Sometimes it's best to get straight to the point, Daddy. You taught me that. Mr. Bill says things like that too. My dream made you angry. I didn't mean to make you so angry. I'm sorry."

"Hey there, I'm not upset with you." My thoughts were a shaken snow globe of emotion and weren't able to follow everything she'd said. For the moment I completely dismissed the reference to a Mr. Bill. I put two fingers to her chin gently lifting until our eyes connected like magnets. "So you were able to control my dream?"

"Not all of it, silly Daddy." Her mercurial nature came through. She smiled foolishly at me. "I was only trying to show you what happened in a way you might understand. I put you on the bus, and you came up with the rest. All those fires and the tree with my faces. I couldn't've thunk up all that. You're a weirdo, Daddy."

It dawned on me that she was talking in a metaphor. Somehow she'd influenced my dream thoughts, maybe with just a nudge, and my subconscious had filled in the details. I thought of the horrible imagery of the tree. Why had I conjured such an image of my daughter?

"Daddy, you've got it both right and wrong. It *is* a met-uhh-for." Suddenly I could feel her presence in my head. It was as if a part of her had turned to smoke and slid into my earholes. "The tree just means I'm going to keep growing. But the god you made in your dream, the bus driver you thought up, you've got them all wrong. They don't look like that, at least not the ones that took all of us away. They have eyes, and they're nice and kind, and they told us to say that they've saved us. They saved us from the uhh-poc-lypse."

Apocalypse. I asked her if that's what she meant. She nodded.

"It was all real confusing when the gods explained it, but later on Mr. Bill told me in an easier way. Mr. Bill said that there is some kind of disagreement happening between the gods."

"Who is this Mr. Bill character?" I asked. My daughter's tone told me it was somebody good, somebody she liked, even trusted, but he was still a stranger to me. "Is he one of the gods?"

She laughed, "No, Daddy. Mr. Bill is just a man. He used to be a farmer. He's the adult I've been assigned to, but he won't let me call him dad."

A guardian of sorts is what she meant. "You shouldn't have called him dad. I'm your dad. I'll always be your dad."

"I don't try to anymore. Mr. Bill won't let me. He said that wouldn't be fair to you or Mom."

"What else does Mr. Bill say?"

"He told me that you and Mom should know that back here on Earth his own children had become good grownups. He misses them."

"Does Mr. Bill know why all this happened? Why the gods are fighting?"

"Yes."

"Can you tell me?"

"Some of the gods have given up on people, and other gods, like the ones that took us, want to keep the experiment going in a safer spot. Mr. Bill *did* tell me that he and I and the others are like a secret.

That we're supposed to rebuild everything on our new home. We're the chosen ones, but we're also a secret to the bad gods."

"But where? Where is your new home?"

She clucked her tongue as if the name of the place escaped her. "There's a river. A lot of the kids want to go swimming in it, but the adults won't let us. Some of the women that wash our clothes down there say they've seen a serpent swimming under the water. Mr. Bill told me a serpent is just a large snake. He didn't know why a snake would live underwater."

"I don't either."

"Daddy, don't be angry, but the gods won't let me stay. I have to go back to help rebuild."

"No," I stated firmly. Once again I corralled her to my chest and squeezed my eyes tight. I stood with her in my arms rocking back and forth like one does with a newborn baby. "No, no, no. I'll hold you for eternity. Why on Earth would they need a child to help rebuild?"

"It's not about Earth, and Mr. Bill said he thinks without children even the best adults would never get it right. Mr. Bill told me to tell you and Mom he promises to love me, that he will do his best with me."

"I'm not letting you leave! I promise I'm never, never, never letting you go. Do you hear me? Never, never, never, letting you go."

"Sorry Daddy, but I'm special. I have to visit Mom, then I'm going for good. Daddy, do you care if I take my juice boxes?"

I ignored this question, instead focusing on living up to my promise. I wasn't letting go of her, no way in heaven or hell. She hugged me back, as fiercely as is possible for a four-year-old girl. I felt her breath on my skin and the wetness of tears on my neck

"You have to understand something, Daddy. There's always an end to things."

I didn't let go of her, yet she was taken from me just the same. I was left holding the air. I fell to my knees sobbing in great hitches as the grief of losing my daughter for a second time racked through my body like detonations.

*

An hour passed before I was able to gain my feet, but out the window the neighborhood was still dark and quiet. I made my way upstairs trying to convince myself I was fortunate to have seen Ellie one last time.

I noticed a sliver of light down the hall. Ellie's door was open a crack. I went to it, gently putting my hand up, but my wife's voice halted me.

"Ellie, do you have a queen?"

Ellie's voice, "Go fish."

"Darn. No match again."

"Mommy, do you have a seven?"

"You must have peeked at my cards!"

I didn't try to peer inside, but I could picture them on the floor as easily as drawing water from a tap. Each would be holding a fan of cards before them, Ellie propped on her knees and in her owl pajamas, and Darlene sitting cross-legged, dressed in sweatpants and a baggy shirt. In the short time it took for them to complete their game, I heard more laughter from Darlene than either of us had exercised in the last six months. I stood there in the darkness and eavesdropped, praying their game would never end.

Eventually, inevitably, they both cheered and clapped. Ellie declared herself the still-reigning champion.

I shivered ice off my shoulders as Ellie's words from earlier struck me with the force of a village crushing avalanche.

There's always an end to things.

"Mommy," Ellie's voice dropped an octave with concern, "I need to tell you something."

I stepped backwards from the door. I couldn't bear listening to Ellie explain it one more time. I turned and traipsed down the hall. I did not sleep.

*

In the morning, I watched the first swatch of sunlight slip through the curtains and invade my sanctuary. I watched it grow as it crawled down the wall until it reached the bed. I rose and shuffled down to Ellie's room. I pulled the owl sheets back crawling into the small bed with my wife.

We held each other without speaking.

We wept hard.

Finally, we slept.

*

316

It was evening when I finally woke. We were still cramped together in the twin-sized bed. Darlene stared straight into my eyes when I blinked out of sleep.

"You've been watching me," I said.

"For about a half hour." She shrugged a shoulder saying *you should expect this quirky behavior from time to time.* The traces of a smile touched her lips. She placed a palm on my cheek. "You looked peaceful."

"That's the first I've slept uninterrupted since ..."

She moved a cool finger down over my lips to shush me. She said, "Me too. Me too."

It showed on her face. The bruise-colored bags that had chronically clung to us both like Marley's chains were gone from beneath her eyes.

"I can't believe this," I said, "but I think I'm actually hungry."

"I guess I should whip something up for us."

Downstairs we agreed on a breakfast for dinner. Darlene opened the fridge to pull out some eggs and let out a yelp of laughter. She said, "You've got to see this."

I stood by Darlene. The package of juice boxes we'd refused to throw out was gone.

"You think they'll get it right over there, wherever there is?" Darlene asked.

Before answering, I opened our kitchen trash. The empty juice box Ellie had drunk the night before was neatly placed on the top. Next to it, and capped, was the half-full bottle of Scotch I'd left on the counter.

I said, "With our Ellie-owl on their side, how could they not get it right?"

Darlene cooked. We ate eggs, toast, and hash browns at the dining table. When we finished, we immediately washed our dishes in the sink like responsible adults.

We moved to the couch, Darlene resting her head on my lap. She was asleep in minutes.

I sat there, ruminating, and stroked Darlene's hair. There were still unanswered questions banging in my head. I tried to puzzle together some answers based on my dream and Ellie's input, but no real answers were coming.

That is until I turned on the news. Now I know one of the answers. When I woke Darlene, I didn't bother to tell her what I'd learned. Our evening had been too peaceful to ruin. Instead, I walked her up to bed. I simply settled her back and came back downstairs to start writing this—my final blog.

Darlene did stir and mumble something as I walked out of the room. She said, "It feels different now."

It sure does feel different.

I've never felt so juxtaposed. On one hand there is at least some semblance of peace with my daughter's *Taking*. On the other is the sensation of helplessness, because I am nothing more than a speck upon another larger speck on a huge and dark canvas able to be painted out of existence with the stroke of an artist's whim.

The most recent news reports are not of another person being swept away into never-never land, but of another hand. This one is not merely a giant hand, but a cosmic hand that scientists estimate is at least twice the size of Earth. It looms above, spinning in space, hundreds of thousands times larger than any era-killing asteroid for which the last decades we've had million-dollar telescopes probing. The scientists' theory is that it probably came through a wormhole. It has a destination. The course it is on is in direct alignment for a perfect hit. They say we might be able to see it with the naked eye by the morning. It is estimated to strike in two days.

Imagine a fist closed around ping-pong ball. That is the kind of mercy I pray it delivers us. I plead to any of you that read this to also pray for that mercy.

Because the dream, the one my daughter partially gave to me, alludes to a permanent forecast of heat, heat, and more heat. That we are about to be pitched like a crumpled paper into a fire.

For me, the prospect of imminent death has unveiled a path to unmatched introspection. I haven't accomplished much with my life, and certainly I haven't lived godly. My professional life has been mediocre at best. More than once fate has presented me with the choice between right and wrong, and I've straight up turned my nose at the choice of clean living in the name of selfishness.

I've also lost a lot of relationships with good people.

But I'm not a terrible person. I'm truly grateful my daughter was chosen over me. Not only because it proves I didn't screw up everything, but also because the new home of humanity is better off with her rather than me. Maybe I wasn't afforded enough time to do so, but I didn't fuck up raising my Elli-owl. That much I was getting right.

Jesus, I love her.

And the ending that's spinning towards us, I'm going to get that right too. Admittedly, poisoning a drink for my wife and overdosing on pills myself has crossed my mind. Given the circumstances I think I'd be forgiven. But no, that would be the easy road, and it certainly wouldn't be an act Ellie could be proud of her father.

I still have faith *my* God is somewhere watching all of this.

Does that sound ridiculous?

Probably it does, but with the end so near, I've nowhere else to turn.

I'm going to fight back with the only means I know. Tomorrow I'm going to hold my wife's hand, because she'll need my strength, and I'll in turn need hers. I implore any of you reading this blog to join us in this fight, to kneel with us, to bow your head with us. For some of you it may have been a long time since you've uttered such words as these. Surely some of you have a different prayer to utter, or different beliefs. To that I simply send this invitation—in your own way. For those that don't, I offer up the words as I learned them.

Pray for mercy with us.
Pray or else we all burn.
Our Father, who art in heaven,
hallowed be thy name,
thy Kingdom come,
thy will be done,
on earth as it is in heaven ...

***

A Taste of Your Own Medicine

by Nidhi Singh

India

It was a warm mid-March afternoon, still as death.

The sea at this hour was out at low tide, leaving a salty, clayish, white beach in its wake. The sun blazed down with a feverish wrath, burning the jagged black rocks that lined the embankment. Little red crabs scurried beneath the slippery boulders, seeking respite from the brilliant burst of fire coming down from the skies. Itchy mongrels sulked in the shade, panting from the heat. Little fishing boats out at sea lurked about chasing the shades of their sails, waiting for the cool night so that they might get on with their business.

Quiet rows of small houses, shaded by plantain and coconut trees, with little fishponds up front, lined the seashore.

Obstinate little flies, common Indian pests, swarmed over Anishta's face, which was ashen and twisted with pain. Sweat dried in craggy rivulets down her hollowed cheeks; strands of once shiny jet-black hair, dry and grayed now, coiled and writhed on her forehead as Valli kneeled by the charpoy and waved a frayed bamboo fan over her. It brought her little relief, as had the blanks Valli got her from the village *vaidya*—a quack with no pretense to modern medicine save a short stint as a clinic compounder where he'd measured out colorful powders and potions into newspaper wrappers or plastic bottles.

A model wife, Anishta had suddenly taken ill, and thereafter slipped fast into delirium and stupor. Valli patiently kept pulling down the edge of her damp sari to cover the bony legs she flailed in pain. Their daughter, unattended and forgotten until she wailed, crawled nearby on the cow dung plastered courtyard, pushing out a little wooden toy cart before her, biting on it sometimes to ease the itching on her teething gums.

321

Valli's mother too lay on a charpoy in a far corner of the courtyard in the shade of the giant peepul tree. An unexpected winged guest, a bright blue *Neelkanth* had perched upon her shoulder, and without a care in the world, was dipping its black bill into the bowl of flattened rice and lentils Valli had placed for her.

"*Ram Naam Sat Hai ... Ram Naam ...*" A funeral procession, chanting the name of the true God Rama, passed outside their house.

The chanting drifted through the fog of her delirium. Anishta painfully turned her head and glanced at Valli with eyes that seemed animate for a moment. Holding her burning, twisted fingers in his hand, he smiled down at her. Bending down, he whispered in her ear, "It's Marich."

He leaned back to observe the shadow of deep grief settling on her wretched face; tears slipped over the edge of her cheekbone and gathered in a tiny pool on the pillow. "I won't be long," he said rising, uncurling the fingers that had gridlocked around his hand—trying to stay him.

*

Dust gathered like a thick film on everything that dotted the ugly Indian landscape—trees, leaves, cars, buildings, clothes, faces— anything that did not move for a minute gathered dust. Sweat glistened on the shiny black backs of tribal girls bent over lawns of guesthouses lining the seashore, as they plucked dead grass and weed. Some of them squatted on the pavements in the shade of parked taxis while the drivers sprawled on the back seats, their feet sticking out the windows, old newspapers covering their faces from the salty, sticky wind.

The tide was coming in slowly now, and the wind had begun to work up a howl, which soon became a constant, loud shriek as it escaped over the mainland like a wild beast.

When Valli returned from the burning *ghats*, Anishta was no more.

*

"Why aren't you running?" the captain barked, prodding the soldier doubled up in a shivering heap on the parapet lining the winding mountain road.

The *sepoy* looked up, his face contorted in pain. He was bathed in sweat even though it was a bracing foggy morning. He clutched his stomach and groaned. "I can't," he managed to mumble through clenched teeth, slight foam gathering at the corner of his mouth.

"What's wrong with him?" the captain spat at the company sergeant major, while still prodding the soldier in his ribs with his thick baton.

"He's unwell, *Sahib*," the CSM replied deferentially.

"So? So what?"

"Sahib," the CSM said, lowering his voice, "people say he's possessed."

"Possessed! What a lame excuse! Even a fly cannot wander into this company line without permission. Sound a couple of chilly canes off his buttocks—he'll come to his senses."

"Sahib, whenever he goes on leave, he gets this problem. He's a fine runner otherwise."

"Don't send him on any leave then. Take him away and sort him out."

The CSM motioned at two men, who, without further ceremony lifted Sepoy Valli between them and hauled him over the tailboard of a parked truck. Later, after the morning parades and roll calls, the CSM marched into the barracks where Valli laid on a nylon charpoy, squirming in a fetal position, his head between his knees.

"What happens to you when you go on leave?" The CSM stood over Valli, tapping his cane on the steel frame of the charpoy.

"I don't know—" Valli turned to face him and managed to raise himself on an elbow. "Look," he said, opening his mouth wide and sticking his black tongue out. Little worms crawled out his mouth, spreading over his face and neck, entering his nostrils and ears. They streamed down the bedposts and toward the CSM's shiny black boots. The CSM stepped back and stomped the slimy stains with his hobnailed boots, cursing all the while. Valli suddenly had a loud hiccup, his breath seemed caught up deep in his stomach when he coughed out with great force a squirming inky ball: the last trail of worms from his mouth. He collapsed back in his bed, exhausted, out like a wet light.

The CSM retreated from the barrack and stepped out into the gray mist that was settling like a heavy blanket over the mountain face. The damp stood thick on the tall green grass, the short day was spent already. He removed his beret, slung it on a tree branch, and wiped the sweat on his forehead. "*Oof*, what's up with him," he asked, standing under the shade and lighting up a filterless cigarette. "Bad oral hygiene."

The orderly NCO, in charge of Valli's platoon, shuffled his feet, tracing lines on the ground. "He screams all night, and he shits blood. Men don't want to use the latrines. He's wetting his bed and jabbers away to himself all the while."

"He looks shriveled."

"Hasn't touched a morsel since he came from home."

"Is it drink?"

"Hasn't touched a drop. We don't issue rum here at the post."

"Don't give him duty with a weapon—he'll shoot himself."

"He's a fine boy otherwise, does whatever you tell without grumbling. Pretty grounded, humble fellow."

"Folks?"

"Decent, poor people. Dad is retired, a respected postmaster. Stays by the sea in Odisha."

"Married?"

"Yeah, recently. Child marriage, I figure. Brought the bride home only last year. Young, very young. Got a small daughter too."

"Happens only when he goes home?"

"Yeah. Gets okay with time, though; recovers in the unit. But it's been getting worse each time. Do you think we should report him? The men understand, but for how long can they tolerate him?"

"The officers won't understand. They don't accept these things—things that can happen in rural areas. They'll say it's superstition."

"Maybe the doctors can help him?"

"They'll put him away in an isolation ward and give him shocks. He'll go nuts. Then we'll not only have a ghost but a crazy ghost up our arse. And you know the manual—I'll have to put an armed guard on him—throw more good men after one problem case."

"What should I do with him?"

"Put him away on temple duties. Let him help out the battalion priest for a few days. Then we'll see. Keep a keen eye on him." The CSM dropped the cigarette butt and ground it under his heel. "And make sure he brushes twice daily."

The orderly NCO followed him as he strolled through the post, snapping at men rubbing their hands in the biting cold, pointing out bunkers and firing hatches that needed fixing. At the platoon boundary the CSM bid the NCO stop. Swinging his cane moodily, he ambled on alone through the narrow mountain track to the next platoon as fat, orange-balled monkeys swung from branches overhead, gibbering away mindlessly.

*

It was dark when Valli set down his trunk on the train platform. He looked around. There was nobody familiar. He looked in the crowd for the glowing face of his bride, or the glazed eyes of his father that sparkled behind horn-rimmed glasses when they saw him, but they weren't there. He found an empty bench and waited.

The unmistakable smell of the sea mingled with fish and paddy fields wafted to his nostrils; smilingly, he inhaled deep gulps of it. It was humid and he could taste the salt as he licked his lips. Just a few minutes in the station and little beads of moisture had sprung up on his arms already. His coarse uniform clung to him like sackcloth and his neck began to itch where the collar touched it. There weren't many trains to Balasore at this hour, and the station began to empty out fast, until it was just him, and a few scruffy scavenger children and stray curs that followed them on the feces and urine-splattered train tracks. Suddenly becoming conscious of the overpowering stench around him, he rose and left.

He hailed down a cramped three-wheeler, noisy as a jackhammer, for a bone-rattling ride home. He was annoyed. He expected to be welcomed at the station—hadn't he written home of his arrival? But moping soon gave way to misgiving as a hundred negative thoughts crossed his mind. Was his father well? Was the child sick? What if his wife was visiting her parents? One could never be sure of the cadaverous postman deciding not to visit your home. But Valli had given him two bottles of army rum the last time, hadn't he?

He, therefore, didn't bother to haggle with the driver as he dismounted at the rusty gates of his house. He banged the iron latch a couple of times to announce his arrival and entered.

Valli passed through the courtyard and entered the living room. His father was watching TV and his daughter was playing on his knee. The old man, a heap of bones in a dirty *dhoti,* rose with delight on seeing his son. They hugged warmly, the daughter pressed between them.

"What's happening here, *Nana?*" Valli asked, looking around the untidy house. "Is she taking care of you?" He stepped back and looked keenly at his father. The old man nodded his head and waved his frail hands in protest, or helplessness, saying nothing.

"You have soda, Nana?" Valli opened the fridge. It was empty save a couple of water bottles, a plate of brown rice, and some fish cooked in mustard curry. "Where's the milk for the girl? Where's Anishta? Have you sent her out to the grocer for it?" He removed a water bottle and sank in the armchair next to Nana. Nana was absorbed in the TV and had turned up the volume as Valli was speaking.

"See what we have here," Valli said loudly, removing a bottle of Old Monk from his trunk and placing it with a flourish on the table. The old man's face lit up. He lowered the TV volume but still couldn't take his eyes off it. Valli poured out two stiff drinks, topped them off with water, and handed one to his father. "Cheers! Can we switch off the TV now, Nana? Where's Anishta?" Valli bent forward and took the baby out of Nana's hands. She snuggled against his chest and was soon snoring softly.

"She'll be back soon. Why, it's quite dark already," Nana said, squinting out the window.

"Why's the house so dirty? Where's the food for the baby? Do you get the money orders I send?"

"Yes, yes. That bastard postman—making eyes at womenfolk." Nana shook his head, knocking back the drink. "I get your letters, but I rarely go out now. Anishta manages everything. She's a good girl— just look around you. That poor single bone has to take care of so much—and the fields. She's gone to get fish for you. Don't get angry with her. Have you seen the crops? The castor stands so tall and proud. Ripe for harvest."

"What about your pension? Aren't you keeping a maid?" he remarked, looking around the untidy house.

"Anishta says we can't afford one anymore—insists on doing all the work herself—won't let anyone enter the house."

"Why? Why weren't you there at the station? Why couldn't she come? I've come after so long. They wouldn't give me leave after the way I fell ill the last time."

"Where would I leave your mother? Who would take care of the baby?"

"Still," Valli scowled.

"How do you feel now, son?" the old man asked, patting his son's hand.

"I feel better in the unit. I've lived here all my life; I love the sea. And now it seems this weather doesn't suit me—or any of us."

"Well, take care this time. Let's drink to us," Nana said, holding up his empty glass. They drank steadily, laughing and talking about good old days when coconut water was still cheap, when mother haggled with Bangladeshi refugees who came on their rickety little canoes and sold pomfrets and prawns on the beach, and when the guns still boomed from the naval firing ranges nearby.

A hush fell on the house when they heard laughing voices outside, the tinkle of glass bangles, and the chime of silver anklets on slim, pirouetting ankles. Valli unconsciously ran his fingers through his hair and straightened up in the chair. The curtains parted, and a dusky, enchanting face peeped in. Anishta, light on her feet, bounded over the hearth and shyly covered her head with the edge of her sari. She touched the feet of both men and stood giggling against the wall, casting coy glances at her husband. She seemed the only one in this house in fine clothes and looking filled out. The weather agreed with her, at least.

"How've you been, eh," Valli asked after her, his anger all gone at her loveliness. Anishta bit the edge of her sari, swayed like a child, and giggled some more.

"Who was with you? Whom were you talking to?" he asked.

The girl froze. "Nobody," she said. "Just some passing fisherwomen."

"Good! You've made friends." Valli rose and took the bulging jute shopping bag from her. He peeked in it. "What did you get?"

"*Illish*," she replied. "Pumpkin and gourd for parents."

Valli helped her empty the contents of her shopping on the kitchen counter. "What are these," he asked, finding vials and wrappers.

"Medicines."

"But there are no markings. Aren't they supposed to be tablets? Where's the prescription slip?"

"He doesn't give," she said, cowering, afraid he'll strike her.

"You're going to some local quack, aren't you? Why don't you go to the army doctor in Balasore?"

"Alone? It's too far." She trembled. Her round eyes became wide with fear and she turned her face protectively.

Valli threw up his arms in frustration. "Your parents should have lettered you. How are you going to teach our child? It's all my fault. I'll get them the medicines—enough to last a few months." He gripped her arms and glowered down at her. Her sari fell off her shoulders revealing bony collarbones on which one could balance an egg, he thought, and a heaving bosom. Pushing her against the wall, Valli pulled down her blouse and planted his lips on her bare breasts, slurping loudly. Her skin tone was much lighter under her clothes where the harsh sun had not cast its burning gaze. She sucked in her breath as his mustache bristled against her baby skin. He released her when he heard his father shuffling about in the other room.

"You are not to visit a quack again. Understand?"

She nodded eagerly, relieved to be spared a boxing on the ears.

He cupped her oval face in his hands and looked deep into her hazel eyes. "After dinner then ..." he leaned close and whispered, his hot rummy breath lingering as he left her to cook the fish.

Anishta smoked the fish in young plantain leaves and prepared it with mustard seed paste, curd, and eggplant, before submitting it to the frying pan for the final assault.

"It's a work of art," Valli said, wiping his mouth at the edge of her sari even as his father burped loudly to show appreciation for the dish served well. Valli finished off his plate before his father did. As he was about to lean forward and pick a piece from his father's plate, Anishta slapped him playfully on the wrist. "Have patience, dear, I'll get you a separate plate," she said, rushing into the kitchen.

"Why can't I eat from my father's fish?"

"I spice it lightly for him. You'll lose the taste. Wait up."

Later, after Valli had put the parents and child to bed, he led Anishta by the hand to the roof where they used to sleep in the cooler sea breeze of the night. The winds had died down with the receding tide and the palms gently brushed across the half-moon that seemed to hang over the edge of the terrace. They could see the little lights of fishing trawlers out at sea peering through the lifting clouds. They sat awhile on the jute charpoy, holding hands, gazing out at the beautiful gloomy expanse of the Indian Ocean before them. Little hillocks rose out of the black emptiness that stretched out as far as the eye could see and then merged into the dark rumbling skies. Valli sighed in peace. He was home. No artist could imitate God in the beautiful things that He had created on this planet, Valli mused.

"Sing a song," Anishta said, curling up on her side, placing her head in his lap.

"All right," he said. Clearing his throat, he began to croon to her in Odiya.

"What does it mean?" Anishta demanded.

"It's just a song, silly bird," he said, "there's no meaning." Bending down, he kissed her on the lips. Raising her, he unwound her sari around her boyish hips and cupped her cool buttocks. He pushed up her blouse and began to suck on her upturned nipples. "Are you still suckling the girl?" he laughed, detaching his face and wiping his lips. She grabbed his hair and pulled him back to her bosom, moaning softly. He rubbed his snout on her moist breasts and drank of her some more. Suddenly, he pulled back and spat on the ground. He wiped his mouth with the back of his hand. He held out his arm against the moonlight and stood up, cursing, "Fu ..." He grabbed her shoulders and turned her to face the moon. Her chest was covered in blood. "What is it?" he screamed.

Anishta first looked down at her naked body and then tilted her head toward the moon, and laughed, as if she were mocking its cleverness. "You bit me, lover," she said.

"No, I didn't, I swear."

"Yes, you did." She lifted her sari from the ground and quickly gathering it about her naked body, she bounded down the rickety spiral wooden staircase to their bedroom where the child lay.

Valli drew water with an aluminum ladle from an earthen pot placed by the bed and washed himself. He fell back on the bed and lay there worrying, his hands cupped under his head.

*

He felt hung over when he awoke in the morning. The night before was hazy in his benumbed mind. He thought a head massage might do him some good, so he sent for the village barber. The barber was chatty as usual, full of gossip about who was beating his wife and who was drinking too much rice beer in the village.

"I need to see the postmaster about Nana's pension ... and my money orders, so give me a nice grooming today," Valli told him when he managed to get a word in between the barber's nonstop patter.

"Why, any problems?" the barber asked, his interest perked up as he examined Valli's head to see how he might shorten the already crew-cut hair. Slashing his scissors against the comb with aplomb, he went to work on Valli's head anyway.

"I think they might be shortchanging Anishta. She can't read, you know. I want to know what happens to all the money sent home. Nana will never complain, you know?"

"It's great to have money, greater to spend it."

"Provided you have it to spend."

"Wasn't your father postmaster himself? They won't stop from robbing their own, is it?"

"People who knew him are long gone."

"It's a bad deal to be a soldier. They're away so long—you never know what fish is frying behind your back. It's fishy, but ..." the barber snorted.

"What do you mean?"

"How much time do you have this leave?"

"Two months."

"That's good for you, then. Your wife won't be lonely."

"She's got my parents, and the baby. Why would she be lonely?" Valli sniggered.

"Yeah, why would *she* be lonely?" And then lowering his voice, the barber said, "She has visitors enough from her old village."

"I'm glad," Valli said curtly, shutting the door firmly on the barber's intrusion into his family affairs for gossip.

"Would *he* be glad, indeed? There's a time to plant and a time to uproot. A time to keep and a time to throw away."

"You speak in riddles, man." Valli began to turn his head but the barber firmly tipped his chin forward with the handle of his knife.

"Don't speak, or you'll be hurt. A time to speak and a time to be silent," he said. Before a confused Valli could come back with a repartee, Anishta's clear voice rang out from the courtyard below. "*Aayi*, come down and have some tea and sweet meats ... and bring along the *nayee* also."

"There, you're done," said the barber, tilting Valli's chin, and examining his handiwork. "Smooth like a girl."

"Let's go," Valli said, flinging off the sheet. "Refreshments await us. You haven't heard of Anishta's sweetmeats, have you?"

"There isn't much I haven't heard about her," the barber smirked. "But first I must clean up the floor."

"Do it afterward." Valli grasped his arm and nudged him ahead down the creaking staircase. Anishta had drawn out a charpoy and placed it in the shade of the old peepul. Two bell metal plates with steaming hot deep-fried flatbreads and dry peas gravy, red hued from the chilies had been laid out. A large copper bowl of hot *jalebis,* covered with a newspaper to keep away the flies, sat by for sweet relief, in case the mouth caught fire. Nana sat cross-legged at one edge of the cot, adjusting his glasses on his nose so that he could eye the repast better. "Come, come," he waved them onward, impatient to begin.

The three men squatted on the narrow cot and began to apply themselves vigorously to the nourishment, licking their fingers as well as whiskers. Anishta sprinted to and fro from the kitchen, barely managing to keep the bowls full. At long last when they were done, the men slurped masala chai from earthen cups loudly, and rubbing their hands over their bellies, talked of this and that.

The skies overcast and the sea breeze salty and sticky on their lips; the ruddy shelduck honking overhead and the frogs croaking below; the rain a-coming, and not else to be done this day, the men dozed for a bit in the cool shade.

Faint rumblings in the distant sea brought the men out of their pleasant afternoon siesta. "I must clean the roof before it rains," the barber announced again, swinging his skinny dhoti-clad brown legs over the cot.

"Anishta will do it," Valli said, stretching, deeply inhaling of the far-off rain in the breeze.

"Never leave these things to someone else. I keep a clean shop, sir," the barber retorted, and clambered up the stairs. Soon after he looked over the parapet, puzzled, and shouted to the somnambulant men below. "Hey, what happened to the shavings and the nail clippings? Have you seen them?"

The two men looked at each other and shook their heads. Nana turned over his side and went back to sleep.

"Strange," the barber came back to the wall after some more searching and fretting.

"Anishta must have swept the floor, Uncle. Come down," Valli said.

The barber wasn't satisfied. He looked around some more and then came down grumbling. Meanwhile, hearing the men awakened and talking, Anishta had also come out, the baby suckling at her half-covered breast, its tiny hands clawing her face. "The wind might have blown them away. Why make a fuss?" she said.

"So you didn't sweep the roof?" Valli said.

"No, not every day," she replied.

"The wind is too light. The floor has been swept clean," the barber said, eyeing her suspiciously.

"So what? It's just garbage done with," Valli said.

"So what? In the wrong hands, mischief can be done. I should have cleaned the floor then only," the barber went out, muttering to himself.

"What's his problem? Weird old man," Valli said. Playfully biting her free breast over the blouse, he guffawed when Anishta howled in pain.

*

Valli hummed moodily when he returned from the post office. He rummaged through the almirah to get the passbooks. He became increasingly anxious as he compared them with the post office statements he'd got from the postmaster. Anishta, sensing him troubled, fussed over him, quiet as a mouse. But he kicked away the stool on which she'd placed tea and vegetable pancakes when he saw in one of the books his face cut out from their joint photograph.

"Where's my photo gone?" he shouted.

"I ... I u-u-used it to apply for the g-gas connection. I didn't have a ph-photo of yours in the house."

He stomped on the fallen dishes with rising rage, and screamed above the clatter. "You said you were unlettered."

"I am," she whispered, her eyes wide.

"Then how come you signed on the post office receipts, instead of your thumb impression?"

"Nana taught me how to write my name. That's all I know."

"Nana? Where's he? And who's this young lout who accompanies you?"

"No one."

"The postmaster told me—come on, tell me!" He crushed her slender wrist in his grip and pulled her down on her knees beside him. He yanked her hair bun till her brows pulled all the way to the end of her forehead.

"It's ... it's Marich ... my ... my cousin from my village."

"A cousin? Where the hell was he all this while? Why does he come? Come on, speak up, slut!"

"Because you're never there. The ... the postmaster makes eyes at me—I'm afraid. And Nana doesn't walk that far nowadays. Marich ... he comes on the first of the month to walk with me ... to get Nana's pension and your money orders."

"The accounts are empty. The statements match perfectly. Everything has been credited. Then where's all the money gone? Who've you given it to?"

"I spent it ... on us. Ouch!" she cried as he gave one final pull, and released her. She trembled like a leaf on a rock face; covering her face in her hands, she feared to be struck. A flood of tears broke out of her almond eyes and trickled through the dam of her small fingers.

"You've been sending money back home to your parents, haven't you?" he yelled.

She nodded and gripped his feet. "They're so poor and weak, Valli! Please, the castor failed again this season—the water is so salty."

Their daughter also began to cry in the other room. His arms hanging loosely by his sides, Valli gazed at his child-wife helplessly. He dropped the passbooks and pulled her to his knees. "Hush," he said soothingly, "there, there, no more, child. See, it's all right. You should've told me, shouldn't you've?'

She nodded, and rested her petite head, thickly decked with wild tresses, on his strong thighs. They were like that for a long time. Later, when Nana came home from squatting in the village square with his friends smoking hookah, Valli brought out the Old Monk and they began drinking.

Valli never again mentioned money to his Nana. The headache from the morning hadn't gone and Valli began to feel a slight hotness rise in his flesh. He could barely peck at the mustard fish curry and rice Anishta had prepared only for him and fell asleep early, strangely exhausted without doing any work.

By morning a full-blown fever had taken charge of Valli. It grew worse and over the next few days Valli went into a delirium, tossing on the bed, hallucinating. His body burnt to the touch, as if on fire, without breaking into a sweat. Nana and Anishta took turns sponging him with cold packs, all day and night. Valli felt as if he had touched the devil himself. He mumbled to himself and felt himself floating near the ceiling, from where he could look down at his body.

He felt disoriented and his thoughts jostled him from one fragmented memory to another at breakneck speed. He drifted in and out of consciousness. He wrenched himself with great effort from the long fingers that snaked around his broken body and tried to stay conscious, but they kept coming back, dragging him into the dark cesspools of his frenzied hallucinations. He threw up every liquid poor Anishta fed him from the soup bowl.

But Valli fought hard and long, and the salve of modern medicine began to ease his anguished spirit. On the fourth day, he finally woke up, when Nana's kindly voice drifted over to him, as if in a dream.

"Where's Anishta," he asked, sitting up in his bed drenched cold with his sweat.

Nana shuffled over to him and held a glass of water to his mouth. Valli felt its coolness soothing his insides, dry as dust. "Rest now, son."

"No, where is she?" Valli asked hoarsely. "I must find her." He flung away the hand-woven linen sheet and rushed out barefoot in the dark. His father raised a feeble arm to stay him, but Valli, his eyes wild and his clothes askew, wouldn't be restrained.

In the gray haze, dull shafts of white streetlights shone off brooding, spinach-dark trees as Valli passed though the sleepy village. Little pebbles bit into his feet, but he charged on, madly along crisscrossing pathways through mustard and paddy fields. When he neared his farmstead, he saw a dull red light from the windows of the barn next to the tube well. Never before had his fields looked so well cared for—a luxurious blanket of yellow and gold mustard in bloom spread over his land. As he edged closer toward the barn, he could make out in the glow of its lamp an outline of two naked bodies entwined on a soft mound of fodder and mulch. He sank on his knees, suddenly unable to go any further. The lovers' whispers carried in the moist breeze over to him. He knew then that one was his unfaithful wife, and the other the man she addressed as Marich, both cavorting vulgarly in the open, with all of nature as a witness.

The couple untangled after a while and dressed. Then they took the path through the fields toward the river, Anishta following the other in her unmistakable, languorous, swaying gait that no wide-eyed man in the village could be saved from. His shame giving him strength, Valli struggled to his feet and began to follow them.

*

334

After an hour's plodding in the riverbank, which was increasingly turning marshy, the river narrowed, and the mangroves became close and dense, almost brushing their faces. Soon they could see white, saltwater crocodiles, lit up by the moon, lazing about in the swamps on the far bank.

Mosquitos bit Valli relentlessly and the heat and humidity made his clothes stick to his body like another layer of skin. After a few hours, the path along the river turned into a small fork and the creek petered off into a shallow pool. The pair ahead rolled up their robes and tied them around their waist and waded across the swamp. Marich led the way. He seemed to glide on the swamp, rather than walk, taking the second step before the first one had completed, making sure both his feet were on the ground at the same time. Anishta hastened after him, carefully trailing his footprints by the glow of the silvery skies on the white swamp.

Valli could see the tracks made on the slippery sands by the swamp snakes and crocs, and fervently prayed not to run into them. The small party soon entered the thick mangroves that grow very closely together. Marich had grabbed Anishta's hand and was steering her on the cattails and reeds that supported them on the marsh.

Before midnight they had crossed over the swamp and reached a firm mud flat surrounded by a spotless pond. A small hut sat in the middle of the ground, a flickering light and curling smoke coming from within it. A loud shout by Marich brought a burning lantern to the door, held by a young boy in black robes. The hut was low, maybe about five feet high. The boy bent and came out towards them. He and Marich exchanged a few words and the boy went back in.

Valli crept forward on his haunches and hid himself in a small bush close by from where he could observe and overhear those gathered about the hut. The boy returned shortly and spread a small rug outside the hut, and set the lantern by it. A tall, skinny *Aghori*—a tantric—soon came out of the hut and greeted the couple by raising his hand in blessings. The couple touched the ground at his feet and took out two bottles of Old Monk—Valli's army-issue rum—a packet of hashish, some hair—Valli's hair—wrapped in a newspaper, and a thick wad of notes—Valli's money—from a sling bag and placed them before him. The Aghori seemed pleased and blessed them again. The party squatted on the rug next to him.

The Aghori was a bearded, skinny sadhu smeared in ash from a funeral pyre. He wore two red dots and a black square mark on his forehead. His chest was covered in vermilion and he wore a white loincloth with four knots. He had loosely tied his matted locks on top of his head over which sat a wobbly black turban. The urchin placed a human skull filed off to a saucer's shape before the Aghori and two steel glasses before the other men. The urchin poured out the local liquor for them while the sadhu pulled out a chillum and greedily filled it with *ganja*—marijuana.

The men smoked and drank awhile, the Aghori often asking Anishta questions about Valli and his life in the army.

"*Swamiji*, when will the work be done?" Marich folded his hands and asked finally. "Other than a general sickness, from which both seem to come out of after some time, there's nothing happening. They are still alive."

"Only when we are prepared to give up everything," the Aghori replied, "are the gods willing to grant us our wishes. I am confident, with time you will succeed. I see you have brought what I sought," he said, poking with the end of his chillum the contents of the newspaper wrapper in which Anishta had neatly bundled Valli's hair, nails, and a small cutout photograph.

"When will the end come? Our daughter is growing. We want to return with her to our village," Marich asked in an ingratiating tone.

"Nothing is hidden from a true tantric, son. I can snatch a person from the blackest pits of the nether world. Let us waste no further time, we are already past midnight, and we have only until two a.m. I will now perform the death-stance." He barked to the urchin to bring him a fresh corpse. "You help him," he ordered Marich.

The urchin and Marich set off in the direction of the marshes across the pond. Many local tribals still preferred to immerse their dead in the holy Brahmani River, rather than cremate them in the Hindu way at the burning ghats upstream. Where the river forked, some corpses got wedged in the marshes and the mangrove roots. The marshes swallowed them and threw them up again after several days.

While the men were gone, the Aghori pushed Anishta down on the ground and forced himself upon her. She struggled meekly under him but soon caved in to his promises, as well as threats to harm her lover and daughter. Valli felt the fever take control of him completely, and he could do nothing more than watch helplessly, his limbs not answering to him at all.

The scene before him sickly evoked in his frenzied mind the first time he himself had known her body. They had been married off, as per custom, when she was only a child. She'd stayed back with her folks till she attained puberty, and then Valli's parents brought her home with great ceremony. Seven un-widowed women had applied turmeric paste on her body, and made her wear a *tilak*, a holy mark on the forehead, with rice, before he could consummate his union with her. Afterward, they had eaten together from a roasted coconut, and she'd offered him saffron milk on the first night.

She must have met Marich when she was growing up in her village, Valli told himself. Now she wants her husband and his father out of the way, obviously. Is it her mind working, or Marich's? He seems a handsome rascal. Anyway, how did it matter—she was still conspiring with him, wasn't she?

By the time the men returned, dragging a corpse by the legs, the Aghori was done with Anishta. Anishta had washed herself at the pond and readjusted her sari, while the Aghori had filled his chillum afresh and was whistling to himself without a care in the world.

The men dragged the corpse inside the hut. Stung by a morbid curiosity, Valli managed to crawl on all fours and reach the low-slung window from where he could peer inside hunched on his knees. On the way, he'd grabbed Marich's still-burning chillum, and inhaled deeply from it, which instantly numbed his pain and lifted the haze in his head.

The hut was brightly lit with kerosene lanterns and choking with heavy incense smoke. Fierce flames spat out of a fire burning in a crack in the baked mud floor, stoked by the urchin splashing local liquor into it for spectacular effects. A mound of brown rice was placed by the fire, painted with red and black stripes at its base, and embedded with limes, fruits, bones, and other strange objects. A wooden stake was buried in the floor, with long white hair tied to it.

The corpse was placed in a corner on the floor, and the Aghori sat on its groin facing the head, chanting his mantras. The others crouched around the fire, fascinated. The urchin tossed into the fire a gooey mixture from a bowl in rhythm with the chants. The bowl looked like it contained a mixture made from standard ingredients:

human excreta, oil, and flesh. They passed on the bowl to the party asking them to make offerings into the fire.

The Aghori next placed a skull on the corpse's head and began to chant hysterically, rocking to and fro, while the urchin lobbed the mixture and liquor into the fire in a livid frenzy. Suddenly the Aghori stopped. He drew a sharp knife and severed off the corpse's arm. He started gnawing on the arm, snarling and gulping down the flesh. After chewing some, he threw the arm at the urchin who placed it in a tin pot filled with water and set it on the fire for boiling.

The Aghori grabbed the liquor bottle and took long swigs from it like a terribly thirsty man. He swung his legs off the corpse and dragged deeply from his chillum, exhausted by the *asana*.

He reached into a small trunk and tipped some green and black powder separately into newspaper pieces, which he folded expertly. He also poured out the contents of the bowl into a small brown glass bottle and handed everything over to Anishta. "The black mixture is stronger, for Valli, and the other for his father. Your job should be done in under a week. If not, next you'll have to bring me either his semen, or blood, and then I will chant the final mantra, which can be very dangerous for all of us—but I don't think that will be necessary. No one has resisted the power of the *shava asana*, the mantra that I have cast on your husband and father-in-law today. That is all now, my children. The dawn arrives, I shall rest now. Leave in peace. May you have many offspring," he said, motioning them to leave.

Marich nudged Anishta, and after touching the Aghori's feet, they left by the same way through the swamp and the fields beyond.

Valli, buoyed by the marijuana, leaned against the hut and waited for dawn before he knocked on the hut's door. He was tired, hungry, and covered in filth, but his head and spirit were quite spotless and lucid now.

*

There was no need for Anishta to burn like this; no need for the candle of life of one so young and beautiful to be snuffed out like this. And there was definitely no need for Valli to be lighting up his child-bride's funeral pyre like this.

The holy Brahmani, placid, and on course to be swallowed by the ocean, lapped at his unshod feet. But Valli felt he was being tossed around in a tiny boat without a life vest—in a black raging storm with crackling thunder and hammering deluge. The incessant wail of mantras on the burning ghats didn't ring; it vibrated, like a cosmic howl, churning up grief and ache. The stench of burning corpses swirled around him, and he could feel the heat of their dying embers cooking the eyeballs inside the skulls. It was as if he himself had been struck a crumbling blow of the undertaker's staff, dispatching his soul on its next flight to another mortal abode.

"Strange for one to die so young, and so suddenly," the grieving village women, beating their breasts as per custom, wailed.

"Oh, what will become of her daughter?"

"What will be Nana's fate? Even his wife has deserted him for her heavenly abode."

*

Soon after the funeral, Valli had packed up a few of their meager belongings and reserved train berths for Jabalpur, where his unit had moved after the field tenure. The captain had accepted Valli's request for priority allotment of family accommodation on extreme compassionate grounds, considering there was no one to look after the child and his ailing father now.

"I am a burden on you, son," Nana bemoaned, as they sat on the platform at Balasore. "You should have left me to live out my last days in the village. How will you take care of the baby alone? You should have remarried, and left your brood at home."

"Never again," Valli said.

"But you'll be lonely, without Anishta, without a wife."

"I see Anishta in her. Don't you think so, Nana?" Valli said, holding up the baby, who looked far better now, smiling to herself in her sleep.

Nana nodded but remained quiet. Perhaps he knew. The girl hadn't taken after his son's features at all.

"We must give this girl the best," Valli said, holding his father's gaze. "Won't we?"

Nana took the baby from him and hugged her close. "Yes, my son," he said, his eyes moist. "Isn't it strange," he said after a pause, "that we should recover, and Anishta should fall ill, as if she'd reaped our maladies?"

"She reaped as she'd sowed, Nana. Perhaps she wanted everything of ours—so she got it. There's nothing strange."

"But there are strange mischiefs afoot—unwholesome murmurs of a powerful tantric being around in these parts ... sudden deaths ...

fields struck down by pests ... water wells souring over ... business ruin. He lives in the swamp by the river. You know of it?"

"He's nothing more than a businessman with strange powers, Nana. So, it's not hard to persuade such a man with incentives to reverse his magic, and prescribe it on the very person who practices it. You can say, Nana, a taste of your own medicine."

***

The Sixteenth Ritual

by Jeff C. Stevenson
United States

When traveling through Romania, you are cautioned to always arrive at your destination before sunset. If the outside light is on, it is a signal that you are too late; the doors will be locked, the windows closed and bolted from the inside.

It's not vampires or creatures of the night that are the cause of all of this; it's simply that because there are no street lights in most rural parts of the country, the roads are easy to get lost on and residents grew tired of strangers pounding on their doors seeking assistance after all was dark. Inconvenience turned to suspicion once the already poor economy sank further and break-ins and violent home invasions in the tiny towns and villages increased. It all finally resulted in the firm edict: Arrive before sunset or wait until morning.

*

Harold Dexter had received a curious email seeking his appearance before the Archbishop of Bucharest. It was a matter "pertaining to the need to immediately validate a document that has been discovered in the village of Predeal, Romania. Upon verification of the item, an evening meeting with the archbishop is requested to review the manuscript. Discuss the contents of this missive with no one. It is to be held in the strictest of confidence."

On two occasions, Harold had traveled from New York to consult with the universities in Romania. He had also spoken at their educational centers and delivered papers on the origins and authentication of religious icons and manuscripts. But he had never been invited to meet the archbishop, nor had he ever received such an urgent yet befuddling request.

341

"Don't they know how long this takes?" his wife, Iris, said, reading over his shoulder. He reached up behind him, turned and pulled her in for a kiss. "You're not supposed to be reading this," he murmured in her ear. "It's to be held in the strictest of confidence."

"Oh, please!" she said, freeing herself, straightening up, massaging his shoulders. He sighed in pleasure. "What could be so mysterious in Romania that you can't tell your wife?"

His phone rang. He didn't recognize the phone number on the screen: 021-315-49-55.

"Harold Dexter," he said cautiously.

"Mr. Dexter, this is Timothy Antonescu, the to the Archbishop of Bucharest. I'm calling you from Romania."

Harold sat up straight, surprised. "Mr. Antonescu! I ... I was just reading your email request." Iris leaned into his phone to hear the conversation.

"That's why I called. I wanted to confirm you had received it." Antonescu spoke with a thick, smoky European accent that called to Harold's mind images of dark bars and suspicious eyes.

Iris gestured for Harold to speak. He cleared his throat, glanced again at the email as he spoke. "So, you have a document you need me to look at. What can you tell me about it?"

"Very little, Mr. Dexter. It was discovered during the remodeling of a home in the village of Predeal. We have not attempted to open the manuscript but we believe it may be of extreme historical value to the Church, so we need its contents verified immediately."

"There seems a sense of urgency about the matter. I need time to get a team together and—"

"No," Antonescu said immediately, as if waiting to say the word. "As I said, we do not want word of this leaking out. We just need you."

Harold frowned, took a moment to compose his response. Iris watched him from the kitchen where she was pouring them each a glass of wine. Calmly, Harold said, "Mr. Antonescu, as you may know, document validation and authentication cannot be done by one person. It involves a team of experts. And we need access to labs for analysis. For example, the ink used in a manuscript needs to be verified as to its age, and we need to study the compounds that were used to create the ink to determine if it is real or forged. And the item

342

must be run through an intensive analysis of microscopy and spectroscopy."

There was no response. Harold felt he was speaking a foreign language that Antonescu wasn't able to understand. He finished off by addressing the immediacy of the request. "You see, it takes months, not weeks, to assure authentication. And it usually involves radiocarbon dating and script analysis of the linguistic style used in the manuscript. Again, it's not a one-man job. A conclusion certainly can't be made 'immediately' as is requested in your email."

Harold stopped, having said all that he could to explain the impossibility of the request. After a moment, Antonescu responded, speaking slowly. "It's our belief, Mr. Dexter, that based on conversations with others who have read your papers and attended your speaking engagements, that you *will* be able to determine the validity of this document simply by examining it. And you will do it swiftly."

Harold shook his head, mildly exasperated; he did not feel he was getting through. "But sir, there's a difference between a document being validated and being authenticated. Of course, I can examine it, give you my opinion, but my reputation—"

"Your reputation will never be at stake since we never will go public with your opinion," Antonescu said calmly. "We simply want you to examine the manuscript, make your judgment. Your name will never be mentioned. We believe this document is authentic; at least, we pray to God it is. We need you to simply look it over and confirm to the best of your ability and with the time available that it is a valid document. Of course, we will pay you handsomely for your expertise."

The amount offered was more than a year's salary. Harold was astounded. Iris heard the sum and her mouth dropped open, she started nodding frantically, mouthing the words, "Say yes!" over and over.

After a few more minutes of discussion, Harold accepted the offer. Antonescu said the check and a round-trip plane ticket to Bucharest would be Federal Expressed to him.

"All the details will be in that envelope. Should you have any additional questions, please contact me," Antonescu said. "And thank you for your help with this, Mr. Dexter."

When the call was over, Harold and Iris hooped and hollered about their apartment. After they settled down, ordered Chinese, and poured more wine, they sat back on the couch.

"Remind me again what you always say," he asked.

"One phone call can change your life," Iris answered.

*

Harold spent the long, first-class flight from JFK to Bucharest reading and researching, boning up on everything he thought he already knew about authenticating ancient manuscripts. He had already cautioned the Church that the task in front of him was impossible, but he wanted to be as prepared as he could be under the circumstances. For whatever reason, those in charge wanted him—and only him—to review this mysterious document and tell them in less than twenty-four hours if he thought it was authentic. He knew his conclusion would be as accurate as correctly guessing the number of jellybeans in a glass jar, but as long as his name wasn't used and his reputation wasn't besmirched by his wild guess, he was willing to make the trip and accept the payment.

Iris had held the check up to the window. "This will change our lives. We can pay off all of our debt, bank the rest, and finally get ahead in our life!" She looked around the cramped, one-bedroom apartment. "Maybe even move to a bigger place."

Harold zipped closed his packed carry-on suitcase, slung his computer bag over his shoulder, and kissed her goodbye. "After you deposit it, don't go crazy and buy anything. I like your idea of getting out of debt."

She hugged him goodbye. "Call me often."

"I'll try, but you know the service over there sucks."

*

The village of Predeal was just over a two-hour drive north of Bucharest. The man who provided Harold his ride and would act as translator was a typical Romanian. He spoke infrequently; his face was an ashen gray map of deep, carved-in wrinkles; his eyes were faded green as if all the sights he had ever seen had been washed away. He had taken Harold's one suitcase, dumped it into the back of the red Sandero hatchback, slammed the trunk, gestured for Harold to climb in, and then settled himself behind the wheel. A hard cough of exhaust

344

and they were off. Harold called Iris, but after two disconnections, he decided to try later.

The man drove quickly through the Prahova Valley, occasionally speaking on his phone, frequently glancing at the rearview mirror, his heavy brow indicating neither curiosity nor concern about his passenger as they swerved and jostled over the rough road. Harold stared out the window, delighted at the sights as they weaved between the dipping and soaring Baiu and Carpathian Mountains. *So different from Manhattan*, he mused. The lush emerald landscape glowed almost fluorescent with the grass and trees in every shade of green. The charming villages with red and yellow roofs contrasted nicely with their surroundings. Haystacks—some more than a dozen feet high— squatted throughout the area or were constantly in the process of being assembled by the farmers. Occasionally Harold caught the eye of a villager when the car slowed between townships; never an exchanged smile, just the sharp flicker of awareness. It was all so picturesque that he regretted that he had never visited the area on previous trips, but there had never been much time when he was doing speaking engagements. He would have no chance during this trip, either.

He pulled out the schedule Antonescu had included in the Federal Express package. First he was to visit the town of Predeal where the document was discovered to see if it had any bearing on its authenticity. Then he was to retrieve the manuscript from the priest who was keeping it in the church's safe; he would then have overnight and the most of the next day to examine the item. Late the following day, the driver would return to transport him back to Bucharest to meet with the archbishop in the evening at his private residence. The next morning, he would take the flight home. It was all impossibly accelerated for what they wanted, but he was here, and he would do the best he could.

An hour later, just as he was attempting to send a text to Iris, the car came to a stop.

"Predeal," the driver announced.

*

A few minutes later, the car rolled to a halt in front of the home of Dorin Anestin.

Mr. Anestin was a widower, lived with his son, Grigore. According to what Antonescu had written to Harold, they were in the process of remodeling a part of their home when they found the parchment in a hollowed-out portion of the wall they were removing. At first they thought it was just old boards, but then realized that the wood planks contained pages that were clamped tightly shut by brass clasps embedded with images of the crucifix. They took the sealed bundle to the local priest who contacted his bishop who, after spending a day examining them, put through a call to the archbishop. By this time, the gossips in the village were visiting Dorin and Grigore regularly, desperate to discover what it was that they had found in the walls of their house that had gotten the attention of the Church leaders.

Dorin and Grigore took a break from their work when Harold and the driver arrived, and after the chauffeur muttered to them, they nodded warily at Harold. The conversation and the translation was short; they really didn't add anything to what Antonescu had already written. They were as curious as the town was about why the Church was so interested in the document, how much was it worth, and would it be returned to them.

The driver seemed curious, too. After translating the questions, he joined the men in gazing at Harold, waiting for his response. He told them they'd have to ask the archbishop; explained again that he was only going to look at the manuscript, it would not become his property, and they'd have to talk to their local priest for any other information.

"*Bani?*" the father asked, both hands open in front of him. He and his son were filthy from the remodeling. It was as if they had intentionally covered themselves in filth and mud; only their eyes and teeth flashed white, the only signs of life from the muck-covered figures.

"Money," the driver translated. Harold's shrug told them again to ask their priest or bishop. He wondered what they would say if they knew the huge sum he had been paid.

*

The priest in Predeal also mentioned bani when he handed over the carefully wrapped package.

Harold had turned to the driver, who knew the answer by then.

After the chauffeur had left, Harold checked into the small, quaint Vila Vitalis hotel. Once he was in his room, he called Iris. She had slept in and was having a late breakfast. They chatted for a few minutes, but he admitted that he was anxious to get started.

"Okay, but after you know what it is, call me," she pleaded.

346

Harold laughed. "Sorry, but it's confidential. You don't even know I'm here, right?"

"Tell me later or I start spending that money," she had joked, and ended the call.

He rubbed his hands together in anticipation. He carefully unwrapped the layers of newspaper until he came to a thick, heavily embroidered cloth that seemed to be the last layer of protective material. Harold pulled on some nitrile gloves in case there was mold or any health hazard that could arise from touching or handling the document. He removed the fabric.

The item was about the size of a coffee table book, secured with ancient, weathered clasps. There was a great deal of corrosion on the cover; he hoped it had not harmed the contents. He gently opened the fragile parchment, teasing it at small increments so as to not damage the clips. The title page, in a faded, yet ornate design, was in Latin. He noticed immediately that the text seemed to have been written on thick, flat pages and aged naturally versus a forgery when the ink is piled up on an already warped papyrus.

Harold took several seconds to make sense of what he was reading. He knew Latin, knew his translation skills were acceptable, knew he was reading it correctly. But the words and what they were communicating astounded him. He grabbed his computer, quickly typed the words into the Latin to English translation. Just to be certain.

He sat back stunned at what the lettering revealed:

XVI. Resurrection

The texts of the Rite of Resurrection contained herein are restricted to the study and use of those who perform this ministry under the direction of the archbishop.

Harold had to hold his hands together to stop them from shaking. He wanted to be positive about what the title page had stated. Seeking clarity, he turned the page to see the contents of the book, to get a more comprehensive understanding of what he thought was before him.

Again, he confirmed his own translation with the assistance of Google. He stared in astonishment at the translated table of contents:

Resurrection—Introduction

Resurrection—General Rules

Rite for Resurrection

Resurrection of children
Resurrection of adults
Resurrection of the excommunicated
Resurrection of the non-converted

He turned back to the title page. *XVI. Resurrection.* He knew there were fifteen rituals in the Catholic Church: baptism, confirmation, communion, marriage, penance, priesthood, exorcism, and so on. Just fifteen, always had been for centuries.

"This must be a forgery," he said to himself. "Never heard of a sixteenth ritual." He sat back in his chair, staring at the parchment before him, mentally preparing for the long night ahead, finally understanding why the Church was paying him so much, and why they wanted an answer immediately.

The Church believed these rituals were given from God, that the ritual of baptism confirmed the divine, that a man became part of the intimate Priesthood of Christ when he participated in that holy ritual, and that demons were cast out of a person when the rite of exorcism was performed.

If this document for a sixteenth ritual—one for resurrection—was authentic, would the Church now believe that with this rite they had the power to raise people from the dead?

*

Late the following afternoon, the sky was red with the fiery approach of sunset. Harold had checked out of the hotel, was waiting out front as the shadows lengthened and stretched out over the area. Like spilled pools of ink, they slowly expanded, gradually surrounding him. Behind him, the windows of the hotel were being closed, bolted, and lights were turned on in the reception area. The glow of the porch light appeared, pushing back the hardening dusk. The sun seemed to be falling faster and faster as the darkness settled in to occupy the courtyard. Overhead, the tree branches swayed, crackled, and made shushing sounds as the wind rushed about.

Harold was relieved when the headlights of the red Sandero appeared out of the nightfall. He had been up all night working, hadn't slept, and spent all day on the document. He was exhausted, looked forward to sleeping in the car for a couple hours before meeting with the archbishop. The driver nodded, grunted some greeting, snatched Harold's suitcase and stowed it in the trunk as Harold wearily settled into the back seat. The idling car was put into gear and soon they were headed back to Bucharest. Harold dozed.

*

He awoke when the car came to a sudden stop, rocking in place as the motor rumbled. The chauffeur hurried out, leaving his door open. The fresh, cold air rushed into the backseat, reviving Harold. He peered through the windshield, saw the driver struggling with an old wooden gate, then finally managing to pull it out of the way of the automobile. He climbed back in. The car began to crunch and sway its way over the road. He nodded when asked if this was where the archbishop lived.

It was pitch black outside; no illumination from any other property, no streetlights or approaching cars to break up the blanket of heavy darkness that had fallen over the area. *I'm literally in the middle of nowhere*, Harold realized as the car worked its way through the secluded vicinity. He called Iris but the call didn't complete, so he sent a text but it only lingered, so he put his phone away. He strained a look out the window to catch sight of the moon, but it was either hidden by clouds or too thin to see. He noticed the driver's shoulders were scrunched up, tense, as he tried to navigate the road in front of him, the weak, pale headlights offering little assistance in cutting through the gloom.

The crackle of the Sandero's tires as they traveled over the pebbles through the impenetrable dark were the only sound and seemed to heighten the sense of isolation Harold felt. He wondered how much farther it was; he had lost track of time since the gate had swung open. He checked his phone. It was almost nine, so they were on time, if they arrived soon. He noticed his message still hadn't gone through, which was annoying.

The car abruptly started to climb; Harold's back was thrust hard against the seat. The motor strained a bit but the wheels clung to the road. He heard the driver mutter sharp words under his breath. The engine groaned a bit harder just as the road seemed to level out. Up ahead, Harold could make out an intimidating shape, a huge mass of something that was darker than the night; it had a small yellow glow in front of it. As they slowed to a stop, he realized it was the house that had loomed behind the dull porch light.

349

Harold thanked the man after he was handed his suitcase, receiving a dismissive grunt in return. Seconds later, the car began its journey back down the hill. Harold knocked on the front door.

"Mr. Dexter!" The door had opened so abruptly and his name had been announced so briskly that Harold was startled. He quickly recovered. "Yes. Yes, I am. Hello, Your Excellency."

"Come inside, it's black as night out there!" The archbishop, chuckling at his own humor, placed a comforting hand behind Harold's shoulder to usher him inside. "The guest room is down here to the right and has its own bathroom. Why don't you settle your stuff in there and then join me in my office, right across the hall, when you're ready."

Harold was grateful for the opportunity to freshen up a bit. He washed his face, then gathered together the pages of notes he had made. He sorted through them, rehearsed what he was going to say, then gently retrieved the document, which he had wrapped again in the embroidered cloth. Once he had all of his items, he stole a glance in the mirror to confirm he was presentable, and left the room to meet with the archbishop.

*

The study was surrounded with books, the shelves packed with tomes, files, and stacks of papers. A desk lamp at the far end of the room and two lamps on either side of the leather sofa near the door provided the only light, which meant much of the area was in shadows. A thick area rug of undiscernible color or pattern led from the doorway to the large desk where the archbishop sat, bathed in pale radiance. Harold had only seen the man for a moment before he had gone to his room, but he looked to be in his late sixties, stocky, bald with thin wisps of white hair scattered about his skull, bright and kindly blue eyes, and a thick Romanian accent that clung stubbornly to his English.

The archbishop stood. "Ah, Mr. Dexter, please sit down."

"Please, just call me Harold." He sat at the desk, just out of the pool of light.

"You've eaten before your journey here?"

Harold nodded.

"May I offer you anything? Some wine? Water?"

"No, thank you."

The archbishop sat. "Good, then I guess we can begin. I know you weren't told much about this assignment, and were instructed to tell no one, correct?"

"Yes, that's correct. And I've told no one," Harold said, thinking of Iris.

"Good. And this may be silly to ask at this late date, but since we both are now aware of the contents of this item, do you have any questions? Are you familiar with the Roman Rituals?"

Harold nodded. "The fifteen rituals which may be performed by a priest or deacon."

"And their origin, do you know how old are they?"

Harold thought a minute. "I believe the first few rituals were discovered in the eighth century." Actually, he was certain but wasn't sure where the questions were leading so he wanted some wiggle room if needed.

The archbishop nodded then leaned forward into the warm glow of the lamp light. "The Church has always known—or suspected—of the existence of additional rituals that were never claimed as part of the original canon of belief."

"Apocrypha manuscripts?"

The archbishop smiled, waved his hand dismissively. "Every religion has apocrypha. Even Confucianism and Taoism or Buddhism have assorted texts that don't hold to the party line or tenets."

"What about this document?" Harold asked, pointing to the wrapped, cloth-covered item that rested on the desk between.

"Yes, what about it?" the archbishop teased. "What do you think?"

"You mean do I think it's apocrypha?"

"No, that doesn't really matter. What we need to know is, do you think its contents are authentic?"

Harold leaned in, joined him in the circle glow. "As I've explained, it would take weeks or months to verify and authenticate it. I only had about a day with it." Harold swallowed, glanced down at the papers in his lap. "Let me tell you what I think."

For the next hour, he reviewed his notes with the archbishop, answered the few questions that were asked, carefully opening the document to point out sections. When he had finished, the archbishop asked, "So, what do you think?"

"I believe it's an authentic document, but I want to remind you that I say that inclusive to all the caveats and doubts and uncertainties I just discussed with you."

The archbishop nodded, a slight grin on his face, his eyes bright with excitement.

Harold asked, "The idea that there are actually more than fifteen rituals would be a major event amongst Catholics, right?"

"Oh, yes. But this sixteenth ritual has been rumored to exist for centuries, so its discovery would be welcomed and celebrated."

Harold shifted in his seat, his shoulders stiff. He had to ask. "Do you really believe that this ritual can be used to bring people back from the dead? I mean, literally resurrect someone?"

"Yes, I do, in the same way I believe in the other fifteen rituals."

Harold tried to think of a response, finally saying, "But ... you'll be a laughing stock."

"Not if it works. Let's see if it works, shall we?" The archbishop reached into the top right drawer of his desk, pulled out a revolver, aimed it at Harold's chest, and pulled the trigger three times. Harold was dead with the second bullet. The impact of the blows knocked over the chair he was sitting in. On the floor, Harold's blood rapidly seeped out of the wounds, blooming about him. The archbishop stood and walked around the desk. He grabbed the lamp. Holding it near the body, he put his fingers on Harold's neck. There was no pulse.

He put the lamp back on the desk, sat, then carefully lifted the ancient manuscript. For the next hour, he studied *Resurrection—Introduction, Resurrection—General Rules,* and *Rite for Resurrection.*

Upon finishing, he yawned and rubbed his eyes. It was close to eleven. He was tired but his mind was still sharp; he had understood all that he had read. Now a choice had to be made. He glanced at his options:

Resurrection of adults
Resurrection of the excommunicated
Resurrection of the non-converted

"Harold, are you Catholic?" the archbishop mockingly asked the corpse. He thought it over, then finally said, "Probably not, so I'll assume you are among the great unwashed, the non-converted." He gently turned to the corresponding page, taking some time to memorize the text. When he was ready, he knelt down next to the body, careful to keep his knees away from the blood. He placed his right hand on Harold's forehead, repeated the phrases for the sixteenth ritual. There weren't many words to say. *Makes sense*, he considered. *After all, Christ only had to say, "Lazarus, come forth!" for that dead man to rise.*

When the brief ritual was over, the archbishop stood, stretched, then aimed the lamp toward Harold's face. He waited, watching. There was no movement.

Five minutes passed.

Ten minutes.

He re-read the text to himself to confirm he had said it exactly as written. Checked on Harold. Still no response.

Then it crossed his mind that perhaps Harold *had* been Catholic after all; the rites for the non-converted wouldn't have been appropriate. After reviewing the different section, he placed his right hand again on Harold and read aloud from the ritual to raise an adult Catholic. As the last word left his mouth, Harold's eyes opened, his body stiffened, and he cried out.

The archbishop gasped. "Ah! So, you were Catholic!" An exuberant chuckle followed, then was transformed into a delighted, full-throated, joyous cackle that lasted for almost a minute. He leaned against his desk and once he had caught his breath, he looked up.

Harold now stood before him, trembling a bit, his chest a blasted mess of blood and torn flesh, but he was alive.

"What have you done to me?" Harold demanded, a simmering rage in his voice.

The archbishop stepped closer. "What was it like, Harold? What happened?"

"What have you done to me?"

"Tell me!"

"It was ... it was bright," Harold managed to say, then he began to weep. He brought his hands to cover his face as he sobbed. "What have you done to me?" the muffled words accused the archbishop, who only stood there perplexed as to what to do next. The sixteenth ritual had worked, but what was he to do with the resurrected man before him? He waited for an idea to form. When one did, he walked past Harold and grabbed from a shelf a heavy bookend in the shape of Romania's national coat of arms. "This'll work," he said, as he brought it down hard on the back of the Harold's head. Once the scholar, now splayed on the floor, was no longer twitching, the archbishop checked for a pulse. There was none.

He straightened up, grunting with the effort. He looked around the dimly lit office. He'd miss his home and the position he'd held for almost three decades, but he had a higher calling, and its time had finally come to be fulfilled. There was much he would lose as he went about setting his home on fire. The books and papers in his study eagerly were set ablaze; many were first editions, priceless and irreplaceable, but it didn't matter.

"There's so much to gain," he said as he quickly moved out of the room that had become an inferno. He knew the destruction of his residence would consume the body of Harold, but if any of it remained, he surmised the local officials would just assume the archbishop had died in the fire, which was fine. He had a new role and a new identity and a new master to serve. As far as he was concerned, his old mortal life had passed away.

With the sacred documents under his arm, he stopped in his bedroom for a few seconds, grabbed his suitcase of clothes and the few valuables he had prepacked, and he was safely out of the house moments before the roof collapsed and the kitchen exploded.

The Sandero was parked just around the bend of the road with the driver asleep. He rapped irritably on the window, startling the man.

"Let's go," the archbishop said.

*

Thirty minutes later they arrived at Snagov Lake. It was after one in the morning; no one was about. Overhead, the far off crescent moon provided the only illumination, faintly glistening off the surface of the lake. The only sound was the constant lapping of the waves, insect sounds.

The archbishop climbed out of the backseat, taking the manuscript with him. He said to the driver, "Stay here. Wait for me. No matter what happens, remain here."

A large metal bridge stretched across the lake. The hurried, hollow clang of his footsteps echoed off the water and revealed his eagerness. It was hard to contain his excitement, and he reached the farther shore in under three minutes. He stepped from the firmness of the bridge onto the cushy soil of the small island, his heart now beating rapidly with anticipation. A rustle in the brush to his right startled him for a moment. Who or what would be awake at this hour? He knew that

Shetland ponies, sheep, turkeys, and other animals roamed the island, but they would all be sheltered after dusk. He waited but the sound didn't repeat itself. He continued on, peering cautiously into the darkness before him. He turned on the light from his phone, pushed ahead with more confidence, soon arriving upon the carefully groomed gardens that clustered about the small building that was surrounded by foliage.

Only a few steps more and he stopped. In front of him stood the monastery, a black silhouette against the barely illuminated night sky. He flashed his light to the heavens and saw several octagonal-shaped turrets. He knew he now stood in the very center of the tiny island. He hesitated. In the thick silence, he heard his breathing, loud with heavy expectancy. He quickly made his way up the crumbling, uneven stone stairs that led to the front of the abbey. He faced the ornate wooden doors and grasped the handles. *Would they be locked?* he suddenly wondered. *After all this time, all this waiting ...*

The heavy doors opened, almost pulling him into the darkness. He flashed his light about. Every inch of wall space was elaborately painted with frescoes, their images in deep blues, golds, and reds, all them ancient and peeling. Massive, elaborately jeweled chandeliers were suspended from hefty chains that were secured to the very top of the monastery. His feet shuffled across the floor toward the back of the church. His hand was shaking; the light flickered about. He tried to steady himself.

He continued forward deeper into the space. His foot nudged something, causing him to almost trip. His light revealed the raised lip of a slightly indented rectangular slab of stone on the floor just in front of the altar. Next to it was an old framed photo and a thick extinguished candle. He eased himself to his knees, fumbled in his coat for a match. It flared in the dark as he touched it to the wick. He turned the light of his phone toward the frame. It housed an illustration of a man in full fifteenth century European royalty garb with large, protruding green eyes, heavy black eyebrows and a mustache that extended to both corners of his jawline.

Vlad Tepes.

A surge of awe swept through the archbishop as he gazed down at the stone rectangle in front of him. This was where Vlad had requested he be buried so the priests would be forced to walk over his tomb as they approached the altar.

"You're really here," he whispered in reverence, his hand stroking the ancient stone.

For decades, the whereabouts of Vlad the Impaler had been disputed. Historians assumed he was likely buried at the Comana monastery in Giurgiu County, Romania. Then it was claimed he was entombed in the monastery at Snagov Lake. So in 1931, access had been given to examine the grave, but the only bones found belonged to small animals and the jaws of horses.

"But they didn't dig deep enough, did they?" the archbishop said quietly, his smile broadening in the dim light.

The candle flame fluttered impatiently. The archbishop gently turned the pages of the sixteenth ritual for resurrection until he came to the correct section. By the light of his phone and the flickering candle, he read the short rite aloud.

*

The driver was a patient man. He was used to waiting for long periods of time for his customers while they went about their business, knew not to ask questions. When the Church needed him, they paid handsomely; certain they could trust him to not reveal where he drove the religious dignitaries.

He had never been to Snagov Lake, and would certainly avoid driving there after dusk if it were up to him. He was not a superstitious man, but he knew his country's history, its legends, and its facts. He didn't like being told to wait at the far end of the bridge from where Vlad Dracula was said to be buried. He wondered what the archbishop was doing alone in the monastery so late at night. And what had happened to that young man from New York? Was he still at the archbishop's home, and was he still expected to drive him to the airport in the morning?

So many questions, none of which he could ask, so no answers were to be had. He would just have to wait.

He rolled down his car window, lit up a cigarette. In the dark quiet of the isolated location, sounds carried. He heard insects, the water lapping. He exhaled smoke rings, a trick he had learned years ago. Perfect circles, four or five at a time.

Gradually, he became aware of something, something approaching, something familiar.

It was the clanging sound the archbishop's footsteps had made when he had crossed the metal bridge; he was now on his way back.

The driver climbed out of the Sandero to stretch before the trip home. The footfalls of the archbishop became louder. There was a resounding echo about them, a blurring of sound. It was different from when he had crossed over to the island, and it took a moment for the driver to realize why.

Now it sounded like two people were crossing the bridge.

***

ABOUT THE AUTHORS

William Ade

William Ade lives in Burke, Virginia, with his wife, Cynthia. He's a newly emerging writer working the craft since 2014. His evolving voice is self-described as "Midwestern Old Man" which is appropriate since he grew up in Indiana during the fifties and sixties. Before launching his writing vocation, he had careers in telecommunications and education.

His stories have appeared in the *Crimson Leaf Review*, the *Rind Literary Magazine*, *The Broken Plate*, *Black Fox Literary Magazine* and *Literally Stories*. Visit his website at billade.com.

Kevin David Anderson

Kevin David Anderson debut novel, *Night of the Living Trekkies*, from Pride and Prejudice and Zombies publisher, Quirk Books, is a funny, offbeat Zombie novel that explores the pop culture carnage that ensues when the undead crash a Star Trek Convention. *Publishers Weekly* gave *Night of the Living Trekkies* a starred review, and the *Washington Post* listed it as one of the top five Zombie novels of 2010.

Anderson's short stories have appeared in more than eighty publications including the Bram Stoker nominated anthology, *The Beauty of Death* from Independent Legions Publishing. His latest fiction contributions have been to the anthologies California' Screamin' from the San Diego chapter of the Horror Writers Association, the upcoming anthology *Automobilia* (2019) and the recently released post-Trump presidency inspired collection, *After the Orange*. His short story collection, *Night Sounds*, will be released in the Spring of 2019, with an introduction by podcaster and voice talent Jason Hill.

Anderson has twenty years of award-winning marketing experience and is an Active member of the HWA. He currently lives and writes speculative fiction in Southern California. To learn more, please visit his website at KevinDavidAnderson.com

Bryan Best

Bryan Best has been writing fiction since he was a teenager. His most recent publication is a play called "Finding Mau Loa" that he sold to the First Baptist Church of Concord in the summer of 2018. It was filmed and will be made available on DVD this coming fall. He has had several short stories published in the U.S., Canada, and Great Britain, and has written two novels with a third in progress. Links and information on Bryan's work can be found on the website: www.bryansbest-author.com. He can be found on Facebook under Bryan S. Best and on Twitter @bsbest_writer. Bryan has a bachelor's degree in psychology, an associate's degree in insurance claims, and currently work as a property claim adjuster. He lives in Maryville, Tennessee, with his family, and mostly has to write once his family is asleep, which is when he can let the really scary things out of his head.

Gustavo Bondoni

Gustavo Bondoni is an Argentine writer with over two hundred stories published in fourteen countries, in seven languages, and is a winner in the National Space Society's "Return to Luna" Contest and the Marooned Award for Flash Fiction (2008).

His latest books are *The Malakiad* (2018) and *Incursion* (2017). He has also published two science fiction novels: *Outside* (2017) and *Siege* (2016) and an ebook novella entitled *Branch*. His short fiction is collected in *Tenth Orbit and Other Faraway Places* (2010) and *Virtuoso and Other Stories* (2011).

His website is at www.gustavobondoni.com.

Chris Dean

There are a lot of places Chris Dean loves to visit, like Yosemite, the Klamath, and anywhere the redwoods touch the sky. This writer traveled western America as a delivery driver and then as an entertainment producer, and Chris liked the driving best. Chris's work has appeared in *Theme of Absence*, *Page & Spine*, and other publications.

C.R. Downing

C. R. Downing, also known as Dr. Chuck Downing, is a nationally recognized teacher, professor, and author. He was San Diego County Teacher of the Year and received the Presidential Award for Excellence in Science Teaching. His science fiction novel, *Traveler's HOT L - The Time Traveler's Resort*, received the Best Science Fiction Novel in the 2014 USA Best Book Awards. A Christian, he serves in ministry at Mission Church of the Nazarene as a Life Group Leader. He has two granddaughters, Hadley and Harper.

Learn more about Downing and his writing at www.crdowning.com.

Gödel Fishbreath

Gödel Fishbreath is a pseudonym of a man who has been in (and out of) science fiction fandom since 1969, the SCA (mostly out) since about 1972, fantasy role play six months after the original D&D box set was published, and furry fandom since approximately 2010.

He has worked as an electrical engineer, and a programmer, with the last such job in 2002. He started getting social security in 2018.

Writing, for him, has been a slowly acquired skill. The two short stories sold so far were published under another pseudonym.
He usually uses Facebook (Godel, no umlauts) to keep in touch with friends.

Aaron French

Aaron J. French is the author of weird, occult, and dark fantasy fiction. His debut novel, *The Time Eater* (JournalStone), is available now. He is the author of *Aberrations of Reality* (Crowded Quarantine), *The Dream Beings* (Samhain), *Festival* (Unnerving), and many published short stories. In addition to writing, he works as a book editor for JournalStone Publishing and the editor-in-chief for *Dark Discoveries* magazine. He has edited several popular anthologies including *The Gods of H.P. Lovecraft, The Demons of King Solomon, Songs of the Satyrs,* and *The Monk Punk & Shadow of the Unknown Omnibus*. Aaron is currently pursuing his Ph.D. in the study of religion.

Joachim Heijndermans

Joachim Heijndermans writes, draws, and paints nearly every waking hour. Originally from the Netherlands, he's been all over the world, boring people by spouting random trivia about toys, comics, and film. His work has been featured in a number of publications, such as *Mad Scientist Journal, Asymmetry Fiction, Metaphorosis, Econoclash Review* and *Gathering Storm Magazine,* and he's currently in the midst of completing his first children's book.

Tom Howard

Tom Howard is a science fiction and fantasy short story writer living in Little Rock, Arkansas, and working as a banking software analyst in the US and abroad. He thanks his children for their inspiration for this story and the Central Arkansas Speculative Fiction Writers Group for their perspiration.

When his four children were younger and traveling in the car for long distances, Tom would tell stories about them as superheroes. This story, and many others, came from his *Superworld* collection of tales jotted down over the years. Meteor Man and his partner, Comet

Queen, are alien members of a superhero group called Heroes, Incorporated, and fight a giant planet-eater called a Destroyer.

This story deals with the concept that the universe is trying to tell us something if we only listen. There is no antagonist, just the heroine fighting herself until she has to take a leap of faith to save the world, arguing with her logical side the entire way. Instead of section breaks, there are news flashes showing how Earthlings are dealing with having a seemingly benevolent alien among them.

Tom is currently working on a *Superworld* anthology containing stories of his children's adventures and has begun writing superhero stories about his grandson and his friends.

Robert James

Robert James is a high school English teacher and author. Since childhood, he has been fascinated by tales of the macabre and fantastic, stories that shine a light where we are afraid to look. For him, stories are about characters—characters we love or hate—and their travails through the extraordinary, the harrowing. His publication credits include "In Dark Places," published by Left Hand Publishers in Beautiful Lies, Painful Truths Vol. I. "The Bells" marks his second commercially published short story. For him, a good story is one that snatches you away for a time. It might scare you, might challenge you, but it always returns you home safe, likely sound, and certainly entertained. He was educated at Seton Hall University, where he received a master's degree in English. His stories range from the hellscapes of horror to the dreamscapes of fantasy, and he is currently working on the second novel in a dark fantasy series. He lives in Bayonne, NJ with his wife, Danielle. You can learn more about Robert James, his storytelling endeavors, and what he's currently reading at https://www.facebook.com/AuthorRobertJ.

Sophie Kearing

Sophie Kearing loves hot coffee, fantastic-smelling paperbacks, and rainy days. Her work has been featured by *Ellipsis Zine*, *Spelk Fiction*,

Horror Tree, and *Sirens Call Publications*, and is forthcoming in *Pixel Heart Literary Magazine* and *Moonchild Magazine*. She looks forward to this winter, when her head-scratcher of a short story, "Rhiannon," will be included in Left Hand Publishers' *Suspense Unimagined* and her children's story, "Zoë Quinn and the Best Christmas Ever," will be included in a holiday anthology benefiting the Avon Riding Centre for the Disabled. Sophie spends way too much time on Twitter and would love to connect with you there: @SophieKearing.

Adrian Ludens

Adrian Ludens is the author of the story collections *Ant Farm Necropolis* and *When Bedbugs Bite*. A third collection, *Cobwebs: Stories of Dread and Disquiet*, is forthcoming. Recent anthology appearances include "This Book is Cursed" and "Terror Politico." Adrian is the program director and afternoon host on a rock radio station. He enjoys hockey, hiking, horror and heavy metal, though it is only a coincidence they all start with the letter h. Adrian lives with his family in the Black Hills of South Dakota. He is convinced both e's in the word 'bee' are silent and dares you to prove otherwise.

Robert Allen Lupton

Robert Allen Lupton is retired and lives in New Mexico where he is a commercial hot air balloon pilot. Robert runs and writes every day, but not necessarily in that order. More than fifty of his short stories have been published in several anthologies or online at www.horrortree.com, www.crimsonstreets.com, www.aurorawolf.com, www.stupefyingstories.blogspot.com and www.fairytalemagazine.com . Several 100-word drabbles based on the worlds of Edgar Rice Burroughs are available online at www.erbzine.com. His novel, *Foxborn*, was published in April 2017 and the sequel, *Dragonborn*, in June 2018. His collection of running themed horror, science fiction, and adventure stories, *Running Into Trouble*, was published in October 2017.

Kat Pekin

Kat Pekin is an emerging speculative fiction writer living and studying in the western suburbs of Brisbane, Australia. She recently completed an honour's degree in creative and professional writing and is currently studying to become a librarian. Kat has a passion for telling stories, creating worlds, and developing characters. Her work has been published in numerous anthologies and her stories have won, placed, or received highly commended in local and Australia-wide writing competitions. Publication in *Suspense Unimagined* marks as her first international publication.

Andrew Punzo

Andrew Punzo lives near Newark, New Jersey, where he attends law school. He wrote for Fordham University's *The Paper* and graduated summa cum laude with degrees in history and sociology. This is his first fiction publication. Andrew is an avid outdoorsman and enjoys reading a wide variety of fiction.

Clark Roberts

Clark Roberts writes mostly short stories in the genres of horror and fantasy. His fiction has appeared in over twenty publications including *Dark Recesses Press, Anotherealm, Nocturnal Ooze, Alienskin,* and *Peaks and Valleys.* He is not a *New York Times* bestselling author, and for now, he's okay with that. He spent much of his teenage years reading the novels of Stephen King, Clive Barker, and Peter Straub. Mr. Roberts lives in Michigan with his wife and two children. Besides reading and writing, he enjoys spending time in the outdoors. He particularly enjoys fishing in the hours of dusk when trout streams whisper, and eyes open in the surrounding woods.

Chris Rodriguez

Chris Rodriguez has retired from the horrors of conventional life. She now lives on the brink of inspiration in a 100-year-old cottage in Pocatello, Idaho. Her works have appeared in various themed anthologies including *Rhetoric Askew*, Kelly Jacobson's, *The Way to My Heart: An Anthology of Food-Related Romance*, Anchala Press's *Flash Fiction for Flash Memories* and several by Horrified Press/Thirteen O'Clock. You can find her latest at https://www.chrisrodriguez-onthebrink.com or https://www.amazon.com/author/chrisrodriguez-onthebrink.

Steve Rouse

Steve has been writing as a hobby for the past two decades and has now had three stories selected for various publications. He is in the process of compiling his own collection of short stories into an anthology for release next year through Walkabout Publ. As a middle school English teacher, his writing began in the classroom in Racine, WI encouraging sixth and eighth grade students to develop their own writing skills. He had the good fortune to have prominent authors Jean Rabe and Stephen Sullivan as friends and mentors, which spurred his own writing in the Sci-Fi and Fantasy genres. His first published story was in their *Blue Kingdoms* series anthology *Mages & Magic* in 2010.

Steve retired in 2015 and lives with his wife, Jean, in northwestern Wisconsin in the college town where they met. Both are happy spending as much time as possible being grandparents to five energetic Minnesotans busy with their own schools, gymnastics, and hockey.

Tom Scanlan

Tom Scanlan lives outside of Boston with his wife, child, and rescued dachshund Louie. He is a graduate of Emerson College and works as a Massachusetts correction officer. His writing explores the incomprehensible truths that lay dormant within and around us like strips of flesh clinging to the skeletons of our worm-addled ancestors. His short fiction has appeared in *The Commonline Journal* and *Bone Parade*. You can find him on Facebook or TomScanlan.net.

Joshua L Shioshita

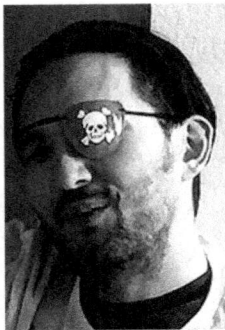

Joshua L Shioshita is a film school drop-out and occasional grunge musician currently residing in the Denver area where he works in an office by day and writes by night. He's addicted to coffee, his two cats, and his wife. He's also addicted to obsessively singing made-up songs in an effort to drive those around him slowly insane. It appears to be working.
You can visit him at
https://www.goodreads.com/UberProductions
Check out his horror themed blog at
http://uberproductions.tumblr.com/
And if you're into bad movies check out @bigboxmovieclub on Instagram which also has links to the podcast he takes part in.

Jonathan Shipley

Jonathan Shipley is a Fort Worth writer of fantasy, science fiction, and horror who ranges from traditional fantasy to vampires to futuristic space opera. Although he self-identifies as a novelist, it is short fiction where he has enjoyed success with sales of over eighty stories. He was a contributing author to the *After Death* anthology that won the 2014 Bram Stoker award, as well as a finalist for the 2014 Washington Science Fiction Association's Small Press Award. He has also been invited to speak at the 2018 World Building Conference in Graz, Austria, which will open up his writing to an international audience. He maintains a web presence at www. shipleyscifi.com where you can find a full list of his publications.

Nidhi Singh

Nidhi lives with her husband in the idyllic Yol Cantonment, an erstwhile POW Camp for German and Italian soldiers during the two World Wars.

Her short work has appeared internationally in Phenomenal Literature, Pen and Kink Publishing, The Sunlight Press, Riggwelter, A Lonely Riot, Mirror Dance, Body Parts, Military Experience and the Arts, Grey Wolfe Publishing, Expanded Horizons, Vagabondage Press, Rigorous, TQR, Fantasia Divinity, Fiction on the Web, Storyteller, TWJ Magazine, Indie Authors Press, Flyleaf Journal, Liquid Imagination, Digital Fiction Publishing Co, LA Review of LA, Flame Tree Publishing, Firefly Magazine, Four Ties Lit Review, The Insignia Series, Inwood Indiana Press, Bards and Sages Publishing, So To Speak, Scarlet Leaf Review, Bewildering Stories, Down in the Dirt, Mulberry Fork Review, tNY.Press, Fabula Argentea, Aerogram, Asvamegha, Fiction Magazines, The Dirty Pool, Flash Fiction Press, Thurston Howl Publications, and elsewhere. She has also authored several novels and translations of Sikh Holy Scriptures.

Jeff C. Stevenson

Jeff C. Stevenson is a professional member of Pen America, an active member of the Horror Writers Association, and a finalist for the Best Published Midsouth Science Fiction and Fantasy Darrell Award. Jeff has published more than fifty dark fiction stories and has been included in anthologies alongside Clive Barker, Ramsey Campbell, Richard Chizmar, Jack Ketchum, Brian Lumley, Adam Nevill, Graham Masterton, Edgar Allan Poe and Algernon Blackwood. Jeff is the author of the Amazon #1 bestselling *Fortney Road: The True Story of Life, Death and Deception in a Christian Cult.* His first novel, the supernatural mystery, *The Children Of Hydesville,* was published in July 2018 by Hellbound Books, who will also publish his suspense thriller, *I'll Come Back To Get You* in late 2018. Jeff also writes mainstream fiction under the pen name of Mary Saliger.

Please Review Our Other Books

If you enjoyed this book, or any of our other books, please feel free to leave reviews. All of our books are available at all major online retailers, including Amazon and Barnes & Noble. You can also leave reviews at Goodreads.com.

Beautiful Lies, Painful Truths Vol. I **Amazon:** http://amzn.to/2reSyIe **Goodreads:** http://bit.ly/2BobVCi	**Beautiful Lies, Painful Truths Vol. II** **Amazon:** http://amzn.to/2ngBq0i **Goodreads:** http://bit.ly/2slkBpP
Realities Perceived Amazon: http://amzn.to/2Dbe1ny Goodreads: http://bit.ly/2nU9hvw	**The Demon's Angel** By Maya Shah Amazon: http://amzn.to/2EVjj7V Goodreads: http://bit.ly/2son5E2
Drawing from the Well By Rachel Bollinger **Amazon:** https://amzn.to/2th8WGE **Goodreads:** https://bit.ly/2M8h57h	**Terrors Unimagined** **Amazon:** https://amzn.to/2OsldAT **Goodreads:** https://bit.ly/2LkLO17
	A World Unimagined **Amazon:** https://amzn.to/2yvJ4vS **Goodreads:** https://bit.ly/2K7b6zj

***

Win A Free Kindle!

If you enjoyed any of our books, please register to review one of our books (and sign up for our e-newsletter). In our newsletter, we give you previews of upcoming releases, discounts, as well as free stuff for our fans! But if you review some of our books, you can also win a FREE Kindle. https://bit.ly/2Fc021g

***

MORE BOOKS FROM LEFT HAND PUBLISHERS

BEAUTIFUL LIES, PAINFUL TRUTHS VOL.I

There's an ironic beauty between humanity's love of Life and fear of Death. Life seemingly brings joy, happiness, hope, and love. Death can end sadness, illness, suffering, and pain. We asked writers to "Let the title and quote take your imagination, your story, wherever it wants to go."

Join them now as an international blend of authors, both fresh and seasoned, bring you an exceptional menu of speculative fiction, mystery, realism, horror, and the supernatural. If your palate varies from the macabre to the dramatic, *Beautiful Lies, Painful Truths* provides an assortment of tasty treasures that will chill, delight, and give you food for thought.

Reviews

★★★★★

"An incredibly amazing anthology.

Every author in this anthology should be commended for their work in this collection. Bringing in life and death into a collection of stories, all by different authors, and how their writing varies, but brings to life, this grand collection. I believe there was a lot of thought put into which authors would be contributing their work, and how this work will be displayed."

Amy Shannon, Author. Writer. Poet. Storyteller. Blogger. Book Reviewer.
Author Blog: http://bit.ly/2yLHuFZ
Facebook: http://bit.ly/2ho273i
Review Blog: http://bit.ly/2iPVV4x
Amazon Author Page: http://amzn.to/2ynn2qM

***

"The quality of the stories read are amazing, with intricate plots in a short story form coming off as so perfect in their construction. The scope of the imagination of the writers just boggles the mind in the executions of stories that make you think. What might be considered 'good' isn't. What is seen as dark and painful is honestly the way it should be. Major kudos to these stories.

"Life is good and beautiful and death is dark and bad. Maybe not. This book presents twenty-four approaches with an amazing array of imagination in the depths of human drama, supernatural, humor, and unexpected twists. These stories will challenge everything you thought you knew—think again.

"*Beautiful Lies, Painful Truths* has stories guaranteed to challenge your view of life and death in mind-boggling ways, taking you down unexpected paths of the serious, humorous, pathos, and the twisted turns of fate. The qualities of the stories are good. The writers are to be commended. An excellent book. Kudos!"
Bruce Blanchard, Book Reviewer
http://bit.ly/2yLBq09
***

"It's an impressive read... It may be about death, but the mood isn't always dark. This anthology spans several genres including science fiction, horror, mystery, and even some humor. Well-written and well-edited, this book may be long, but it's hard to put down."
David Watson, Book Reviewer

REALITIES PERCEIVED

Nothing's more dangerous, or delightful, than invoking a cadre of talented authors to create short stories that defy our perceptions of reality. Do we create our own truth? Or does our view of it shape our world? Neither heroes nor heavens, victims nor villains, may grasp the true nature of our being.

From science fiction, to horror and the supernatural, to dramas about the fabric of our existence, this international fusion of artists will thrill you with an eclectic selection of tales that cross all genres. Sit back and be prepared to have your perception of reality both challenged and distorted.

Reviews

"... it kept me on the edge of my seat and I did not want to put it down even to eat or sleep. You have a great book here."

Lori Kibbey
Book Reviewer

BEAUTIFUL LIES, PAINFUL TRUTHS VOL.II

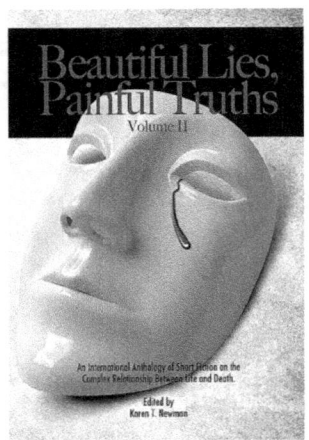

Most believe that Life promises light, bliss, and wonder. Death scares most with its shadow of mortality, darkness, and destruction. But what if those may be, if not lies, just facets of the complicated entities that bookend our existence? Life does not mock Death, but feeds it. Death is not the cessation of Life, but an alteration of existence. What would you do if faced with either truth?

An international galley of authors brings us a second repast of tales featuring the complex relationship between Life, Death, and humanity. From the supernatural to the sublime, these writers, both novitiates and accomplished, serve up a banquet of speculative fiction across a wide spectrum of genres. Beautiful Lies, Painful Truths Volume II will continue to feed your craving for the fantastic.

Reviews

"You have to love an anthology that can give you well-written stories no matter what the genre is and it looks at important issues in addition to death such as love, religion, and redemption."

David Watson, Amazon Book Reviewer

"This collection is a recipe for a lost weekend as I found myself wanting to read 'just one more' until by nearly midnight I had finished all sixteen. I will recommend this to my friends and fellow bibliophiles without reservation."

Natalia Corres
Book Reviewer, Twitter.com/Ncorres

"I read the first volume and was more than excited to read a new collection. Life and death is not just black and white, but all the in-betweens and as the title alludes, both are beautiful, but also full of lies and truths."

Amy Shannon, Author. Writer. Poet. Storyteller. Blogger. Book Reviewer.
Author Blog: http://bit.ly/2yLHuFZ
Review Blog: http://bit.ly/2iPVV4x
Amazon Author Page: http://amzn.to/2ynn2qM

THE DEMON'S ANGEL
By Maya Shah

Neha was excited to enter her sophomore year in high school. That was until the boy she went out with sprouted wings, and Lucas, the man who raised her since she was a baby, turned into a demon.

Neha is far from human. She is an angel, the natural enemy of demons. An angel raised by a demon has never been heard of before, which makes some angels see her as a threat. Neha not only has to prove that she does not know anything about demons, she has to prove that she is on the side of the angels.

And she is. So she thinks.

This Young Adult supernatural thriller follows the tribulations of the teenaged Neha as she learns both the truth about her past and herself.

Reviews

★★★★★

"Intensely unique.
The character Neha is something very remarkable, she has depth and grows as a character, especially when she feels she has to prove herself. She thinks she's proving herself a good angel to the other angels, when in fact she's also proving it to herself. Neha is not your typical teenager, nor typical angel."

> **Amy Shannon,** Author. Writer. Poet. Storyteller. Blogger. Book Reviewer.
> Review Blog: http://bit.ly/2iPVV4x

***

"This flight of fancy with engrossing plot twists tempts anyone ever dumbfounded by a parental deception."

> **Wendy Landers,** Book Reviewer
> Author of Just Let Time Pass
> www.wendylanders.com

***

A WORLD UNIMAGINED

Beyond what is conceivable to what might be is a universe full of the unexpected and the unexplainable. From science fiction to science fantasy, the location of this realm of creation and the mind is...

A World Unimagined.

An international manifest of authors, both new and experienced, crew this voyage to the other side of the unbelievable with stories unique and thought-provoking. This anthology of science fiction short stories transports us to the future, the past, and to cultures and civilizations undreamed of. Set your imaginations to stunned and your minds to light speed.

Reviews

"An eclectic menagerie of *X-Files* material. My favorite was the alien invasion of the Vietnam War's Hanoi Hilton."

Wendy Landers, Book Reviewer
Author of *Just Let Time Pass*
wendylanders.com

"Science Fiction is the great cosmos governed only by the power of What If. It requires minds seeing beyond our world of limitations and creating through imagination different species and stories boggling anything we ever thought. The stories here prove the writers included have done just that. They lay the backdrops of science and provide the fiction of imagination bringing the reader into other worlds and hopefully opening up their minds.

"... for the record, science fiction doesn't usually appeal to me. These stories do ... very nice. If these can turn me on, the book is definitely worth reading."

Bruce Blanchard, Book Reviewer
https://www.facebook.com/bruce.blanchard2

***

DRAWING FROM THE WELL
By Rachel Bollinger

A collection of parables, poems, and anecdotes to enhance your spiritual journey. Author, Rachel Bollinger walks you through her personal challenges and triumphs, referencing scripture and entertaining you as she walks closer to God.

Join her as she draws from her well of experience, faith, and victories on a journey of faith and discovery.

Reviews

"We all journey through dark nights of the soul. In this lovely collection, Rachel shares some of her most challenging life experiences and how she coped and grew in grace through the unchanging Word of God. Rachel's memories, in story and verse, are honest, brave, and witty. I came away understanding that the grief I hold in my heart has a permitted place to live."

Susan V. Smith, Amazon Reviewer
https://amzn.to/2JuDfmz

MINDSCAPES UNIMAGINED

Open the door to any genre and you will find places where the unimaginable and the unexplained collide with reality. These stories take you far past that point. From the horrifying to the macabre to the edge of real madness, you will travel to...

Mindscapes Unimagined.

An international bevy of authors, new and experienced, weave tales both fantastic and exciting. This genre-bending collection of short stories blurs the line between what can be and what can be imagined. No monster, dimension, or mortal villain is off limits. When you are ready to risk sanity and sleep, start on the first page.

Reviews

★★★★★

"*An adventure in reading*
Mindscapes Unimagined is a collection of stories from a grand variety of writers. This collection contains stories stemming from the imagination that blends horror, paranormal and science fiction into one great collection. Most of the authors in this collection, I haven't read before, but I will definitely keep them in mind for future writings. I found the order of the stories very interesting, as one led into another. As Rouse wrote in his story 'Hodag,' 'Did you not just see what joy I brought to these less fortunate? They have broadened their lives, enriched their experiences through my eyes and my story,' it worked perfectly with the concept and collection of the stories. I enjoyed each one, enticing and captivating as the one before it, and yet its own story and imagination of the darkness.

"This collection is definitely a menagerie of stories, from different minds, mixing dark and light, and blending it perfectly. Some are first person, and others are written in third person, and with most stories, it makes a difference and takes a story where it wants to go. I always embrace the anthology that has many different authors, points of views, stories that are shown and not told, and this is no different."

Amy Shannon
Writer. Author. Reviewer.
Amy's Bookshelf Reviews
Facebook: https:// https://bit.ly/2C2YSpS
Blog: https://bit.ly/2mat8sy
Amazon Author Page: https://amzn.to/2ENvyGu
Author Blog: https://bit.ly/2g7KQYn

***

Coming Soon from Left Hand Publishers:

SUSPENSE UNIMAGINED

Not all monsters have fangs, fur, or horns. Many times the worst demons are as real as tomorrow's headlines. From criminal suspense to psychological thriller to just plain scary, these short stories of pulse-quickening fear will drive you to...

Suspense Unimagined

An international fusion of authors, new and experienced, craft tales of terrors unimaginable and thought-provoking. This anthology of suspenseful short stories drags us down paths both inconceivably possible and more horrifying than the supernatural. Unclench your knuckles for a ride to inspire you to think and cringe.

***

www.ingramcontent.com/pod-product-compliance
Lightning Source LLC
Chambersburg PA
CBHW061303170626
46817CB00001B/33